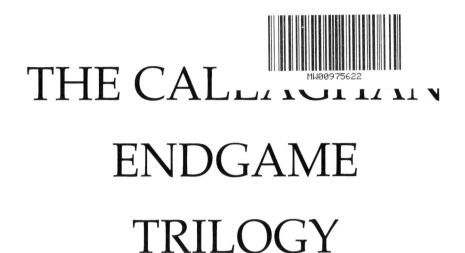

THE CALLAGHAN

ENDGAME

TRILOGY

by

KIM EKEMAR

The last three of seven books in
The Callaghan Septology
covering the terrible fate
of losing your identity
and the right to recover your stolen life.

THE LAST THREE BOOKS OF
THE CALLAGHAN SEPTOLOGY:
THE CALLAGHAN ENDGAME TRILOGY
Copyright © Kim Ekemar 2022

All rights reserved.

ISBN 10-digit: 1717396968
ISBN 13-digit: 978 -1717396969

A NOTE ABOUT THE TEXT IN THIS WORK:
The text in this novel has British English spelling.

Edition 2211-01

Published by
Bradley & Brougham Publishing House
2022

The Callaghan Septology

consists of two tomes:
The Callaghan Tetralogy
and *The Callaghan Endgame Trilogy,*
making it a series of seven books, as listed below.

The Lost Identity Casualties

PART I: Fragments of a puzzle
from a forgotten past.
PART II: The reward from exacting revenge
is in the details.
A book about betrayal and vengeance.

*

Where the Bones
of a Buried Rat Lie

PART III: If you dig deep enough,
you will find yourself in a hole.
PART IV: Faced with the truth.
Revealed by the lies.
A book about power and persecution.

The Quarry at the Crossroads

PART V: Hope clings to bridges of straw,
while those of iron will conquer the abyss.
PART VI: Deadlines turned devious
from double-dealing and deceit.
A book about the pursuit of money and justice.

*

The Tollbooth in the Labyrinth

PART VII: Pursued in the pit of the past
on a journey with no recourse.
PART VIII: The furrows of the future
should be ploughed with patience.
A book about lives lost and recovered.

*

Callaghan in the Cross Hairs

PART IX: Money comes and goes.
The art is not how to make it,
but how to spend it.
PART X: Freedom rides an elusive steed,
while money mounts a different horse.

A book about plots
and ill intentions.

The Hourglass Running Out of Sand

PART XI: Even the longest journey starts
with one foot put in front of the other.
PART XII: Catching a viper by the neck
renders it unable to use its fangs.
A book about survival and comeuppance.

*

The Final Facedown

PART XIII: In a game of life and death
pawns and kings alike are fair game.
PART XIV: Life is a lottery
with the winners impossible to predict.
A book about challenge and resolve.

PREFACE

Over the years, *The Callaghan Septology* grew from a single volume to a tetralogy, and then on to what I'm now adding a trilogy.

Why?

Because, after finishing the first book in the series, *The Lost Identity Casualties* – which can be read as a stand-alone book (although it's my sincere hope that this circumstance won't discourage readers from reading the six sequels in the series) – I found myself curious about what was next in store for the protagonists. Hence the following three instalments that complete the tetralogy. After finishing these, a brief time later I found myself once again wondering about the fate of the main characters, so I sat down to, this time simultaneously, write the additional three sequels.

The framework of *The Callaghan Septology* is meant to highlight today's ongoing, real, tragic, cynical, to not say terrible events and actions that have increased around the world in the last couple of decades: terrorism, people trafficking, drug trafficking, organised crime, illegal immigration, money laundering, corruption, impunity and much more.

The world's first face transplant took place in France in 2005, and every aspect concerning such surgery has, in preparation for these books, been extensively studied to present the reality surrounding one. I can confirm that, in April 2018, a second face transplant performed on a single patient was publicly reported to have been successfully made.

There are many true historic events included in the narrative. To mention a few: the fate of the London Bridge, the criminal Kray twins, the ever-changing landscape of the competing Mexican cartels and their capos, online Internet frauds and some particular terrorist actions in Europe and Morocco. Hopefully, there are also some notes on happier issues for the reader to discover, like the kindness expressed by ordinary people.

The septology contains many characters, which I personally have found to be one of the more fascinating aspects while writing it – just like it is in real life to encounter interesting people from all walks of life. Although I don't think the progress of the story, with the introduction of both fictitious and real people, is difficult to follow, I decided to tread a cautious path and add a complete list of its 171 actors. They're included – no matter how extensive or brief his or her part is – as long as they are mentioned by their names. Don't get alarmed by the number – only twenty-six of those mentioned have any significant role throughout the story (they are marked in bold in the overview that can be found at the end of the book). Also, in the overview I decided to add the years of their births and deaths, but only as long as these have been mentioned, or alluded to, in the text. (I leave it to the reader to imagine the ages of the remaining participants.)

After carefully having considered the option, early on I decided to include the day and the date when each event takes place. Halfway through, I began to regret having made that choice. Despite making it clear exactly when something occurs, it became a nightmare to edit out orphans and widows in the printed version. Nor could I afford to make a casual mention when something took place, i. e. conveniently making it a Sunday or a Monday or a Tuesday. So, the mention of the day and date is very real and precise and not a diary of sorts, and it was made with plenty of both discipline and agony.

A careful revision has been made by my editor Mark Swift, whose excellence in executing this task cannot be overstated after I personally had done my utmost to, in multiple revisions, edit the text. Still, from past experiences, it wouldn't surprise me if some unforgiving eyes will find and complain about a missing comma, point out an unintentional misspelling or suggest an improvement to be made among the half a million words this series represent. I, for one, think the narrative should be more important than petty complaints of such nature. I'd like to add, though, that after Mark Swift's thorough edit, I find a complaint of such nature highly unlikely.

A few additional observations: The text is written using British spelling, so an American audience, in particular, should be made aware of this. Complete sentences written in italics are thoughts made by the person in question. (This doesn't apply to single words marked in italics, which usually indicates a stress on the word or an expression in a foreign language.) Different countries have different punctuation rules. In dialogues, the comma is placed before the closing quotation mark in the US. In British English the comma is placed after the dialogue's ending quotation mark (which, in my view, is infinitely more logical).

With that I leave you to read about the unusual fate and story of Matthias Callaghan, a man born to a life of privilege and the curse of his given name – a narrative taking place in our truly turbulent times at the beginning of the 21st century.

Kim Ekemar, Mexico,
April 2022

CALLAGHAN IN THE CROSS HAIRS

by

KIM EKEMAR

The fifth of seven books in the septology
covering the terrible fate
of losing your identity
and the right to recover your stolen life

PART IX

Money comes and goes.
The art is- not how to make it,
but how to spend it.

Wednesday July 3, 2013

"Vasily, I think I've found a solution to our money-laundering bottleneck", Mikhail Berlosky cheerfully announced as he entered Vasily's exquisitely decorated office at the Arexim headquarters. "As you know, the restaurants and the laundromats are no longer sufficient to handle the increased volume of cash from our sales. Besides, I'm having a constant headache where to store the money before going through the motions to make it legit."

"I'm all ears", Vasily replied, sounding bored. His state-of-the-art sound system was playing a melodramatic symphony by some Russian composer, although Berlosky was unable to tell who.

"There is a lease available for a locale that until recently functioned as a branch of one of the major banks. It has a vault, and best of all, a loading area at the back." He sat down opposite his boss.

"What's your proposal, then, Mikhail?" Vasily said, his thoughts elsewhere.

He's more interested in the boring music he's playing than in this truly inspired idea I've come up with, Berlosky thought with dismay.

"We'll rent this place, and front it with a perfectly legitimate financial corporation. Its activity will be to give small loans to private citizens at an annual rate of, let's say, fifty or sixty per cent. Like the credit card companies."

"Sorry, Mikhail – it doesn't sound very exciting."

"That's because you haven't heard it all. Besides actually lending to the general public, we can add any number of fictitious customers. This is where we'll convert our profits from the drug transactions to a taxed and impeccably respectable capital."

"I don't follow you … we need to launder at least two hundred and fifty million pounds a year, and you're telling me that we can solve this by lending peanut amounts to individuals?"

"Yes", Berlosky replied, leaning forward with a glint in his eye, "because we're going to set up branches in several countries within the European community to cover the now quite substantial business we conduct on the continent. Don't worry, we'll more than cover the two hundred and fifty million pounds."

He rose to leave.

"Oh, by the way, Pyotr needs more people for accounting – business is growing by the day."

"All right", Vasily replied with a giggle. "See if you can get Sonia to find any trustworthy people that we can bring in from Moscow. And we might as well transfer her to London, too. I've come to the conclusion that I need a personal assistant."

Monday July 8, 2013

After handing over detailed prospect of the property up for rent to Vasily and Berlosky, the real estate agent led the way into the former bank facility at 128 Moorgate.

"It will take some investing to get the locale back in working order", the agent said as they observed the severed computer cables and peeling wall paint. "That's why the owner offers a reduction on the rent the first six months."

The main room, where the bank's clientele had previously queued for a cashier, was high-ceilinged and its marble floor was intact, Vasily noticed. Beyond this space, there were four more rooms, a kitchen area and, most interesting of all, a large vault guarded by a thick steel door.

"Is the vault working properly?" Vasily asked, trying his best to sound disinterested.

"It is", the agent replied. "The combination has been reset to zero by the former leaser. It's a steel-reinforced nineteen ninety-four Beckingshire vault, and it comes with a manual how to operate it."

They continued through a wide corridor until reaching another steel door that the agent opened using two different keys.

"And here is the loading area, which is accessed by vehicles from South Place Mews behind the building."

It was a large hall with a dock designed to receive vans and small lorries. The garage could hold up to three vehicles at a time.

Berlosky looked at Vasily triumphantly, signalling 'what did I tell you' with his eyes. Vasily silently admitted that the idea Berlosky had come up with was a beauty. The locale was ideal for handling money out of sight from curious eyes.

"Now, about the rent, the ..."

"We'll take it", Vasily interrupted the agent while distractedly flipping through the prospect that listed all the benefits of the property up for rent. The last page detailed the provisions for the contract, which Vasily was too disinterested to read.

"May I ask what your business here will be?" the agent asked, surprised over the quick decision.

"An investment firm", Berlosky told him with a broad smile that revealed his gold-capped eyetooth.

*

"I'm very pleased, Mikhail", Vasily congratulated him with a giggle once they were back at his flat at Park Lane. "You have come up with a solution to several of our current problems."

"I told you so", Berlosky beamed. "Here in the UK, we will pick up the cash from the dealers and transfer it in vans to be unloaded behind closed doors at the back of Moorgate, then count it before we store it in the vault. By the way, we need to get some more cash-counting equipment … I'll think of something … we'll need to get them through some discreet channels. A constant guard of five armed men should be enough to protect the place against any robbery attempt. The large room up front is where we'll receive people making personal visits asking for loans, the actual ones, that is. In the backrooms, we'll have people handling the logistics of the fake ones, both domestic and those made on the continent. Besides, I'm thinking of taking advantage of the room height of the entrance floor and build a second floor where Pyotr will conduct accounting for all our activities. Oh, and I think the time has come to give Pyotr clearance to handle all incoming and outgoing cash. And, just in case, I'm thinking of creating an escape route from that second floor into the adjacent door, just in case."

"Why is that?"

"Probably an unnecessary precaution, but just the same, you never know whether it will turn out to be a wise one. Just think about it, at first glance just about everything is important: the money, the contacts, the distribution network, the suppliers, you name it. But at a closer look, you'll agree that all this can be replaced, albeit with some effort involved. However, what can never be substituted is the accounting ledgers – they're the artery of the matter – "

"Artery?"

"The core information of our business", Berlosky replied, somewhat irritated. "I'm giving priority protection to what I believe is our most vulnerable asset."

"You're absolutely right doing so, Mikhail", Vasily complimented him after quickly thinking through the point made by Berlosky.

"I'm glad you see it the way I do."

"How do you plan to handle the continental operation?"

"We'll create ten or so subsidiaries to our new British investment company across Europe. Nowadays, Arexim has enough legally declared capital to fund the new company with, let's say, a hundred million pounds. These subsidiaries will be virtual, because everything will in reality be processed from London. Using the information that Allan provided us with when he hacked into various customer bases, we'll set up short-term loans to individuals that we'll invent, at a sixty per cent annual interest rate. I think that's the maximum rate you can charge without attracting attention. The loans will be wire transferred in bulk to the subsidiaries once a week. After three months they will be returned with interest, and then we'll start the cycle all over again."

"When the money is transferred, it must be withdrawn to pay out the supposed loan, Mikhail", Vasily challenged him. "That's a lot of small-amount cheques."

"We can automate that; I'll talk to Boris about it. The average loan we'll make will be the equivalent to, let's say, twenty thousand pounds. Laundering two hundred and fifty million in a year that has as many work days, means lending a million pounds a day. Sixty per cent annual interest on a twenty-thousand loan is twelve thousand, or three thousand on each trimester loan. This means we need to create roughly twelve thousand borrowers a year, not counting the real people who look us up here in London. In practice, we're talking about writing about fifty cheques a day, or five cheques from each subsidiary. It's not impossible."

"So, our subsidiaries make those cheques –"

"No, we'll bring all the cheque books to London and write them here", Berlosky interrupted him. "Remember that the subsidiaries will only exist on paper besides a plaque outside some lawyer's office."

"Where will these cheques be deposited?"

"We'll issue them to the bearer and send them weekly to our various offshore accounts like the ones on Isle of Man, Panama and the Cayman Islands. When the loans come due, we'll make cash deposits into the subsidiaries' accounts, and then we'll send the money back to the London parent company that will declare the profit. That means we'll be converting twenty-four thousand pounds that we have in cash from the sales, and pay tax on merely four thousand, that is, the apparent interest."

"Now, if I take on the part the devil's advocate: what if

something goes wrong and the cops finds out about the operation?"

"We'll salvage what money we can, of course, and let the managing director I intend to personally hire take the blame."

"I may start calling you a genius, Mikhail", Vasily complimented him without attempting to hide the admiration in his voice. "The handling of all the cash has certainly become a headache lately."

"I hope I will see some bonus when the operation is in place", Berlosky smiled, consciously flashing his gold-capped tooth. "One more thing: we have to concentrate our operations to Germany, Austria and a few other countries that have no limits for cash deposits like France and Portugal do." He sighed. "It means that we still have to transport cash from some countries to others."

"All right, check with the lawyers and get the scheme going." Vasily giggled. "You have my blessing as long as nothing goes wrong."

Tuesday August 20, 2013

Another twenty-five thousand quid safely in my pocket, Paddy O'Hare thought, contented, as he landed the old cargo airplane on the unmanned airfield Bolt Head in Cornwall that consisted of nothing but hard dirt interspersed with grass. The airfield was ideal for the kind of flying that Paddy was doing – no one around to question his work, no one to check his cargo. It all depended on his discreet approach from overseas carrying the cargo, of course. When the weather was favourable, he flew beneath the coastguard's radar so low that he almost dipped the wings of his aircraft in the waters of the Atlantic. This required considerable skill, and that's why he had been hired by the Russians to fly illicit drugs into the UK to their mutual satisfaction. Paddy didn't care much for the drugs, but he had considerable appreciation for the monetary reward that came with each successful flight. The poor bastards that sniffed or injected the stuff? The thought made Paddy shrug. Everyone was allowed a choice; his preferred one was Irish whisky. He was in it for the money, not to save the world or its people.

After landing, he taxied to the space where he had agreed with the airfield's manager that he could park the plane. There, three jeeps and a dozen people stood waiting to unload the cargo. *It's a neat deal*, he thought. *Besides the generous landing and overnight parking fees, paid in cash, the manager is happy to see his usual salary tripled while he looks the other way.*

Dawn was making itself noticed. Paddy stretched and yawned after the airplane came to a halt. It had been a long flight, covering nearly two days back and forth, with hardly any sleep. Still, with an average of two to three flights a month, the money he was making more than made up for his occasional lack of sleep.

Hamza, his assistant and fixer of any in-flight problems that arose, opened the hatch. The men on the ground quickly loaded the packages he handed them into the back of an old jeep. When they had finished, Hamza knocked twice on the wall separating him from the cockpit. Paddy taxied the plane to the rented slot among the other private aircraft, most of them owned by amateur enthusiasts.

Paddy was the eldest of the seven sons his father Patrick O'Hare had procreated with as many women. He didn't know much about his father, except that he had possessed a golden tongue and a twinkle in his Irish eyes that was able to turn the head of the most stubborn lass that had earned his interest. Paddy's mother had remained single until the day she died, which was shortly after Paddy had turned fifteen. From then on, he had to make do as best he could, until the day he had struck gold with the cocaine cargoes.

Paddy had always had a passion for airplanes. As soon as he had reached the required age for flying lessons, he had paid for them with the modest inheritance left to him by his mother. Since he had a flair for flying, he received his licence in record time.

He had scraped by for ten years by working as a waiter in different establishments. During weekends, he had participated in different events celebrating flying, and, on the rare occasions his purse allowed it, he had flown to France and Belgium in a rented aircraft.

His breakthrough had come when he was 28. A man with a Russian accent had approached him after an event in which Paddy had flown a pre-war airplane. After some introductory small talk, the Russian had come to the point: would Paddy be interested in a well-paid job of flying some packages that the police should be unaware of?

After hearing the details of the offer, Paddy decided to give it a try. He was tired of waiting on people and paying for flying. The proposal promised both money, time in the air and adventure – the very things he looked for in life.

Thursday November 25, 2010 – Wednesday September 11, 2013

Ahmed hadn't heard a word from his boss, Abdul Mahfouz, after he had travelled to Switzerland around Christmas in 2007. A month later, he got worried and began searching for Mahfouz's whereabouts. He depended on Mahfouz for his daily bread, which consisted in smuggling drugs, tobacco, alcohol or whatever else was in demand, from Morocco to Spain.

Nearly three years passed before he found Mahfouz's wife, Ghalib, now living in a small house in the modern part of Marrakech. As he accepted the customary mint tea from her, he reflected on the obvious improvement her life had recently seen: a nice house, expensive furniture, her teeth fixed, and an indescribable sense of self-assurance.

Since the windfall after her husband's death, Ghalib had taken immense steps forward, both in her own mind and in the perception of her family and neighbours. They were in awe of how this poor woman with nothing to offer but her basket-weaving had suddenly flowered into a woman full of confidence. She had paid a fortune to get her teeth mended.

With unaccustomed fierceness, she had refused loans to her daughters' husbands when they had pleaded with her for money. Nine months later she had bought an already operating ten-room *riad* and made this Moroccan boutique hotel produce more than she could spend. It was as if she, in her middle age, suddenly had grasped the mechanisms of capitalism.

While sipping their tea, Ghalib told Ahmed, showing no regret whatsoever, that Abdul had suffered a heart attack in a place called Switzerland. His death had blessed her with a well-deserved widow's pension, she added.

The news left Ahmed, not yet 30, in a spot. If Mahfouz, who had possessed all the necessary contacts, was dead – in what way could he now make his living?

Soon after his afternoon tea with Ghalib Mahfouz, Ahmed stumbled upon a new, and even more profitable, way of making money. After selling his speedboat, and with the financial help from Ghalib, he bought an old fishing vessel large enough to hold a hundred people – "a hundred and thirty, really, if you make the right arrangements, and anyway it's a short trip, two days at the most" as he had explained to Ghalib when pleading for the loan. He managed to persuade her. Thus he started his new business venture in 2011, the same year that Muammar Gaddafi fell from power and was killed. Thanks now to his own contacts, he received people smuggled overland from south of Sahara and shipped them from Tripoli to the coast of southern Italy. The business had over the past two years increased to the extent that he and

Ghalib had been able to buy a larger ship, one able to take up to 400 passengers if packed tightly.

To his dismay, Ghalib had got wind of the profits involved, and now refused to let Ahmed repay her loan to him. Instead, she wanted an equal share against the financing of another ship or two. *The surprising turns life takes*, Ahmed at one point thought, *the widow of his former boss turned out more astute than the man who had kept her under his thumb.*

Friday September 20, 2013

At an early age Ralph Trollope had decided he would dedicate his life to art. The revealing moment in his life was at school, when he had been shown a painting by Salvador Dalí depicting a burning giraffe. The painting had fascinated him, more than anything because it was such an incomprehensible thing to set fire to an exotic African animal, an act he up till then had never been able to imagine.

Ralph soon discovered that he didn't have the talent to paint giraffes or, for that matter, any other exotic thing that tickled the imagination. During his teenage years he did, however, find that his true talent was bartering. Ralph was a natural-born businessman. After graduating from university, he went to live in a shabby flat on the outskirts of London. From there he worked as an assistant at a printer's house and spent his free time looking at art. Sculptures, graphics, photographs and many other artworks; but more than anything he was attracted to oil paintings. In these – especially the classics – he felt that there was something eternally attractive that, with the right knowledge and a smooth tongue, could be turned around with a tidy profit at the end of the deal.

This attraction the world of art had on Ralph made him take the plunge into investing in an art gallery of his own, using borrowed money. He was wildly successful, financially speaking – not because Trollope was an art genius, but because he entered the London art scene at the right moment. For a few years, the prices of everything related to art simply exploded.

Then, as always in speculative commodity markets, prices imploded. Trollope soon found himself desperate for an exit to his debts and commitments, and he was lucky to find one in Jeffrey Foley.

Jeffrey Foley was a distant acquaintance of Trollope's who had learnt of the latter's financial misery. They happened to be members of the same club, and one evening Foley asked Trollope to share his table. It didn't take long for Foley to come to the point.

"Ralph, I know someone who's interested in selling a Constable painting that is not on the market because, to be frank, it was pinched a few years ago. With your contacts, would you be interested in brokering a deal with some client of yours who isn't too concerned about its provenance?"

For a while Trollope thought hard about the eventual consequences, but he quickly came to the conclusion that he personally wouldn't touch the stolen painting, and that the profit he stood to gain outweighed any risk by far. He accepted.

Encouraged by his sudden fortunes, Trollope thus embarked down the extremely profitable road of selling stolen art – one he didn't regret for a single moment once he had begun to see the results.

It must be said about Ralph Trollope – by this time portly and amply adorned with a prominent double chin despite his mere 49 years – that most of his business was dealing with art that was perfectly legitimate. Even disregarding his shadier dealings, he made a very good living trading artworks with unquestionable provenance. However, Trollope had an inclination to go beyond the legal frame that regulated him and all other citizens, merely because he felt cleverer than "the system".

Trollope managed a gallery on Clifford Street in central London, one that was his own in every respect. It also had the advantage of being within walking distance from London's most important auction houses of art: Christie's on King Street, Sotheby's and Bonham's on New Bond Street and Phillips in Berkeley Square. Occasionally a buyer dropped by, who after an hour or a second visit bought the artwork that Trollope most eloquently described to "most assuredly be one of the central works of the painter" in question. Trollope's sincere peering over his half-moon glasses while delaying the mention of the price was beyond doubt his most effective strategy when it came to close a deal.

However, Trollope wasn't satisfied with the bread-and-butter business that his rather undistinguished gallery managed to maintain. Now, after years of fencing stolen art, his side business had become ten times more lucrative than his official business when it came to returns. He was recognised as trustworthy by those who had stolen artworks to sell, and – as the thieves sooner or later had to admit – to sell a stolen painting, you certainly need the right contacts.

It was only to some extent that Trollope had these convenient contacts. He was always on the lookout for new prospects. One of his most successful ways of finding a buyer was to visit preview shows of works about to be auctioned at Sotheby's and Christie's.

In the end, it all comes down to three things, Trollope repeated his mantra to himself. *No one wants to be found out. Someone wants to make a deal. Everyone wants to come out on top.* He was thinking this while he discreetly studied the prospective clientele at Sotheby's who had come to study the paintings of its upcoming Impressionist & Modern Art auction. Walking from artwork to artwork at a slow pace, he pretended to look at the paintings. At the same time, Trollope tried to judge any potential new customer with sufficient resources to be of interest to himself.

It was a technique he had successfully developed to near-perfection over the years. When finding someone interested in a particular artist, painting or period, he began grooming this potential customer by offering something similar at a lower price. It wasn't fool-proof, and it didn't always work, but it wasn't the profit or loss from the sales of legitimate artworks that spurred Trollope. Once the customer was hooked making deals of smaller magnitude that soon became obvious winners, Trollope introduced him to "a once in a life-time opportunity" – an artwork lost for decades, reported as stolen, but at a bargain price. Greed was a powerful motivation, he knew, and Trollope never made the offer until he knew the customer well enough to be certain there was no risk in making it.

A diminutive man across the room, lingering in front of a large Picasso painting going for the estimate of 33 – 36 million, caught his eye. Behind him two disinterested men with high cheekbones and of apparent Eastern Europe origin looked bored. *Someone with two bodyguards and an interest in a 30-million-plus Picasso sounds just like my cup of tea*, Trollope thought cheerfully and began to contemplate how to get within chatting distance of his mark.

As he moved closer to his target, who now had continued into a subsequent room, he heard the man giggle after saying something to one of his companions. Trollope was surprised. He had never considered that men giggled; it was something little girls did.

*

"It certainly is a marvellous work of art", Vasily heard the large-bellied man with bushy eyebrows say without watching him. "He was a synaesthete, you know, so he painted what he heard."

Vasily and the stranger who had offered his opinion were standing in front of a Kandinsky painting with an estimate of 5 – 6 million. Immediately after hearing the stranger's words, Vasily could imagine that the colours and flowing paint could make up a symphony. It interested him. It was as if a door had suddenly been opened to him.

"It's a very interesting painting, and your observation intrigues me", Vasily replied as he turned towards the stranger. "Can you elaborate on your remark that Kandinsky was a synaesthete?"

"Oh, I didn't mean to interrupt your tour among these truly fantastic artworks, sir", Trollope said as he turned and lowered his gaze to meet Vasily's. "Please accept my apologies for my spontaneous comment. But, to answer your question, a synaesthete is a person who perceives multiple sensory information. In Kandinsky's case, he saw colours when he heard music. There are also other examples of synaesthesia."

Vasily turned to study the painting again. It overwhelmed him that he could suddenly see music on a piece of canvas.

"You've just made my day." Vasily said and giggled twice. "I wonder why I didn't see this before!"

The man's giggling made Trollope feel uncomfortable. He brought out a small case in which he carried his business cards.

"My name is Ralph Trollope and here is my card, sir. My business is art and I happen to have two similar works by Kandinsky should you be interested to look at them. May I ask whom I have the pleasure of addressing?"

Vasily accepted his card, and with another giggle found one of his own in the breast pocket of his suit.

"It may be that I'm interested to see what you have to offer," he said, studying Trollope as he handed over the card.

Trollope made out the name Benyamin Bogdanovich beneath the logotype that spelled Arexim.

When Vasily later walked out from Sotheby's and was ushered into the Mercedes by Vladimir and Ilya, who then rushed to get into their own car, he was thinking hard about the man he had just met. There was no doubt in his mind that this Trollope was a racketeer in the art business. Vasily's sixth sense told him he could become useful.

Saturday September 21, 2013

Paddy adjusted the bowtie and studied his appearance in the full-length mirror. His unruly locks needed a haircut, he noticed, but there hadn't been time for that. He had arrived home late the previous night after another rewarding cocaine flight. He combed his wet hair the best he could to paste it to his head and hoped he looked respectable enough to be best man. Six months ago, his brother Frank had met this actress, Julie Cross who – and there was no way to deny this in Paddy's view – looked absolutely gorgeous. He had met her on two occasions, and if his brother hadn't decided to marry her, he would have gone after her himself.

He heard the wedding ceremonies shaping up outside

and looked at his watch. He had less than five minutes to present himself downstairs. Chosen to be their best man, he was to hand over the ring to the bride, and Frank had warned him that he'd better not be late – or else.

*

Yuliana looked adoringly at Frank, her husband-to-be.

A year ago, after spending three years in the US, she had decided she wanted to return to London – her true home despite all that had happened to her there. She had met Frank through some friends, and she had found him very charming with his Irish ways. The one exception was when he started talking about financial issues – his favourite subject and one that she abhorred. They had eventually reached an agreement that he would avoid the topic when she was present.

She had fallen in love with Frank. The brusque separation from Matthias still smarted, but with the years the hurt she felt was diminished by her increased need for a loving companionship. Frank was a man who enjoyed life, and he had swept her off her feet. He had taken her to places in Ireland to explain his heritage; he was cultured and well-educated; and he had introduced her to important people in finance and politics. She didn't care much for his friends, but she found Frank to be an exceedingly charming and self-assured man.

When he asked her to marry him, she smiled sweetly and asked him to give her a day and a night before she gave him her answer. Frank had looked upset when he left, but Yuliana knew she had to think through her present and past situations carefully.

How much can I tell him? How much SHOULD I tell him? Once again, she found herself in a quandary where she hated her life so much that she couldn't talk about it. The rapes in Spain; her revenge many years later; the glowing satisfaction she had felt after executing it. Yet, the part of her life that she hesitated most about revealing was the more than two years she had lived happily with Matthias Callaghan. How could she explain this to Frank, who only knew her as Julie Cross? And there was also the small but important detail that, to be able to reside in the UK, she used a false Hungarian passport in the name of Julianna Kovács. Ever since Matthias had arranged for her to be deported back to Romania, after discovering that her real name was Yuliana Korzha, she could no longer use it in the UK.

She eventually came to the conclusion that the difficult things in the past should remain where they were, and opted for not mentioning neither the bright nor the dark days of her relationship with Matthias to Frank. *It's simply best not to dwell on any of the intimate details that ruled my past,* she decided.

She settled on accepting his proposal and explaining to him that Julie Cross was merely a stage name, and that her real name was according to her Hungarian passport. However, while still a young child, her parents had divorced, and she had moved with her Romanian mother to Bucharest. That's why she spoke Romanian and very little Hungarian.

And she no longer had any living relatives, nor had she been married previously. That was true in a sense, because her marriage to Matthias had been annulled since she had used her Julia Cross identity to marry him. *That should cover all the essential facts*, she thought, *and I won't mention anything else about my life before travelling to America, except perhaps for some anecdotes working in London theatres.*

Tuesday September 24, 2013

Vasily's single most important problem was what to do with his constantly growing income. During the last year he had made 20 per cent more than the previous year, and the increase for the coming one looked as if it would be even greater. His present yearly gross earnings were around 400 million pounds, and after paying commissions for laundering, some token taxes on official revenue, salaries, bonuses and other overhead costs, Vasily estimated that his net income was close to 250 million pounds.

For the past year he had invested in setting up additional meth laboratories around Europe, expanding the sales organisation and purchasing franchises to launder the proceeds. Berlosky had come up with a scheme that avoided the stiff commissions previously paid to crooked bankers and others to clean up the profits. He had invested the money in franchises that handled a lot of cash, which meant fast food restaurants, pharmacies, ice cream parlours, shoemakers and, appropriately, laundromats. Through three offshore investment companies that Arexim had set up using Mossack Fonseca in Panama, the franchises had been acquired whenever they became available. Although Vasily left the day-to-day running of these businesses to Pyotr, his chief accountant, who in turn was supervised by Berlosky, the logistics were tedious. In hundreds of small business outlets, the actual income was multiplied on their balance sheets using cash deposits from the drug sales. It implicated having agents who, for a commission, made the deposits in the UK and elsewhere in Europe. The three companies that owned the franchises were based in Ireland. Ireland had been chosen on the recommendation of their legal adviser Longhorn, who had pointed out that this country had a mere 15 per cent corporate tax – the lowest in Europe. On occasion, Vasily had doubts over the complex set-up and wished for something simpler. The new solution that Berlosky had come up with, laundering larger sums through loans to individuals, sounded promising. If it worked out as projected, Vasily was determined to sell off the franchises and simplify the myriad of small businesses that he had long ago lost track of.

At present, he was able to launder about a third of the money he made. The remainder – including a considerable amount of bank notes now occupying significant space in the Moorgate vault – was a constant headache. He was aware that the present increase in his business proceeds called for careful planning. Firstly, he must find a way to prove to the tax authorities that he was able to carry on with his lavish lifestyle thanks to an income that he declared and was being taxed for.

Secondly, he needed to invest his accumulating wealth of undeclared money in something worthwhile. Vasily disliked the notion that his money, stacked on pallets in secret warehouses, wasn't producing more wealth. There were three things in his mind that made sense as investments: properties, a yacht of impressive proportions and artworks.

He already had his tentacles out for opportunistic buying of estates, buildings and villas all over Europe, including Russia. This involved a lot of coordination with payments either in cash or by wire transfer from tax havens and setting up legal identities to become the official proprietor, allowing Vasily to maintain the control from behind the scenes. At the same time, he needed a way to not lose track of the acquisitions he was making in this whirlwind manner.

The idea of buying a yacht appealed to him for several reasons. He had read an article about how the world's billionaires competed trying to best one another by having the largest private yacht built. The price tag for a reasonably big yacht was several hundred million dollars, which would take care of a large chunk of the excess cash he wanted to get rid of. Vasily also imagined himself as a captain aboard a ship, something that he had fantasised about since he was a child.

He was also sincere about investing money in expensive artworks by recognised artists. He considered that investment in art would be both lucrative long-term and, on a personal level, a hobby for pleasure.

Vasily told a secretary to call Ralph Trollope and arrange a meeting that same afternoon. An enthusiastic Trollope replied that he would be delighted to receive him at his art gallery.

It was caution that made Vasily contact Trollope. He didn't want to be involved in buying expensive artworks at auctions and thus attract unnecessary attention from the police or the tax authorities. Vasily knew that the best approach would be to use an intermediary, preferably someone who was a known art dealer. Trollope seemed a good choice. During their brief encounter, Vasily had intuited a streak of dishonesty in the man. It was only a question of confirming whether Trollope could be trusted with the tasks Vasily had in mind.

Vasily entered the art gallery on his own, leaving Vladimir and Ilya waiting in the Mercedes outside. Trollope received him effusively and offered him a choice of gin, whisky or tea. Vasily opted for a cup of tea. After some slight hesitation, Trollope told his assistant to make tea for two.

They strolled through the gallery at leisure, cups in hand, while Trollope pointed at the paintings on the wall and made learned comments about them. The place wasn't large, four show rooms in all. At the end of the tour, Trollope fished a key out of his pocket and opened a door.

"I told you I have a Kandinsky not very different from the one we saw at Sotheby's", Trollope said with a wink. "In here is where I keep the special objects for true collectors."

It was a windowless room. The specially designed furniture, covered with protective green felt for the storage of framed paintings in different sizes, lined the walls. Trollope began to slide the artworks from the niches until he found what he was looking for.

"Here is the Kandinsky I told you about!" he exclaimed with a smile. "Say, isn't it a beauty?"

It was smaller than the painting at Sotheby's, but the colouring was exquisite. Vasily immediately took a liking to it.

"You are right; it is similar to the other one."

"It was painted the same year, and of course I have the documents that show its provenance."

"How much do you want for it?" Vasily asked.

"I will let you have it for four point four million pounds, which is a lot less than the estimate at Sotheby's." He had accepted the painting in consignment from the seller who wanted 3.6 million for it, and he would go as low as 3.7 million to make a quick hundred thousand quid.

"However, the other one is larger, and just because the estimate is higher doesn't mean it will sell."

"If it sells, there will also be a commission to pay to the auctioneer", Trollope countered, unperturbed.

Vasily kept thinking while he studied the painting.

"I'll tell you what", he eventually offered. "I'll buy this painting of yours for four million even. If you manage to buy the other Kandinsky and the Picasso while representing me anonymously at the upcoming Sotheby's auction, and at a price within their estimates, I will pay you the additional ten per cent."

Trollope's head swam at the unexpected proposal. He immediately realised that he had found what every art dealer dreams of: a golden goose.

"May I ask how you will pay for this one?" he queried.

Vasily decided to risk it.

"This painting of yours, I will pay in cash. If you're successful at the auction, you'll receive a wire transfer made to your bank account to enable you to pay for them. How does that sound?"

Trollope's eyes narrowed. Although tempting, this offer was highly unusual. He immediately realised that the money must be funds that the taxman was unaware of. Then again, the diminutive man standing in front of him was a Russian national, and he had heard many stories of the oligarchs who had robbed billions through deals and corruption selling oil, natural gas and other commodities. Or maybe Vasily was a front for one of them?

He shrugged. Why should he care where the money came from? If he secured the purchases at the auction, he would make 800,000 pounds tax free, which could be invested in art easy to displace without HMRC knowing a thing about it. He merely had to convince the seller of the Kandinsky to accept the money in cash, but he was convinced it wouldn't be too difficult. After all, nobody wanted the taxman to have a share.

"Your proposal is attractive, Mister Bogdanovich", Trollope finally said. "I think I can agree to those terms. When would you like to make the transaction?"

Vasily giggled. His evaluation of Trollope's character couldn't have been more precise.

"Why don't you bring the painting to my office the day after tomorrow, where you will get paid?" he said and made for the exit.

Thursday September 26, 2013

When Trollope was ushered into Vasily's office, he was impressed by its unexpected opulence. It made him more than nervous. Had he gone beyond his capacity of doing multi-million deals with people who obviously were working the wrong side of the street, or had he actually found a way to secure a windfall?

He had come alone, despite plenty of apprehension in doing so. Trollope had reasoned that, even if he had appeared with half a dozen bodyguards, he was vulnerable because he was convinced these people had significantly more resources than he would ever have. Trollope understood perfectly well that, once he had entered this high-stakes game, he was committed to its rules. There was a lot of money to be reaped, but there would be no turning back.

After shaking hands, Trollope stripped the painting he had brought of its carefully applied packaging materials. He held it up to Vasily, who was standing at the other side of the room before approaching the painting to study it up close.

"Very well, Mister Trollope, I think we're in business, you and I", Vasily finally said with a grin that looked more ominous than he had intended.

Nevertheless, the calm way Vasily had said it, and the

realisation that there now was no exit after accepting to work with a big-league operator, made Trollope stealthily wipe drops of sweat off his forehead. However, despite his anxiousness, his perception of the financial reward he would reap from now on extinguished any doubts he might have had.

"Now, please allow me to pay you the agreed sum", Vasily, dapper in his suit, told him as he led the way out of his office.

Close by there was an unoccupied office space. Vasily held the door allowing Trollope to enter first. Inside the bare room there was nothing except thirteen identical, blue suitcases. Vasily opened one them, replete with five-pound notes.

"I promised you cash payment, and here it is", Vasily clarified, giggling when he saw Trollope's jaw drop. "To facilitate the removal, I ordered that the bills should be put inside something easy to carry. You decided to come alone – a discretion I certainly appreciate – but it seems to complicate the removal of the money that's now rightfully yours."

Not in his wildest imagination had Trollope even begun to think of how much space four million pounds would occupy, especially if the payment was done with notes in small denominations.

Later, when he had arranged for the money to be transferred to his art gallery using a rented moving van, he did a quick check of the amount he had received. Eight suitcases with five-pound notes, four suitcases with ten-pound notes and one suitcase with twenty-pound notes. *All untraceable, of course,* he pondered with a sigh of satisfaction as he sat down at his desk to call the seller about the successful sale.

Monday October 5, 2013

The Aeroflot jumbo landed at Heathrow with a screeching sound when it made contact with the asphalt runway.

Sonia Malkovich and the three accountants she had vetted – after putting in considerable time and effort – began their disembarkation. After nearly an hour of queues and immigration screening, they were met outside by three cars and Pyotr Litvinoff. When their luggage had been stored, the identical black Mercedes sedans travelled in caravan in the direction of London City.

"I'm happy to have you here", Pyotr offered. "It will be a considerable relief to have your people working to help us diminish the internal paperwork."

Sonia didn't answer and continued to stare straight ahead. She didn't know Pyotr except by name, and she felt that, before anything else, she should get her orders directly from the man who had hired her two years earlier – Vasily Ivanovich.

Friday November 29, 2013

Boris, Arexim's computer wizard, had decided that the easiest way to handle the fake contracts for the subsidiaries was to programme them for the next twelve-month period using a software he specifically designed for the task. On Berlosky's instructions, he let his software randomly assign loans in a range between 12,000 and 30,000 euros. These were matched to a list of names Allan had once downloaded from Amazon's server. The list had at the time been considered useless by Boris, because it didn't contain the customer's credit card information, merely names and shipping addresses. He now found it handy for what he had in mind.

In addition, he fed the programme the black dates from a calendar, excluding all bank holidays. He then copied the dates, applying them to the following five years. After making some internal trials simulating fictitious loans by cheques and repayments, he felt satisfied that everything worked as he wanted.

"It's ready now", Boris told Berlosky. "All wrinkles have been ironed out. I've done at least twenty trials and there is nothing that doesn't work as expected."

"Good Boris", Berlosky said. "I will tell the boss."

Thursday December 12, 2013

Once he had got started, Trollope found it increasingly easy to work with Vasily. Vasily rarely bargained the price he was offered, and he appreciated Trollope's expertise and contacts. Since Vasily was wary regarding the limelight that came with the acquisitions of expensive paintings, he was happy to rely on an art dealer to find him high-quality works that interested him. His flat on Park Lane had eight rooms, and there was still plenty of wall space that needed to be covered.

One afternoon, after having requested a meeting beforehand, Trollope was shown into Vasily's office. He had arrived carrying a thick book under his arm. The Kandinsky painting he had sold to Vasily hung behind his desk, illuminated by newly installed lighting.

"I know you're fond of whisky", Vasily greeted him and waved his hand towards an exquisite handmade cabinet that carried several bottles and crystal tumblers. "Please help yourself."

Trollope accepted the invitation and served himself from a bottle that claimed its content to be twenty years old. Over the past months he had managed to sell Vasily two more paintings, a Gustav Klimt and a Joan Miró. On top of that, he had successfully bid on the Picasso and the Kandinsky at Sotheby's. The Picasso had sold within its estimate, but over the phone he had needed Vasily's approval to go up to 6.8 million for the Kandinsky. This merely proved that Vasily had made a bargain earlier buying the other Kandinsky from him, Trollope later claimed. Vasily had replied by giggling approvingly.

"You wanted to see me", Vasily now said and sat down on the leather sofa opposite the art dealer.

"I have been approached by someone who is offering a Picasso from his cubist period", Trollope began, carefully phrasing his words. "The price is very – very! – attractive, but, alas, there is a minor detail."

"And that is? Vasily asked, sipping his tea.

"A part of the provenance is missing."

"Meaning?"

"Here is a picture of the painting", Trollope said evasively and opened the coffee table book he had brought. He turned the book around and pointed at a full-page illustration. "It's called *Le pigeon aux petits pois*. In my opinion, it's one of his best works from his cubist period."

Vasily studied the reproduction printed on glossy paper. It was without doubt magnificent. The measures below its title indicated its size to be 54 by 65 centimetres. *It would be perfect for the flat*, he thought.

"I like it. Tell me more."

"Like it? It's one of his masterpieces!" Trollope exclaimed. "And, as I said, its existence was recently made known to me together with a heavily discounted price. You see, its provenance can only be documented for its first ninety-nine years –"

"What you want to tell me in a roundabout way," Vasily interrupted him, raising his eyebrows, "is that it's stolen. And now you've come to me to offer it?"

"I thought I should at least bring it to your attention", Trollope, on the defence, weakly explained. "You told me to be on the lookout for opportunities, and I thought this would be one you'd be interested in. But, you're right, I shouldn't even have brought it up – "

"How much is the asking price?" Vasily asked, still studying the illustration.

"Twenty million. It would go for at least twice as much at

auction."

"Save for the little nuisance that you can't auction it off since it's hot goods", Vasily giggled, looking up. "Tell your seller I might be interested at five million, on the condition that I can look at the original first-hand before any deal."

"Five million? I don't think –"

"I won't go higher." Vasily stood up to indicate that the discussion was over. "Arrange for the showing, should the seller be interested."

*

Trollope stepped out of the building housing Vasily's office and hailed a cab. On his way home, he thought about the offer Vasily had made. He had to convince Yonathan Birn to take 4 million, or 4.5 million tops, if he was going to make a decent profit. Yonathan had told him he wanted at least 12 million pounds for it, which he considered a fifth of its true value. On the other hand, Trollope knew perfectly well that it wasn't easy to offload stolen artworks as well known as this Picasso, which was confirmed by its status as unsold for more than three years.

Along with four other masterpieces, it had been stolen from the Musée d'Art Moderne in Paris in 2010, in a theft that at the time had been addressed as "the heist of the century". The thief, nicknamed "Spiderman" and whose real name was Vjeran Tomic, was arrested the following year, but by then the stolen artworks had been passed along to middlemen attempting to sell them for whatever they could get. The joint value of the paintings was eventually determined by the authorities and the insurance company to be 104 million euros. Tomic, who had earned his nickname by scaling buildings to rob the apartments of Paris's wealthy residents, confessed to the police that he had been hired to break into the museum to steal a particular painting by French cubist painter Fernand Léger. When the museum's alarm system – which had been defective for several weeks without repair – didn't go off, Tomic decided to also cut another four paintings from their frames "because he liked them". Despite Tomic's arrest, none of the stolen paintings had been recovered. And now Trollope had found the perfect customer for them.

Perhaps I can bundle it with the Modigliani from the same heist, and ask for ten million? Trollope asked himself. He decided to contact Yonathan to see if the Modigliani painting was still available.

Friday June 27, 2014

"Mikhail, I feel an urge to look at more options to invest my proceeds", Vasily told Berlosky over dinner at Gordon Ramsay's Michelin three-starred restaurant. "I want you to find ways to invest in gems – in particular expensive ones."

"Gems?"

"Diamonds, sapphires, emeralds, anything that seems to be a good investment. Expensive gems have the great advantage of occupying a fraction of the space that dirty-

47

smelling pound notes do, don't you agree?"

"Of course, Vasily, it's a good idea", Berlosky replied, as he suspiciously munched on the unfamiliar minuscule dish that had just been served as part of seemingly never-ending helpings of the *menu dégustation* that Vasily had ordered for them both. Personally, he preferred pizza. "I'll look into it right away. I think I know just the person to contact."

Sunday August 10, 2014

At the graveyard, the humidity on this grey afternoon threatened to convert itself into rain at any moment. Georgie listened to the priest's words floating upon the foggy air. *Words, carefully phrased, intended to strike the delicate balance of telling the truth while praising the qualities of the deceased. Not an easy task,* Georgie thought while picturing himself in a similar casket in fifty years' time.

As the mourners moved away from the burial site after the ceremonial, Georgie kept repeating to himself that he now was completely on his own. Fate had left him with the riches his Uncle Jeremiah had accumulated during his lifetime, bequeathed to his father upon Flint's death. Now, with his father also dead, Georgie no longer faced any restrictions spending Flint's fortune. *You never know for whom you're working,* he smiled to himself, and silently sent Uncle Jeremiah a grateful thought. The more he considered his new situation, the better he liked it. His father had been too old, too weary and too cautious to spend more than a pittance of Flint's legacy, and whatever he had spent, had mostly gone to pay medical bills.

Nearly five years had passed since Flint had been found dead from a heart attack with his face on a plate of food. Georgie's father wouldn't allow Georgie to squander more than a little extra of Flint's fortune – and then only when he was travelling abroad. "It's too risky", Phil had insisted. "You're a police officer, and the moment you start spending more than you earn, someone will take notice and suspect you of taking bribes or of some other crime."

Georgie acknowledged this to be true. Now that his dad was dead, the obvious solution was to create a second home abroad and resign from the Metropolitan Police. It had to be done credibly, certainly, to avoid any suspicions of the life he looked for spending the spoils that Flint had hoarded.

Together with the other two dozen or so of his father's friends and distant relatives, he left the graveyard and walked into the pub for his dad's wake.

Monday August 11, 2014

"I'm sorry about your loss, George", Detective Inspector John Blackmoore, Georgie's immediate boss, greeted Georgie when he entered the office at Scotland Yard.

"I really miss my dad, sir, and lately I've been thinking I should take his advice, the one he always insisted on making."

"What advice would that be, then?"

"He always said I should study. Dad said his greatest

49

regret was not to have paid more attention to his own education, and he didn't want me to share that regret."

"What, then, is your intention?"

"I want to honour my father by pursuing a university degree. I wish to take a leave from the Yard for a couple of years and then return better educated and with a chance to rise in the ranks. I might even get your job one day, if I'm lucky!"

"That'll be the day, George", Blackmoore grimaced. "Don't misunderstand me. I'm all for you and other people to get more education, but I'd hate to lose a reliable officer like yourself."

"Thank you kindly for the encouragement, sir. I still haven't thought this through, but I think I'll ask for a leave starting next summer."

"All right, that means you have plenty of time to reconsider it."

"No, that's the time I need to get my life organised. Besides, I need to reinforce my savings if I want to take time off for university."

Sunday August 17, 2014

"I washed my hair twice this morning, and I can still find the rice in it that Jack was the most ardent to throw", Samantha said as she embraced me from behind in front of our twins. "Hey, is anybody up for Chinese food tonight? Courtesy of Uncle Jack! Just tell me, and I'll shake my hair."

50

I laughed, pleased that she was in such good mood. The children, now three years old, began throwing their breakfast corn flakes at her.

"So, boys, did you like your mom and dad's big wedding party yesterday?"

"I liked the cake!" George shouted.

"No, the fireworks. Because that's what makes a wedding, George," Owen retorted.

Despite their close physical resemblance, we had both detected that, while George was exuberant and enjoyed expressing himself for hours painting, Owen was more silent, thoughtful, even philosophical at times, despite his young age.

When I had got my real identity back after laying bare my story at the London Metropolitan Police headquarters, it had become possible for me to marry Samantha. Finally, after several years, there no longer existed any legal hindrance to do what I wanted: marry or travel or apply for things using my real identity.

I looked with longing at Samantha as she admonished the children to stop throwing corn flakes, or else. All of sudden I felt that I had never been happier, despite all that I had gone through. Yes, I had to continue my daily diet of ciclosporin. No, I didn't dare to return to the United States, or to countries with which the United States had extradition agreements, although the passport I had used when Thumps had been killed had been my father's. Yet, what did all this matter, when I was living happily with my wife and children in Sydney, Australia?

Our construction project with Jack at the helm was about to reach its successful conclusion, and the investment was beginning to show profits. Jack was already talking about another project, grander still, on the outskirts of Sydney. After discussing it with Samantha, I had let Jack know that we could be persuaded by the idea. I liked working on a large construction project. More than leadership, I had learned, it needed careful supervision: to avoid theft of tools and materials; to exact the necessary performance from the workers while treating them with fairness; to not cede to constant and inevitable excessive demands of additional money or time off. I enjoyed solving problems, and a large construction site presented a large variety of these.

"Look, Samantha, I think I'm going to have a look at how our own future home has advanced, now that there are no workers around", I said and rose from the table.

"You do that, dear", Samantha replied with a smile. "The boys will keep me busy."

I left the small house where the four of us lived, really Samantha's bachelorette home that by necessity had been converted into a four-person household. Accustomed in the past to living in an eight-room penthouse in London with a butler in a flat next door, the cramped space we now occupied was truly getting on my nerves. With the increased sales of the properties from our joint venture with Jack, the money had started its reverse flow, and together with Samantha, we had decided to build a large house on a cliff overlooking Sydney Harbour. It was the first time I had ever partaken in a construction project that required creative solutions on a day-to-day basis. I took pleasure every minute in doing it.

Wednesday September 3, 2014

"Remember me? Do you remember my dad?" Georgie asked as he faced the man he had met on only one previous occasion. The man in question was a fragile-looking forger by the name of Milton Cooper.

Milton looked up at him with a keen eye.

"Yes, I recall, you came here once, maybe twenty years ago, a young lad then. Your father brought you. A premium customer, your father. Always paid on time, never had complaints, and not even once did he cause me problems with the coppers."

"I'm here to see if I can contribute to the family tradition. I need a passport or two."

"So, you need a passport or two", Milton sighed. "And what kind of passports would that be?"

Wednesday September 17, 2014

Alistair Stewart was a stooped man in his mid-sixties who lived in one of the seedier districts of Greater London. He was lean on the verge of looking famished and had large, pleading eyes that fooled even the most cunning cop. His disguise was his physical presence, and, perhaps because of it, he was one of the most successful fences in the capital.

Georgie had met him on four occasions when accompanying his father. The first time as a young boy, but the last time as an out-of-uniform constable. Since then, more than fifteen years had passed.

Contemplating his future, Georgie had given himself until the end of May the coming year to dissolve his present, gloomy life and, without raising any suspicions, convert it into his idea of luxury and endless pleasures, now that he could afford it. One of the many issues he faced was how to launder Flint's treasure trove into untraceable cash. The gold and the jewels he had helped his father retrieve weren't something he could just go to a pawnshop or a metal broker to get cash for. He had quickly realised that he needed a fence to cash in on Flint's inheritance. The only one his father had seemed to trust was Alistair Stewart, so Georgie had decided to look him up.

Alistair blinked several times at the man who had entered the simple locksmith operation that acted as the front for his real activities. The young man, not yet forty, with tousled brown hair and matching puppy dog eyes seemed familiar to him. Then he remembered: it was Phil's son. The last time he had seen Phil and the boy was, what, twelve or fifteen years ago?

"Hello there, Alistair", Georgie smiled at him, "I'm Georgie. My dad used to do business with you. Phil Jones, if you recall."

"I remember my old friend Phil very well", Alistair said, giving him a hesitant smile. "How's he doing these days? I haven't seen him for a bit."

"Alas, the hearse took him to his grave this past summer", Georgie replied with a sad look on his puppy face.

"It grieves me to hear the news, lad. I always respected your dad for providing me with good business and paying me fair and square for my services."

"I'm here willing to continue the tradition, Alistair", Georgie said, "though I'd prefer a more discreet environment to discuss the issues at hand, if you don't mind."

"Of course", Alistair replied and rose from his chair. "We should go into my office. Follow me."

Alistair unlocked a door and led his visitor through a corridor to another locked door. After he had opened it, Georgie was stunned with the elegance inside that contrasted the outer office: mahogany walls, leather furniture, the latest in computers, classy paintings on the walls …

Alistair pointed at one of the easy chairs and seated himself in a swivel chair behind his desk.

"So how can I be of any help to you, Georgie?" he asked, then added: "Don't worry about speaking freely, this room is soundproof in every respect."

"I know you helped my dad cash in on some jewellery of questionable origin", Georgie began. "It so happens, that he bequeathed me more of the kind, and I am at my wits' end how to convert it into money. That's why I thought of coming to you."

"You did well, lad. But first of all, let me understand what it is that you have to offer."

55

Georgie reached into the inner pocket of his jacket and brought out a small package.

"Some samples for you to consider before we get down to the main business."

Alistair carefully opened the package to reveal a dozen gem stones: six diamonds, two emeralds, two rubies and two sapphires.

"These are samples from different batches, to allow you to appreciate any differences in quality", Georgie offered.

After finding a loupe in one of his drawers, Alistair fastened it in his right eye. Beneath the light of a lamp with the Kelvin degrees set to daylight illumination, he made a note about each stone after having studied it with great care.

"So, what do you think?" Georgie asked.

"I think some of the stones are good, while others are not so good", Alistair replied and switched off the lamp. "Since they don't have any provenance, it'll take some time to unload them. How many carats do you want to sell, in all?"

The question caught Georgie off guard. Should he tell Alistair that he had about three thousand gems that he wanted to sell? No, he decided, it was better to do this piecemeal; perhaps even use some other fence to balance things out.

"I don't know how many carats, but in all I have about a hundred and twenty stones."

"Leave these with me and I'll tell you how much I can get you for them. I need to study them more closely. If the rest of the gems you have match the ones you're showing me now, it'll give you an idea of how much you can expect. Fair enough?"

Georgie thought about Alistair's proposition for a brief moment. Considering the amount of gems he had in his possession, the samples didn't present much of a risk. Besides, he doubted that Alistair would make a run over a handful of stones, and his daddy had trusted him for many years.

"That's fine with me. When will you tell me what these ones will fetch?"

"Come back in a week." Alistair rose. "Now, let me show you out."

After letting Georgie out of the shop, Alistair returned to his office and began scrutinising the gems with more care. There was one nagging detail that he couldn't get out of his head while he studied the stones under his powerful microscope.

Four years earlier his nephew Sid, together with twenty others, had been caught in a drug-related police operation. The sting had landed Sid in prison for twelve years.

Alistair had a clear recall that one of the arresting officers was Georgie, Phil Jones's son.

Sunday September 21, 2014

"After the Rabbit was caught being too interested in puppy love", Berlosky told Vasily, "we have run out of inside information from the Metropolitan Police."

"Then you'd better make some effort to find ourselves a new source", Vasily replied disinterestedly, without raising his eyes from the newspaper flown in from Moscow that morning.

"It's not that easy", Berlosky protested. "It takes time to set up a first-class informer to provide us with top-level intelligence."

"Well, if you can't do it, I'm sure I'll find someone else who can", Vasily yawned while doubling the newspaper. "Either you come up with a solution, or you'll be replaced by a person who delivers what I need."

Vasily yawned again, looked briefly at Berlosky and left the room.

Berlosky doubted that Vasily could replace him so easily after all the years he had worked in the organisation. At the same time, he knew that Vasily could be ruthless if someone working for him didn't give him the results he wanted. Berlosky racked his brain for some entrance to a corrupt cop. He decided he needed to make it his top priority from now on until he found one who could take the Rabbit's place.

Wednesday September 24, 2014

Alistair looked up as the bell discreetly announced a customer entering his shop. He recognised Georgie.

"Hallo there, Georgie boy, good of you to look in again", Alistair cheerfully greeted him.

"How could I not, considering I recently left a small fortune here with you?" Georgie replied in the same playful veneer.

"Yes, you did, my boy, you certainly did. Let's withdraw to my office to discuss it further, shall we?"

When they were seated in his secret den, Alistair moved to open a small cupboard from which he brought out several small white jeweller envelopes. "I have studied them with interest. To sum it up: some are quite good, many more are mediocre and most of them are not of a particularly good quality."

"If you were to give me an approximate value for the lot you've examined, what number would you come up with? Now, understand this question of mine in the context of my possible future interest of allowing you to purchase five times as many stones."

Alistair involuntarily smiled. He was used to people coming to offer him gems with a questionable history. Georgie was no different.

"I'll tell you what I would pay for the lot, and then you leave with what you brought me, with no charge for the evaluation. I consider it to be worth sixty thousand pounds if I were to purchase them from you today."

The amount – much higher than he had expected – took Georgie's breath away.

"In case I were interested, how would you pay me?" he asked.

"The same way I paid your father when we were doing business in the past, I thought", Alistair responded, smiling. From his reaction, he knew that Georgie would accept his offer, which was about a fifth of the real worth. After some shuffling with acquaintances in his business, he estimated he could make more than 200,000 pounds passing on the gems.

"But, whichever way you want, Georgie. Your father preferred cash, I seem to remember, but perhaps you'd prefer to opt for some of the more modern ways of payment?"

"OK, let's do it. Cash is fine with me. I'll pick it up Thursday next week, if that's all right with you. If everything goes well, I'll bring you a few more stones to consider, all right?"

"Sounds perfectly fine to me", Alistair said as he rose to show him the way out. "Whatever you need, consider this your second home."

Sunday October 12, 2014

Julie Cross was back in London after what had been a couple of successful years on Broadway in New York. Cameras clicked and flashes fired as she walked onstage to scattered applause for the promotion of her upcoming musical *New York, New York*. The theatre, where she was going to perform next, had arranged a press conference to promote the new show she would appear in.

Trudy Swift, bored with the assignment of covering the event even before it had begun, sat sprawled in the theatre seat noisily chewing gum. The reporter who usually covered entertainment events was in bed with the flu. For lack of other newsworthy stories to follow up on, Trevor Burns – editor-in-chief at the *Daily Mirror* – had asked her to stand in for her sick colleague.

Trudy, a skinny 28-year-old self-taught journalist with a keen intelligence and a penchant for everything black – clothes, lipstick, hair (cut short), nail polish, boots (army style) – deeply disliked writing for the paper's social pages. She felt it was beneath her dignity as a serious newspaperwoman. She wanted to dig into political conundrums, upper echelon crimes, twisted corruption cases that led to the downfall of important people, and more such in the same vein. Despite her young age, she was quite respected by both Burns and her colleagues at the paper. More than anything, because she doggedly pursued her conviction of what was rotten once she had got the scent of an important story. Trudy also had a talent for nailing the essence of a story, writing articles with very concise words – hence Burns's respect for her despite her youth and rebellious presence.

The murmur of voices from the press corps, an estimated thirty-five in all, went quiet as the producer of the theatrical work announced the leading star. *She's still quite good-looking for being one so old,* Trudy reluctantly admitted to herself as she listened to the actress give a short speech promoting the upcoming musical. Although Trudy didn't like covering arts and social events, she was nevertheless a professional, and she had done her homework looking up the actress. Julie Cross was 44 years old, she knew. She had recently returned to London after three much-applauded years on Broadway. Wikipedia – which Trudy didn't consider a reliable source by far, but she found the online encyclopaedia convenient for looking up general facts that she needed fast – claimed that she was an actress and singer born in Spain to a British father and a Spanish mother, and who had arrived in London in her teens. Wikipedia also listed the successes that she had had over the years, from her beginning in small roles to her triumphant years in New York. She had recently married a banker, Frank O'Hare.

What could be more fitting, now that she was back in London after her three-year stint in the US, than to star in the musical *New York, New York*?

Tuesday October 14, 2014

Three youths were standing on Wapping Lane, smoking and talking loudly while stomping their feet to keep the cold away. Georgie approached them, cap pulled down over his forehead and a scarf wrapped around the lower part of his face.

"Hey, lads, can you do me a favour if there's ten quid in it for you?"

They all looked at him suspiciously as if he were some kind of pervert. Georgie caught their looks and the message they broadcast.

"I need to ship this envelope with some urgency, but I have a problem. My old lady works in there", he said, nodding at the DHL facility half a block away. "I just can't get inside because the other night she caught me red-handed chatting up a lady friend of hers, if you see what I mean. So, if you're game, there's a tenner up front for just walking inside and handing over the parcel."

It didn't take much to convince the teenagers, who anticipated spending the money on beers despite being too young to enter a pub. Georgie gave the keenest of the teenagers enough to cover the shipping cost and added the promised ten-pound note for their trouble.

Standing hidden behind a corner across the street, he watched how the three youths entered the courier office. Five minutes later they came out empty-handed, laughing and shouting to each other about the easy money they had made.

The padded envelope, addressed to Detective Inspector John Blackmoore at the New Scotland Yard, contained a generic USB stick and nothing else. With his wry sense of humour, Georgie had put down Abdul Mahfouz as the sender. If Blackmoore would attempt to find the real person behind the remittance, at best there would be a description of three young boys who had no connection whatsoever to himself.

The fact that I specified Mahfouz as the sender will be certain to raise Blackmoore's interest, Georgie thought with glee over his cleverness. *There's no way that this ubiquitous USB stick can be tracked down, nor the digital message. Flint is dead. The only obvious lead for the investigators will be to pick up Callaghan, which should result in the issue of his arrest warrant. You have it coming, Callaghan, and it only serves you right for double-crossing Uncle Flint and cheating him out of what was going to be my inheritance. Yes, the bottom line is that you swindled me out of money that today should rightfully be mine.*

He was sending the USB stick to Blackmoore with a

sense of mischief more than one of vengeance, just to see what it would lead to. Now that he was a rich man, he also relished the power that came with money. Georgie felt that he could do just about anything, and this was his first test to prove whether this was true.

Thursday October 16, 2014

Detective Inspector Blackmoore yawned as he sat down behind his desk. He had come to the office earlier than usual this morning because of new cases that required his attention. Then he saw the package with a DHL label on his desk.

Inside it, without any explanatory letter, there was a USB stick. He connected it to his computer. When he listened to its contents, he immediately came out of his drowsiness. He listened to it three times before he was satisfied that he had understood every detail.

*

"Jones", Blackmoore called out, "do you remember the case we were never able to solve, the one regarding the lawyer Rathbone who was strangled in the spring of two thousand and nine? Well, this morning I got an anonymous voice file that clearly indicates that the murder was performed by Thompson, the thug who shot to local fame by being killed by a giant cactus in Arizona. In addition, it charges Jeremiah Flint, now deceased, to have ordered the murder. More important still, Flint accepted to arrange the murder in exchange for economic benefits offered by someone who wanted Rathbone's death. Now, if that's not an interesting bouquet of characters, I don't know who would qualify! I want you to listen to this."

Georgie sat through the session listening to the same tape he had heard dozens of times before.

"It sounds very grave", he said when it ended.

"Grave?" Blackmoore asked, looking at him. "Here's unequivocal proof of a murder set-up, and the best you can come up with is 'grave'?"

"Well, it's a serious matter that's been buried for a long time", Georgie joked.

Blackmoore wasn't a man who appreciated double entendre and merely stared at Georgie.

"What would you like me to do, then?" Georgie asked him evenly. "Thompson is dead and, as you just pointed out, so is Flint."

"The person who instigated the murder is still on the loose. Now, you too were present when Matthias Callaghan came clean here at the Yard a couple of years ago and admitted that he had assumed Mahfouz's identity. Since the real Mahfouz died in two thousand and seven, it must have been Callaghan who made a deal with Flint to have Rathbone done away with! It also checks with the account that Flint and the false Mahfouz co-signed at the bank."

"That sounds about right, sir, but to be completely sure I'd like to go over the records that were archived."

"Of course you should, Jones, just like I have done this morning. I might have missed something, and it's always safer to have four eyes going over a case before we reopen it."

"Yes, sir, I'll get on it right away."

"When you're finished, I want you to immediately issue an order for Interpol to apprehend Callaghan."

"Yes, sir", Georgie responded, smiling inwardly. "Count on it."

"There's one more thing. Have this envelope analysed. As you should recall, Callaghan told us a long and wild story how he was given a face transplant when he was in a coma. The bizarre thing is that the face he was given, and the identity he adopted, was that of Abdul Mahfouz. Somehow, someone has once again decided to appropriate his name by putting it down as the sender. Also, check with DHL to see if they have some CCTV images from the person who handed in the package.

"What shall I put down as the charge in the arrest warrant, sir?"

"Alleged conspiracy and instigation to commit a first-degree homicide."

Friday October 17, 2014

The pieces are coming together, Georgie thought happily. *I've got extra passports in the names of James Stuart and Peter Forrester; I've cashed in enough diamonds to cover expenses and more for the next year; and Nathalie adores me and my new Paris flat. Life is certainly looking up compared to being a flatfoot at the Yard. I'll keep a low profile in London, and travel on my new passports to Paris on my free weekends. Then I'll give it – what, another six months? – before I resign from the force on the pretext that I want to pursue a higher education.*

Georgie's view on life had taken on a whole different dynamic since his father's funeral. He realised now that he had never ventured to override his father's decisions, like the important one about spending the inheritance Flint had left them. Well, his father had used very little of the inheritance, and now that he was dead, it meant that Georgie – unknown to anyone else on earth as far as he knew – could spend it all alone. *Thanks to Uncle Jeremiah, I've become one of life's lottery winners,* Georgie reflected, sending a thankful thought to Flint's unknown whereabouts, which he suspected were further from heaven than its opposite.

His first action that morning had been to confirm to Blackmoore that the arrest warrant request for Matthias Callaghan had been sent to Interpol.

Tuesday October 21, 2014

Ilya Furo, who reported directly to Mikhail Berlosky, drove his boss's Mercedes car, carefully avoiding the puddles from the latest rain. He pulled up by the kerb and stopped in front of the address where he had been sent on his errand.

When Ilya entered the locksmith shop, Alistair Stewart peered suspiciously at him as if he didn't recognise him, despite Ilya's dozen previous visits.

"What's the matter, *tovarich*, are you forgetting who your best customer is?"

Alistair merely mumbled something about how nothing was secure these days before he unlocked the door to the corridor that led the way to his office.

"So, what can I do for you?" Alistair asked once they were inside the soundproof room.

"This time we want to increase the order", Ilya said. "The three purchases we've made so far were only trial orders to see if you would deliver the promised quality. The gems we got matched your description, so you have nothing to worry about."

"Worry? Why should I worry? The only thing that gives longevity in my line of work is delivering the promised goods."

"And so you did, on three occasions", Ilya replied. "That's why my boss has charged me with a purchase of twelve million pounds of top quality diamonds."

"My, my, isn't that a pretty sum!" Alistair replied, amused. "I'm sure I can't produce gems to that amount in a hurry. It'll take me plenty of time to do so, and I will need some guarantee that you won't renegotiate on the purchase."

"How much do you want as down payment?" Ilya asked. "Oh, and don't for a second think you can go for an extended holiday before delivering on any advance payment."

"Of course not", Alistair sighed. "Who do you take me for? You sound just like that young copper who came in the other day and …"

"What young copper?" Ilya sounded alarmed.

"Don't worry, this copper was selling me gems that were far from legitimate. I hear he struck it rich when a distant relative of his died.

"I see", Ilya said, intrigued. "And who was this copper?"

Alistair looked him squarely in the eyes for twelve seconds.

"I'm not in the business of revealing names. Not yours, nor anyone else's."

Wednesday October 22, 2014

"I've made the deal with Alistair Stewart as you wanted", Ilya reported to Berlosky. "Two million pounds as down payment. The diamonds will be delivered two weeks later against the balance owed, ten million that is. I did make it clear that he'd better not cheat us on the quality of the stones."

"Good work, Ilya", Berlosky replied, "I'll have the money prepared for Thursday. Did he mention anything else of interest?"

"Not really … well, he did say that he was fencing gems for a cop."

"For a cop, you say?" Berlosky's interest was immediately roused. "That sounds interesting. Why don't you give me the details?"

*

Two years had gone by since Berlosky had started looking for someone inside the Metropolitan Police to replace John Stopper. Stopper was the cop he had baptised 'the Rabbit' who now was convicted of and incarcerated for sexual abuse of children. To Berlosky, Ilya's information sounded promising indeed: a cop who was selling diamonds to a fence was certainly an encouraging venue to explore.

Berlosky told Ilya to wait outside while he entered the little locksmith shop. Alistair Milton looked at him suspiciously. It was the first time they met.

"I've come to confirm that the two million quid you want up front is being prepared as we speak", Berlosky offered as an introduction that he was bona fide. "The cash will be delivered to the agreed address on Friday. Ilya, with whom you've been dealing, has the necessary instructions and will supervise this and the upcoming payment. We are satisfied with the quality you've given us so far, but don't let us down on this one. It would destroy the beginning of a successful partnership."

Alistair merely nodded his agreement and waited for Berlosky to come to the point of his visit. It was obvious to him that something else was on the Russian's mind besides a veiled threat to deliver the promised goods.

"I'm interested in some information. I was told by Ilya that you have a cop who is selling you stones."

"I don't give out that kind of information. Besides, why should I cut you in on who my suppliers are? So, you can skip the middle man?"

"Don't get me wrong, Alistair – I'm not at all interested in buying anything from this cop. We rely on you to assess the quality of the stones, because, simply put, we don't have that knowledge. Why would we place a twelve-million-pound order with you if it wasn't so?"

"Why do you want to know about this cop?"

Berlosky hesitated at first, but decided to be frank.

"I was thinking that maybe he can help me straighten out an issue or two that I've had with the police. It's worth a try. Now, to make this easier for you, I'm willing to pay for his name. I'll give you twenty-five thousand quid up front, and later the same amount again if he turns out to be what I'm looking for. How does that sound?"

Berlosky reached inside his jacket and pulled out wads of money held together with rubber bands.

Alistair had been around a long time, and he had survived up to his retirement age. He knew perfectly well that Berlosky and his lot were dangerous people. It took him ten clicks from the pendulum of his grandfather clock in the corner to decide that there was no way out of this, except to accept the offer.

"His name is Georgie Jones."

Friday October 24, 2014

Berlosky ordered Boris to make an exhaustive research regarding Detective Sergeant George Jones. Boris didn't find the task too difficult: there was plenty of official information to be found about him just by digging into the Metropolitan Police's web site. He also found several images of him searching Google Images. By cross-checking information, he found an address, that his father had died a few months earlier, and that Georgie had been the sole heir.

Boris then looked up Georgie's father to see if he could come up with something else of interest. There turned out to be plenty. Philip Jones had been in prison twice for robbery, the second time around with a sentence of 10 years. After his release for good behaviour, there was nothing for 30 years until Boris stumbled upon an inheritance he had received in January 2010. When he had exhausted the information available on the Internet, Boris took his investigation to Berlosky.

"If you want more details", Boris told him, "I must either hack into the Metropolitan Police server, or you should send someone to follow this Georgie Jones."

"All right, I'll make the decision after I've read through your report."

After Boris had left, Berlosky rapidly eyed the documents. Georgie was a bachelor, 38 years old and a detective sergeant with the Metropolitan Police. He drove a seven-year-old car and lived alone in a modest house in one of London's suburbs, with plenty of mortgage still to be paid off. His father had died earlier the same year, but Boris's investigation didn't reveal where Georgie had got his stolen gems from, or if he had more of them for Alistair Stewart to fence.

Then, on the last page, one item caught his eye: in 2010, Georgie's father, Philip Jones, had inherited a pub called The Lion's Head on Upper Street in Islington from a certain Jeremiah Flint. *What a coincidence,* Berlosky thought, recalling the day five years earlier when he had been ordered by Vasily to pick up Flint for interrogation. *Of course, that's where he got the diamonds from.* Berlosky remembered Flint as a local gangster boss who had given them some information about Mahfouz and Callaghan. *If Flint left Georgie's father the pub, he probably let him inherit the fenced jewellery as well. And now that Phil Jones is dead, it's no surprise that his earthly belongings have gone to his only son, Georgie. And now Georgie, young and unmarried, wants to cash in and have a fun time with the money. well, it really stands to logic. He'll be the perfect replacement for the Rabbit who, alas, will remain languishing in prison for years to come.*

Berlosky picked up the phone and dialled Boris.

"Boris, find out why Jeremiah Flint left his pub to Philip Jones when he died, and if there were any other heirs."

He then called for Oleg Volkov, his lieutenant, to come to his office.

"Oleg, I want you to stalk a man called George Jones without letting him know that you're doing it", he instructed him. "Find out what he spends money on, where he goes, where he sleeps, who he meets, anything and everything. Here is his home address and a picture of him."

"How much time will you give me?" Oleg asked.

"A week, tops", Berlosky replied. "Oh, by the way, I

think you should know that he's a police officer with Scotland Yard, so proceed with caution."

Saturday October 25, 2014

With Vladimir driving, Oleg arrived outside the address where Georgie lived just after five in the morning. They sipped on their hot coffee that Vladimir had brought in a thermos until it was a quarter to seven. At this hour they saw a man, matching the photo Berlosky had given Oleg, come out through the front door before locking it. He carried a medium-sized suitcase. A taxi arrived at the same moment, and Georgie got into the car.

Dawn was just about to arrive. The weather was foggy with light rain. Forty-five minutes later the cab pulled up in front of St Pancreas station. Oleg ordered Vladimir to stop five cars away. He got out with the small bag that he brought as a precaution, with necessities and sufficient change of clothes for three days, and told Vladimir to return to Arexim.

He overheard how Georgie bought a Business Premier ticket to Paris at the Eurostar ticket counter before looking up at the big clock inside the terminal. When Georgie got on the escalator to the upper floor, Oleg hurried over to the ticket counter he had just left. He waited impatiently behind two couples, one elderly and one younger with two small children in a twin carriage. The latter took their good time fussing about the children, not finding the wallet and dropping some loose change on the floor. When they finally but ever so slowly

74

removed themselves from the counter, Oleg asked about the next train leaving.

"It leaves in twenty-five minutes. You may just make it if you hurry. Do you want first or second class?"

Oleg thought quickly. Georgie was travelling first class, and he didn't want to bump into him unnecessarily.

"Second class", he said and put some bills on the counter.

Oleg ran up the escalator two steps at a time. At the security check, he threw down his overnight bag in front of the X-ray machine, pulled off his belt and put it on a tray together with his mobile, his watch and some coins.

"Your shoes as well, sir", the security guard admonished him after three persons before him had passed the metal detector without removing their footwear.

Oleg swore silently and hurried to get his shoes off. The guard offered him another tray. He passed the detector without causing it to beep. Oleg glanced at his watch as he picked it up. Eight minutes until departure. Without bothering to tie his shoelaces, he walked fast to the passport control, where he produced his fake Belgian passport. After it had been checked, it was handed back to him with a curt nod that he was allowed to pass.

He couldn't see Georgie on the platform. Oleg jogged along the train until he found the carriage he had been assigned and got on the train. Sweating lightly, he found his seat and sat down with a sigh of relief. There was a newspaper in the pocket in the seat in front of him, which he started reading as the train started moving.

Ten minutes before the train's arrival in Paris, Oleg walked through the carriages until he came to the one right behind the section with the first-class passengers. He made sure to be the first one off the train and hurried along the platform towards the exit where he stopped. Covering his face with the newspaper he had found on the train, he watched the Eurostar passengers as they walked by. When he detected Georgie, he let him pass before throwing away the newspaper and starting to follow him.

Outside Gare du Nord, Oleg watched how Georgie got into a grey Mercedes taxi. A man approached Oleg and asked him where he wanted to go.

"You drive a cab?"

"*Oui, monsieur.*"

"OK, let's go. See that cab over there? Don't lose it and I'll pay you twice the fare on the meter."

Oleg's cab driver turned out to be Bulgarian and very slow at shifting the gears on his diesel-powered Renault. To Oleg's despair, he could see that Georgie's taxi driver was considerably more agile moving through the heavy traffic. A heated discussion between the taxi driver and himself in a mix of French, Russian, Bulgarian and English didn't help. Approaching the eighth arrondissement, Oleg had to admit he had lost Georgie.

Still upset with the driver, he got out of the cab. He threw a couple of euro bills through the open window and walked away ignoring the insults the driver was shouting after him. At the crossing, he noted the name of the streets where he had lost Georgie's taxi: Avenue Niel at the corner of Avenue des Ternes.

What should he do now? How could he find Georgie?

*

After arriving at the address he had given the cabbie, Georgie paid him and went down into the underground garage, where he pulled off the protective cloth that covered his impeccable, yellow Lamborghini. He had owned it for a mere three months and was still in love with its beautiful curves. He spent half an hour merely sitting in the car, inhaling the rich leather and listening to the excellent sound system.

Forty minutes later, Georgie took the old-fashioned elevator on the ground floor to his new home on the fourth floor. The flat was located three buildings away on the same street as the garage. He quietly unlocked the door and stepped inside. His watch showed 12:52, local time. After discarding his overcoat and leaving the suitcase in the hallway, he crossed the three-room apartment and opened the door to the master bedroom.

Standing on the threshold he heard Nathalie snoring lightly. As usual she slept covered by nothing except the green silk sheets that he, at her insistence, had bought a month earlier.

After admiring her youth and her beauty, Georgie sat down next to her and gently shook her.

"Nathalie, wake up."

"Oh, *chéri*", she replied sleepily and put her arms around his neck without opening her eyes. "I'm so glad that you're finally here. Come to bed, won't you?"

*

It occurred to Oleg that the taxi that had taken Georgie might be stationed outside Gare du Nord and would return for more fares. He hailed a new cab and asked the driver to be taken there. He waited for thirty-five minutes until he saw the grey Mercedes, with its sign lit to indicate that it was free, stop at the end of the taxi queue. Oleg walked up to the car and motioned the driver to lower his window.

"I believe you had a customer this morning, a man not yet forty that you picked up here at Gare du Nord." Oleg didn't speak any French, so he spoke slowly in the hope that he would be understood.

"Yes, monsieur, perhaps I did, but what's it to you?" To Oleg's relief, the driver spoke passable English. He thought quickly.

"What's it to me? Only that he has made a cuckold of me, seducing my wife, that's what!" Oleg tried to sound impassioned. "I want to confront him, so I followed him to Paris, but I lost him in the traffic."

The driver looked slightly amused at the prospect of a drama involving an incensed husband snubbed by his wife's lover.

"So, what's it got to do with me?" he asked.

"I'll pay you twice your fare if you take me to the address where you let him off", Oleg said angrily. "I want to discuss a thing or two with this … this lowlife."

The cabbie couldn't see any harm in it. It was good money, and he might also pick up some juicy details during the ride that he would be able to share along with some laughs with his pals.

"All right, double fare and I'll take you there. But you have to pay a hundred euros up front, mister."

Forty minutes later, the driver of the grey Mercedes stopped outside the garage where he earlier had dropped off Georgie.

"I saw him go in there", he said and pointed at a door that was part of a larger garage door. The story Oleg had told him was still ringing in his ears. It would certainly make for a great laugh over lunch.

When the taxi had left, Oleg eyed the building. He wrote down the address in a notebook and tried the door to the garage. It was locked. There was one entrance door on either side of the garage, both with names next to the buzzers to announce visitors. He wrote down the names of everyone. They all sounded French. *Maybe he's renting something second-hand?* Oleg wondered. *Or he's visiting a woman who lives here? But why would he enter by the garage if he wants to see some girlfriend?* He decided to wait across the street until someone came out.

It was a long wait. At least he had some information: an address in a fancy part of Paris. A couple came walking on the opposite side towards the garage. Oleg stiffened when he recognised Georgie, and pulled back into the shadow of the entranceway. Georgie had his arm around the waist of a stunning brunette who walked slowly and provocatively as if she owned the world. She laughed gaily at something he said. Georgie opened the garage door with a key and disappeared inside while she waited rummaging for something in her handbag. Oleg heard a roar a second before a yellow sports car emerged from the depths of the garage. It paused next to the woman. Georgie got out and hurried over to the passenger door to hold it open for the woman, who couldn't be a day over 22. As if getting into a Lamborghini was the most natural everyday thing that people do, she did so while simultaneously tapping in some information on her mobile without a glance at the car. *That would be rich, even for Vasily,* Oleg thought with a wry smile, now that he had located Georgie.

He hastened to scribble down the registration number of the sports car before it raced away.

Monday October 27, 2014

"This Georgie Jones, he went to Paris over the weekend", Oleg began after entering Berlosky's office at Arexim. "He has a yellow Lamborghini stashed away there, and he took off in it with a girlfriend of sorts on Saturday, not returning until Sunday afternoon. Then he went back to his drab, cramped lodgings in a depressive part of London. Something doesn't check, does it?"

No, it doesn't, Berlosky thought.

"Give me the details, Oleg."

Oleg did as he was ordered. Berlosky dismissed him, saying he would call for him if there was anything else he needed.

Berlosky interlaced his fingers behind his neck and placed his feet clad in handmade kid leather boots on the twenty-thousand-pound antique desk to be able to think better. *Georgie drives one of the most expensive cars made, yet he is living in a house heavily mortgaged. By and by he's selling off diamonds through a fence. Boris has told me Georgie's father and Jeremiah Flint became stepbrothers after Phil's mother and Georgie's father got married. It all fits together well, doesn't it? Now, how can I convince little Georgie that he must start cooperating by giving me useful information?*

At this point, his thoughts were interrupted by Vasily's entrance. Vasily frowned when he saw Berlosky's boots on the desk but made no mention of it.

"I need your opinion on something important, Mikhail. Come with me."

Berlosky followed Vasily into his office and slumped into one of the plush easy chairs. Vasily handed him a sheaf of papers and sat down.

"What is this?" Berlosky asked.

"These are copies of the passports used by three Mexicans who recently entered the UK to find a way to harm our interests", Vasily explained. "They work for the Zetas. I don't know exactly when they arrived, only that it must have been during the last five to ten days. Nor do I know their present residence. The one thing I know for certain, though, is that the Zetas are now upset that we have chosen to work with the Sinaloa cartel. I suspect that these three Mexicans are here for one, or possibly two, reasons: The Zetas want to start supplying our competition, and it wouldn't surprise me if they have orders to kill me, and perhaps you, too. With you and me gone, it would allow them to quickly take over our market share, and give el Chapo's presence in Europe a serious blow in the passing."

"How do you know this, Vasily? What makes you so certain?"

Vasily looked at him stonily without replying. Berlosky took the hint. Vasily wasn't going to reveal his sources even to him, despite his many years in the organisation.

"Give me a couple of days to see what I can come up with", Berlosky said after a long, awkward pause. "Oh, by the way, I believe I've got some good news for you", Berlosky said as he rose. "I've finally found ourselves a replacement for the Rabbit. I expect to make contact with him in the next couple of days, presenting him with some convincing arguments that he must come to work for us."

Thursday October 30, 2014

Oleg had continued to watch Georgie's daily routines, and, among other things, reported to Berlosky that Georgie more

82

than occasionally went with a few others to The Red Lion, a pub not far from Scotland Yard, after finishing work at five. He was usually the first to leave to take the tube home using Westminster station. This information helped Berlosky figure out a way to approach Georgie in an inconspicuous way.

He chose a spot close to the Westminster underground station entrance and waited until Oleg called to say that Georgie had just left the pub. As he approached, Berlosky recognised him from a recent photo given to him by Oleg. He stepped forward when Georgie was close and purposefully bumped into him, hitting him hard on the shoulder. Surprised, Georgie cried out.

"I am *so* sorry, sir", Berlosky excused himself and started brushing Georgie's overcoat. "How clumsy of me, I didn't watch out. But now that we've got to know each other closer, ha ha, I insist on buying you a drink, to present myself properly."

"Who are you?" Georgie asked in a hostile tone.

"I'm a businessman who's an expert in negotiating deals about almost new Lamborghinis", Berlosky grinned, flashing his gold tooth.

Suddenly pale, Georgie was visibly shaken.

"What do you mean?" he asked weakly.

"I think you know perfectly well what I mean without asking me questions. If you don't think I'm serious in wanting to discuss a deal, I can add that I'm particularly interested in cars with Paris number plates. Do you happen to have one on offer?"

"What do you want?"

"Yet another question from you", Berlosky smiled and shook his head. "Before I reply to this one, I suggest that we retire to a more private place. Do you see that hotel across the street? There's a bar next to the reception that is discreet. Should you be interested in listening to the details of a proposal I have, join me there in five minutes."

Berlosky led the way without looking over his shoulder to see whether Georgie would obey him. He didn't need to. Oleg was watching Georgie closely and would tell Berlosky if Georgie would choose to not follow him into the hotel bar. Once Berlosky had disappeared inside the lobby, Georgie still looked bewildered, Oleg noticed. Oleg stood watching him from outside the tube station stomping, his feet in the evening cold. After a few minutes, he saw how Georgie made up his mind and began to saunter towards the hotel.

An obvious threat, Georgie thought, peeved, wondering who the stranger was. Although his English was good, there had been a certain Eastern European accent to it. The stranger had walked as a self-assured man with not a single worry in the world does, the palms of his hands facing backwards and his feet pointing outwards. He was clean-shaven, broad-shouldered, overweight but not obese, with thinning hair that was greying at the temples.

Georgie had registered all these details about Berlosky before he had disappeared inside the hotel. Four minutes later, Georgie followed him through the entrance door. To the left there was a sign pointing the way to a bar called Checkers.

The bar's interior, with its wainscoting and thick wall-to-wall carpet meant to make the place feel intimate, was somewhat depressing by its unfortunate combination of dismal colours. Berlosky sat facing him in a booth in the far corner. Just as Georgie entered, a bartender placed two tankards of lager in front of Berlosky.

Dragging his legs until the bartender had returned behind the bar counter, Georgie sat down opposite Berlosky. He didn't touch the tankard while Berlosky took a deep gulp from his. His pulse racing, Georgie intuited that the information the man in front of him was about to share could only mean trouble.

They both kept their silence, waiting for the other to talk.

"I'm curious to know how a detective sergeant employed by the Metropolitan Police with a yearly salary of, let's be generous, thirty thousand quid", Berlosky finally opened the conversation, "can afford a three-hundred-thousand-pound luxury car."

"Who are you? What do you want?"

Berlosky sighed.

"You only have questions, and no answers, right?" His voice hardened. "Yet you followed me in here, because you know that I'm aware that your finances don't add up. So, since you don't have the courtesy to inform me, let me oblige myself with the answers to your questions."

Berlosky took a swig from his tankard. Georgie watched him, concerned.

"One: I'm your new partner. You will pass on to me

information of certain police activities ..." Berlosky saw Georgie frown at the prospect. "No, no, don't wrinkle your nose – I'm sure you didn't turn down Flint, you know, old Jeremiah who left your dad the pub in Islington and a lot of jewels when he croaked five years ago. I don't doubt Flint's success was due to a well-placed source inside Scotland Yard, what do you say?"

"I have no idea what you're talking about", Georgie replied, stalling, because in part he wanted to get more information but also because he was afraid that their conversation was being recorded.

Berlosky laughed.

"Oh, yes you do. I had the privilege of meeting with your Uncle Flint some six months before he died. He had some interesting things to share with ... me." Berlosky had nearly made the error of saying "us". He decided to try one of his hypotheses on Georgie. "For a fact, I know Flint had a collection of some very pretty diamonds that eventually ended up in your pockets, and which you now are selling off to afford a yellow muscle car and an expensive lover in a very rich neighbourhood in Paris. Why Paris? Because you don't want your improved status in life to be too obvious to your colleagues where you work ... Or, what is your personal opinion on the subject?"

With every fact detailing his new life, Georgie quickly understood that the man sitting opposite him had kept him under surveillance for some time and now was familiar with most of the secrets he so assiduously had tried to protect. *How was this possible?*

"What shall I call you?"

Berlosky laughed pleasantly, now that it was clear that the fish had swallowed his hook. He thought for a moment.

"Call me Mister Fisherman, if you please." *His smile is that of a shark,* Georgie thought.

"And what can I do for you, Fisherman?"

"Show some respect – it's MISTER Fisherman!" Berlosky growled at him, in a show to make Georgie understand that he was the subordinate in their new relationship. "What I want you to do – as long as you want to avoid upsetting the applecart of your present, pleasant life – is simple: you will give me information that is of interest to me."

Georgie kept quiet while he watched Berlosky extract a document from the inner pocket of his leather jacket.

"Don't worry, it's nothing complicated and it won't get you into trouble", Berlosky continued, now again smiling benevolently. "I want you to search the Scotland Yard server, or, if necessary, the British immigration authorities' records, for the UK entrance and the whereabouts of these three men." Berlosky looked Georgie in the eyes with his hardest stare.

Georgie looked at the paper and read the names typewritten on it. He didn't recognise any of them.

"If you give me this information", Berlosky lied with a straight face, "I won't bother you again."

Georgie felt relief. *I can do this and nobody at the Yard will be any the wiser,* he knew.

"By the by", Berlosky said as Georgie rose without

having touched his beer, "from now on your code will be 'Minnow'. Get used to it."

Monday November 3, 2014

Berlosky, impeccably clad for once in a bespoke suit made by a Savile Row tailor, watched as Frank O'Hare at his invitation sat down opposite him after having shaken his hand. They were meeting in one of the smaller offices in the previous bank locale, now leased by the newly founded Full Sails Financing Ltd. There were distant noises of drills, hammers and other tools used by the contractors who laboured on renovating the premises.

"I'm sorry about having to meet you with all this racket going on here", Berlosky opened their conversation, "but we want to get our operation up and running as fast as possible."

"Oh, I understand perfectly", Frank said.

Frank was a burly man with an open, honest face that made people instantly take a liking to him. His eyes were pale blue and his hair thick and wavy. *He doesn't look a bit like his brother*, Berlosky thought as he compared him with Paddy, the pilot who worked for them. His immediate impression of Frank was that he indeed looked like a perfect fit for the job he had applied for, and this impression was reinforced during the interview. Frank had ample experience in the banking and finance sector, he projected enthusiasm and, more than anything, Berlosky found that there was a streak of ingenuousness in the applicant that was perfect for the plans he had made.

"I'm impressed, Mister O'Hare", he said at the end of the interview. "I have no doubt whatsoever about your capacity or capabilities. You're hired. Mind you, we'll start up operations early January parallel to a huge promotional campaign across Europe, and I want you here for preparations a month earlier. Will that suit you?"

Frank O'Hare looked overwhelmed at the immediate decision to employ him.

"Yes, I'm very pleased of course … but we never discussed my salary …"

"How about five hundred thousand pounds a year plus a five per cent bonus on the net income?"

Frank's jaw nearly fell to his chest. It was three times more than he had earned in his previous employment. He rose with a broad smile and extended his hand.

"Accepted, sir! I'm very pleased to be on board! Count on my best efforts!"

Monday November 10, 2014

When Georgie handed over the requested information about the three Mexicans who had recently entered the UK, he thought he had closed the door of extortion behind him. He was not only naive about it; he was dead wrong. As most victims of extortion soon discover, it's the other way around – once you have entered the game, you're hooked, and there's no way out.

Berlosky was an expert at this particular game. At first, he pounded on something insignificant that was perceived as something only remotely illegal. Then he put in another demand, in the wake of the previous, this time slightly more arduous. From there on, he built up the requests until the victim no longer had a way out. If he or she went to the police, they would be imprisoned for years. And should they choose not to comply, their anonymous handlers would give them up. Classic Mafia strategy.

Georgie didn't feel much choice when "Mister Fisherman" once again accosted him and insisted on a meeting at the same depressing hotel bar where they had last met. This time, however, Georgie came better prepared.

They met at the same table as on the previous occasion, with Georgie arriving fifteen minutes after Berlosky, as agreed. Without a word, Georgie threw down the Manila envelope with the requested information on the tabletop before he sat down. Berlosky opened it to briefly eye the photocopied information of the three recently arrived Mexicans he was interested in.

"This is excellent, Minnow, just what I wanted", Berlosky told him with a smile. "I'm hungry. Do you want a pizza? No? But I want one, because a lot of time I have to struggle with fancy food that only upsets my stomach, if you know what I mean. There's nothing like basic food don't you agree? By the way, if you're not ordering a pizza, you can concentrate on the best way to inform me about how the Liverpool customs office operates – down to the most minute detail, if you please."

Wednesday December 3, 2014

After some very careful calculation concerning the safe transport of the two artworks from their hiding place in a Croatian village to London – a task that had required serious negotiation and meticulous planning for several months – Trollope delivered the Picasso and the Modigliani paintings to Vasily. As was to be expected, Vasily himself was nowhere to be seen when he made the delivery in an agreed-upon warehouse near the Thames. Six thugs against him and one of his helpers, Trollope noted, shivering with anticipation of something about to go bad, but then nothing did.

Vasily's goons didn't even bother to check the contents of the cardboard tube he handed over. Apparently Vasily was more than confident that he would deliver as promised. If not, Trollope imagined that he soon would be found wrapped in chains at the bottom of the Thames, or worse. Besides, although Trollope didn't suspect this, Vasily planned to use him as an intermediary for various ventures that Trollope wouldn't learn about until the time was ripe. Vasily also counted on Trollope's greed and business sense to want to continue doing lucrative deals with him instead of hanging on to difficult-to-sell stolen paintings. And, despite Trollope's ignorance concerning Vasily's plans, Vasily was absolutely spot on in his assessment of Trollope's character.

Three hours later, with the help of Sonia, Vasily took pleasure in hanging his latest acquisitions on the walls of his Park Lane flat.

Wednesday December 24, 2014

I dressed the Christmas tree with the kids while Samantha was busy in the kitchen together with our domestic help, a Philippine woman with excellent recommendations who had recently been employed by us. I had a hard time understanding why, in the heat at the middle of the Australian summer, we were trying to simulate wintry Nordic customs by bringing a pine tree that diminished our living space even more, but Samantha refused to listen to my arguments. She was adamant about the traditional yule festivities for our children's sake, thus putting an end to the discussion.

We were still living in Samantha's bachelorette flat, a two-bedroom and sitting room semi-detached house with a small garden surrounding a pool. The cramped spaces had obliged me to work evenings and weekends away from home, at Jack's office in central Sydney. When I wasn't busy supervising the construction project we partnered with Jack, Samantha's brother, I had done my utmost to find a new home that met the criteria we had agreed on. Apart from an acute need for more space: rooms for the children, a large kitchen, an extensive garden, a study for Samantha and, on a personal note, my own work space to allow myself some urgently needed breathing room, we wanted an extensive garden.

After a few months of searching, I had stumbled upon a glorious plot of land on the outskirts of Sydney with a breathtaking view over its harbour. Of course, this affected the asking price: it was twice as high as the land further down the precipice that didn't count on the same view. Although I, out of habit more than anything, negotiated the price to see how low the present owner would go, I was from the outset set on buying it. Since I was willing to pay cash, using a major part of the money I got from selling my property in Italy, I managed to get a 3 per cent discount. Not a lot, it seems, but by the time I was finished with the construction a year and a half later, the land value had gone up 20 per cent.

Fortunately, Samantha was equally enthusiastic after I had done my best to outline my vision of our new home. Before buying it, I had stridden among the underbrush and the long grass to point out where the different rooms would be built, but more than anything it was the view that had convinced her. Now, after a year and a half, construction was nearly completed. I estimated that we could move in in about four months, i.e. in April the coming year.

So, there we were beside our German-inspired Christmas tree sipping hot punch or lemonade depending on our age. Then the time came to open the heaps of gifts the American-inspired Santa Claus had left the previous night in the incredulously small stockings over our non-existent Australian chimney because the hot weather really didn't call for one.

"It doesn't matter what you and I know", Samantha had whispered angrily to me when I had tried to bring up the absurd situation. "It's the magic the boys will believe in for a few years from now on."

I resigned myself to experience the Australian version of Christmas by spending time in the pool with the children until

Samantha said it was time to see what Santa had brought Daddy. We went inside, and sitting around the kitchen table, beaming she brought out a small parcel wrapped in white paper and tied with a red bow.

"Open it, open it, open it!" George and Owen chanted.

I did, and inside there was a velvet box with a pair of gold cufflinks. I couldn't help associating them with the elderly ladies who had shown their appreciation for my dad's attentions by gifting him similar items. Samantha, of course, didn't know this.

Each cufflink had one ruby, two emeralds and two diamonds incrusted in the form of a quincunx, with the ruby at the centre.

"They're beautiful, Samantha", I told her as the children clamoured to see what I had been given.

"Remember the course I've been taking the last eight months?" she asked with pride shining in her eyes. "I told you it was pottery, but actually it was jewellery design. I made these for you with the ruby symbolising my heart, the emeralds your eyes and the diamonds our children."

"Besides being a talented designer", I told her, truly amazed, "you're also a poet. I'm in awe."

She looked pleased at my praise.

"What an incredible gift! What an amazing and profound thought", I told her.

"I'm glad you like them."

"Well, Santa brought you and the boys something as well", I said and brought out an envelope. "It doesn't compare with this thoughtful, artistic gift of yours, but at least we will do it together with the children."

She opened the envelope and rapidly scanned the first page. Her eyes shone.

"We're going to Italy, boys!" she shouted. They shouted along with her, not understanding much beyond the fact that something exciting was going to take place.

"Since we're now coming full circle with the construction project with Jack", I explained, "and the boys still aren't old enough to attend school, I thought we'd take a well-deserved vacation in Europe. I've rented a house in Tuscany for a month, and, after that, we get back to Sydney to move into our new home, which will be ready by then. How does that sound?"

"Marvellous!" Samantha cried and threw her arms around my neck.

"Marvellous!" echoed George and Owen.

"Marvellous, then, it shall be", I solemnly declared, without an inkling how wrong I was.

Wednesday February 9, 2015

On the third day of his newly appointed assignment, FBI Special Agent Solomon Vaughn read through file number twenty-two of the twenty-eight he had been told to review. Apparently the agency was once again flush with funds, because so far, the cases he had perused were four to ten years old, with no activity after the initial year or two. Since these cases apparently had been judged to be either unlikely to solve or difficult to prove, they had been shelved in favour of cases more likely to lead to arrests.

Case number twenty-two stood out as more exotic than any of the others that Vaughn had studied. The allegation stated that a British subject carrying an illegal gun, proven to have killed a big shot in narcotics trafficking, had been killed by another Brit who had pushed a giant cactus on top of him. *That definitely requires steely hands,* Vaughn thought as he tried to imagine someone pushing a cactus with its spines mortally wounding the victim. The allegation was evidenced by fingerprints and photographs of a supporting rubber hose showing it had been cleanly cut through. Before falling on top of the victim, the cactus had been secured to the balcony of the room rented by the alleged killer, known as Matthias Callaghan. Callaghan was assumed to be the killer, despite never having been registered at the hotel, because he later crossed the border into Mexico in the same Mercedes noticed at the hotel.

Callaghan hadn't been travelling alone. He was accompanied by another Englishman, who had paid for everything at the spa using a debit card in his name. Callaghan's other companion was an Australian woman, who various employees at the spa had confirmed was using their facilities located far from the incident when the death occurred.

Besides the overview, which Vaughn found to be laudably specific, there were copies made from the passports of Samantha Kirby, born in 1980, Andrew Reese, born in 1961, and Matthias Callaghan, born in 1953. The prints were copies made from their entry to the United States on May 15, 2009.

There were additional copies of their exit from the country, to which none of them had ever returned. Andrew Reese had taken a flight from New York to Paris on May 24, 2009, paid for with a debit card that he had ceased to use afterwards. Kirby and Callaghan had left the country by car on the same day, crossing the Mexican border at Nogales after declaring 41,500 dollars in cash. The coming weeks, there had been intense contact with the Mexican police, but the couple had simply vanished into thin air – there were no records that they had ever exited the country.

Some elements of surprise in the summary stimulated Vaughn's fascination. Killing by pushing a cactus – that's certainly an unusual murder weapon. One of the persons involved goes to Paris, never to be heard of again. The remaining two – an apparently glamorous couple with a 27-year age difference, travelling in a conspicuous sports car – disappear immediately upon entering Mexico. *For six years no one had bothered to thoroughly investigate them,* Vaughn mused. *I will bring in the murderer. It will be a feather in my hat when I do.*

On further examination, Vaughn realised that all three passports had expired since they left the United States. This meant that, to be able to travel, they must have asked for passport renewals. He made a request through Interpol, which responded that there were no such requests from Reese or Callaghan, but there had been a renewal of Kirby's passport.

For further details, he was asked to contact the Australian police.

Thursday February 10, 2015

"So, what's it going to be?" N'douro challenged Omar. "We'll soon be leaving. If you want to come with me, you'd better come up with the money fast."

Without looking up, Omar continued to pedal the homemade contraption that allowed him to form the clay into assorted pots that his siblings were going to sell at the market. His greatest desire was to go to Europe to work and make a lot of money to send home to help his impoverished family survive. There were thousands of stories circulating in the bazaar about neighbours and friends in Mauritania who had made it across the Mediterranean to get rich in Holland and Germany and France. The money they were sending home was the indisputable proof that convinced even the most sceptical.

At 22, Omar was the eldest of seven brothers and sisters. His mother suffered from arthritis and could no longer participate in making pottery, a skill that she had previously taught all her children. Omar's father rarely got out of bed since a bullet by chance had hit but not killed him when he was in Rwanda on some business. As far as all practical issues were concerned, Omar was the head of the family. He also considered that his younger sisters and brothers were likely to survive with their present way of living, but with no improvement whatsoever in sight. The only way to make life better, as he and millions of others like him in Africa knew, was to travel to Europe. However, N'douro asked for 1,500 euros to take him there.

Omar suspected that N'douro was a bad apple and not to be trusted. On the other hand, he knew of no one else who had the contacts to send him to the lands where money grew on trees.

"I'm working on it", Omar replied. "Count me in."

So far, he had managed to put together two-thirds of the money by selling his bicycle and his TV set, besides adding his not very impressive savings and counting on the promises of several relatives to lend him money against his pledge to pay them back with substantial interest. Still, he needed to find another 450 euros in addition to enough travel money to sustain him until he could get his first salary. There was a last resort, but Omar was postponing it in the hope of finding some better alternative. This last resort was going to the professional moneylenders. His reluctance to do so was twofold: The interest rate was exorbitant, and Omar's family would become the guarantee for the money owed. If the money wasn't paid back within the stipulated time, one or several family members could be either maimed or killed. Still, thus was Omar's faith in making money hands over fist once he got to Europe, that he was willing to risk this if there was no other option to be found.

"Believe me, I'm working on it", he repeated. "When will we be leaving?"

"Within a month, Allah and the weather allowing", N'douro replied haughtily and left the poor Harantine. The Harantines, or "black moors", were the descendants of slaves that the Bidhan, or "white moors" – proud descendants of the Berbers – had once dominated.

A Bidhan himself, N'douro despised the Harantines but not their money.

Friday February 13, 2015

When Vaughn's team began to dig deeper into the information concerning Callaghan's escape from the murder scene at the Arizona spa, they came up with several findings not previously considered. Presented to Vaughn for his consideration, he could only shake his head when he realised that the original investigation had been so sloppy.

The last time anyone had sighted Callaghan was at the border control in Nogales. Since then, there was no confirmed sighting of him, nor any transaction by credit card or similar. *So, the last time Matthias Callaghan was ever seen or heard from was on May 24, 2009,* Vaughn pondered. *Six years is a long time without any news whatsoever of someone rich living like a jet-setter. Perhaps he was killed and buried in Mexico by some Mexican cartel? Is there a possibility that he was involved in trafficking drugs or money laundering? If either would be true, I'd probably hedge my bet on money laundering.*

His Australian sidekick, though, is a different ticket. Was she just a convenient mistress or did she play some important role? In her case, we know she used a debit card somewhere in Mexico called Ixtapa a week after she entered the country, and a day or so later, the card was stolen from her.

The Mexican authorities are officially quite strict about filling out forms when you enter and exit the country, but, considering the level of corruption in the country, there's probably very little difficulty if you want to avoid complying, especially if you can afford it. But where would Callaghan go if he didn't remain in Mexico? Or perhaps he got beheaded there by some cartel, by accident or because he was considered to be either competition or a nuisance?

The red sports car that they drove into Mexico, rented using Reese's card, had a year later been found among other vehicles after a shootout at a ranch in Sonora. The undercover operative had been collaborating with the DEA and the Mexican marines, which had turned out to be surprisingly effective. The Mercedes had been confiscated among twenty more vehicles apprehended at the ranch, along with assorted guns, stacks of cocaine packages and mountains of money.

Was the rented Mercedes an indication that Callaghan was part of the drug cartel?

Callaghan had also declared that he was carrying 41,500 dollars before crossing the border into Mexico. Doing so had not been illegal, but, in Vaughn's mind, *at the very least it was an indication of something fishy. Nobody carries that much cash across a border known for drugs and money laundering, unless there's some serious financial interest involved.* One of Vaughn's researchers had contacted the Mexican Immigration authority, which had replied that their records showed that Matthias Callaghan had entered the country without declaring that he was carrying an amount in excess of ten thousand dollars. Since the money had been registered leaving the US and not reported upon entering Mexico, it only strengthened Vaughn's impression that Callaghan was involved in the drug business.

A request from Vaughn to the DEA came back with a negative response: they had no information whatsoever that related to Matthias Callaghan.

*

After working his way through three secretaries, Solomon Vaughn waited impatiently for Chief Inspector Sterling Dunaway with the Australian police to pick up the phone.

"Dunaway."

"This is Special Agent Solomon Vaughn with the FBI. I need to talk to you about an Australian subject who was present at a deadly incident here in the United States – to be more precise, in Arizona in two thousand and nine."

"What happened? Why the delay contacting us? It's been six years, hasn't it?"

"As far as the delay is concerned, we've experienced budget shortages for political reasons. It wasn't until recently that I was assigned this and some other cases that were shelved in the meantime. A British citizen, accompanied by the Australian woman who I'm interested in talking to, is wanted for questioning in connection with an alleged murder."

"Who exactly are we talking about?"

"The main subject's name is Matthias Callaghan, a man who's been on the run from American justice for quite some time. The Australian we're interested in talking to is Samantha Kirby."

"What did Callaghan do?"

"He allegedly killed a man by pushing a cactus on top of him."

"Pushing a cactus … that certainly sounds like an extraordinary feat to me. Well, if you send my secretary the paperwork through the proper channels, I'll look into it."

Without bothering with a polite word of goodbye, Dunaway hung up on him.

Vaughn sighed and looked at his watch. It was almost six p.m. He decided to deal with the issue after the weekend.

Sunday February 15, 2015

From long years of experience, Haroun was accustomed to guide his dromedaries across the part of the Sahara Desert that began in Southern Morocco and after forty nights of walking ended in Mauritania. Then he made the same journey back to Morocco. The caravan he guided on invisible desert paths usually consisted of 100 to 120 dromedaries. This time he was guiding his largest ever – 147 dromedaries.

The supervision of some thirty additional dromedaries didn't provoke the least apprehension in Haroun. Guiding caravans was something his family had done for centuries, and there was even a story told by his grandfather that *his* grandfather had taken more than a thousand camels across the Sahara and thus funded the family fortune.

Not that Haroun had seen much of that family fortune. With an average of twelve children for every couple since his great-great grandfather, the only abundance left to enjoy was his offspring. Still, he was grateful that his own father had shown him how to safely cross the Sahara.

This immense desert, the largest in the world, meant death for those who didn't know it and was a blessing in disguise for those who did. Twice a year, Allah and temperatures permitting, Haroun travelled south by night with his dromedaries and a handful of drivers. The dromedaries were loaded with cooking oil and other basic necessities, which he traded for textiles, carpets and jewellery in Southern Morocco and Mauritania on his way back. For a fee, he also guided people from Mauritania across the desert to Morocco.

As he prepared to set out this year, he had borrowed thirty camels from a trusted neighbour in exchange for a sum of money that Haroun felt was exorbitant. Nevertheless, he needed the animals, and the profit he was about to make this spring didn't make it worthwhile to rebuke his neighbour about the excessive price. *The sun shines on everyone*, he sighed, *especially if you're in Africa.*

Monday February 16, 2015

Special Agent Vaughn read through the reply from Interpol that had come in earlier that morning. It concerned his query about Andrew Reese. Being a UK citizen pertaining to the European Union, he had in 2009 exercised his right to work in Italy. The work description he had given at the time of his application to obtain his Italian permit was "caretaker". His present address, unchanged since his residential application, was a villa in Umbria, central Italy. Still early morning in the US, Vaughn managed to contact his key liaison at the US Embassy in Rome. Forty minutes after he had explained what he wanted to learn, Vaughn got a call back explaining that the villa in question had been sold in June 2013 to a retired couple. Apart from the owner couple, there was no one else living at the property.

Vaughn asked his liaison to request a copy from the notary's ledgers showing the property's owners for the past two decades.

Wednesday February 18, 2015

Vaughn read through the reply from the US Embassy concerning the Italian property that Andrew Reese had indicated as his address.

A childless family, owner of the property for fifty-five years (not counting the family's previous fourteen generations), had sold the estate to an Englishman by the name of Charles Rathbone, solicitor by profession, in 2001.

Some legal issues, which Vaughn didn't quite grasp, had in 2008 resulted in the involuntary transfer of the property to eventually end up in the hands of – and here he had to read the paragraph twice to make sure he understood the chain of events correctly – Matthias Callaghan, born in 1971. Said Callaghan had later, in 2013, sold the property to its present owners.

This made Vaughn tell his secretary to discontinue any incoming calls to be able to concentrate at what he himself considered to be his strongest suit: analysing. Alone in his office, puffing on an empty pipe because smoking was not allowed inside the building, Vaughn considered the case as far he had been able to determine it. As he went through the known details, he arrived at more questions than conclusions.

Assuming that Reese did live on the Umbria property after returning there from Phoenix, he must have left soon after. Where did he go from there? In what way was he involved in the murder of Thompson? Why did he leave the US immediately for Paris in such a haste, while Callaghan and the woman continued to Mexico? Was it Reese's task to cover something up in Italy?

Thursday February 19, 2015

Harry Jordan was a billionaire who, despite his immense wealth, didn't feel particularly happy about the fact despite having lived the past fifteen years exactly the way he had always dreamed of doing. This needs some explanation, because he had more money than he could ever spend: he had an extremely attractive wife who was twenty-nine years younger than himself; he lived on a yacht that required a crew of twenty when sailing (which he had only done briefly on two occasions); and he had a coveted mooring place in Monaco that now would fetch five times the amount he had paid for the privilege when he had acquired it.

Harry was an American who had made his money by starting running errands for the New York mob in the fifties. He had begun his career delivering messages, flowers to their wives and sweethearts, and packages holding cash for the bosses. Eventually he had moved up the ladder and had become responsible for a greyhound racing track. His protector was an old school Italian Mafioso, Luigi Monticalli, who noticed something in him that Harry had not yet discovered. Harry was a genius with numbers. Monticalli introduced him to some friends on Wall Street, and it wasn't long before Harry was making big money in the bull markets after the Second World War. To pay his benefactor for the introduction, Harry gave the ageing mobster valuable tips on every occasion some opportunity presented itself.

And the opportunities were plenty during the increasingly more complex financial markets in the eighties and nineties. He moved on to real estate, using the mob's money to acquire properties and in the process cleanse it from its dubious origin. Harry's success in doing so earned him a lot of respect from the people at the head of the mob families, whose understanding of money earned translated into respect merited. However, due to the changes, competition and jail time for some important figures in the New York crime scene during the last decades of the 20th century, Harry figured he would be much better off if he could pull off one great stunt and then retire. After vacationing three times in France, he had become an ardent Francophile. With his money, business acumen and financial inside information ... who could stop him?

In 2000, at the age of 59, he made the big move that he during nearly a decade had carefully planned for. The mob bosses weren't happy. They had believed in his magic proficiency of keeping their portfolios alive with constant double-digit profits, and now that he had disappeared with a large portion of their investment money, they became deadly disappointed. Overnight, Harry Jordan became non grata, which he knew was only to be expected. Days before this happened, Harry fled to Europe in a meticulously designed and well-executed plan to elude any of those sure to be upset by his disappearance. Through complex manoeuvres, he not only managed to transfer a large fortune into several offshore bank accounts but also to avoid the mob's revenge. Still apprehensive of the mob's detection that he had played foul, he opted for the most luxurious, discreet and least traceable asset where he could continue a life of luxury. His definition for such an asset was a 157-foot yacht that had once belonged to Panama's disgraced president Noriega, and it was delivered to him in Panama City. Harry had immediately begun extensive refurbishing and ordered it moved to Monaco, where he had previously secured the right to a permanent mooring place. Thanks to his careful planning, Harry felt that there was no one who could possibly threaten him.

However, Harry soon discovered that there was a different price that he had to pay, and it had nothing to do with money. He found that, despite having one of largest yachts anchored in Monte Carlo, you don't socialise easily. He spent many nights at the casino, where his losses far exceeded the few occasions he ended up with meagre winnings. Sure, there were hangers-on and bimbos and slick young men with hot deals constantly making offers that no one in his right mind would accept. Still, he refused all the hare-brained scheme that came his way, because money had lost both its lustre and its importance the day he made his first billion.

A billion dollars had been the "moon" that he spontaneously had set out as his target when asked by Luigi Monticalli what he wanted out of life.

Although he could now enjoy everything he could ever wish for, either by buying what he desired or by simply exposing his enormous wealth, Harry missed the everyday action in New York. It wasn't the same living in a country where, despite private lessons in French, Harry was at a disadvantage culturally. Everything he needed was delivered anonymously to the ship. He had also become increasingly reluctant to stray far in case someone would put two and two together and reveal his true identity to some vengeful offspring of mob members he had crossed back in the days in New York.

Since he had moved to Europe, Harry had multiplied his fortune by financing weapon deals for African and Middle East countries. Sanctions imposed by the US and the Europeans had helped immensely, of course, pushing up prices to new, unheard highs. Harry had come to appreciate arms dealing as a much straightforward way of making double digit profit, with no questions asked after the merchandise had been checked for its efficiency. Still, it should be stressed that at this time in his life, he was now making business out of habit rather than out of interest.

Fifteen years on, he still lived on his impressive yacht that had left its Monte Carlo harbour on two occasions for brief excursions. On and off, his wife as of the past fourteen years, Ludmila, visited the yacht, although with time her interest in doing so had become less frequent. She preferred spending time purchasing perfection, visiting stores in Paris, Rome and London. Money? Harry knew that he had more than enough to last him twenty life times. Women? When Ludmila was present, he was in awe of her class, looks and emotional intelligence, although he did his best to hide it. At other times, that is when she was not around, he kept two high-class escort service companies on their toes as their best-paying customer.

Ludmila had been born in Kotor, Montenegro, when the country was still under the thumb of the Soviet Union empire. Her good looks took her to Berlin, then to Paris, and then on a visit to Monaco into the welcoming arms of her future billionaire husband. Ludmila had a weak spot for any photographer seeking to take her picture, so her image frequently appeared in European magazines (under strict instructions from Harry to not use his surname but her maiden one) and not seldom with a mention that she was among the best-dressed jet-setters in Europe.

While Harry preferred to be cooped up on his yacht in Monaco, and only on occasion leave it to play at the Monte Carlo casino – usually with an eye-raising loss – lately Ludmila had reduced her visits to the yacht to two weekends a year. These tended to coincide with her need for an increase of spending money. Harry thought he could control her through the amount of money he gave her. Nevertheless, the reality was that Ludmila expertly made up such perfect narratives concerning her economic needs with Harry believing her, because he was now an old man with too much meaningless money and she was a younger, beautiful woman that he had acquired and who deserved his attention.

Monday March 16, 2015

"Mikhail", Vasily said, "I want you to take the next available flight to Nouakchott."

"Nouakchott? Where is this place? Why am I being punished?"

"Please be serious for once. It's not some punishment – it's business. It concerns the big cargo we're waiting for that is about to arrive in Nouakchott, the capital of Mauritania, next week."

111

"What language do they speak in Mauritania?"

"The two main languages are Arabic and French, and then there are several local ones."

"Well, then you better send Henri, our Algerian distributor in Lyon. I'm absolutely confident that he knows either of these lingoes much better than I do."

"There's too much money and too much merchandise involved to send some second-rate, unknown dealer to supervise this delivery. No, I need someone I can trust to be present. You're my choice, Mikhail, and we won't discuss it further. Just don't mess it up."

Wednesday March 18, 2015

Haroun looked around as the camp was being dismantled before beginning the journey back to Nouakchott from the south of Mauritania. He felt pleased with himself because, not only would he have a record crowd of 220 refugees who had paid him 500 euros each to take them from Mauritania to the meeting point in Morocco, but never before would he carry such valuable cargo on his dromedaries. His only costs were the rent that he had to pay his neighbour for lending him thirty camels, the simple food for the people he was taking across the desert and some inevitable commissions to the recruiters. On top of the regular bartering trade of cooking oil for handicraft, he calculated that he this year would net more than 100,000 euros from the transfer of the people eager to get to Europe.

Still, compared to the new business that so conveniently had presented itself, the profit from the people transfer was a mere puff in the wind. For carrying the eighty sealed packages to Morocco, he was being paid five times as much. It had suddenly become profitable to know one's way around the desert, and in thanks he sent a brief prayer to his deceased father who had taught him how to cross it safely.

Although Haroun on good grounds suspected that the eighty bags were a drug consignment, he couldn't possibly fathom the immense value it would have when sold by dealers across Europe. The high-grade, nearly pure cocaine had been produced in a jungle laboratory in Colombia before being sold to the Sinaloa cartel in Mexico. Part of their deal was delivery by the Colombians in Panama, where the Mexicans took possession. There it had been loaded onto a cargo vessel with destination Nouakchott, Mauritania, from where Haroun would be responsible for its safe journey north into Morocco.

At the going rate, Vasily had calculated its worth to be around 250 million euros once it hit the streets in Europe. He stood to net a third of that sum.

Thursday March 19, 2015

Depressed, Allan studied the bottle with anise liqueur he had just bought at his local grocer. He wondered if he would be able to go through with his decision that no doubt would bring down the Russians' wrath. On the other hand, if he

113

didn't do it, Allan was convinced that he was destined to forever remain in their power delivering them illicit gains from hacking and phishing over the Internet.

Decided, Allan leaned over and googled the City of London police. "I commit crimes by hacking other web sites", he wrote, "although the main income from my activities comes from phishing for innocent people's online identities. I'm a slave to the people who control me. Please, I urge you, free me before they come for me …"

Having finished by pushing the send key, he poured a good portion of the bottle over his laptop's keyboard, and the remainder into his PC, making sure the liquid dripped into the disc drives. While letting the two computers soak for a minute or two, he went to look for some paper towels in the kitchen. Upon his return, he placed the towels on the desk and turned his laptop upside down.

After the sugary liqueur had ceased dripping on the paper towel, Allan tried the keys. Nothing showed on the screen, but when he hit the keys again, they provoked a deep, alarming sound from the computer. Satisfied, Allan closed the screen over his laptop.

He then turned his attention to the PC, which was equally unresponsive.

*

Boris burst into Allan's house half an hour later, more upset than Allan could remember ever having seen him.

"You cut off computer?" Boris accused him. "Not good. Bad choice. Now my boss cut off your feet."

Boris went over to Allan's laptop and tried to revive it, but to no avail.

The same instant the doorbell gave off an insistent ring. Allan walked over to the front door. Boris was busying himself with Allan's laptop and didn't pay him any attention.

When Allan opened the door, he found two policemen looking at him in a no-nonsense way.

*

Allan and Boris were taken to the nearest police station for questioning. While Allan freely admitted his illegal hacker activities, Boris refused to say anything except insisting in Russian that he wanted to speak to his lawyer. Based on Allan's declaration, both were later that day detained for further investigation.

Friday March 20, 2015

"We have a problem on our hands, Vasily", Berlosky announced as he entered Vasily's office at Arexim. "Yesterday our golden-egg-laying hacker Allan was picked up by the police."

"You don't say?" Vasily replied while he briefly looked from the Moscow newspaper that he daily had flown in from Russia. "Well, it was good business while it lasted, wouldn't

115

you agree?"

"The situation is far worse than losing Allan. Boris was with him when the cops arrived, and now both have been detained."

Vasily folded the paper and put it aside.

"Boris won't talk."

"But Allan will embrace the opportunity, surely", Berlosky said. "I still don't know how this may affect our different operations, but we need a contingency plan just in case something goes wrong. Besides, Boris is our communications genius, we need him here."

"Allan doesn't know a thing about our real operation. Let him rot in jail for all I care", Vasily replied, stroking his chin like he always did when he was contemplating a problem. "But, you're right, we need to get Boris out of there eventually. What's the best way to approach this issue?"

"Let me talk with Longhorn, who over the last year has been taking over more of our legal issues. However, remember I have a flight to Africa on Sunday, and it'll be at least four days before I'm back."

"Boris won't talk. If he was clumsy enough to be caught, he can sweat it out in a comfortable British cell for a couple of days and nothing worse will come from it. You have to concentrate on what's most important, and right now the overall priority is the shipment about to arrive in Mauritania."

Sunday March 22, 2015

The London flight to Mauritania landed in Nouakchott in the early afternoon. It was the first time that Berlosky visited the African continent, one that he had always perceived to be suffering from insupportable heat in a clammy jungle environment. Although humid, due to its location next to the Atlantic Ocean, to his surprise Nouakchott greeted their arrival with a pleasant temperature and no jungle at all. A third-world country, no doubt, but he rapidly found that Mauritania's capital lacked none of the modern conveniences as long as one was prepared to pay for them.

Accompanied by Vladimir and Ilya, they were met at the airport by their local contact, Bamba Boubacar, who spoke French and halting English. A Mercedes took them to the best hotel in the city, the Hotel Semiramis, where the three Russians checked in using fake Belgian passports.

Monday March 23, 2015

After breakfast, which Berlosky found to be "too African" for his taste, Bamba drove him to a decrepit warehouse in the port. Vladimir and Ilya followed in a rented lorry that had seen better days. Two men were waiting in a van outside the entrance. Inside, another four members of the Mexican cartel making the sale waited by a 40-foot container in the otherwise empty building. Berlosky's Mauritian contact pointed at the unbroken seal and said in French that he had bribed the customs agents who had wanted to inspect. The bribe he claimed to have paid was three times the actual sum, but it was of no consequence since Berlosky anyway didn't understand a word he was being told. The ensuing conversation would have been a total disaster if it hadn't been for one of the Mexicans speaking passable English.

Bamba brought out a large cutter, which he used to remove the seal. When the doors had been opened, Berlosky could see dozens of pallets inside, stacked several tiers high.

"Refrigerators", the Mexican who spoke broken English told him with a joyless grin. "Me, I'm very sure you much interest in five pallets way back, numbers forty-four up to forty-eight."

Bamba had gone to find a forklift and came back a few minutes later. He began unloading the pallets. Forty minutes later, Berlosky had the five pallets of interest lined up in front of him. Each pallet carried four tall refrigerators. The Mexican brought out the specially designed screwdriver needed to unscrew the back of the appliances. There were four taped packages stacked inside the spaces usually occupied by the compressor.

Berlosky made a small cut in one of the packages and carefully sniffed the cocaine on the blade of his knife. He smiled and nodded at Vladimir and Ilya, who began to randomly choose a package from each refrigerator. Vladimir opened the bag he had brought and placed an instrument on the floor of the container that none of the Mexicans had seen before. It was a sophisticated equipment to measure the chemical composition of the white powder.

After testing twenty of the random samples, Vladimir nodded his approval to Berlosky.

"On average, ninety-six per cent pure."

Berlosky looked at Ilya, who, with the help of Bamba, was counting and weighing the packages.

"Just three more, and we'll be finished", Ilya said, red-faced from the effort. "But it looks like there are no surprises. Four thousand kilos, give or take a gram or two."

Berlosky flashed his golden tooth in a big smile.

"*Viva México!*", he yelled. "You delivered, and now we're in business."

"No, not yet, *compadre*", the Mexican who spoke English warned him, keeping one hand inside his jacket pocket. "There's the little detail that you pay us or you not get the *merca* out of here."

"Of course." Berlosky brought out his mobile and dialled a pre-programmed number in his address book.

"We've checked the goods", he told the person who took his call. "Everything is hunky-dory, exactly as promised." He listened to voice at the other end. "OK, just send me a message to confirm the payment."

Berlosky switched off his phone and turned to the two Mexicans.

"I suggest that you talk to your boss in about ten minutes. By then he should have been able to confirm the reception of the twenty-five million dollars."

*

Vasily sat down by his laptop computer in the study of his Park Lane flat and entered the site of Arexim's Isle of Man bank. He went through the security details before being able to proceed with his session: secret questions, password and voiceprint. When he had been approved, he entered the details of the transfer, and ten seconds later his bank on the Isle of Man confirmed that 25 million dollars had been transferred to the requested Mossack Fonseca account in Panama.

Two more minutes passed before Berlosky received a WhatsApp message that merely stated the word "Done". He informed the Mexican who spoke English that the transfer had been made.

"Now, all you have to do is confirm it with your boss. You know, the Speedy Gonzalez way: quick-quick. Nobody wants to wait around here more than absolutely necessary, agreed?"

Fifteen minutes passed as the Russians and the Mexicans stared at each other without speaking. Then the Mexican's phone rang. He answered it immediately.

"*Sí. Sí.* OK. OK." The Mexican relaxed and allowed a brief smile of relief to show as he disconnected.

"I think I now understand your lingo better than I thought I ever would", Berlosky laughed. "I'm glad your boss is OK with the deal. Vladimir, bring in the lorry."

Bamba eyed the refrigerators as the lorry backed into the warehouse. It was clear that these were going to be abandoned after the more valuable merchandise had been removed, and he knew just the place where they would fetch a good price. *A most welcome bonus*, he noted, *on top of the 5,000 euros I'm being paid.*

Counting them, Berlosky waited patiently while Ilya and Vladimir stacked the eighty bags inside the lorry.

"All right", he told Vladimir, who was going to drive the lorry. "Let's get to the meeting with this Haroun guy. I'll be behind you watching out for anything suspicious. Now, let's check the radios to see if they're working."

Never losing sight of the lorry, Berlosky kept the distance as they crossed the city. The vehicles arrived at the huge camel market on the outskirts of Nouakchott that was the agreed spot for the rendezvous. Berlosky dialled the number Vasily had given him and waited impatiently for his contact to pick up the phone. Exasperated he tried the number again and again. On the fifth attempt, he got an answer.

"Haroun speaking," said a tranquil voice.

"Yes, Haroun, I've been trying the better part of this morning to get in touch with you," Berlosky exploded. "We have important things waiting to get done, so you better speed up your caravan to get here!"

"No camel will walk faster if you shout", Haroun replied. "If you cross a desert, it's not the speed that counts, only that you make it to the other side."

"Don't start insulting me with some ignorant camel proverbs!" Berlosky shouted at the telephone. "Where are you? We should unload this as fast as lightning and get those camels of yours going at once."

"I'll meet you at the market in a quarter of hour, *inshallah*."

The fifteen minutes turned out to be a little over an hour before Haroun and his dromedaries finally made their majestic entrance at the market. They made a sight that impressed even Berlosky: one hundred and forty-seven fully equipped dromedaries and twenty drivers clothed for the desert to keep them in order.

"Here I am, at your complete disposal", Haroun said and bowed slightly before Berlosky. He was dressed in a light blue djellaba and wore a mauve turban wrapped around his head and his neck. Berlosky had by now regained his calm. He instructed Ilya and Vladimir to help load the 80 packages containing the cocaine onto the twenty dromedaries reserved for this purpose, amounting to 200 kilos per animal. When everything had been secured, he took them both aside.

"The time has come for me to leave you. You will stay with that caravan as if your lives depend on it. Don't for a minute lose sight of our cargo."

"You never told us we had to go with the cargo across this desert!" Ilya protested. "I don't think I'm up to sitting on a bloody camel for a month!"

"Well, it's your choice", Berlosky replied without a trace of sympathy. "Either you cross the Sahara watching out for our interests, or you have to answer to Vasily personally. Or, I could save you the misery of trying to explain yourselves to him right away by placing a bullet between your eyes."

Neither Ilya nor Vladimir protested further. Instead, their

faces took on a resigned look of suffering at the thought of what was lying ahead.

Wednesday March 25, 2015

Upon his return from Mauritania, Berlosky went to see Jason Longhorn. He was immediately received by the lawyer, who did all formal work through his associate after his professional disgrace of being disbarred. To Longhorn's surprise, despite the disgrace the law firm had obtained considerably more and better rewarded work, principally by Arexim, which was now their premier client.

"You've done good work setting up the Full Sails Financing company and its branches across Europe", Berlosky began after they were seated in the law firm's main conference room. "Now I have a completely different task for you ... let's see if you're up to it. If not, don't hesitate to tell me that it's out of your league."

"I'm eager to hear what this unusual challenge might be", Longhorn replied, confident.

"I want you to cut through all the red tape that prevents Boris Orloff, one of our staff, from being released on bail. He's in custody right now, awaiting trial. You should get him out as quickly as you can, no matter the cost."

"What is he accused of? Where is he held?" Longhorn asked.

"He was arrested together with Allan Gould in Allan's home, where they ... where they were doing some research on a joint project. The police claim Gould has confessed to phishing and hacking under duress, while Boris hasn't opened his mouth except to demand legal counsel. When you get him out on bail, we will fund you, although officially it will be your firm that will post the surety."

"I have to study the details", Longhorn argued, "but it sounds to me that this could have ramifications into immigration, privacy concerns, illegal access ... well, a number of legal issues –"

"I don't care about learning the details, I merely want results", Berlosky interrupted him with and got up. "Call me when you need the money."

Sunday March 29, 2015

The house, which we were leaving for the last time to move into our new one upon our return, was in turmoil. Bags were being packed, the children kept running around in excitement and there were last-minute details that needed to be ironed out.

It was still late afternoon, but I admonished Samantha that the kids needed to go to bed as soon as possible, since our flight left Sydney at six in the morning. This meant leaving home at the impossible hour of three to get there at four. Samantha merely shook her head and smiled, as if indicating that "everything will take of itself". She was one of the most laid-back persons I knew, and, believe me, Aussies in general are considered more laid-back than any other population in the world.

I have always felt capable to work under stress, solving issues. But to watch Samantha taking measured control of everything to get us organised as we were leaving our cramped house to go on a vacation and return a month later to move into another, filled me with a sense of wonder. We were going to put up the house for sale upon our return, as soon as we had moved the last of our furniture to our new home, which by then would be completely ready to receive us (well, the garden would take some additional time). We had already packed a lot of our belongings into boxes that we had moved to the garage of our new home along with some of the furniture. Upon our return, I'd supervise the packing and removal of the remainder. Samantha had cancelled the phone service, and we agreed that it wouldn't be necessary to get a landline installed in our new house – our mobile phones were more than sufficient.

To top the day off with yet another of her surprises, Samantha curled up next to me that evening.

"I have some news of importance to share with you, Matthias", she whispered with a smile. "By mid-October the boys will have either a sister or brother."

Monday March 30, 2015

The aircraft kept up its steady drone that had finally made Samantha and the twins go to sleep. By now we were halfway through the flight to Rome. Our vacation in Italy would be more than welcome after a few tough years with a lot of work and occasional cash flow issues.

No one was looking forward to our first extensive family vacation more than I. The years on the run, the birth of our boys, the clearance of my name, learning the ropes in the construction business ... it was all either exhausting or exciting or engrossing, but now I needed a pause. I had chosen Italy for sentimental reasons, because that's where Samantha and I had become lovers. I longed to see old vineyards and the rays of the sun slanting over afternoon fields and the ever-blue morning skies and going to the Saturday market to buy ham and vegetables ... just like I had done as a young boy when travelling through Italy with my grandfather, I realised. I could only wish that George and Owen were old enough to remember this experience later in life. If not, well, I wouldn't mind coming back – Italy and its history fascinated me.

By now the construction project in which Samantha and I had participated, initiated by her brother Jack, was about to be wrapped up. Sixteen of the twenty properties on offer had been sold, and now Jack wanted to reinvest the profits in a much, much larger construction site. It was a very interesting, once-in-a-lifetime waterfront project in an abandoned docks and dilapidated warehouse area some forty minutes from central Sydney, for which the local government was willing to discuss tax benefits with the developer.

At the same time, my personal project – building a house for my family overlooking the Sydney port – was coming to a conclusion. I had given my last and very detailed instructions how I wanted the changes Samantha and I had agreed on to be done by the time we returned from Europe. Of late we had both shouted at each other that we needed to get out of her old bachelorette pad – there simply wasn't enough space for the four us now that the kids were growing up.

I've always had a hard time when it came to sleeping on airplanes. I fished out an inflight magazine from the pocket at the back of seat n front of me. Distractedly I leafed through it until an article caught my eye: "Upcoming auctions of 20th century and contemporary art". It caught my eye, because with some of the profits we were now making, I wanted to once again make investments in artworks – this time for our new house with its many naked walls. I had been obliged to sell the paintings I had owned in London because I could no longer live in Europe, and there had been no practical way of taking them with me. Now that I once again had begun to breathe financially, I thought quite a lot about returning to buy quality art that interested me. Naturally, I knew I should get Samantha's approval before I did, but I didn't perceive this to be a major hurdle.

This article was followed by another, headlined: "Stolen masterpieces, never recovered". The general topic was interesting. It dealt with the multi-million-dollar business of art theft, with the booty ending up in either private collectors' vaults or not seen at all for perhaps a generation or two. There was also a list of the most famous paintings stolen and never recovered. It began with a walkout theft from the Louvre in 1911 that caused da Vinci's Mona Lisa portrait to become the most famous painting in the world; then went through World War II war crimes; covered various museum thefts where the appalling security made it a piece of cake to walk away with multi-million-dollar paintings that weighed next to nothing; and finished with the so-called "heists of the century". The conclusion covered museum secret buybacks; ransom negotiations to free political prisoners; thieves who made their livings travelling the world to steal artworks; and the futility of reselling stolen, well-known works next to images of works never recovered: Rembrandt's only seascape, several Picassos and van Goghs, a Modigliani, and various other 19th-and-20th century works.

The constant humming from the jet motors finally made me sleepy. Five hours left before landing in Rome. I decided to try to sleep the remainder of the flight.

The line when we got to immigration at Fiumicino Airport was at least twenty people long, and I noticed how the lack of quality sleep was making both Samantha and myself irritated over the smallest thing. I longed for a comfortable bed at the hotel I had reserved.

Slowly the line got shorter, and ten minutes later I was finally able to shove our four passports into the aperture of the immigration officer's cubicle. The officer studied our passports carefully, before picking up a phone. He said something in rapid Italian that I was unable to understand. Behind me, one of the twins began crying. Samantha tried to quieten him, but instead he hit his brother. Now both twins were crying, and I could tell from the way Samantha spoke that her tolerance was depleted.

"Mister Callaghan, please follow us." The order was given by a uniformed man who at the same time grabbed my upper arm from behind. Another official grabbed my other arm. "You can leave your hand luggage with your wife."

"What is all this about"

"I know nothing except that we're here to execute an arrest warrant. You will have plenty of time to discuss it with the police, I'm sure."

130

PART X

Freedom rides an elusive steed
while money mounts a different horse.

Tuesday March 31, 2015

Representatives of the Italian justice system told Samantha that the extradition of her husband to the United Kingdom was expedited the very moment they spoke.

Still unable to understand the full implication of the situation since no one cared to explain the details to her, Samantha rushed to the nearest travel agency to buy tickets to London for herself and their two children.

*

A lawyer, assigned to me by the Italian authorities, explained to me, in staccato-inflected English that included extended pauses to underline his arguments, that I was subject to a European Arrest Warrant. This particular warrant was a procedure put in place in 2004 to speed up extradition proceedings within the European Union. I found his remark about the implementation of such a warrant quite worrying. According to the lawyer, the European Arrest Warrant was only permitted if the accused faced an offence incurring a sentence of at least one year in prison.

"What about my passport?" I asked him. "It was never returned to me."

"It's standard procedure in these cases, I assure you", the lawyer assured me in what must have been his most convincing voice. "Now the British authorities will receive it, and when they find you … well, not guilty of anything, they will return it to you. It's very simple really."

I felt as if I wanted to throw him through the barred window of my holding cell.

"You're a very cheerful man", I told him, smiling sarcastically. For some obscure reason, he looked pleased upon hearing my observation.

*

The Italians who interrogated me had only done so in a casual way. I had been told by them that I was held on murder charges presented by the British police. Naturally, I had

132

denied all knowledge of the charges I was accused of – that is, to have masterminded the killing of Charles Rathbone on March 20, 2009. When I responded with questions to find out what the police knew, these were ignored. After a surprisingly brief interview, I was left alone in a depressing holding cell at Fiumicino Airport, enlightened only that my extradition to the United Kingdom was being processed in the meantime. It became obvious that I wasn't going to face the tough questions and whatever proof the police had until I was on British soil.

The red tape caused by the extradition process at least allowed me time to think through my situation and prepare my answers.

Friday April 3, 2015

"Jack, oh Jack, I need you to pick up the twins in London as soon as you possibly can", Samantha implored him over the long-distance call.

"What happened, Sam?" Jack asked her, alarmed.

"Matthias has been detained by the Italian police and I still can't get a grip on what's going on", Samantha replied, tears scurrying down her cheeks. "The point is; I can't handle the kids' needs if I also have to find out a way to get Matthias out of this … this … horrible situation."

"Calm down, Sam! Of course I'll pick up the twins. Where do you want me to meet you?"

"Matthias will be taken to London tomorrow or the day

after. Can you meet me there? I'm at my wits' end here. Call my mobile when you arrive. Dear Jack, thank you, thank you, thank you!"

*

The release of 11.5 million documents, immediately baptised *The Panama Papers* to the Panamanian government's resentment, made headlines around the world. The Panamanian law firm and corporate service provider Mossack Fonseca's negligible cyber security had made it possible for a hacker to access the documents of the rich and powerful around the world who used the firm to hide assets in tax havens.

The first wave of information mostly concerned politicians and world leaders. When Harry Jordan read the news on board his yacht in Monaco, he was instantly worried that his own setup through Mossack Fonseca would surface in the news. However, to his relief there was still no mention of him or the company that owned his yacht.

Doubling *The New York Times* newspaper flown in every day, he decided to make some drastic changes of the yacht's official ownership to avoid the disgruntled friends with long memories from his past in the New York mob to get a lead about his present whereabouts. *Better safe than sorry,* he thought.

Saturday April 4, 2015

Five days after my arrest in Rome, I was flown, handcuffed, to London. A police van, a Black Maria no doubt especially equipped to transport hardened criminals by the look of it, delivered me with blaring sirens to a prison with a location that no one bothered to give me the name of. Inside, I was registered, photographed, fingerprinted, searched and assigned the basic tools for any rookie prisoner: prison clothes, soap, toothpaste, toothbrush, a towel and a manual with the prison rules. After having stripped, I was told to put on the standard prisoner garments. I was led by two warders to a solitary cell. By then it was dark outside and everyone was silent, as ordered to be at this hour if they wanted to avoid additional punishment.

The experience was one of humiliation.

*

"Look, Trudy, there may or may not be something worthwhile in this tip I just got", Trevor Burns said, looking up as Trudy walked into his editor cubicle. "A Brit was extradited to the UK from Italy last Saturday, charged with a murder that happened years ago."

Trevor Burns, the editor-in-chief at the *Daily Mirror*, looked over the rim of his reading glasses at Trudy Swift who had stopped in front of his desk. As a reporter, he liked her: she was inquisitive, had imagination, could give a tale a different spin, and she had a talent for fact-checking that most reporters her age couldn't be bothered with.

"Who's the bloke? Anyone I should know?"

On the other hand, Burns disliked Trudy for her attitude and her provocative way of dressing: piercings, hair tinted matte black, wearing nothing but black garments. Her face, only a shade less pale than that of a corpse, was in urgent need of a charter trip to Mallorca. Besides, she was endlessly and defiantly chewing gum in a way that could drive a man with lesser patience crazy.

"His name is Matthias Callaghan. Look him up in our archives. See if you can find something of interest related to his arrest, then report to me."

Sunday April 5, 2015

Dressed in his usual, elegant tuxedo, and with Ludmila still in Paris, Harry Jordan travelled in his Rolls-Royce the short distance to the Monte Carlo casino for another night of gambling. After a slow start, most incredibly, he started winning nearly every bet he made. Feeling more excited in years, he threw down thousands on the roulette numbers. His bets were infallible, and after winning more than two million euros, he ordered the most expensive champagne for everyone inside the casino. The next bet he made paid for the champagne and much more. Harry was euphoric. Then he felt his heart protesting his euphoria. He staggered and fell over the heaps of chips stacked in front of him at the gambling table.

The casino's standby medical team, which arrived instantaneously, could after prolonged resuscitating efforts only confirm that Harry Jordan had died of a massive heart attack.

When the news of his death eventually, some six months later, reached the ears of those who now were in charge of the mob in New York, they cursed Harry for having cheated them out of their revenge by pulling a simple heart attack.

Unbeknown to the enemies who cursed him after his death, in the end there were only two persons (besides their lawyers) who in any way would see any benefit from his demise – Ludmila Jordan and Vasily Ivanovich.

Harry Jordan's heart attack resulted to be not only news, but in the case of his widow, exceedingly fortunate such. As Harry's only heir and with the help of a dozen lawyers, Ludmila immediately began to make all necessary steps to transfer her deceased husband's patrimony to her own name. She soon found out that the one asset she had inherited to be a white elephant was the yacht in Monaco. Since she had nearly drowned in a swimming pool as a young girl, she simply detested the idea of being on a ship at sea. The problem was that the huge yacht represented a considerable lump of the total assets Harry had left behind.

Tuesday April 7, 2015
After three days at Wormwood Scrubs – as I had now learnt the name to be of the infamous place I had been taken to –

more than anything, I felt resignation over my recent fate.

The police accused me of having ordered Charles Rathbone's assassination while impersonating Abdul Mahfouz. How could they know this? There was nothing I could do except to spar with the interrogators who questioned me about Rathbone's murder. I had no idea how they after all these years had found some clue that indicated that I in some way had been a participant.

After some initial confrontation, during which I didn't admit to anything suggested by the police, I was finally allowed time alone with David Sandhurst, who I had appointed as my legal counsel. Among a lot of the troubling things he told me regarding my situation, the most worrying was the printed transcript, with me as Mahfouz requesting Flint to kill Rathbone. The recording was at best inconclusive, he said, but the accusation and the circumstances were loud enough to have been picked up by the traditional media, the social media platforms and the vultures managing the gossip columns using either. In short, the #millionairemurderer hashtag was now making its unstoppable rounds around the world.

As much as I intensely disliked the announcement of my situation across the social platforms, I knew that there was nothing that could be done about it. I could merely keep quiet and wish for some new scandal to break soon to get the Twitter-ready vampire thumbs to change the subject interest. My hope was that, in a week or two – that is, as long as I didn't feed the news about me with some new scandal – my story would be forgotten. Still, it was a serious attack on my integrity that, guilty or not, would linger on the Internet for anyone who would bother to look me up. In other words, my life and my reputation were now forever in tatters, and perhaps beyond remedy.

On a more worrying level, though, I wondered how anyone could have discovered that it was I who had negotiated with Flint to have Rathbone killed six years earlier. As I had suspected at the time, he had recorded our conversation, but I was pretty sure the motorbike had drowned out the words. Yet the police now had a transcript of the exchange. I had made my deal with Flint as Abdul Mahfouz, and I couldn't for my life think of any possible way for him to have found out that I was anyone but Mahfouz. There must be some other way the police had discovered about our meeting.

I couldn't make head nor tail of the situation.

Wednesday April 8, 2015

The following morning, supervised by armed prison personnel, I was moved from the First Nights Centre to a single cell in the prison's D wing. A little later I was told to join other prisoners and walk to an area where food was served twice a day. That's when I saw Allan again, after so many years. He hadn't noticed me yet, and I wondered if he would recognise me now, considering the time that had passed and the many faces I had worn.

139

I was standing last in the queue with perhaps ten other inmates between us. Allan acted as if he had been in prison for some time, because he knew the drill without the need of being shouted at by the officer supervising us. After getting his serving, he went over to a solitary table in a corner while not letting his eyes off his food. That is, with one exception. When he went by a man with his head shaven clean ahead of me in the queue, he did cast a quick glance at him, looking as if being afraid of being thrashed. His mouth became more set and he walked a little faster. *Interesting*, I thought. *Allan must have passed some disagreeable times with this fellow.*

When the bald man had got his plate with food and left the queue, I got a better look at him. His face had Slavic features with high cheekbones and blue eyes. Eastern European, without doubt. He went to sit with some other inmates at a table far from Allan.

After I had been served the breakfast of grit, fruits, bread and coffee, I chose to sit down at the very same table where the bald man ignored the chat of two other inmates. On purpose, I chose a chair that only allowed Allan to see my back. I waited in silence to see if the bald man would start talking to me. He didn't, so I decided to speak up.

"I'm Matt", I began. "I was transferred to this wing this morning, so I don't know much about what's going on in this place. How long have you been here?"

"Three weeks", he reluctantly replied after a pause. His accent was clearly Russian, which explained Allan's hostile glance earlier.

"Three weeks? I was hoping to get out long before that, you know, by getting bail. How do things work around here?"

"You sleep. You eat. They interrogate. You wait a lot."

"Sounds boring. By the way, since it looks like we're going to be together here for some time, what shall I call you?"

"Boris", he said and rose to return his tray to the area where you were supposed to leave the unwashed dishes.

I did the same, and was then ordered back to my single-occupant cell. Once inside, the door was slammed shut behind me.

*

Being one of the last to arrive for dinner, Allan got a shock when he realised that Boris was sitting at a table talking to his former partner Matthias. *Why is Matthias here? What has he done? How come he knows Boris? How can I avoid them?* These and more questions swirled in his head as the robust, no-nonsense woman behind the counter brusquely threw a portion of mashed potatoes on top of the greasy sausages and overcooked carrots previously served.

He went to an opposite corner in the dining hall, as far away from the two people he least wanted to meet. *What can I do? What are they talking about? Are they discussing me? How can I get out of this circle of hell?*

Contemplating suicide as a solution, the depressed Allan decided he would first request to be moved to some other penitentiary.

141

Friday April 10, 2015

Vaughn sighed as he put aside the printout of the complete records of the debit card that Andrew Reese had used on US soil. Not that there were many transactions. The VISA card had been issued by Barclays Bank in London on May 13, 2009, in connection with the aperture of a new account. There was only one deposit ever made into the account – 50,000 pounds on the day it had been opened.

Two days later the card had been used for the first time, paying for a limousine service from JFK International Airport. From there on, there was a flurry of activities paid for by the card: theatre tickets, meals in expensive restaurants, clothing and other purchases in upscale stores, and an impressive expense charged by the Waldorf Astoria for a five-day stay. *That's how the rich live*, he reflected and sighed again.

The list continued with flight tickets to Las Vegas and more expenses similar to those in New York. There was the amount of 20,000 dollars withdrawn at the Paris Las Vegas Casino, presumably to play the tables – or maybe purposely to have cash to avoid leaving a trail when moving on into Mexico? Callaghan had declared 41,500 dollars when he had crossed the border on the last occasion he had been confirmed seen.

Then there were charges for the rental of two cars, gasoline and meal paid for in Lake Havasu City, more gasoline at a roadside station further south in Arizona, and the charge made by the spa hotel facility on May 24, moments after the alleged killing had taken place. Later the same day, two single

142

tickets in economy class were purchased for passenger Andrew Reese only: one from Phoenix to New York City, and the other from there to Paris.

After this intense spending spree, there was only one more charge made to the account, this one by Avis on June 19. It was for 8,460 dollars to cover the deductible for a stolen Mercedes that had been rented in Reese's name.

Left in Reeve's Barclays account, which since then hadn't been used for nearly six years, were 10,625 pounds. A small fortune, no doubt. Vaughn wondered why it had been left untouched for such a long time.

He concluded that Reese must have acted as a personal assistant to Callaghan and the woman. It seemed obvious that the money deposited in Reese's account had been paid by Callaghan. It looked as if Callaghan had had no intention of returning to the UK, and didn't want to leave a paper trail behind after he had arrived in the US. Was it because Thompson, a known London gangster, had made Callaghan go on the run?

*

After visiting Boris in prison, Jason Longhorn called Mikhail Berlosky. Longhorn said he had news and wondered if they could have a late lunch together, after he had made a visit to the courthouse? Berlosky said they could meet at the pizzeria in Covent Garden. Four hours later, Longhorn arrived and found Berlosky nursing a beer at a corner table.

"So, how are things going with bail for Boris?" Berlosky asked after they had ordered.

"The paperwork is being processed", Longhorn said, "but things haven't been made easier by Allan Gould's tales to the police of cruelty and modern-day slavery. He's told the police, and I quote, that 'Boris was his supervisor, who in turn obeyed the instructions of ruthless Russians gangsters'. However, I think my efforts making Allan look unreliable in the eyes of the authorities is working quite well, and, besides, he has no real proof to support his story. I'm pretty sure Boris should be out in a week or two."

"That sounds good."

"However, the main reason I wanted to see you is because of something else I learnt today."

"I'm all ears."

"Remember Matthias Callaghan?

"I do."

"Well, it turns out Callaghan has been put behind bars in the same place as Boris and Allan."

As he spoke, Berlosky watched the pinball emotions in Longhorn's face go through its phases of resentment and animosity. He knew perfectly well that it was Callaghan who had tricked Longhorn into losing his licence to practice law.

"That's quite an interesting twist. What's he in prison for?"

"I don't know the whole story, only that he's accused of a murder committed years ago here in London."

"A murder? Do you know who the victim was?"

"A solicitor by the name of Charles Rathbone."

Rare was the occasion Berlosky found himself speechless. Longhorn wondered why Rathbone's name had been such a surprise.

"I was at the courthouse before I came here to ask around", he continued. "His lawyer is David Sandhurst, who is working on getting Callaghan out on bail."

Saturday April 11, 2015

"This story will sell copies – don't doubt it", Trudy claimed sarcastically as she threw down a printout of said story on Burns' desk.

The editor picked up the pages and adjusted his glasses. Trudy sat down uninvited in one of his visitor's chairs and in the process ripped another hole in her jeans. Assumed by her contemporaries to be designer jeans, they were in fact just old, worn and about to cease functioning for their intended use.

"To sum it up, this prince charming named Callaghan used to be very rich, then he got into trouble and sailed abroad to calmer waters, and years later he's back again accused of masterminding the murder of a lawyer who hasn't yet been named but apparently nobody liked", she offered as an advance review of her typewritten story while studying the grime under the peeling black paint of her finger nails.

Burns looked up and looked at her over the rim of his glasses.

"I can't believe that I'm hearing you say this, Trudy", he

accused her. "You can do much better than putting up a bored face and reciting conclusions a five-year-old can come up with."

"Well, it *is* a boring, everyday crime story as I see it. If you don't like my take on it, perhaps I'll just walk out of here and you can give it to someone else."

This time without answering, Burns read through the page and a half that Trudy had put together.

"His father sounds more fun to write about, though", Trudy said in an offhand manner and yawned.

Burns looked up and studied her sharply.

"Why do say that?"

"He was a bloke who blew an inheritance of several hundred million in a decade or so, and then he had to resort to escorting rich old ladies twice his age. Quite a gigolo in his time, it appears. He was all over the papers ten, fifteen years ago."

"Why do you bring up him and the old ladies?"

"Well, apart from sounding more fun, he's good-looking, he's a playboy and he's dead."

Burns couldn't help smiling at her cheek.

"You know, I'm beginning to understand what you're hinting at – there could perhaps exist some interesting connection between the son and the father. Some human angle … Why would a millionaire son allow his father to survive as a gigolo, then leave the country and years later be arrested? See if you can dig deeper into this. We'll run the main story tomorrow, and I'll give you the chance to run follow-up articles for a week or two, should they turn out to be promising."

"Will do", Trudy said with a wry smile, got up and left his office.

Sunday April 12, 2015

"Vasily, we have not one, but two or maybe even three problems on our hands", Berlosky greeted him as he stepped into the sitting room from the elevator that Sonia had allowed to arrive at the penthouse. He handed Vasily a paper and pointed at the headline on page three: "Millionaire jailed for murder". He sauntered over to the bar and asked Sonia to serve him a glass of tequila.

"You have to switch firewater every now and then", he said, smiling, when she asking raised an eyebrow.

"Why is Callaghan in jail, Mikhail?" Vasily asked, curious, after he had read Trudy Swift's story in the *Daily Mirror*. "This article mentions that he killed someone?"

"I don't have all the details, Vasily, but what I've learnt from Longhorn is that he was arrested as a suspect for killing none less than our former solicitor friend Charles Rathbone."

"A suspect in the murder of Rathbone!" Vasily giggled in response to the unexpected news.

"Now, how about this: he's awaiting trial while spending time in the same jail as Boris and Allan."

"Mikhail, that's incredible!" Vasily cried, rubbing his eyes. "Life is certainly full of surprises!"

"Longhorn is still working on getting Boris out on bail", Berlosky said, pleased with Vasily's reaction. "Last Friday Longhorn met with him. Among other things discussed, Boris said that Allan Gould has been spilling the beans to the cops."

"What does Longhorn say? Can he get Boris out on bail?"

"He says he's confident he will. It will, however, take another week or two before bail will be granted due to court procedure. He also told me that Callaghan has instructed his lawyer to do the same. What do you want me to do with Allan and Callaghan?"

"Why, kill them, of course", Vasily exclaimed, making a sign with his hand across his throat. "Why should we risk our business with either of these two *tovariches* who already know too much for their own good? Get rid of them!"

"It means we have to put up the surety to get Allan out as well. Longhorn told me the bond for Boris is going to cost at least eighty-thousand pounds. Money that will be spent and lost, no doubt."

"You know better than to worry about money."

"OK, I'll see what I can do", Berlosky said.

"You'll do better than that, Mikhail. You should make sure that both are dead before they compromise any of our activities."

Monday April 13, 2015
"Good afternoon, everyone", Burns greeted the men and

women around the conference table as he entered the room with a smoking tea cup. "Let's see what we have for tomorrow's edition, shall we?"

Each reporter made a summary and, in some cases, pitches for continued investigation of the news in their particular field.

"What about you, Trudy?" the editor-in-chief asked when it came to her turn. "By the way, let me mention that I've thought about what you told me a couple of days ago, and I think you hit it spot on. The Callaghan-arrest-and-extradition story that we ran yesterday was really one that comes thirteen to the dozen. What have you found out since that will make the follow-up more interesting?"

"I've looked into the Callaghan family history", Trudy began. "The son, recently arrested, and his father, share the name of his grandfather – Matthias Callaghan. The grandfather was a great industrialist; the father evolved into a sybarite and a terrific spendthrift. What took the grandfather half a century to build, he spent in a decade. The son has been successful in the computer business, from which he retired after a making a considerable fortune."

She sat up in the chair and looked around the table.

"That's just a brief background, so you can understand the main players", she clarified, without making any excuse. "Here are some interesting titbits about the youngest Callaghan. He was married for more than two years to a famous actress, and you'll never guess who. By the way, Trevor, I've suddenly realised that I'm now thankful that you dispatched me to interview her six months ago. It has given me a different perspective, you know."

They all look keen to learn who the actress is, she noted contentedly, *although Trevor of course immediately knew who I'm referring to.*

"Julie Cross, no less, of *Umbrellas* and *Beauty and the Beast* fame, and recently back in London from Broadway to sold-out shows of *New York, New York*. But that's not all: although they were married in two thousand and six, the marriage didn't end with a divorce – it was annulled. Another interesting fact about Callaghan is that he was declared dead at the time of the annulment, something that later was corrected. Apparently it wasn't he but his father who died … a confusion from having the same name, perhaps, although it does sound a bit strange, doesn't it? Another odd detail is that the particulars about all of this have been protected in a so-called closed material procedure and cannot be accessed by the general public. That's how far I've got."

There was a murmur of appreciation around the table as she finished. More than one thought it sounded like a juicy story that their readers would lap up.

"It certainly has elements that look newsworthy", Burns said, before wrapping up the meeting. "The celebrity wife who never was his wife, the playboy father who squandered a fortune, the Internet millionaire who wound up in jail accused of murder, the secret documents that would explain who died and who didn't. Make it concise but don't spare any details, Trudy. All right everyone, back to work."

Tuesday April 14, 2015

Allan hadn't seen Jason Longhorn since he had come to his house to hand over the cheque for seven million pounds three years earlier. Now Longhorn was sitting across the table in an interrogation room together with a younger associate, who had presented himself as Brett Stevens. Since Allan never had revoked his previous power of attorney, Longhorn's law firm could still represent him in court.

"We are here to get you out on bail, Allan", Longhorn began.

"What on earth for?" Allan blurted. "To return back to … into … the horrible slavery that the Russians exert? Not on your life!"

"Calm down, Allan – please, calm down", Stevens said in low voice while moving his hands palm down towards the tabletop. "We're not here to make your life more miserable. We're here to help you get out of jail."

"Paid for by whom?" Allan questioned him in a shrill voice. "Let me guess? The very same Russians that have made my life miserable over the past six years!"

"Actually, we've come with the intention of completing the government's required pro bono programme", Longhorn lied. Stevens shot him a glance as if wondering what he was talking about, but he didn't say anything. Still upset, Allan didn't notice.

"You see, all law firms are encouraged to do some work for clients without resources, pro bono that is, and like most law firms in our profession, we adhere to that principle. Since

I have worked with you in the past and now am aware that you're passing through a difficult financial situation, Brett here and I decided that it would be an honourable undertaking to take you on, pro bono, considering your present situation."

Stevens – incredulous, since it was the first time he had heard Longhorn's explanation being the reason for now sitting in the interrogation room with Allan – looked sideways at Longhorn, but he prudently kept his tongue while making a mental note to ask him later. On purpose Longhorn hadn't informed him, because Stevens didn't have knowledge of the full extent of their law firm's dependence on the Russians.

Allan didn't listen – he simply didn't digest the meaning of Longhorn's words. Instead, he started babbling about his hellish years during which the Russians had taken advantage of his skills while keeping him under house arrest.

Longhorn listened to the unhinged Allan pouring out his grievances while jotting down the essentials on a legal pad with the intention to later share them with Mikhail Berlosky. *Who has heard of a prisoner refusing to leave jail when bail money has been put up for him?* Longhorn wondered. *Once the judge has been convinced that Gould is not a flight risk, of course he will grant him bail. Whether Gould wants it or not, he's going to be released very soon.*

Monday March 23 – Wednesday April 15, 2015
After the caravan had begun its journey northwards at dusk, it

didn't take many hours before Ilya and Vladimir understood the reality they were going to endure for weeks to come. They were travelling by night. They did so because, as Haroun with his seemingly endless patience had explained when Ilya asked him why, the heat during daytime was too forbidding. This in spite of this time of year being the most favourable season for crossing the desert.

The Russians did not exert any particular surveillance of the valuable merchandise they were supposed to watch over. Instead, they were simply, hour by hour, doing their utmost to survive one of the harshest climates in the world. Besides, who was going to hijack a camel caravan in the middle of a desert? With unbearable temperatures during the day, and bitterly cold nights that they spent swaying on the backs of dromedaries as if in an endless dream, they lived through a kaleidoscope of nightmares. Their daily confrontations had been the dusty, barren plains when they had set out, which gradually had turned into sandy, barren hills. On occasion, sudden desert storms – short-lived examples of the upcoming Sirocco – whipped their path. It was the only time when the monotony was replaced by sand that entered the smallest space imaginable in their bodies, no matter how well they tried to cover themselves up. That's when Ilya and Vladimir learnt to appreciate their djellabas and the return to the journey's monotony.

However, most of the nights consisted of swaying on their dromedaries, or walking beside them, below a night sky that Haroun proudly pronounced to be the only million-star hotel in the world. Ilya and Vladimir had a hard time sharing his enthusiasm. Then again, as Haroun understood perfectly well, they were city boys whose closest experience to a desert up until then had been as toddlers in a sandbox.

Now, after twenty-three days of incessant suffering, the only consolation that Ilya and Vladimir had found from traversing the desert of Mauritania and Western Sahara into Morocco was their shared cursing of the impossible choice between their two options of crossing it. Either they could be carried by a dromedary that by nature was about half a meter wider than the legs of a human were supposed to be spread, and thus enduring the unwanted acrobatics for a twelve-hour night trip; or they had to walk in ever-shifting sand that was even more tiring for the legs than sitting on a dromedary.

Haroun had explained it succinctly to the usually taciturn Vladimir on the occasion the latter had complained about the uncomfortable travel circumstances.

"People weren't made to walk in the desert, they were made to ride dromedaries. Dromedaries were designed to walk in the sand, because they have large, flat hooves. Humans never bothered to develop large, flat hooves, because they are better off riding the dromedaries."

When Vladimir recounted this to Ilya, Ilya could only shake his head and lament that they were still doomed to traversing the desert hell for another two or three weeks, if they didn't get lost.

"Perhaps we're better off staying on the beast", Vladimir sighed. "These animals always find water, they have a great

154

nose for finding water, I've been told. And I urgently need a lengthy bath to wash off the smell of them."

"They have a great nose, all right", Ilya replied, touching his own while trying to adjust his uncomfortable position in the makeshift saddle that likely never had received a scrubbing. "That's easy to confirm just by looking at their ugly faces. I heard someone refer to them as 'ships of the desert'. It's a very precise description. Travelling on one inevitably makes you seasick."

"I hate this robe that Haroun made us put on."

"The djellaba? Yes. It stinks of camel and rancid cooking oil. But I guess it's more practical than city clothes in the desert."

At least the hardships made them bond closer than they ever had been, since otherwise they had little in common apart from being Vasily's employees. Vladimir was tall and gangly, had a melancholic outlook on life, and strangely enough – considering his choice of employment – had an ascetic approach to life. He was saving up money for an early retirement and a comfortable *dacha* back in the motherland, where people shared his way of thinking. His actions were contradictory in that he was working abroad in a violent, ruthless business in order to achieve a peaceful life with no worries in the region where previous generations of his family had been serfs and later farmers living in poverty. *To achieve a life without hardships, you first have to live them*, Vladimir had pondered more than once. *Riding this horrible animal for nights on end will count as just one more*, he decided as his dromedary grunted.

Viewed from a great variety of aspects, Ilya was quite the opposite of Vladimir. Six years younger, Ilya had a great appetite for life: food, drink, women, jewellery, cars, long siestas and no worries beyond living the moment – and probably in that order. A man in his mid-forties who had been comfortable with his growing midriff, he was perfectly aware that he would reappear at the other side of the seemingly eternal desert restored to the starved looks of his youth. Someone had long ago explained to him the Latin expression *Carpe diem*, and Ilya had liked the concept so much that he had worked on memorising the words to (in his mind, at least) perfection, with an Italian-inflected pronunciation acquired from watching the Godfather movies: "Relax-ah, ya gotta be more-ah … caarpe diiem, *capice*?" This was Ilya's preferred way to transmit his worldview that he didn't care about some blurry tomorrow. Considering his present circumstance on an extended trip through the driest place on Earth, riding an uncomfortable animal that he rejected every aspect of from the smell to how it had made him hurt every time he had the relief to climb off it, he felt the challenge even greater than Vladimir. The food provided was invariably dried fruits and couscous. The drink was restricted to water, in very measured portions. Women? This was an all-male expedition, supposedly for funding future encounters with the fairer sex. Sometimes he had sincere doubts that being an enforcer in the drug business was really worth his efforts. *Perhaps I would have been better off as a night club manager or something,* he occasionally dreamt.

Nevertheless, oblivious of everything that separated them, riding through the Sahara had the formidable effect of firmly bonding the two through their shared experience that, despite all their discomforts, also inspired in them an awe of the star-bright universe they nightly journeyed through.

The reality, imposed on them by Berlosky with the threat of Vasily's merciless retribution, impacted them in more than one way. Besides the landscape monotony and the drastic temperature changes between day and night, there were the invading smells of the beasts of burden, the unwashed bodies that shared their tent and the scents of mysterious seasoning floating on the air when food was prepared over open fire that inevitably opened their appetite. Then there were the prayers five times a day. The shouts and mumbling from their travel companions in the hundreds, inside the makeshift tents and other shelters that shielded the travellers from the relentless sun, prevented Ilya and Vladimir to go to sleep at dawn. During the day, the lengthy and insistent prayers woke them up on four more occasions before it was time at dusk to force their aching bodies up on the camelbacks again.

That morning, when the caravan stopped for the coming day's rest, Haroun walked up to the two Russians.

"We have now left Mauritania and entered Western Sahara. Half of our journey has been accomplished, and no problems so far. Everything is going according to plan."

After his briefing, Vladimir and Ilya, with every muscle hurting, had difficulties imagining what could possibly be

157

more punishing than to force a man on top of a dromedary and doom him to ride it through a desert with no end in sight.

Thursday April 16, 2015

Invited by their old business partner Sergei Gagarin – who continued to launder money through his three London-based Russian restaurants – Vasily, Berlosky and Sonia arrived at the Caspian Sea a little after seven. Although the amount that Gagarin laundered had become insignificant during the years of Vasily's aggressive expansion, Berlosky had persuaded Vasily to keep him on. It's always good to have a reliable friend who hails from the motherland, Berlosky had argued. At first, Vasily had merely shrugged, but after meeting with Sergei, he found the middle-aged man to be good company and full of entertaining anecdotes. The growing friendship led Vasily to meet with Sergei at least once a month, very much enjoying his company, his wit and his canny eye for the preferred tastes in food, beverages and companions of his guests. The company this evening, which took place in one of the principal restaurant's private dining rooms, had been expanded to include Sonia and Oleg, and a trusted assistant that Sergei vouched for. The gargantuan dinner, with everything on the house, was intended to mix pleasure with business. Sergei was looking for a way to get a larger slice of the business Berlosky and Vasily were expanding in giant leaps, according to what he had learnt through the grapevine.

To begin with, this evening was no different from any

other pleasurable time spent together at the restaurant, with the exception that the company was larger than usual. The astute Sergei, jovial and deft at leading the conversation surreptitiously towards discussing his interest at heart – something that Vasily with amusement noted as the evening proceeded – had them enjoying themselves royally. After the blinis with caviar, the oven-baked salmon, the roasted wild boar, the twenty-odd side dishes and the dessert, Sergei estimated that the moment had come to expound on the true theme of the reunion. Everyone asked for coffee and liqueur, except Vasily, who said he would accept another glass of the exceptional red wine they had been served with the wild boar.

The waiter wrote down everyone's wishes and disappeared.

*

Misha felt miserable. *Miserable Misha, Misha is miserable,* he repeatedly told himself as he raced through London at excess speed in the Ferrari that his father had bought for him the day he celebrated turning eighteen. He was used to his parents doting on him, although now, at nineteen, he considered his mother suffocating in her attempts to overprotect him and his father rich enough to buy everything that Misha fancied.

That evening he, as usual during their heated relationship for the past three months, had taken his beautiful, slim-limbed girlfriend three years his senior to dinner. Before picking her up in his car, one that impressed everyone he

159

knew except this girl in particular, he had spent a long afternoon smoking hashish with two friends of his. At the restaurant, as the effect begun to wear off, he repeatedly rose, excusing himself to go to the gents. There he inhaled a fair amount of high-quality cocaine. The girlfriend wasn't dumb, and perhaps more than anything felt upset that Misha didn't offer her a taste. After a disastrous meal, during which they argued so loudly that the stern head waiter had to ask them to lower their voices, Misha asked for his car. He drove them to their preferred discotheque, leaving the Ferrari parked illegally by the kerb outside. As always, the presence of his car was the automatic free entrance ticket to the club. Since it was still early, barely ten o'clock, the queue of hopefuls consisted of a mere handful who were held back by the bouncer as part of the strategic marketing ploy.

After ordering a bottle of champagne at a privileged table overlooking the still empty dance floor, Misha went off again to cheer himself up with more cocaine. When he returned to the table, he offered his cheers and brought his glass too violently against his girlfriend's, which made it break. Broken glass and champagne sprayed over her dress, one she had bought a day earlier. Misha for some reason found it hilarious, and burst out laughing. The girl became furious and began screaming quite ingenious insults at him.

Ten minutes later she had disappeared in a cab and Misha got into his car alone. He felt miserable: his girlfriend had just humiliated him by shouting that he couldn't drive his car, that he was a show-off and that his problem was mixing too much hashish with lines of cocaine that, she had nagged, when added up in one evening, was longer than the queue outside the discotheque would be at midnight. He had done his best to defend himself, claiming that the dent in the Ferrari that he had almost parked in time that evening, was easily repaired.

Misha managed to bring his powerful sports car to a halt outside the Caspian Sea without hitting anything else that evening and, after some trouble getting out while trying to get his bearings, threw the keys to the valet to have it parked. He entered his father's restaurant, was effusively greeted by the captain whom he chose to ignore and sauntered somewhat unsteadily to the bartender with the intention of ordering something strong that he could dilute with tears of self-pity.

Before he had the opportunity to decide on which liquor he would test this time, the waiter of confidence that his father employed for important business meetings appeared.

"I need three Hennessy VSOP, two Grand Marnier and another glass of the Chateauneuf-du-Pape you served earlier."

"No problem with the cognac and the liqueur, but I'll have to go down to the wine cellar to see if we still have some bottles of that particular wine", the bartender replied. "It will take me some time, though."

"Well, you better hurry up, there are some important, not to say impatient, people in there – not least the boss."

"I'll go and find the bottle of wine while you fix the other drinks", Misha heard himself offering to help out. "I'll even have a glass of the very same myself."

The employees looked at him suspiciously, before they with an invisible shrug and a raised eyebrow, nodded their consent. He was the boss's son, after all, and who were they to contradict his orders?

The bartender gave Misha the key to the wine cellar. He stumbled down the staircase to the vaulted cellar in the beautiful 18th-century building with its rows of bottles of spirits and wine. He found the section where vintage wines were kept and began reading the names written with chalk on small blackboards.

By now Misha had forgotten what chateau-wine he was supposed to fetch, so he chose at random. *No one's going to notice the difference,* he assured himself, *I'll just pour it into a wine decanter.*

The rustic wine cellar, which maintained a constant, cool temperature, also had some tables and chairs for sampling sessions. Misha sat down, opened the bottle with a corkscrew he had found and inhaled the pungent bouquet that wafted up in his nose. *Smells like wine, all right.* On a shelf where assorted glass containers were kept, he chose a decanter and poured the wine. Just to be perfectly sure he was serving quality stuff, he took a deep swig from the decanter before wiping its opening with his sleeve. *Good wine. Should try it more often.*

The waiter had already returned to the private dining room with the other beverages, the bartender told him when he reappeared from the cellar.

"Don't worry, I'll take this one there myself", he replied.

"Just hand me another wine glass."

He got it and turned towards the closed door to the dining room where his father entertained his guests. Somehow he had made the movement too abruptly. Misha began to feel queasy from the evening's overindulgence. He nevertheless made a brave effort, reached the door a second before the waiter opened it and let him pass. A few heads turned as he entered.

"Who was asking for ... for ... for ..." Misha felt a wave of renewed nausea overwhelm the milder version he had experienced before entering and stumbled as the stomach cramps came and went as a prequel to the want of vomiting. The glass he had brought fell to the stone floor and broke. He managed to hold on to the decanter, but as he doubled over, he poured a good portion of the wine over the person who was sitting with his back against the entrance.

Chairs scraped against the flooring as those present, distressed, got up. No one was more aghast than Sergei, Misha's father. The only one who outwardly seemed unperturbed was Vasily, the victim of the shower of wine.

The enormity of what had just happened, combined with Vasily's ominously calm reaction, saw three seconds pass with no sounds in the room except for Misha's unsuccessful attempts to vomit. Then everyone started talking at the same time until Vasily raised a hand to silence everyone.

"Sonia, can you go to my place and get me a change of clothes", he said, calmly, his words more sinister since they were spoken without his customary giggle. His face was deadly pale and the pupils of his eyes seemed to have become one with his irises.

Sonia immediately rose and left. Sergei strode across the room and slapped his son hard across his face. It was spontaneous, it was necessary and he hated himself for doing this to his only son in front of his guests. At the same time, he knew he had to demonstrate an immediate and violent action to the inexcusable act of spoiling the silk suit of one of Berlosky's closest men and his own well-prepared evening to expand his business.

Just to be clear, Vasily had chosen to let Berlosky take the lead in all negotiations, while he himself acted as one of Berlosky's advisers. It didn't make him anonymous, but it made him unimportant in the eyes of people who shouldn't be in the know, which was Vasily's point.

Misha was chased from the room by his father. Minutes later, the bartender appeared with a generous glass of the correct wine that Misha had overlooked. Subdued small talk eventually renewed the interrupted evening, until Sonia appeared with Vasily's change of clothes half an hour later. Full of excuses for his son, Sergei showed Vasily to a private bathroom where he could get changed.

As he closed the door behind him, Sergei merely shook his head. The opportunity he had planned so minutely for had slipped out of his hands the moment he thought he had held it in his palms. *At least a minor miracle avoided having Misha pour the wine over Mikhail Berlosky,* he inwardly sighed. *Although not at all good, not good at all, fortunately he only soaked that adviser of his in wine.* He shook his head. *I have to talk to Misha. This can't go on. He has his toys and he's young, but now the time has come for him to grow up.*

Friday April 17, 2015

"Vasily, Sergei called me this morning", Berlosky opened the conversation as they met in Vasily's flat before lunchtime. "He's ashamed and upset and, I think, quite frightened that you might harm his boy for what happened last night."

"Well, it wasn't one of the most pleasing moments I've gone through", Vasily replied dreamily, stone-faced and un-giggling. He was sitting dressed in a thick embroidered Japanese silk robe in front of an elaborate waterfall that he had ordered to be installed in a space next to his bedroom. *Sitting down, his hands are placed palms up resting on his thighs,* Berlosky noticed, but he didn't know what to make of it. *My boss is harder to read than an encyclopaedia,* he decided. *As usual, I need to play along and see what he eventually comes up with.*

"Actually, it was the most humiliating experience that I've had since I decided to leave Russia for London. What makes it more insulting to me, is that the show wasn't put on by one of the bumbling idiots who live in this country, but one of our own. I'm thinking of the appropriate punishment, and of course his father is worried to death."

"Let me put it this way, Vasily", Berlosky implored. "The boy is barely nineteen, he's tasting too much of the stuff we are offering wholesale in this country, and he became sick the

165

moment he entered the room, not out of disrespect, but because he's a spoiled junkie. His father is begging me to not punish Misha. He's willing to listen to some well-considered advice that will teach his son a lesson. By the way, Sergei doesn't know that you're the boss; he thinks I've been making the decisions ever since Yuri was put out of misery."

"So why are you lobbying so hard to save the whelp's neck, Mikhail?"

"For two reasons: his father goes a long way back with us, and he has always remained loyal. And the kid didn't try to humiliate you on purpose – he was high and drunk, and he's just another teenager who needs to be disciplined."

"All right, Mikhail, well spoken." Vasily's reply was accompanied by a giggle that Berlosky relished after not hearing one for nearly twenty-four hours. To Mikhail, it wasn't the yoga position that meant that Vasily had regained his usual posture of equanimity, it was his customary giggle. "But one of these days I will have to impose a punishment … I don't know yet what or where or how, but tell Sergei that he doesn't need to fear that something too severe will happen to his son."

The guru had spoken. Mikhail took his cue and left when Vasily shut his eyes.

*

When Samantha entered the conference room at New Scotland Yard, Georgie rose from his chair to greet her. He was immediately taken by her freshness and her beauty, only imperceptibly marred by the frown of worry above her eyebrows. *Perhaps some four, five years younger than myself,* his experienced eye judged. He went around the table and offered her a chair, before returning to his own seat.

"I'm so sorry that we have to meet here, in this way, under these circumstances", Georgie began, hesitating. "I'm Detective Sergeant George Jones, and I've been given the task by my superior, Detective Inspector Blackmoore, to brief you regarding the concerns you have presented to the police over your husband's detention."

"I'm very much worried about the way he was arrested at the airport and then extradited to the UK … I don't think my husband was allowed his legal rights in the, to say the least, hasty transfer. And, more worrisome yet, I still haven't been allowed to speak with him. As a matter of fact, I still don't know where he's being held."

"As we speak, he's in custody at Wormwood Scrubs."

"That's a prison, isn't it?"

"Unfortunately we don't have sufficient space here at the Yard, so sometimes we have to ask a larger prison complex to accommodate persons who are going through the legal process before coming up before a judge and a jury."

"I still don't completely understand on what grounds Matthias was arrested in Rome. Could you enlighten me?"

"Of course", Georgie replied, giving her a melancholy smile that he years ago had discovered worked wonders on women he was interested in. "I have copy here of the plaint that the prosecutor has presented to the court."

He found the paper in his briefcase and handed it to Samantha.

In horror, she read that Matthias, while posing as the deceased Abdul Mahfouz, was accused of having hired gangsters to murder a lawyer called Charles Rathbone.

"Is this true?" Samantha half-whispered after finishing.

"As far as the police are concerned, it covers what we have learnt so far", Georgie confirmed. "There is, of course, still a lot of ongoing investigation that may change the final conclusion."

"What can I do? What should I do now?" Tears welled up in her eyes.

"If you give me your London address and mobile phone number", Georgie said, seizing the opportunity, "I promise I'll be in touch with you should any new development occur."

Samantha gave him the name of her hotel and her mobile number. After thanking him with a sad smile, she rose and started for the door. Georgie couldn't help but admire her figure that at this point still wasn't revealing her pregnancy.

*

Allan was ordered by two warders to step out from his cell. When he asked them where they were going, the warders merely ignored his questions. They led him inside a nondescript room that he had never seen before, where two men in civilian clothes waited.

"Your bail application has been approved with the condition that you wear this anklet monitor", one of them told Allan and waved the device in the air. "There are a few other conditions, too, which I will explain to you in due course. Sit down on that chair and roll up your trouser leg."

The news of his release on bail only accelerated the anxiety that nowadays never left Allan. The two uniformed warders left.

"I've been granted bail? Why is that? I prefer to remain in prison. I don't want to leave!"

"Well, you don't have much choice", the other man snickered. "Her Majesty's Prison Service won't be paying for your upkeep any longer, gov. Your solicitor requested your release on bail and put up the surety. Eighty grand, a little bird tweeted in my ear, so surely your rich friends on the outside can afford your future board and lodging, too. Eighty grand ones, not bad at all, eh; it means you must be one of those important blokes. Now, roll up that trouser sleeve of yours!"

Dumbfounded by the news, Allan obeyed the warder. *Those "rich friends" who have put up that amount as surety to secure my release – they have to be the Russians! They want me back, slaving away at phishing scams. I can't allow it! I can't do it! I can't live like that again!* His hysteria began to build as he understood that, while pretending that he had Allan's interests at heart, Longhorn was working for the very same people Allan dreaded and wanted to get away from. It was Longhorn's firm that had posted the surety for his bail, without even bothering to get Allan's consent. *Of course it must have been Boris's people who had put up the money!*

Once shoved outside the prison complex, he spotted his partner from the failed Internet café venture, Bruno Fenwich, in his dilapidated car. Despite their disappointing business venture, Bruno had remained a friend. After being fitted with the anklet, Allan had been allowed a phone call. He couldn't think of anyone to call to pick him up from prison with the exception of Bruno. Allan quickly got into the passenger seat, and nervously asked him to drive away from the place as quickly as possible.

Bruno watched him, concerned, as Allan kept studying the mirrors for cars that could be following.

"What's the matter with you, Allan?" Bruno asked, puzzled. "You've just got out of jail, and now you're more paranoid than I remember ever having seen you."

"Look, Bruno, I'm really thankful that you agreed to pick me up", Allan responded, nervously, "but there are some things that … that don't feel right to me. I can't go home. I think my life might be endangered."

"Endangered? What on earth for?" Bruno sounded alarmed.

"Just a feeling … the way things developed while I was on the inside", Allan answered in a slightly higher pitch than he normally spoke. "The thing is, I'm not allowed to move out of a ten-mile radius from my home in Wimbledon, but I don't dare to go home."

"I think I know something that perhaps might be a solution for you on a temporary basis", Bruno said after having thought about it for a minute. "I know this place not far from your house. It's one that rents flats to tourists on a weekly basis. Mind you, it's not the most elegant of residences, but maybe it can work for you until you get back on your feet again. Do you want me to take you there so you can have a look?"

"Sounds good, Bruno, please do." There was a hint of relief in Allan's voice, Bruno noticed.

The residence turned out to be a three-storey building with flats having one or two bedrooms, a sitting room and a kitchen. There were a dozen flats or so on each floor, all which opened to a corridor at the centre of the edifice. The building itself was old, probably built in the decade following World War II and later refurbished to fit its present business model. There was a somewhat grimy aspect about the place that Allan didn't like, but on the whole he found it would serve his immediate needs. *I can hide here for a couple of weeks,* he figured, *while making plans for the future.* Meanwhile, since he was within the stipulated radius of his home address, he would be compliant with the bail conditions.

Later, he thought, *I'll think of some way to get rid of this nuisance around my ankle. As soon as I have come up with some way to regain my life.*

Saturday April 18, 2015

Two warders led me from my cell down long corridors before motioning me to enter a small visitor's room. Samantha rose

171

as I entered it, looking disturbed as one of the warders removed my handcuffs. The room was bare except for a table screwed to the floor and a couple of chairs.

"No touching allowed", one of them hissed.

The warders leaned against the wall as we took the chair opposite one another. It was very uncomfortable not to be able to even hold hands while the smirking warders strained to overhear what we were saying.

"Jack came to London for the twins", Samantha began with a murmur. "I couldn't see how I could care for them while frantically looking for a way to reach you and understand what is going on."

"You did the right thing", I replied, half whispering in a low voice. "I'm not sure what happened, but someone has his mind set on framing me for something I didn't do."

We discussed this and a lot of practical things until her hour-long visiting time was up. As Samantha was escorted out of the room, she could see how the other warder secured the handcuffs on my wrists before taking me back to my cell.

Monday April 20, 2015

"I've finally been able to wiggle your bail request past a court approval", Sandhurst told me. "For it to happen, you must accept and meet the following four criteria: you need to post a surety that still hasn't been determined, but which I estimate will be a couple of hundred thousand pounds; have a permanent address in London; twice a week present yourself

172

at the local police station; and wear an ankle monitor until the trial takes place."

"Whatever it takes – I can't stand being locked up this way", I replied. "I'll ask my wife to arrange a transfer of the money to whatever account you indicate. As for a permanent London address, I'll ask her to hunt for a suitable flat that I can rent."

"What about a twenty-four-hour monitor wrapped around your leg that must be kept charged at all times?"

I merely shrugged. Of course I had to accept it, or otherwise I would remain in jail. The trial, Sandhurst had previously explained to me, was a long time away, perhaps up to six months.

"It wasn't easy, I need to tell you", Sandhurst continued, "to get you out on bail in the first place. It took some effort convincing the judge that an unconfirmed tape recording and circumstantial evidence weren't enough to keep you remanded in custody. What is important though, despite the limitations you'll be facing up until the trial, is that you will no longer be locked up."

"I'm very grateful, David", I praised him, perhaps allowing a too obvious hint of a sarcasm slip through.

I wasn't sure that he perceived it, though, and anyway, it hadn't been directed at him personally. My bitterness was about the slow, outdrawn process of the British legal system; the utter lack of compassion or empathy – whether guilty or not – that the warders, judges and police showed those arrested and the not yet convicted. The supposed rule that you are innocent until proved guilty simply didn't apply. No smoke without fire, as the saying goes, which in practice meant that anyone charged with a crime was guilty until the court decided the contrary.

*

"I just received a call from my new contact inside Scotland Yard", Berlosky announced triumphantly as he stormed into Vasily's office unannounced. "They're likely to let Callaghan out in a couple of days, probably this coming weekend. He'll be on bail, awaiting his trial likely to take place in four or six months."

Vasily smiled as he took in Berlosky's information, and – as always when he contemplated how to act on unexpected news of importance – he processed it in his head until he had determined how he could best use it to his advantage.

"What about Allan Gould?" he finally asked.

"He was released on bail last Friday. He's being monitored by the police. I'm confident my informer will allow me to know his movements."

"Keep me up to date, will you?" Vasily did some more thinking. "What happened to Boris? Wasn't he locked up in the same place?"

"Yes, and he's still inside."

"Why hasn't he been able to get out on bail, too?"

"Longhorn has told me that the judge will rule on it any day now."

"Good. Then let's proceed in the following way", Vasily said, standing up while straightening his impeccable tailored suit. "When Boris gets out of jail, keep him somewhere until I make up my mind on what to do with him. As for Callaghan and Gould, as I've told you before, I want them disposed of without anyone noticing that it happened. It occurs to me that, should you be able to get them on the upcoming flight to Africa, the pilot could drop their bodies while he's flying over the Atlantic. A complete, definite disappearance feeding the fish with no one having a clue to what happened. Certainly there will be a lot of unanswered questions. Yet, the two ex-partners are on conditional bail awaiting their respective trial, and if they have disappeared, it's probably because they have escaped together. Sounds reasonable?"

"Vasily, you're a genius", Berlosky confirmed while giving him his widest smile, which allowed his golden-capped implant to reflect his true admiration for his boss.

"I want you to use One-eye to get rid of Gould, and I think the time is ripe to initiate Misha, both to please his father and oblige him to join the rank and file. He needs to be disciplined, so make sure he follows your orders to take care of Callaghan. I haven't forgotten his past little prank, and if it weren't for his father and your intervention, I'd probably have Misha dropped in the Atlantic, too. You can set it up any way you like, as long as both Gould and Callaghan get killed and Misha learns to follow orders. Understood?"

"Sure, Vasily. Easy as pie. I'll take care of it."

"One more and very important detail, Mikhail. I want

you to make sure I get impeccable proof that they are dead. That means photos of the bodies, their wallets, ID cards, valuables they wear, whatever. Understood?"

"Count on it Vasily", Berlosky grinning so broadly that he once again managed to flash the gold in his eyetooth.

Tuesday April 21, 2015

"Love, I was told by Sandhurst this morning that my bail request is likely to be formally approved by the court tomorrow sometime after noon", I told Samantha on the second of the three weekly sixty-minute visits she was allowed. "If all goes well, I'll be released not later than this weekend. In my case, the surety for the bail has been set to two hundred and fifty thousand pounds. Can you arrange that sum before the weekend? Draw on the funds from our construction company as a personal loan to me ... and hopefully Jack won't disagree. I'll pay it back later, of course."

She must have heard the desperation in my voice because she did her best to calm me.

"Finally some good news, Matthias, and don't worry about the money. I'll get to work on putting it together the moment I leave this depressing place."

"Sandhurst told me that, if everything runs smoothly, I'll probably be released on Saturday morning after being fitted with an ankle monitor. Of course my passport will remain confiscated, and I won't be able to move outside a restricted area in London until the trial is over."

"What date is the trial set for?"

"Sandhurst estimates it'll be at least four, perhaps six, months before I'm going to court unless we can convince the prosecution of dropping the case with something unexpected at the preliminary hearing", I said and sighed. "Meanwhile, we have to think about practical matters. You can't stay here all this time; you need to go back to the kids in Australia."

Samantha didn't answer at once.

"Yes, I need to do that", she finally agreed. "But I'll be back for the trial."

"We'll cross that bridge when we get to it", I replied. "You're going to have a baby, remember? Changing the subject – what about the lodgings that I called you about yesterday?"

"I've found a decent furnished two-bedroom flat in Hammersmith. The rent is outrageous, but of course this is London. It will anyway be a bargain compared to staying at the Savoy for half a year."

"Take it for six months, whatever the cost. Tell Sandhurst to make out the contract with me as the tenant. He's already got my power of attorney to sign this kind of contracts.

One of the warders supervising Samantha's visit warned us that the time was up.

"Call me as soon as you know when you will be released, will you?" Samantha implored as she made an attempt to hug me farewell.

"No touching!" the guard watching us yelled. "Follow the rules!"

"Of course I will, darling", I promised while containing my anger as Samantha stepped away in obeisance. Reluctantly, she walked in the direction of the warder's stern finger, with me already missing her as she walked out of the room.

Wednesday April 22, 2015

The most irritating detail Jason Longhorn perceived about his evolving, and quite frankly very lucrative situation nowadays as a professional, was the need to work through Brett Stevens. Since he had made Stevens his associate six years earlier, the sense of the partnership – that is, the invitation from him as the founder to one of his junior solicitors to join the firm – had shifted to his disadvantage. It had been Longhorn's solution after having been disbarred, which was something it hadn't taken Stevens long to discover, bright lad as he was. Since Longhorn could no longer act as a solicitor in the courts, he was obliged to work through Stevens. In practice, he was now Stevens's legal assistant. Stevens wasn't late in exploiting the fact, and by 2015 he treated Longhorn with the courtesy of an associate only because he was a shareholder in the firm. Brett Stevens had, by all means and perceptions, become the principal decision-maker at the law firm.

Over time this had embittered Longhorn even more, because he realised that there was nothing he could do to amend his situation. He had sought reinstatement as a member of the bar with a carefully worded plea. It had nevertheless been rejected. By now, he had come to realise that he was never again going to act as a licensed solicitor, and therefore would have to depend on others when acting in the legal circuits.

The official removal of his credential didn't take away his knowledge and study of the law, of course. The roles within his firm had changed, yes, but he was still very much at its centre. Brett Stevens made the court cases, but Longhorn found the customers. The firm's recent and most valuable customer, Arexim, now represented close to half of its revenue.

Brett needed him, Longhorn knew, as much as he needed Brett. He also realised that the growing dependence on Arexim and the Russians was making their firm increasingly more corrupt with every new demand.

And then, not forgotten by far, there was his personal issue with Callaghan who had tricked him into getting the signatures of false witnesses.

Thursday April 23, 2015

The surety for Boris Orloff's bail had been set to 82,000 pounds. The money was promptly forwarded by Berlosky to the Longhorn & Stevens law firm, which immediately made the corresponding deposit to the authorities' account. Eighteen hours later, Boris was allowed to walk out of prison.

Boris signed the receipt for the belongings returned to him, got his copy and walked with his usual swagger behind the warder who was taking him to the prison gate. His right leg had been fitted with a tracker device, not unlike the one he had seen Berlosky fasten on Allan years ago. So now, he too, was under supervision. It was something that Boris didn't like in the least.

Longhorn had informed Berlosky that Boris was going to be released that day after posting the surety the previous day. Boris found Oleg waiting outside the prison.

"They put a monitor around my leg", Boris complained as he got in the car.

"When the time is right, we'll remove it, don't worry", Oleg assured him. "I was told by Mikhail that Callaghan is still in there."

"I heard he's getting out this weekend", Boris said sourly. "I guess I was lucky to get out before he did."

Friday April 24, 2015

"Thanks for putting together the surety, Samantha – half an hour ago I was finally notified that my release has been formally approved", I told her over the phone that I was allowed to use up to three minutes. "This means that in a little less than twenty-four hours from now, I will walk out of here. For some obscure, legal or surreal reason, I'm told that I won't be allowed to make further calls between now and my release. I'd very much appreciate if you will be at the prison gate to pick me up tomorrow at ten o'clock, because you have no idea how much I long to once again see a friendly face up close."

"Count on it, darling", Samantha said as her voice broke, and through the earpiece I thought I could pick up the sounds of the tears scurrying down her cheeks.

*

The mobile Berlosky used exclusively for calls between himself and his new informer, Georgie Jones, rang with the first bars of "Rule, rule Britannia". He liked the attitude of his "Minnow" – it was so much more accommodating than the condescending "Rabbit". There was no need to strong-arm Georgie like he had been obliged to do every now and then with John Stopper, who recently had received a sentence of fifteen years in prison.

"To give you an update on the things you last asked me about, there have been some developments that you might find interesting", Georgie began. "Matthias Callaghan has fulfilled the conditions necessary to be released on bail, and he will walk out of Woodworm Scrubs tomorrow at ten o'clock. The other titbit I got for you regards the whereabouts of Allan Gould since his release. According to the signal from his ankle monitor, he's not moved from a building on 395 Saint Mary's Road in Wimbledon for several days."

"Good work, Minnow", Berlosky flattered him. "Now there's only one more little favour I want you to do for me. I want you to put a call through to Callaghan's wife, who's staying at the Savoy."

Despite that her belly barely showed her pregnancy after ten weeks, Samantha was lying on her back wishing to feel the growing baby when her hotel phone rang. She looked at her watch. It was a little after eight in the evening. The reception wanted to patch through a call for her – would she accept it? She confirmed that she would.

"This is Detective Constable Peter Scarborough with the Metropolitan Police. I'm sorry to bother you at this time, but I've been asked to inform you about your husband's imminent release from custody."

"Please explain yourself, detective."

"The court has approved the release of your husband on bail as of tomorrow Saturday at ten o'clock."

"I do appreciate your call, Detective Scarborough", she replied, "I received that very same information earlier today."

"Then you are already aware that your husband was transferred from Wormwood Scrubs to Belmarsh this afternoon, as part of his conditional release?"

"No, I wasn't. What does that mean?"

"Since it would be very impractical for his return to Wormwood Scrubs, his release will take place at the Belmarsh prison."

"Where is this Belmarsh place?" Samantha asked, irritated by the unexpected change.

"It's located south-east of central London, just past Greenwich."

"I'll look it up. Thanks for informing me."

"I'm glad to be of service, ma'am."

Saturday April 25, 2015

Still early, two warders arrived to take me to a room where two civilian policemen were waiting.

"We have been instructed that your release is subject to wearing a monitor", one of them announced after they had introduced themselves. "This means that we will put this device around your ankle."

He showed the ankle bracelet to me.

"Let me explain to you how it works", the other one said. "It's a homing device that every minute sends out a cellular signal that contains location and some other essential information. This means that, if you move out of the limits that you've been limited to, the police will be alerted that you've overstepped your allowed range – in your case, the Hammersmith area as marked here on this map."

He waved a piece of paper at me. His companion indicated that I should sit down and put my right leg across my left thigh.

"It won't be tight enough to cause you discomfort, and you will be able to pull up a sock between your calf and the monitor", he continued. "At the same time, it will be sufficiently tight for you to be unable to pull it off. It's also tamper-resistant. Should you remove it, a possibility that is usually the first thought that pops into the mind of anyone obliged to wear one of these devices, it will cause a circuit break that immediately notifies the police."

While he was talking, his colleague pulled up my trouser leg and fastened the tether just above my ankle, over my sock.

"It's waterproof so, wearing it, you can shower without problem. It also comes with a charger that you're required to carry with you, to ensure that the monitor is charged at all times. In case you for some reason have, for example, a medical issue or some other emergency, you must first contact the police before moving outside your restricted area. Again, I advise you that, should you not comply with the instructions, you will be rearrested and automatically waive your right to any future bail. Is that clear, or do I need to explain any part of what I've just told you?"

I was becoming increasingly irritated with the patronising way he spoke to me as if I were a common thief, but I held my tongue. What I wanted was to get out of this dismal place and recover my freedom, despite its limitations.

"I understand perfectly", I finally conceded between clenched teeth. The anklet had been securely fastened around my leg. "There's no need to repeat any of it."

After the two policemen had left me, I was taken to another room where the objects that I had been obliged to deposit upon entering the jail were returned to me and for which I had to sign a receipt. The items consisted of my clothes, wallet, the cuff links that Samantha had given me at Christmas, my mobile and its battery that I had detached upon arrival to avoid its depletion, my watch, a keyring and some change. I was also instructed to sign a release form. Without bothering to read either receipt, I stuffed them into the breast pocket of my jacket.

"Those posh cufflinks surely look as if they belong to some fancy toff", the sleazy-looking warder taunted me with a jealous sneer.

In an act of defiance, I took my time fastening them onto my shirt sleeves in front of the warder without addressing him with either a look or a word.

I stepped outside through the imposing – confidence-shattering, really – entrance to Wormwood Scrubs, where I had been kept jailed for the past three weeks pending the investigation and the pre-trial, and breathed the fresh air. There was a light rain, so I pulled my trench coat over my head while peering into the parked cars and a single cab looking for a ride. Samantha wasn't there waiting for me as she had promised. I called Samantha to tell her I was waiting for her outside the gates as agreed, but that I couldn't see her anywhere.

"I don't understand; Matthias ... I got a call from the police last night that you had been transferred to the Belmarsh prison facility as part of your release programme, and that's where I am right now. And now you're telling me you're still at Wormwood Scrubs."

"Let's not make too much of a fuss of this. There must have been some administrative error. The important thing is that my bail has been accepted and that I've been released. Tell me, where is Belmarsh?"

"Well, it's some twenty minutes past Greenwich, leaving central London – "

I sighed.

"You're almost two hours away from me, love", I said. "I'd say that we're more or less the same distance from the Savoy. I'll catch a cab, and let's meet there."

"I'm so sorry, Matthias, I really wanted to be there for you – "

"Hush, darling, we'll see one another in an hour anyway, so let's not make too much fuss about this insignificant setback, all right?"

Boy, did I miss the Australian sunshine. Here I was, standing in the permanent drizzle that in my mind exemplified the British weather every time I stepped on its soil.

I waved at the lone cab in waiting, and he moved towards me, too slow for my liking. Meanwhile, I was getting wet to the bones.

"Hop in, gov. Where to?" the driver, who wore a cap pulled down over his forehead, asked.

"The Savoy Hotel, please, it's on – "

"Don't you worry, gov. I know exactly where it is."

Another proud London cabbie who gets offended when he's given directions, I thought. As he started driving, the doors automatically entered into a locked position. I didn't pay it any attention, since I knew security issues had evolved significantly over the last couple of years. The glass partition between the driver and myself was closed, but five minutes after I had got into the cab, it was shoved aside, as if the driver wanted to speak to me. Instead, he threw a glass container through it. The container landed with a heavy thud on the floor, between my feet, where it broke. The driver quickly slammed shut and secured the cab's glass partition. A gas began to spread in the passenger compartment. I frantically tried to open the door next to me, to no avail. I did my best to avoid inhaling the gas, but, then again, for how long can a person hold his breath?

In desperation I brought out my phone, clumsily trying to call Samantha's number. I felt how my fingers and my mind simultaneously went numb. Then the mobile phone slid out of my hand as I no longer could resist the overpowering desire to slip into a profound and dreamless sleep.

*

Misha, who was driving the stolen cab, watched in the rearview mirror how the unconscious Callaghan slumped over in the backseat. The xenon gas had overcome him in less than four minutes, he noted after checking the clock on the dashboard. This gas, Oleg had explained to him, was a harmless one that was commonly used as a quick and overpowering anaesthetic. Misha's assignment was to drive the stolen cab, which previously had seen its number plates altered with black masking tape, and throw the canister into the passenger area once Callaghan was in it.

So far so good, Misha thought, still nervous about not

living up to Berlosky's expectations. It was his first serious job for the Russian mob, and it had been given to him – after some serious afterthought, he knew – because his father had intervened when he had made a fool of himself. Misha now knew that his father laundered money for the organisation that Berlosky headed. He hungered to belong to Berlosky's team, because he wanted to be someone of importance. Misha had no talent to speak of. He had been lazy throughout his school years, which against all odds had lasted nine years, and he had no interest in pursuing a career that required either mental or practical training. *Now*, Misha thought, almost bursting out in song after glancing at the man slumped sideways in the backseat, *I've finally discovered what I want to do.*

Misha turned the cab into a deserted parking lot next to a building that was in its first stage of construction. After releasing the electric locks to the doors, he got out of the driver's seat. When he opened the door to the backseat, he sniffed suspiciously in spite of having been told by Oleg that, as all noble gases, it was odourless. Misha then went over to the backseat door on the opposite side and opened it. Oleg had warned him he should make sure to ventilate the passenger cabin before getting inside. The man Misha had been ordered to pick up while guided on his mobile by someone on Oleg's team in a car close by didn't move. Briefly he wondered if he had killed him, but then he recalled Oleg's explanation that xenon gas was an anaesthetic, which made people go into a deep sleep for long hours while surgery was performed on them.

When Misha was satisfied that the backseat had been aired sufficiently, he went inside the car and patted the man's calves. The right one was fitted with a bulky bracelet, which he with some difficulty removed sawing through it with a large Swiss Army knife. He knew from Berlosky, that the minute the monitor was cut off, an alarm was being sent to the division at Scotland Yard supervising those on bail wearing anklets.

Misha threw the monitor into a heap of scrap construction materials, closed the doors, and got back behind the wheel. He made sure all locks were secured before returning to the traffic for the remainder of his four-hour drive.

*

Misha was bubbling over with excitement as he called Oleg to report his thundering success of overwhelming the jailbird who an hour earlier had stepped outside Wormwood Scrubs.

"Good", Oleg approved of Misha's recount after having to listen to the boring details he couldn't care less about. "Now take him to his final destination as you were instructed. Then, get rid of the cab by destroying it. Don't leave your finger prints or DNA because that will land you a twenty-five-year prison sentence. Then walk away from it for at least an hour – without any undue haste, mind you – then take any public transport you can find to get back to London. Do you

189

understand what I've just said?"

Oleg was only pulling Misha's leg, because he had already figured out how to get rid of the cab.

"Yes, loud and clear." Misha suddenly sounded more subdued and duly worried, Oleg noted with a smile.

"Keep driving, Misha, and don't mess this opportunity to get back in the good graces of your bosses. I will alert the pilot that you're on your way."

Sitting in Berlosky's office when the call had come through, a smiling Oleg shared with his boss how the enthusiastic Misha had described to him how he had picked up Callaghan before knocking him out in his backseat with the gas container.

Berlosky had opted for xenon gas because a medic with knowledge in chemistry had told him it was the perfect substance if you wanted someone knocked out for three hours, a day and even longer, depending on the concentration mixed with oxygen when inhaled. In itself, the gas is non-toxic, it had been explained to him, and when inhaled with oxygen the xenon dissolves in the blood and penetrates the blood-brain barrier to cause a mild to full surgical anaesthesia depending on the dose. Depending on the person subjected to it, secondary effects could occur.

Berlosky didn't care the slightest about any after-effects using the xenon gas. It had just been a convenient method to ensure that Callaghan was at their disposal. Vasily wanted Callaghan dead, and now he was as good as.

Allan felt frantic at the prospect that the Russians might have sent someone to pursue him, after the long years they had kept him prisoner in his home. His incarceration by the British police after admitting the hacking thefts the Russians had obliged him to perform had no doubt made them more dangerous than before. Despite the monitoring device he now wore, he felt closer to freedom than he had in years. Yet, he knew, he wouldn't be fully free before he could make sure that the Russian Mafia menace had gone away. He needed to disappear. He had to look for a return to a long-lost normal life. Yes, a normal life was all Allan desired, but he still hadn't figured out how he could achieve it.

The flat he had rented was all right. The only thing he needed was some groceries while he was holed up. He put on a cap and a pair of sunglasses to hide his face, and for the second time dared to walk the twelve minutes it took him to get to the nearest supermarket.

He was trying to act normally, but other shoppers couldn't help noticing how nervous he appeared. Allan repeatedly looked left and right for perceived threats and in a low voice conversed with himself. However, although other customers avoided him, no one reported his odd appearance to the police or to the supermarket manager.

Allan felt convinced that one or two of the large, grim-looking Russians he had got to know over the past and very decidedly grey years in his life had been ordered to bring him back into their fold. Or worse, cutting off his limbs like they had done to Matthias. Why else would they have told Longhorn to apply for the bail that he didn't want?

He paid for his purchases, exited the supermarket, pulled his cap even lower over his face and walked rapidly towards his temporary accommodation. Relieved, he entered the building and heard the door click shut behind. Instead of taking the elevator, he preferred to walk the two flights of stairs to his flat. Except for an old lady swabbing the floor, he met no one as he walked down the corridor towards his temporary lodgings. The bare arms of the old lady were heavily tattooed, which he found curious and momentarily distracted him from mulling about his future.

"Good afternoon", he muttered as he passed her, once again returning to his thoughts about how he could get away from London without the police chasing him down.

"And a good afternoon to you, too, sir", the cleaning lady replied and looked up as he passed her. Allan glanced at her and felt a brief moment of pity for the woman who, apparently in her seventies and with a dark blue eyepatch covering her left eye, had to work cleaning floors at her age.

Allan put his hand inside his trouser pockets to pull out his keys. He didn't see how the cleaning lady at the same moment reached inside the bucket next to her and pulled out a Glock 17 fitted with a silencer, and, surprisingly agile for her age, stood up and squeezed the trigger grabbing the gun with both hands. The single bullet, fired at close distance, traversed his skull from the base of his neck to become lodged behind his forehead. Allan toppled over and died instantly.

With no emotion whatsoever, the old woman brought out her mobile.

"The job is done", she said as soon as the call was answered. "You can pick up the package outside the recently rented flat."

"Good work, One-eye", Berlosky replied. "We have some people nearby that will take care of the package in the next few minutes."

*

After instructing Oleg to arrange for the pickup of the body and its immediate relocation to Bolt Head, Berlosky placed a call to Vasily.

"Everything is going according to plan, Vasily", Berlosky informed him. "Both Callaghan and Gould have been incapacitated and are on the way for Captain Paddy's special treatment."

"What about our half-blind professional?"

"An extraordinary woman, all considered. One-eye delivered the baby as promised and didn't blink with her remaining eye when the opportunity came in sight. She executed the trick we asked her to perform."

"Yes!", Vasily giggled. "A one-trick pony ... but what a trick!"

*

Samantha returned to the Savoy forty minutes after catching a cab outside Belmarsh. Matthias wasn't there waiting for her – neither in the lobby nor in her room. She called the reception desk to ask if he'd left her any messages, but the answer was negative.

As the hours rolled by, she became increasingly worried. Every five minutes she called the number registered on her phone when he had called her earlier that day. No reply, no encouragement to leave a voice mail – nothing. She tried his WhatsApp, and could see from the two check marks that her message had been delivered. They weren't being read, however: the colour of the check marks remained grey. *His phone is working, so it's not a battery issue,* she concluded while trying to get to grips with the situation. *On the other hand, for some reason he's not reading the message. Three hours have now gone by since he should have arrived. Where is he?*

Anguished, she intuited something bad must have happened to Matthias.

*

After four hours of driving, Misha arrived at the rural airport in Cornwall. With the help of Hamza, he removed Callaghan's unconscious body from the cab and loaded him onto the plane supervised by Paddy.

Less than an hour later, another car arrived. This time it was Vladimir and Oleg getting out. Oleg opened the car's boot and shouted at Paddy to arrange for the body inside to be moved onto the aircraft. Since the day he had got to know him, Paddy resented Oleg's way of ordering him around, but, as on previous occasions, he didn't challenge him. Paddy found his job too rewarding to risk a confrontation. Instead, he ordered Hamza, who he noticed was becoming increasingly jittery, to help Vladimir carry the black body bag with Allan's corpse into the cargo hold of the airplane.

After they had completed the task, Paddy examined the cargo space inside the plane. He saw the body bag containing Allan, the unconscious Callaghan and the additional fuel tanks that would enable him to travel the extra distance back and forth to southern Morocco. As far as Paddy was concerned, everything was as it should be.

"Everything's in order. I'm ready to leave", Paddy announced after his inspection. "I'll see you here tomorrow evening."

He got into the cockpit and went through the checklist before starting up the engines. Everyone outside receded as the noise and the wind from the propellers increased. Paddy taxied to the point of the sole runway where he, according to the weather information, was most likely to hit a head wind.

*

"Trudy, I want to see you in my office", Burns' voice came over the intercom.

Two minutes later she stood before him, as always wearing a rejecting grimace at the thought of being ordered around by anyone with an authoritative voice. *She's getting a new tattoo made,* Burns observed when he saw the half-finished design on her bare shoulder. *A pity, she would be quite pretty without the piercings and her general self-mutilation.*

"I was informed a few minutes ago that Matthias Callaghan was released on bail this morning and then immediately went underground. There's a new arrest warrant out for him. I want you to drop anything you have and follow up on this story."

Why do these things always happen on weekends? Trudy thought. Plans had been made, she needed to see her friends, but as a freelancer she needed the money even more.

*

"So, what are you going to do with the stolen cab?" Oleg asked Misha.

"I was thinking that I'd drive it to the coast here nearby, set it on fire and push it over a cliff into the Atlantic", Misha, sounding proud, shared his vision that he had chewed on for the long journey to Cornwall. "Then I'll walk for an hour or so until –"

"You're going to push a burning cab over a cliff?" Oleg wondered, amused. "How are you going to do that?"

"It's just figure of speech, of course. I'll pour petrol over the car after I've put a brick or something on the accelerator, and when the moment is right, I'll put it in first gear – "

"Don't bother going through with your complex plan

that will be unravelled by the police in a minute", Oleg laughed as he puffed on his cigar, placed a fatherly arm around Misha and led him towards the stolen cab. "Vladimir, follow us in the other car, will you?"

Halfway on their way back to London, Oleg ordered Misha to turn off the main road. Ten minutes later, they arrived at a large metal scrap recycling facility that announced itself as "King of Steel – the Metal Recycler".

"It's misspelled", Oleg joked. "Everyone knows this place as the 'King of Steal'. You'll see."

Oleg got out of the taxi after telling Misha to wait. He returned accompanied by an obese man who wore a cap turned backwards that only partly covered his shoulder-length, unwashed blond hair. The fat man kept talking incessantly without expecting an answer. A smoking cigarette between his lips kept moving in time with his words.

Oleg and the man stopped when they reached the cab where Misha and Vladimir stood waiting.

"This is the car I want you to scrap", Oleg was finally able to put in. "There's a thousand quid in it for you as long as we can have the pleasure of watching it being demolished in the jaws of your monster press. What do you say?"

"At first glance, it appeared to me as if this cab was in working condition, but, after a closer look, I guess the time has arrived for it to go through the King of Steel's recycling process."

Fascinated, Misha later watched how the cab was crushed into an unimaginable small and compact block of metal. Unknown to all present, Matthias Callaghan's mobile, left undiscovered in the car, suffered the same fate as the cab.

*

Once in the air flying southwards, Paddy shouted to Hamza to enter the cockpit. The noise in the thirty-year-old cargo plane was deafening at best. He had to yell several times before Hamza finally lumbered into the cockpit and took the co-pilot's seat.

"Here's what you need to do", he shouted over the engine noise. "One of our passengers is still alive – why I don't know. Take this syringe and inject him with the content."

"What is it?"

"Heroin – enough to make a horse start dancing the hula-hula", Paddy said, grimly. "The thing is, we've been told to dump the two bodies over international waters, which won't be safe to do for another hour or two. At the same time, I feel uncomfortable that one of the blokes we will dump is still alive. That's why I want you to give him this shot."

"OK, boss."

Hamza got up from the co-pilot's chair and staggered back to the cargo load as the aircraft began to hit unexpected air pockets.

God, how I hate these complicated missions, Paddy sighed. *I only want to fly contraband, be it drugs or anything, and now it's come down to this.*

Soon after Paddy had got them airborne, Hamza had begun to claw his face, regretting that he hadn't given himself the usual fix before taking off. This time had been different, though, with all the important people present. Hamza had thought he could wait until they landed in Morocco in the evening. Nevertheless, his craving for a fix was growing greater than he had imagined. Hamza knew that there was no way he could wait another couple of hours. He realised that he had miscalculated the timing, and now his body needed an immediate fix.

To grab the syringe, the one that Paddy had expressly said was intended for the fellow next to him who was barely breathing, was not a difficult choice for Hamza. *I'm supposed to throw the two bodies from the plane once Paddy has got the aircraft far enough from land. Why should I waste perfectly good smack on someone who in an hour or so is going to perish in the middle of the ocean anyway?*

Hamza prepared himself by tying his left upper arm with a strip of rubber and beating the veins with the fingers of his right hand. After having found one, he injected the heroin meant for Callaghan. The effect was almost immediate. Hamza fell backwards and found himself in the most amazing setting he had ever been.

*

"Hamza, how are things going?" Paddy shouted at his walkie-talkie an hour later, trying to be heard over the noise the engines made.

He was nearing the spot where he had planned to get rid of the bodies. There was no answer from Hamza. Paddy repeated his question. There still was no answer.

To avoid radar detection, he was flying at less than a hundred feet above sea level. The head winds were gusty to say the least, but Paddy needed to understand why Hamza didn't reply to his calls over the walkie-talkie. The airplane wasn't equipped with autopilot, so he would need to take it higher before making some arrangement to leave the plane flying on its own. If he did, he risked being detected by either Spanish or Portuguese radar. They were now flying slightly beyond the midway point to his destination. After judging the distance, he still had to fly with the remaining fuel, Paddy considered it safe to turn westwards away from the continent. The weather had now become ominous and unpredictable, with a promise to soon unleash its fury. Rain began to hammer the windows of the cockpit. After fifteen minutes of flying westwards at a low altitude, he took the aircraft up to 2,000 feet, above the clouds, where he levelled it. When detected by the radar people, which he knew was only a question of a minute or two, they would challenge him for his flight plan and identification. Since the aircraft's transponder had been removed, there was no way they would know who he was unless he told them. By heading the opposite direction, away from Portugal, he hoped they wouldn't second-guess that his real destination was Morocco. Paddy didn't want fighter jets to come looking for him. At the moment there were no strong winds, so, with a specially prepared wire that he used for occasions like these, he secured the control yoke to hooks on each side of the flight deck. It was a makeshift solution to maintain the cruise altitude, and Paddy knew he couldn't trust it for more than a couple of minutes at the most.

Leaving the flight deck unattended implied that anything like sudden squall could make the plane go into a tailspin or veer off course. Paddy, worried, knew that he nevertheless had to check on the total silence at the back of the plane. Surrounded by the strong humming of the plane's engines, confiding in his improvised autopilot that risked at any moment to dip the airplane's wings into the violent waters of the Atlantic, Paddy rushed down the short corridor that led to the cargo space. Inside, he stumbled over Allan's black body bag before seeing Callaghan and Hamza's equally inert bodies.

Paddy ran over to Hamza. He had long suspected Hamza to be using drugs, but he had never known how serious it might be. He gazed into the face of the dead Hamza – wintery pale, glassy-eyed, mouth gaping as if in surprise. Paddy cursed under his breath as he found the empty syringe lying next to him. He immediately puzzled the story together. Instead of shooting up the unconscious man with the heroin, Hamza had used it on himself, without realising that the concentration had been large enough to kill a stranded whale.

What could he do? There was neither time nor opportunity for him to throw the bodies overboard on his own with the plane flying on a makeshift autopilot that depended on a shoestring. In the distance, he heard a voice calling out over the radio to report to ground control. He had to get back to the cockpit. Sweating after the revelation and a brief check for Hamza's non-existent pulse, Paddy ran through the airplane to renew control of it.

Ignoring the calls on the radio to identify himself, he began to take the aircraft down while still flying westwards. Constantly checking his altimeter and his distance from land, when he was ninety-two feet above the sea and knew that he couldn't be seen on radar from the Iberian Peninsula because of the Earth's curvature, Paddy circled until he was heading south-east. After twenty minutes, the insisting voice on the radio began to break up, which to Paddy's relief indicated that he was leaving that particular airspace.

What shall I do now? he wondered, sweating despite the low temperature inside the cockpit. *Hamza was the one supposed to cast them overboard ... it leaves me with no alternative. I must dump the bodies when I arrive at the destination.*

Well, perhaps it's not too bad, a thought consoled him after having determined the solution. *The desert is a place as solitary as any ocean.*

*

Hours later, after having flown well beyond Agadir and then north-east across the scarcely inhabited Western Sahara, Paddy landed the plane on a small, improvised airfield in southern Morocco at the edge of the desert.

He had left Cornwall at 1:30, and it was now half an hour

before sundown. Paddy felt tired. He looked at his watch. *Enough time for a snack and a wink,* he thought, *after unloading the excess baggage.* The handover of the consignment was agreed to take place when the first rays of dawn hit the desert dunes.

Paddy went to the cargo space and opened the hatch. Outside the heat was overwhelming compared to the British weather he had left behind. One by one, he dragged the three inert bodies across the floor of the aircraft and threw them outside. He jumped down from the aircraft and, sweating profusely, Paddy went through the pockets of the three men. His perfunctory search found nothing until he got to Hamza, who had already collected everything of interest and value from the other victims. Paddy stuffed their rings, phones, watches and wallets into his pockets before bringing out his own smartphone. He took four pictures of each man from different angles. With the sweat scurrying in the hot dry air from the effort, he dragged the bodies one by one to a sand dune close by. When he was done, he scooped sand over them with his cupped hands until he was satisfied they were as good as invisible. *Never to be found unless you come within spitting distance,* he thought as he studied his work. Exhausted and thirsty, he returned to the aircraft to empty a large bottle of tepid water while longing for a cool pint of Guinness.

Now he was ready to meet the caravan. The propellers started with a roar. Without taking off, Paddy taxied the airplane to the opposite side of the improvised desert airfield. He took it as far away as possible from the bodies he was leaving behind, now forever damned to their anonymous destiny once the desert had overtaken them.

*

By nightfall, Samantha had grown worried enough about Matthias not showing up that she decided to go to the police. Her repeated phone calls to his mobile remained unanswered. She knew something was wrong. Matthias would never keep her in the dark about his whereabouts for an extended time.

At the police station, she was obliged to wait for twenty minutes while the policeman was taking notes from the two complainants that had arrived before her. The first was a girl in her late twenties that pulled a pram with a young boy. She had an unwashed appearance and spoke with a shrill voice about her boyfriend's abuse. The next in line was an older man who mumbled statements that the police officer several times had to ask him repeat. The old man finally left with a sigh, looking even more troubled than when he had arrived.

"I'm worried about my husband, Matthias Callaghan, who hasn't shown up at our hotel although he was supposed to get there shortly after noon", Samantha explained to the officer on duty. "He hasn't called me and I don't get any answer when I try to reach him. It's not like him at all."

The police officer appeared to have heard a similar story at least a hundred times before and didn't look as worried as Samantha wanted him to. He eyed the blond woman in front of him, trying to judge her. She was very attractive, he noticed, and seemed to be in full possession of her wits.

"When did you last see him, miss?" he asked while jotting down Matthias's name.

"He was released from the Wormwood Scrubs prison early this morning", she reluctantly replied, blushing slightly. "It concerns a temporary detention over some migration misunderstanding. We had agreed to meet immediately after his release. That was eight or nine hours ago."

"I see", the officer said, non-committed. "Please give me his date of birth, a detailed description and, if possible, a recent photograph of him."

He interviewed Samantha for another fifteen minutes about more details of the missing person. As soon as Samantha had walked out from the station, he passed on the information to a secretary who uploaded the information onto the national register of persons not accounted for.

She caught a cab outside the police station and asked to be taken back to her hotel. During her journey, her vacant glance happened to land on a large billboard promoting a show in London's theatre district. With a start, she sat up when she read the name Julie Cross as the star of the show. The name immediately rang a bell – Matthias had told her he had been married to Julie before he had met her.

Using her mobile for information, Samantha soon learnt that the show, in which Julie Cross was the protagonist, ended at 4 p.m. on Sundays.

Sunday April 26, 2015

Haroun shouted in Arabic to four of his camel drivers to hurry up the unloading of the consignment the animals carried. Haroun's underlings dragged the packages across the sandy ground and threw them down by Paddy's feet next to the airplane's cargo hold. Although the morning was still fresh after the recent sunrise, Paddy sweated as he pulled the bags of cocaine across the floor to stack them for the trip back to the UK. To secure them, he used straps fastened to the interior of the hull. When he had loaded the last package into the cargo hold, the space was one-third full. Haroun waited patiently in the shade of the wing outside, not letting Paddy out of his sight for a second. To reassure himself that Paddy wouldn't try to take an undesired shortcut from their agreement, he had ordered his drivers to place ten dromedaries in front of the airplane.

Paddy swore at the thought of having to do the work of the stupid Hamza who had overdosed on their trip down to Morocco. He briefly wondered if he could claim Hamza's pay, too. It would only be fair, really, in view of all the extra trouble he had to go through.

After counting the eighty packages and inspecting them for any tampering, Paddy nodded his approval to Haroun, who waited patiently for him to finish. Two of the dromedaries grunted at each other in what Paddy perceived as their discontent with the human race in general and his own presence in particular. He wanted to get out there as fast as possible, so he went to the cockpit for Haroun's money.

Paddy searched under both seats and removed two large duffel bags. In them were bundles of high-denomination bills totalling 500,000 euros: the agreed-upon sum for Haroun's services. He handed the bag over to Haroun, who hunched over it using his flowing burnoose to shield the money from the sight of the others travelling with his caravan. Taking his time, Haroun verified the stacks of euro bills, until he was satisfied they approximated the amount agreed upon. He rose, nodded to Paddy and shook his hand.

"It's always a pleasure doing business with men who keep their word", Haroun told him as farewell. "Tell your boss he knows where to reach me, should he wish to repeat our successful transaction next season." To express his pleasure over the transaction, he added that Allah was sure to protect Paddy on his journey home. Two dromedaries began to bale at each other as if to underline the sincerity in Haroun's well-wishing.

Paddy ignored him, wishing only to get the hell out of the godforsaken desert that was melting him faster than an ice cube. As he was ready to mount into the cockpit, Paddy saw two men in Arab garbs walking determinedly towards him.

"You will take us back with you", Ilya told him. "Berlosky's order."

Briefly Paddy studied the two dirty, sunburnt travellers, each clad in djellabas and carrying a small bag.

"Now then, who are you?", he asked with an Irish brogue. "I don't mind reminding you that I've never seen your lot before! And, who is this "Berlosky" you garble about?"

After forty-five days in the desert, Ilya felt a desperate longing for the benefits of advanced civilisation, which in his present state of mind essentially boiled down to an extended, hot bath with no sand present.

"Don't try to be funny, mister pilot, whoever you are", Ilya growled as he took a menacing step closer. "We were asked to watch over the merchandise that you just loaded onto your plane. I suggest you make immediate contact with our London boss."

The determined edge in Ilya's voice made Paddy climb into the cockpit and risk a brief satellite call to Berlosky.

"Starman, two pigeons want to get off their camels and climb the stairway to heaven. What do you say?"

There was some static and a prolonged pause.

"Bring the pigeons home", a voice that vaguely sounded like Berlosky's ordered him, "as long as it doesn't affect the stardust."

Paddy signalled to Ilya and Vladimir to climb on board and then got the propellers running. Exhausted and aching all over from the uncomfortable desert trip, they obeyed him and seated themselves on the piles of cocaine packages. As Paddy went through the checklist, he could see how Haroun motioned his men to remove the dromedaries and get the caravan going again. The propellers started running with a roar.

The sunrise coloured the desert sand dunes red as Paddy raced the airplane across the makeshift strip and noisily got it up in the air.

As Paddy banked in the direction of the ocean, he and his passengers could observe how the caravan started north to enter the forbidding landscape of desert dunes.

The Callaghan Septology VI

THE HOURGLASS
RUNNING OUT OF SAND

by

KIM EKEMAR

The sixth of seven books in the septology
covering the terrible fate
of losing your identity
and the right to recover your stolen life

PART XI

Even the longest journey starts
with one foot put in front of the other.

Sunday April 26, 2015

Berlosky munched on a toast spread thick with his favourite bitter orange marmalade as he browsed the morning paper. Then his eyes hovered over the headline that read "Millionaire fugitive". After recapitulating the back story, the article stated that Matthias Callaghan, apprehended for the alleged murder of a renowned London solicitor, had not presented himself at the local police office as his bail conditions required. Moreover, he had removed his ankle monitor immediately upon being released from prison on bail. *Even the press is confirming that Misha did a good job, being his first ever,* Berlosky mused contentedly. *And now that annoying Callaghan, with his tendency to pop up everywhere where he wasn't wanted, has finally been put to rest.*

*

The *Daily Mirror*'s black headline on its front page was much bolder. It blasted "Millionaire murder suspect skips bail". *Nothing news-worthy of national importance today, then,* Georgie thought as he bought a copy at the newsstand. The front news was followed up by several speculative articles on the inside pages. After stating "facts" discovered about Matthias Callaghan, they all ended with a hinted conclusion that Callaghan must be guilty of the murder he was accused of, since he hadn't reported to the police and now no doubt was on the run.

Georgie read the background articles with more interest than those with speculative information of no substance. If they were to be believed, Callaghan came from a wealthy family. His father had been something of a jet-set playboy, while his grandfather had created a multi-national company. Apparently, the grandfather's riches had been squandered by his son, but then his grandson had later become wealthy in his own right with an Internet application. For the last couple of years the now-accused Callaghan had been out of the public's eye after moving abroad. Out of the public's eye, that is, until he was arrested entering Europe via Rome's Fiumicino

Airport.

As he, amused, eyed the story in the paper, Georgie thought of his wonderful idea to inform Scotland Yard with a copy of the tape when Callaghan negotiated Rathbone's death with his deceased uncle. *Serves him well,* Georgie decided with a smile, *for cheating Uncle Jeremiah out of a small fortune that I would otherwise have inherited.*

*

I was brought to consciousness by an ear-deafening roar. I wondered where I was. My eyes were full of sand. There was a weight across my chest that prevented me from moving my arms. I blinked as the shadow of an airplane passed over me, and then there was only the brilliant, blue sky. The noise from the airplane faded, and soon there was no sound at all besides my heartbeat. *A most welcome sound,* I drowsily thought. *I'm alive.*

I struggled to free myself from the weight on top of me. There was sand everywhere: in my shoes, inside my clothes, even in my mouth and ears. Finally I could roll away from under the dead weight that had kept me pinned down. *Dead weight is the right term, all right,* I thought with horror as I understood that it was the body bag encasing someone deceased that had restrained me. Standing on my knees, sluggishly making attempts to brush the sand off of me, I noticed another body half hidden close by in the sand. *Somebody tried to kill me along with these two men,* I realised.

Aghast, I tried to clear my head from the drowsiness so I could remember something that could explain the strange, surreal situation, but all I could concentrate on was how tired I felt. When I looked around, I saw desert dunes. It was getting warmer in the sun. *Have I been abandoned in a desert with two corpses? Why? How is that possible?*

Taking a deep breath, I crept on my hands and feet to one of the bodies and rolled it over. The dead man was thin and wiry and looked like an Arab. I couldn't recall ever having seen him. His bare arms had tattoos and needle marks. *A junkie?* I crept over to the body bag, the one that had covered me when I woke up. I pulled down the zipper and felt overcome with alarm and nausea when I recognised Allan. I felt for his pulse, but I couldn't find any.

I staggered some distance away from the bodies and sat down. I felt tired and only wanted to sleep, but I knew I first had to come to terms with my situation. I looked at my watch only to find that it was gone. So was my wallet. The heat was building with every minute, and the shadows slowly disappeared as the sun continued its course across the sky. My cuff links twinkled in the sunshine when I removed my jacket. *What shall I do?*

I had no food or water, and there were no buildings as far as I could see. I needed to find shelter from the sun and access to water. These had to be my absolute priorities. It meant that I had to walk until I found both. I wasn't dressed for a desert hike, so I went over to Allan and threw down my jacket. I stripped him of his shirt and wound it around my head and face until I had covered all of it except for my eyes. It made me associate to my times at St Puys, when I had gone through the face transplants. That, in turn, made me realise that I needed my ciclosporin pills or I would be in trouble. I now recalled having walked out of the prison in London, after being handed my personal belongings. Why had I been allowed to keep my cuff links if everything else had been stolen? Perhaps the thief hadn't suspected anything of value would be found underneath the cuffs of my jacket.

What could I do? With not a soul around, I started walking, aimlessly. The position of the sun, of course, was a telltale, but I didn't know if I had been abandoned north or south of the equator. Where was I heading? Into unknown dangers or welcoming arms? How many days had passed since I had been abducted? The questions that crowded my mind somehow didn't sound too relevant. My only worry should be survival.

As I walked along the improvised airstrip, I could see the sand dunes to my right. The airstrip came to an end, and I continued across the barren land strewn with pebbles along the edge of the desert. Trying to stay calm and use logic, I observed my surroundings as I plodded on. I couldn't be in Europe, I knew, because there doesn't exist a place on that continent with the intense heat and a desert like the one I had been left in. Australia, which by now I knew pretty well, had deserts that were hot and extensive, but they were flat, not with dunes like here. I tried to recall any desert in Asia, but the only one I could remember was the Gobi one, located in

China. I strongly doubted that I had been taken to China. I could be in the Middle East – Saudi Arabia or Yemen or some other sheikhdom. However, discarding all other options, the only reasonable conclusion I could reach was that I had purposefully been abducted in a London cab to die of thirst in an African desert. As far as I could recall, there were only two deserts of any importance on that continent – the Namib and the Sahara. And, if I had been abandoned in Sahara – boy, was I in trouble.

I tried to visualise a map with Sahara on it. From east to west, the desert stretches from Egypt to Morocco. From north to south, it covers parts of a dozen or so countries including non-Arab nations. But – where was I, really? If I had been dumped in Sahara, the only assumption I could make was that I would be in the northern hemisphere …

Survival was the only thing that mattered.

With nothing better occurring to me, I trudged ahead towards what I presumed to be north – towards the Mediterranean Sea, Europe, the UK … Struggling forward in the sand one step at a time, I realised that this was exactly what Africans wanting passage to Europe were paying for. It also dawned on me that I had now turned into one more of the needy people who were desperate to get to Europe. I had no documents to identify me, no phone to communicate, no money whatsoever … how could I possibly make it back home? To Samantha, to my children?

I walked along the edge of the desert for hours, with its truly impressive sand dunes to my right and with nothing moving except for me and the sun across the sky. Despite having Allan's shirt wrapped around my head, the sun's relentless heat made me feel as if both my skin and my blood were boiling. No house, no people, no birds, not even a stray camel in sight anywhere. Nothing. The air vibrated with heat. I had walked for three or four hours when I judged the time to be noon. The sun was bearing down on me, relentlessly. It must have been forty degrees Celsius in the shade – except there was no shade to be found. Allan's shirt was soaked with sweat from my forehead.

Overcome with weariness and heat, I slumped on a small drift and covered my hands by burying them in my armpits.

*

After a sleepless night, Samantha was feeling increasingly distressed about Matthias's disappearance. She knew that he never would vanish without giving her some clue where he would be. They were a happy couple living in Australia with twins he adored – how could he? Impossible. In her mind something had happened to him. Nevertheless, she was absolutely clueless who or what could be behind his vanishing, or any reason for it.

Exhausted from tossing and turning in her bed from her worries, she fell asleep at dawn and didn't wake up until 1:30 pm when the housemaid knocked on her door asking for permission to make up her bed. The housemaid was given strict orders not to come back until the following day. In an awful mood, Samantha took a shower and got dressed. She looked at her watch. It showed 2:50.

On an impulse, she went to the lobby where the concierge had someone whistle for a cab waiting at the nearby stand. Samantha told the driver to take her to Shaftesbury Avenue in the West End. With a deep sigh, the driver complained as he wriggled back and forth to find an alternative route in the heavy traffic. The complaints were uncalled for. The taxi took twelve minutes to reach the destination. Samantha repented not having asked the concierge about the distance. If she had, she would have walked the less than half-hour it would have taken her to get there.

After Samantha had paid the cabbie and got out of the taxi outside the theatre, she found that the show in which Julie Cross appeared wouldn't finish until an hour later. Allowing for time afterwards to remove makeup and a change of clothes, Samantha estimated she had at least an hour and a half to kill before Julie Cross would come out. Since she hadn't eaten anything since the day before, she decided to pass the time in a nearby pub.

Having ordered fish and chips and a bottle of mineral water, she again went through the confusing situation. *Matthias was released from prison, but not from the one I was told. Why? He called from outside the prison, after his release, and said he would take a cab and see me at the hotel in less than an hour. Perhaps someone else picked him up … even taking advantage of the situation? He hasn't answered his mobile … did he lose it?*

Samantha left her plate half-finished, with a great sense of displeasure over the oil-saturated fare. She looked at her watch. The show had finished by now, and she was unsure when Julie Cross would step outside. She hurriedly asked for the bill, paid it and left.

It had started to rain, and she didn't have an umbrella. The changing weather immediately added to her misery. Samantha found the backstage door where she supposed Julie Cross eventually would exit.

While she waited, Samantha was suddenly overcome with nervousness at the prospect of meeting Matthias's ex-wife this way. What could Julie possibly know about Matthias's recent disappearance? Still, since Samantha didn't what else to do after reporting her concerns to the police, there was a mix of intuition and curiosity that made her want to meet with Matthias's previous wife. She would learn something, anything, a lot, whatever it took to find him.

*

"So, maybe you would like some water?" I heard someone close to me ask. "Berber custom is to never allow a man to go hungry or thirsty. I invite you to drink and have food at our camp. Please, come with me."

Hearing his words from a distance, I forced myself to open my eyes. They felt glued and sandy, and I tried to focus them on the face belonging to the man who had spoken to me. He was dressed in a long, light blue cotton robe with a white shawl around his neck. Wound around his head was a mauve cloth that served as a turban. Behind him towered a huge camel.

"I appreciate your kind invitation", I responded hoarsely – the first words I had spoken all day. He handed me leather skin and said, "Drink."

Which I did, until it was nearly empty. Nothing in my life has tasted better than the water in that leather skin.

It was late afternoon and the air had begun to cool somewhat. After drinking the water, I began to feel refreshed and curious about my surroundings again. After nothing but sand and the blinding sun since I had come around that morning, I felt my hopes rise at the prospects of making it back to … to wherever Samantha was waiting for me. I still felt weak and confused.

"Where am I?" I asked him. "Who are you?"

The man laughed.

"I'm Haroun the camel driver to those who know me well. I don't know how you came to be here without knowing where you are, but I've heard and seen stranger things during my years in the desert. Welcome to the Sahara."

"I need to get back to my country in a hurry … England … do you know how I can do that?"

He laughed again.

"Everything is possible, my friend, as long as you can pay for the service." Despite the hard reality revealed by his words, he looked compassionate about the state I was in. "You should talk to Moammar. I'll introduce you to him. He is taking a group of people who share the same desire you have to reach European shores."

*

Yuliana exited from the back-stage door fifty minutes after the show had finished. She opened her umbrella to shield herself from the drizzle that promised to keep on for days on end and descended the staircase. When the weather was fine, there was usually a large crowd waiting for autographs and selfie pictures. Today's dismal weather had only brought a lonely woman unprepared for the rain with her jacket kept over her head.

As she arrived at the foot of the staircase, their eyes met. To Yuliana, she didn't look like the usual star-struck autograph-hunting admirer. The woman's hard gaze and set jaws signalled something different, and for a brief moment Yuliana again felt that dreadful apprehension from the time she had been courted by Jaime Hernández.

"I'd like to talk to you about a matter of urgency", the blond woman said as tears began rolling down her cheeks. "I know that you were once married to Matthias Callaghan. I'm his present wife, but I'm also at my wit's end. A day ago, he disappeared from the face of the earth, and I don't know where to look for him. I don't really know anyone in London, so I could only think of you."

"But … Matthias died many years ago!" Yuliana gasped, consternated. "You must be mad!"

"I may have told you I'm at my wit's end, but that doesn't mean I'm mad,", Samantha replied, tears rolling down her cheeks while she dug into her handbag for a handkerchief.

"Should this be true, I would have a thousand questions to ask you," Yuliana said in disbelief.

Not knowing what to think at the shocking news that her former husband was still alive, and re-married to boot, Yuliana told her they'd better talk in a nearby hotel bar. She shared her umbrella with the unknown woman, instinctively trusting her.

After they both had ordered a glass of white wine, Yuliana studied the fetching woman seated in front of her. She was perhaps ten years younger than herself, and she could understand why Matthias had been drawn to her. She had introduced herself as Samantha.

In her Australian accent Samantha, hesitatingly at first, began to tell Yuliana the basics of her relationship with Matthias.

"We met on a flight some time after your divorce, on the last day of August in two thousand and eight."

"That's something that I can't comprehend … Matthias died in July that year." *Mere days after he made me sign the papers annulling our marriage and having me deported to Romania,* she thought. "His father told me so."

"It's complicated … you are of course aware of the surgeries Matthias went through?"

"I am", Yuliana replied reluctantly, vividly remembering Abdul Mahfouz's face as Matthias's bandages came off. "The face he got was far from the one he lost."

"I never knew him with the transplant face he first received –"

"What do you mean by 'first'?" Yuliana asked in a sharp voice.

"I don't know how to tell you this in any other way … Life hasn't been kind to Matthias."

"Please explain."

"Matthias went through a second transplant, and the donor was his murdered father."

Yuliana's gasp was filled with incredulity as she stared at Samantha.

"His murdered father? A donor? But I met his father on two occasions the following year … How was he murdered?"

"You may not remember me after all this time", Samantha said gloomily, "but on one of those occasions that you met him, I was present. Does the inauguration of a Japanese restaurant ring a bell? That wasn't Matthias's father, it was Matthias carrying his father's face – something I didn't learn until many years later, I might add."

Yuliana digested the information in silence.

"And, as for the murder", Samantha continued, "although this may be hard to believe, the assassin of Matthias's father later came looking for me and Matthias", she sniffled before adding: "In the USA."

Yuliana knitted her eyebrows over this, thinking that perhaps after all the woman wasn't in her right mind.

"I have to think through this unexpected news later,

because it has so many implications that I need to reflect on …
surely you understand?"

"I'd like to show you this picture", Samantha said and
brought out her mobile.

After a quick search among the photos on it, she held out
the phone to Yuliana. The picture showed her, Matthias and
the twins smiling at someone's camera in front of a swimming
pool. In the background, there were indications that the house
was in the last stages of construction.

Although hard to accept after her belief that Matthias
had died seven years earlier, Yuliana reluctantly began to
embrace the idea that Samantha was telling her the truth, no
matter how incredulous it sounded.

Both remained silent for some time.

"But you didn't come here to explain to me these things
from the past", Yuliana finally said. "Tell me, what is it that
you wanted to talk with me about?"

"Matthias was arrested in Italy recently, and later
extradited to the UK", Samantha answered, after having
decided that she needed to be blunt about it. "The charge is
very murky, but he's accused of ordering a murder committed
by someone in the London underworld. He was released on
bail yesterday. Nevertheless, he disappeared into thin air the
moment he stepped outside the prison gate."

Samantha began to cry again.

"I don't know what to do next. I've already gone to the
police and reported him missing. I simply can't believe he has
skipped bail or that he would stop communicating with me."

Well, I can, Yuliana thought, still smarting at the memory about the way she had been cast aside.

"If there's one thing I'm confident about", she spoke aloud, "it's that Matthias was always a very resourceful man.

"I know, I know", Samantha moaned, "but I suspect he's once again become a victim of the Russian Mafia."

"The Russian Mafia." Dazed, Yuliana sipped her glass of wine. All the bad memories from the past came back to her, ripping apart the carefully sewed-up shroud where she had buried her most unpleasant experiences. Matthias carrying her rapist's face. Abandoned by Matthias. Matthias having her deported. The castration of Spanish. Her flight to the US.

So this is what I have to live with, forever, she thought. *Like Samantha and Matthias, we all have to live with whatever role we have been assigned to act in real life. How frightening.*

As they sat in silence, occasionally sipping their wine, Yuliana stealthily studied Samantha. Physically, she was quite different from herself. Samantha wore her blonde hair short, compared to her own dark brown that she wore shoulder-length. She was at least a head taller than Samantha. Samantha was more spontaneous, and less restrictive about herself, Yuliana granted her, before she with a sigh accepted that her jealousy should be buried in the past with so many other things that she refused to think about.

She hadn't seen Matthias for many years in the belief that he was dead, and, now that he wasn't, it seemed logical to her that he had found a new partner. Still, there was a part inside her that couldn't help feel jealousy against the younger,

227

very attractive woman who Matthias had married and who had borne his children.

To Samantha's consternation, Yuliana's eyes suddenly filled with tears. *The children I was unable to have because of the abuse when I was forced into prostitution after being traded to Spain from my childhood Romania,* she remembered.

"It's not like him to vanish like this", Samantha offered, "as I'm sure you know. What should I do now? I've reported his disappearance to the police, to no apparent avail. You knew him … intimately, of course. Can you think of anywhere he could have gone, or why he would abuse his bail provisions?"

"I haven't seen or heard of Matthias in a million years, I didn't even know he was alive until you just told me. How would I know where to find him?"

Then Yuliana began to, very silently, cry. She cried because, oblivious of the lauded successes she had achieved by treading the boards basking in applause for her talent, she now remembered nothing but the injustices life had presented her.

"Tell me, Julie", Samantha urged her, placing a hand on Yuliana's sleeve, "how did you two meet? Why did you have a fallout? I'm so desperate to understand the part of Matthias that I've been excluded from. Could his past be the key to his present whereabouts …?" She lowered her head and began to cry. "I'm so sorry, I have no right to ask you these questions, but I feel so … powerless …"

"I understand", Yuliana replied, softened by the

desperation in Samantha's voice. "Believe me, I understand. Before I came to the UK, I was a vulnerable young girl who was lucky to be taken in by a couple who became my substitute parents."

"How did that come about?"

"It's a long and very sad story, but the essence of it is that there are good-hearted people in this world who will help you." Yuliana's eyes took on a dreamy look. "Violet and Alexandru were the kindest people I ever met, and they took me in and treated me as if I was their own daughter ..."

"As their own daughter? Meaning?"

"They didn't have any children of their own, although Violet told me that, in a previous marriage, her only child had been stolen from her –"

"What do you mean ... stolen?" Samantha gasped.

"She told me that she and her husband were in Istanbul when someone managed to snatch their three-year-old daughter at some bazaar with a lot of people."

Samantha felt cold shivers descend on her back when she heard this. *Could it be possible ...? No, the coincidence was too great.*

"Please, tell me a bit more about the young girl that was lost", she pleaded after having absorbed Yuliana's information.

"I really don't know too much about it", Yuliana said before sipping on her glass of wine. "Why the interest?"

It cost Samantha several moments of silence before she could overcome the awkwardness she felt.

"When I was a little girl, I was apprehended in Turkey by some people who later, presumably, sold me for profit", she finally blurted. "I … I … was reminded by your story that I could have been that little girl." Samantha burst out in tears and covered her face with her hands.

"Imagine, here I am crying over a past I don't remember", she sobbed after collecting herself, "when the only thing I want is to find Matthias again."

Yuliana leaned across the table and put her hand on Samantha's arm and gently squeezed it.

"I have no idea where Matthias may be or what happened to him, but what I can do is find out more details about the child Violet lost in Istanbul. Would that help in any way?"

"Thank you", Samantha replied behind tears before getting up. "I'm so sorry, I've taken up your time and …"

"Nonsense. Just give me your phone number, and I'll do my best to get more information. You see, Alexandru and Violet made me their sole heir. Isn't life ironic?"

*

Walking beside Haroun riding on his camel, we arrived at the nearby camp as the nightfall was about to arrive. He shouted in Arabic to some of his helpers, who were sitting around a campfire eating. True to his word, moments later I had a plate with hot stew and a generous portion of water.

At first it hadn't struck me as unusual that the man in

mauve turban had spoken to me in English. Soon enough, it became apparent that I stuck out like a sore thumb among everyone else in different shades of brown and black that protected them from the unforgiving desert sun. I was the only European, so of course he would address me in English.

Later, Haroun took me to Moammar, with whom he exchanged a couple of phrases in Arabic. Moammar turned out to be a shifty operator who in the most obvious way was looking for the fastest manner to turn a profit. I soon understood that he wasn't in any way troubled by other people's hardships: the only thing he was interested in was how to make a quick quid.

"Haroun says you want travel come sea, then come Europe", he told me in broken English.

"Yes, that's right. Can you fit me onto one of your lorries?"

He ignored my question.

"Not possible. If pay good, maybe everything possible."

A negotiator trying to get the utmost from a half-dead man dressed in rags.

"Of course I'll pay for your services. What do you want?"

"Money!" he laughed, revealing missing teeth.

"Well, I don't have any money on me", I said, "but I can offer you something better."

He looked at me, smiling and expectant.

"OK, you show."

"First tell me what your regular fee is for taking people

from here to Europe."

He studied me for a moment, as if to gauge how much he could possibly charge me.

"Normal business, five thousand euros."

"I don't believe you. I shall ask the others here how much they paid."

"OK, OK, two thousand euros."

"I'll give something worth much more", I told him and held out one of my cuff links to him. "This is gold with diamonds, emeralds and a ruby. It's yours if you take me to Europe."

Moammar took the cufflink and studied it in the light of the nearby fire. The diamonds seemed real to him, after having probed them with his tongue. He had learnt this trick to distinguish a diamond from its imitation, cubic zirconia. On the immediate contact, the diamond offered a colder experience. It was like the difference in walking on a floor made of stone to one made of wood, he knew.

They were cold enough, he admitted to himself, and they seemed to be of good quality, although he knew a microscope would be needed to verify his assumption. Moammar prided himself in knowing everything about precious stones, because in the past he had spent three years smuggling blood diamonds out of Angola.

"One thousand euros, no more. This pay you go Tripoli only."

The halting conversation made me doubt that Moammar had ever seen a pair of cufflinks, or he would have asked me for the missing one. I decided to play along without revealing all my cards.

"All right, keep it and take me to Tripoli."

The one cufflink had probably cost Samantha five times as much as Moammar charged me for the transfer to the Libyan capital.

Monday April 27, 2016

Frank O'Hare had on occasion wondered about a – perhaps insignificant, but nevertheless inexplicable – detail that he had detected among the activities of the company that he'd been hired to run as its CEO. As an experienced banker, he found it increasingly dubious that *every* three-month loan made by Full Sails Financing Ltd to its customers across Europe had been paid on time. It was a statistic hard to believe considering an average of 50 loans a day to private citizens. The first loans had become due a little over three weeks ago. All 610 loans had been paid on the exact day they were due. He had decided he would ask Mikhail Berlosky, the company's president, about this extraordinary feat. Were the customers chosen by analysts or some software he didn't yet know about?

However, before he got the opportunity to meet with Berlosky, there was a second questionable issue that raised a red flag. Thirty-seven contracts had been electronically signed, approved and uploaded to Full Sails Financing Ltd's central computer by its various branches across seven countries on the continent. It was his job to authorise and oversee the payment of the loans to the various branches. What bothered him was that they had all been closed on Friday April 3.

How is this possible? he wondered as he stared at the computer. *Nobody works on Good Friday. It's the one bank holiday everyone in Europe observes.*

What Frank had discovered was Boris's mistake to consider the Easter holiday for the weekend in 2014 to be the same in 2015, not taking into consideration that, since the 4th century AC, Easter is a moveable feast.

*

Detective Inspector John Blackmoore studied the extensive report that had been sent to him about Matthias Callaghan skipping bail on his computer screen. He still didn't know what to think of Callaghan's disappearance. In Blackmoore's experience, it seemed uncharacteristic contemplating both the man and what statistics had taught him over the years. As far as he could recall, not a single person in British criminal history had removed his or her ankle monitor within thirty minutes upon leaving custody.

Blackmoore also remembered the interview years earlier that Callaghan had volunteered to give to clear up past investigations and to regain his good name. *A strange story, that: going through face transplants as if he were changing the shirt on his back.* Still, Blackmoore found it incredulous that a clever man such as Callaghan would opt to disappear immediately after being released on bail. *Perhaps there's something I'm missing?*

A patrol car had been sent out to search for Callaghan when the surveillance centre had noticed that the signal the monitor emitted revealed that it had been removed. The anklet had been found next to a construction site. The thick strap securing the device to his ankle had been cut through, and there were blood stains on it. The blood type matched Callaghan's. The charger for the monitor had not been found.

Despite his doubts, Blackmoore felt fairly certain Callaghan must have removed the monitor himself because he was guilty and afraid of being convicted for Rathbone's murder. He began reading the three-page analysis of Matthias Callaghan's restricted movements and activities since he arrived in Europe.

I can see only two options, Blackmoore mused when he had finished reading. *Callaghan made a run for it immediately after leaving jail, because he's guilty of the murder that he's been accused of. He has left, or is about to leave, the country by some unknown means, despite having been reprieved of his passport. There exists of course the possibility that he has decided to remain hidden somewhere in the British countryside.* If he were, in Blackmoore's experience Callaghan would sooner rather than later reveal his whereabouts when he contacted friends or relatives that the police would automatically keep under surveillance.

Or, although Blackmoore found it farfetched, *he could have been abducted, extorted or killed by someone* – a scenario that Blackmoore had to acknowledge, however improbable, had to be considered as a possibility. Callaghan had arrived in Rome from Australia, where he had been apprehended immediately by the Italian police and later extradited to the UK. *In the case of the abduction scenario after Callaghan exited Wormwood Scrubs, who could possibly have the information, the time and the logistical acumen to arrange for such an elaborate scheme between March 31 and April 27? No – impossible. Callaghan disappeared immediately after leaving jail. And the cab that picked him up has still not been found.*

Blackmoore felt overwhelmingly convinced that Callaghan had staged his own disappearance. No doubt an intelligent man, Callaghan had arranged it in such a way that he thought the police would look the wrong way. *But,* Blackmoore thought, *he won't be fooling me.*

In case he had already managed to leave the UK, Blackmoore decided to send an alert to Interpol for the apprehension of the fugitive Matthias Callaghan.

*

Berlosky stepped out of the elevator and entered the sitting room of Vasily's penthouse flat. Vasily was sitting on a luxurious leather sofa with one leg across the other, studying the daily paper. He looked up, and deduced from Berlosky's smile that he was bursting with good news. Vasily folded the paper and signalled to his closest associate to take a seat.

"Everything has worked out according to plan … more or less", Berlosky grinned at him after having made a quick detour to the bar where he knew the chilled vodka was kept. He found it in the enormous refrigerator Vasily had installed next to a painting of a blue horse by some German painter that gave Berlosky hallucinations.

"As you know, two days ago Misha picked up Callaghan in a stolen cab when Callaghan was released from jail." To confirm the statement, Berlosky put some pictures on the table, taken across the street by one of Oleg's men as Callaghan waved down the cab. "Callaghan was gassed unconscious inside the car and was driven to the airport, where Paddy was ready to take off for Morocco. A little later, Allan's body, after One-eye's successful kill, arrived and was loaded onto the plane."

"And they were dropped far from shore over the Atlantic, as I ordered", Vasily said as he stifled a yawn, expecting the usual confirmation from Berlosky.

"Well, not exactly", Berlosky admitted, slowly moving his head from one side to the other while making a grimace. "Not that it matters, they're dead all right, which was the whole point of this operation, wasn't it?" He placed more prints on the table between them. "You see, they were disposed of in a different kind of sea. A sea of sand."

"What happened?" Vasily asked with a sigh, still not looking at the photographs. A neat and precise man in any undertaking, he profoundly disliked deviations from orders given or from plans he had put a lot of effort into. On top of this, there was also a narcissistic streak that permeated Vasily's being: he was the intelligent superior being who had crushed Kiril before taking his place at the helm of Russia's largest crime organisation. Yes, business was growing exponentially, thanks to his vision. And, daily he was becoming acutely aware that his weak point was not his vision or knowledge or intelligence, but his dependence on stupid thugs who were inept at sharing that vision or knowledge or intelligence – or to perform even the simplest orders.

"When he got back, Paddy explained to me that, while in the air, his co-pilot injected himself with heroin meant to kill Callaghan and overdosed. Since Paddy was alone, he had to concentrate on flying the aircraft to Merzouga in Morocco, which – if you remember – I constantly reminded him was his number one target. 'If you need to improvise', I told him, 'your number one priority is to deliver the merchandise to me.' Then I said: 'If you don't – don't bother to come back.'"

"So far, so good, then", Vasily nodded patiently, waiting for Berlosky to get to the point.

"Definitely!" Vasily assured him before throwing back the glass of vodka he had brought from the bar.

Vasily waited, accustomed to his countrymen's faith in raw alcohol to solve either their difficulty of describing the reality, or using it for evasive purposes – "Only one more toast, *tovarich* …"

"Well, the excellent news is that we have unloaded the cocaine from Paddy's aircraft, and it's now on the way to six different distribution centres …"

"Mikhail, it appears to me that you skipped the part that at this moment is of most interest to me", Vasily sighed and

238

sipped his tea. "I'm exhilarated that the transfer of our cargo went well, but, try to stay focused. I want to know what happened to Allan and Callaghan."

"Oh, oh, oh", Berlosky said in a mocking tone while he tried to look preoccupied. "These guys are as dead as lead as we speak, Vasily." He triumphantly threw down the last batch of the pictures he had brought.

"Look at these!" Berlosky insisted.

Vasily took another sip of tea, which suddenly seemed a bit too tepid for his liking. It vexed him, just like Berlosky's news vexed him. Mikhail had been given specific orders, and whatever the result, they had not been carried out as he had been told. Vasily knew he had to address the problem, the sooner the better, but as usual decided to not say anything until he had had time to think it through. He put down his teacup and grabbed the photographs that Berlosky with a swagger had left in a pile between them.

The photographs showed three men lying on a background of sand with their eyes closed. One of the men, who Vasily recognised as Allan Gould, lay inside a black body bag, zipper lowered just enough to show his face. He didn't recognise the other two men, and quizzing looked up at Berlosky.

"That's Paddy's assistant on the flight leaving Cornwall", Berlosky confirmed, stabbing his index finger at the photo. "He was the one who helped himself to too much smack on the way out and overdosed. As I said, that's why the bodies of the other two couldn't be dropped at sea ... All alone

239

on the aircraft and flying low to avoid radar detection, Paddy has explained that he couldn't just let go of the steering wheel or whatever it's called on airplanes."

"Hrm, I can see his point", Vasily reluctantly approved. "And now they are certified as dead; not at sea but buried in the desert?"

"That's right", Berlosky replied, "dead and buried. The Sahara may not have the extension of the Atlantic, but it's the world's largest sea of sand."

"Who's this?" Vasily asked, pointing at the third man pictured in the photos.

"At first it seems a stretch of the imagination, but, no – that's Callaghan. Another facelift, no less. I didn't believe it myself at first, but I've checked it out. As you can see from Ilya's photos when he left prison and got into Misha's cab, it's the same man."

"I see that it's same man getting into the cab who winds up in the desert. What I don't see is the man I myself, together with you, met in the flesh at Victoria station a couple of years ago."

"Callaghan had us fooled, I have to admit", Berlosky said as he got up to serve himself another vodka.

"Fooled?" Vasily grimaced.

"For the two occasions we met, I think he got some disguise to make us believe that the face he showed us was his true one", Berlosky called out from behind the bar. "Very clever. We never had reason to suspect it, since we only knew that he had made his second transplant that ended as the video of the first one."

"You don't have to remind me, Mikhail. I remember it vividly."

"Well, I did some digging into his background before I came here to see you", Berlosky said and returned to the table where Vasily waited. "It's hard to believe, but Callaghan somehow managed to get his original face back during his second transplant."

"What do you mean ... his original face?" Vasily asked, narrowing his eyes.

"Look at this magazine clipping."

Berlosky placed a copy of a page from "The Internet Insider's Monthly Review" in front of Vasily. The photo above the article showed Matthias Callaghan shaking hands and smiling together with another man. "Callaghan and Caruthers shakes on VOIP app sale",the headline announced. There could be no doubt that, although younger-looking in the magazine article dated 2006, it was the same man who now lay dead in the Sahara Desert.

"I have a hard time believing this", he told Berlosky, amazed and to a growing extent vexed with himself for having allowed himself to be fooled. "How could he possibly have pulled that one off? No wonder he wanted to erase the end of the second transplant video."

"By some good fortune, my new contact inside the Metropolitan Police was present a few years ago when Callaghan made a statement to come clean about certain offences he was credited with. What I learnt from him is that

Callaghan's lookalike father was knifed to death by someone, so Callaghan took advantage and inherited his face."

Vasily was not one to be either impressed or easily shocked, but to Berlosky's satisfaction, he noted his boss's dropped jaw and the incredulity in his eyes. Vasily picked one of the photos that pictured Callaghan dead.

"And now Callaghan is dead and buried", he mumbled. "In a way, what a pity. He was an interesting opponent."

"Mummified in the sand", Berlosky confirmed, laughing. "Perhaps some archaeologist will dig them out in a thousand years and announce them to be specimens of interest. By the way, here are the rest of the things you wanted as proof that they're dead."

After pulling out the items from the plastic bag he had brought, he placed the emptied wallets, their contents and assorted jewellery on the table. There were also two small glass flasks that, according to their labels, contained ciclosporin pills.

*

Samantha's mobile rang. It was Yuliana.

"Hello Samantha! As promised, I've spoken with some people about the disappearance of Violet's little girl. You can judge for yourself from the information I have gathered. Fortunately, being Monday, I don't have a show today. Are you free to meet with me?"

"Of course I am!" Samantha exclaimed, excited, feeling

butterflies in her stomach. "What about afternoon tea here at my hotel?"

"I'll be there", Yuliana replied. "Let's meet in the Thames foyer at two o'clock, shall we?"

*

Just before lunchtime, Detective Inspector John Blackmoore was swivelling back and forth in his office chair while once again contemplating the mysterious disappearance of Matthias Callaghan. A newly delivered videotape confirmed that he had been picked up by a cab with the plates X518TGG, recorded by a CCTV camera outside Wormwood Scrubs. A quarter of an hour later, his ankle monitor had been removed. Since then, no one knew the whereabouts of Callaghan. Still more intriguing was that the taxi plate recorded by the CCTV camera didn't exist. Blackmoore's best guess at the moment was that the cab had been stolen and a set of false number plates had been attached.

This left Blackmoore with a still more challenging question: had Callaghan known that he was going to be picked up by this particular cab with its false number plates?

Was Callaghan abducted? Blackmoore mused. *Or did he stage his abduction? Did the driver help him cut off and discard the monitor? The answer to the last question is probably yes. The technical report indicates a knife was used to saw through the anklet, yet Callaghan left prison without carrying any such tool.* Still, there were many questions that remained unanswered.

Blackmoore, who always appreciated the finer points of a substantial lunch, decided with a deep sigh that these had to wait until he had satisfied the rumbling originating from this stomach.

*

Samantha was waiting nervously sitting at a table near the glass dome in the Thames foyer. So many things were upsetting her life now. Matthias vanished. Although speaking daily with her children, she missed them. Almost three months pregnant. And the news Yuliana was going to share with her … would she find out who her real parents were? She felt terrified.

Yuliana arrived, looking very elegant and distinguished. More than a few pairs of eyes turned to watch her, both because of her beauty and for her being a famous actress.

After exchanging greetings, they ordered tea from the head waiter. They shared some small talk until a waiter arrived with a tray laden with silverware, finger sandwiches, scones with cream and jam, and pastries.

"Violet, who took me in and cared for me when I arrived in London, was married twice", Yuliana began when they had been left alone. "Her first husband was Harold Winthrop. Violet was forty when their only child, a girl named Sandra, was born on January thirtieth in nineteen-eighty. In June nineteen-eighty-three, Violet and Sandra accompanied Harold on a business trip to Turkey. One day they visited the Grand

Bazaar in Istanbul, where they lost the girl."

Samantha was ignoring her tea and scones and stared at Yuliana with her fists pressed against her mouth. Her knuckles were white. She was unable to speak.

"Amazingly, Violet's mother is still alive, now ninety-six years old with a mind and a memory as crisp as a fresh carrot", Yuliana continued, getting emotional when she saw tears well up in Samantha's eyes. "I met with her this morning, when she told me what I'm now telling you before she gave me these pictures."

She pushed a dozen photographs across the table and drank some tea in silence while she watched Samantha study the faded colours in the Kodachrome pictures of a blonde little girl at the age of one, two and three. Looking at them made the colour fade from Samantha's cheeks, too.

"Harold died from a broken heart in nineteen eighty-six, Violet told me."

"I'd … I'd like to meet Violet's mother", Samantha stammered. "Can I?"

"Of course you can", Yuliana confirmed, accompanied by one of her melancholy smiles.

*

Inside the large tent that Moammar, the Arab, had set up two days earlier upon arriving, Haroun, the Berber, studied him with experienced eyes. After more decades than he cared to remember of crossing the Great Desert, he had learnt when men were acting honourably and when they exclusively pursued the spoils of greed. Haroun had no doubt whatsoever that Moammar belonged to the second category, so he was very much on his guard. He was particularly apprehensive about the half a million euros he had been paid by the Russians that still hadn't been secured.

"How was your trip across the desert?" Moammar asked him while chewing on a date. "You've come a long way, old man." He spit the pit on the carpet spread inside the tent, something that Haroun found extremely offensive. Still, he kept his outward calm.

"Not hotter than usual", he stated, "and I've brought you an even larger crowd of men willing to pay for their passage to Europe than I have in any previous year. That should make you both pleased and a tidier profit than you envisioned."

"I do appreciate your concern and your well-wishing for a modest increase in my profit for the ungrateful task of fulfilling this rabble's dream of a better life."

Haroun sipped his tea before he nodded thoughtfully at his host. He had instantly recognised the false claim for what it was, and he wanted to get out of there as fast as possible without raising any suspicion that his most valuable cargo was something very different from the would-be European immigrants.

"As you know, I travel at night. Dusk will be arriving within short, and I have preparations to make before I leave. If you don't mind, I'd like to settle the amount of your commission immediately."

"You are a man of business, foremost, just like myself", Moammar beamed. "I appreciate the increment in the business, of course."

From inside of his garb, Haroun brought out a large leather purse. Inside it there were two hundred and ten 500-euro notes.

"Here is your share, Moammar, and do not have any doubts it will be larger still next season. It's all accounted for. Two hundred and ten men. One hundred and five thousand euros. Since you made a deal directly with the one we found in the desert, I'm sure you understand why I haven't included him."

"Of course. As always, it's a pleasure doing business with you."

After Haroun had stepped outside Moammar's tent, Moammar smiled to himself. *Things are going great.* Since Ghalib had inherited the money upon Abdul Mahfouz's death, she had needed someone to make wise investments on her behalf with the fat bank account she now possessed. Ahmed had suggested to her that people who wanted to go to Europe were willing to pay good money for the trip. She had paid for the second-hand lorries and the ship, expecting half of everything they made. Yet there were always ways to skim off some extra money for himself, like the piece of jewellery he had been paid by the Englishman.

Life is good. Business is good. And, if you think about it, helping people travelling to get rich in Europe, well, it should really be considered charity.

*

After having slept through the day and being restored by the water and the food offered to me, I began thinking more clearly about my situation. I had paid my way to continue to some unknown African port in the Mediterranean where I would somehow find passage to Europe. How many days that meant spending in the sun, I didn't know. I had no sunscreen or other solar protection.

At the back of my head, there was also the increasingly nagging worry that I was the only white European among hundreds of impoverished Africans. I still had one of the cufflinks in my possession, my only means to pay my way to return to Europe. What would become of me if that last single item of value I still owned was taken from me?

Worse, I felt a growing concern about the lack of the ciclosporin I needed to prevent rejecting my face transplant. Of course I was worried. I clearly remembered Dr Sternmacher's stern warning that I "needed to take it every day for the rest of my life – or else".

The person sitting next to me, a young man with a friendly face and skin as black as the night now surrounding us, touched me playfully on the shoulder.

"You're going home, friend?"

"I guess I am", I mumbled. I was tired and suddenly perceived a distant yet curiously present pulsing in my fingers and face. "I need to go home or I will face some very serious consequences."

"Life is a very serious matter, never to be taken lightly", he said, grinning. "I know, and that's why I'm going to Europe. I need to send money to my family that cannot be made in Mauritania. The wars in Somalia, Nigeria, Rwanda, Burundi and other places in Central Africa has spilled over the borders to my country.

"Where in Europe do you want to travel?"

"Wherever there is work", he answered, now contemplative. "I'm told London is where you can make the most money, but that it's very difficult to get across the English Channel."

"You speak very good English", I asked him. "Where did you learn it?"

"I helped taking Doctors Without Borders into war zones in nearby countries. In exchange they taught me both English and French, can you believe?"

He laughed, and it was such a pleasant, joyful laughter that added another small link to the bond I felt with him in our common misery. He exuded goodness and no ill will. I felt a liking for him, and not just for the situation we both shared.

"Perhaps you got the better end of the exchange – if you make good use of your knowledge, proficiency in languages tends to add up to a better salary."

"Speaking languages pays you better?" he asked, interested, and leaned forward.

"Any skill in demand will make it easier for you", I reassured him, "and speaking foreign languages is one of them. I'm trying to get back to London myself. I still have friends there. You seem to be a bright young man. Perhaps I can arrange something for you."

"That would be wonderful, of course", he said with a polite smile that indicated that he didn't believe me.

It dawned on me that I no longer looked the prosperous business man, but rather the ragtag and penniless refugee without a future trying to enter Europe. That was what I would remain, at least for some unforeseeable future, unless I died trying.

"My name is Matthias", I told him. "What's yours?"

"I'm Omar", he replied, "and if you permit me saying so, the sun has not been very kind to you. Your face and your hands have been ravaged; try to keep them covered like the rest of your body. Your skin wasn't made for Africa, like mine."

I looked down at my hands and felt an infinite sadness coming over me, because I realised that every word he had spoken was true. Damned by circumstance, toyed by destiny – what had there been in my life that I could have changed for the better?

"I will give you something to protect you, and it will also alleviate the scratching irritation you will otherwise soon start to feel", he continued and started rummaging inside his sizeable backpack. He held up a small glass flask with a dark, viscous liquid inside.

"My grandmother's recipe", he said triumphantly. "It cures anything from sore feet to bellyaches."

"What is it?" I asked, suspicious.

"Mainly coconut oil, and then there are some herbs and grasses."

He signalled me to hold out my hands and rubbed some of the oil on them. A minute later the slight throbbing and the itching I had felt, had gone away. Then he applied it on my face.

It didn't take long before I was feeling much better, and then the toll of my past long days took me into a deep, blissful, unworried sleep.

I woke up to loud shouting. Men with rifles aggressively motioned everybody to quickly get on board the lorries. I counted seven vehicles. The darkness had by now completely enveloped the improvised day camp. The people got up from around the camp fires, folded their makeshift tents and dragged their scarce belongings to the nearest lorry. I followed suit – not that I had much baggage to drag along.

A bearded man, whose swarthiness offset his surprisingly white teeth, stood smiling broadly illuminated by the headlights of two large lorries. He spoke in Arabic, and I couldn't understand a word he said. At the end of his short speech, about half of the emigrants he had agreed to get to Europe cheered. Presumably he had told us we were in his very good hands, and that shortly we would tread European soil. It wasn't a hard conclusion to come to. Why would those desperate to travel to Europe who did understand Arabic cheer otherwise?

Shortly afterwards, our motorcade rolled north, towards the Mediterranean. I estimated that there were thirty of us riding in the back of each lorry. Above us, a tarpaulin would serve as sun protection when dawn arrived. The sides and the back were open, allowing for the air to flow freely to cool us passengers. In the driver's compartment of each lorry, there were either two or three menacing-looking guards with rifles.

I was riding on the back of the fifth lorry. As our caravan advanced along the dirt road, the rushing night wind was refreshing after the hot daytime desert air. By and by, everyone on the lorry began to look for the most comfortable way to settle into some kind of half-sleep on their bags and belongings, while ignoring the bumps in the road. The stars were blinking above us, clear and undisturbed by light except for the headlights of the vehicles. Eventually, I too fell asleep, sort of, sitting with my back against the side of the lorry.

Tuesday April 28, 2015

The lorries continued along the desert overnight. Riding in my uncomfortable position half asleep, I noticed that we were climbing uphill and downhill across a mountain range. The air became considerably chillier, and we all huddled together to keep warmer. No one spoke. Then dawn arrived with a rosy promise on the horizon to heat up the day. The lorries stopped and we were told to jump down. I could see a couple of palm trees next to a well. It was a place obviously used as a resting place on previous occasions. Some of the men rambled over to the well and sent a bucket down it to fetch water, which they poured over themselves. Soon there was a queue of men who wanted to follow the example.

Some of the men with rifles pointed at a pile with bottles of water, and no one was allowed to take more than one. The tepid water tasted like glory. A fire was started next to each lorry and kettles with some sort of stew were heated. The stew turned out to be chicken, or at least it tasted like it was. It wasn't the most succulent thing I've eaten, but, then again, I was in no position to complain – I had hardly eaten anything for days.

An hour later, with the lorries refuelled from the large jerrycans secured on the cabin roofs, we were once again on our way. I was in a better mood now, although I had no way of knowing where we were. Around noon, we were on a narrow dirt road crossing a mountain pass. The lorries came to a halt in front of two uniformed soldiers with rifles across their chests. It took me a while to understand that it was a checkpoint between Morocco and Algeria. A yawning officer, with his jacket unbuttoned over an unwashed undershirt, appeared from a small hut while putting on his peaked military cap. Moammar, who was the undisputed boss of our motorcade, got out of the leading lorry and greeted the officer. They seemed to know each other and shared some small talk and a smoke. The officer laughed at something. Moammar brought out a package, which he handed to the officer.

The officer looked pleased, nodded amicably and waved at his soldiers to let the seven lorries through.

We continued along the almost invisible dirt roads that sometimes took us up in the mountains and sometimes skirted endless sand dunes. While the morning air was still fresh, there had been loud conversations among my fellow passengers. When the heat set in, it ceased – it took too much effort to speak. The other passengers studied me, the only European, with curiosity. *Why on earth would a European want to be smuggled into Europe,* they were no doubt thinking. *A criminal? A spy? A legionnaire?* I could only shrug at their guesses. There were only two things that mattered to me as things stood: my life and my remaining cuff link to pay for the final journey out of Africa. Once back on European soil, I would find some way of getting back to London.

At nightfall, we stopped again for water and food. The people smugglers took turns at the wheels; apparently they were in a hurry to get us to our destination. By now every muscle in my body ached from the uncomfortable ride. However, what worried me most was the increased pulsing in my fingers. The absence of ciclosporin was beginning to make itself increasingly noticed.

*

The more that Special Agent Solomon Vaughn studied the different angles of Matthias Callaghan's involvement in the death of Richard Thompson, the more intrigued he became. What at first had seemed to be a simple case of murder, albeit with an exotic weapon, had taken on new dimensions. Among the usual exchange between the FBI and its European counterparts about ongoing cases and surveillance, a small but interesting piece had landed on Vaughn's desk. It concerned the son of the suspect who had killed Thompson, and it had been channelled to him only because he carried the same name as his father.

Immediately after Matthias Callaghan had been released on bail on April 27, the ankle monitor he was carrying as a condition for his release was removed. He had not been seen or heard from since. That was three days ago. The disappearance added to Vaughn's professional incredulity. Just like the three people present at the spa when Thompson was killed, and who immediately afterwards took off, now the son of the main suspect had gone missing, too. Vaughn had been unable to track down Samantha Kirby in Australia, and Callaghan Senior had completely disappeared since he had crossed into Mexico after Thompson's killing. Andrew Reese had years ago reported his address as one in Umbria, Italy, but had vanished since then.

Four disappearance acts related to the same case? Vaughn shook his head in belief. *Not on my watch.*

Not being US citizens, and due to the legal restrictions he faced, he wouldn't be able to interview any of the people involved in the case unless they volunteered to or entered US soil. There was one thing he could do, though. Attaching a copy of the passport he had used to enter USA and later to cross into Mexico in May 2009, Vaughn put in a request with Interpol to arrest Matthias Callaghan, born in 1953, on the suspicion of murder.

Wednesday April 29 , 2015

Early in the morning, we passed another checkpoint, this time to cross Algeria's border with Libya. Moammar disappeared inside a building to pay the official his bribe. Ten hours later, we could see the Mediterranean Sea beyond the country's capital.

What little I saw passing through Tripoli didn't impress me. The rebuilding of the city after the revolution against Gadaffi didn't seem to have taken off. At least they hadn't done so along the streets where our seven lorries were driven.

Our motorised caravan finally came to a stop. Waving their rifles, the guards started shouting at everyone to get down. We were motioned into a huge warehouse close to the sea, located in what had the aspects of being a suburb to the capital. Watched over by the armed men that Moammar had brought along on our journey, we were ushered into the building where there were remnants of small-sized fishermen's vessels in need of repair. Inside, hundreds of other migrants were sitting or lying on the floor. We were told in harsh voices to sit down in a semicircle before Moammar, who then addressed us in French (significantly more fluent than his English, and presumably he did so because most of his clients came from former French colonies) flanked by his glowering, rifle-wielding soldiers.

"You will stay here one night, maybe two. Then, early in the morning, I'll drive you to the quay where the ship is waiting to take you to Italy. The trip will take two or three days, depending on the weather. You will be given water and food for three days before we leave. Now you will have supper. *Inshallah*."

The temporary barracks that we had been herded into was surrounded by a fence and guarded by armed men. My new-found friend Omar seemed worried about me and my green eyes and fair skin.

"You will get yourself into trouble, sir", he half-whispered to me. "They always look to kidnap people who look like you. You know, for ransom. Just look around you. There's not a single white man here except you."

His plea sounded so honest that I couldn't avoid professing my doubts that there was anything I could do about it.

"I can't help how I look, and now you're telling me I'm in danger", I told him. "So, what precautions do you suggest I take?"

Omar furrowed his forehead until his face lit up again with his contagious, toothy smile.

"We must make you look like the rest of us, so you won't stand out!"

With a quick laugh, he ran off. Five minutes later, Omar came back with some grease and a foul-smelling liquid in a PET bottle.

"The smell will wear off after a couple of days", he promised, "and I guarantee you no one will recognise you unless they look into your ... not very African eyes."

"I can't put that on!"

"Suit yourself, sir. It's your decision."

Of course Omar was right, which I realised after a few hours of contemplation. I certainly was the ugly duckling among the motley crew from Sub-Saharan Africa. They all looked at me, I imagined, wondering how a white European – with the privileges that come implied with that origin – was travelling with the poor and the desperate for work.

I eventually allowed Omar to apply the concoction on my bare skin, which didn't exactly acquire the tone of my fellow travellers, but fulfilled its purpose reasonably well if you didn't inspect it too closely. The smell was hideous at first, which Omar explained was because he had stolen some engine oil from the diesel trucks. To this he had added something he didn't want to tell me. Anyway, I was now less conspicuous before our last leg to Europe, and, as Omar had promised, it didn't take too long before I got used to the smell after it had begun to fade.

*

"Sir, today I handed in my application to the human resources department requesting a temporary leave", Georgie told the superior officer sitting at his desk. "I just wanted to make sure you knew."

"Temporary leave?" The chief inspector, to whom Blackmoore also reported, raised his left eyebrow. "What is this? Why on earth would you like to leave the force, even if it's intended to be temporary?"

"Since I'm keen on making a career within the force, sir, I

258

do believe it will be of great convenience to that purpose should I be able to get a degree or two while I'm still young. I did tell Detective Inspector Blackmoore last year of my intentions. Do you disapprove of this, sir?"

"As it is, the times are moving too fast for my liking these days, Jones, and it's not my call to disapprove of the changing times. I congratulate you on your ambition to get a better education, and I do hope to be here to meet you when you get back from your studies. In my opinion, we need more laddies like you."

When Georgie left his chief inspector's office, he couldn't help letting out a chuckle. *If the old man only knew,* he thought. *I've got more money to spend in a day than he will make in a year. And I'm going to spend it as if every day will be the last, because, if I don't – for whom would I have been saving it for? Surely Uncle Jeremiah is as good an example as any.*

After having given notice of his departure, he was still leaving the door open should he one day need to go back for information. *One more month, and then I'll finally be free to enjoy Uncle Jeremiah's fortune – and not a single soul at Scotland Yard suspects a thing.*

Thursday April 30, 2015

The chief of police in Marrakech, Mustafa Goulla, looked tired as he languidly kept moving his ivory fan in front of his face. The appearance was deceptive. He had been born with the characteristic brown bags beneath his eyes that was a heritage

259

in the Goulla family, a genetic trademark, so to speak, that induced the false impression of his constant weariness. Perfectly aware of the image he projected, Mustafa Goulla had more than once used this misleading air to his advantage.

The Goulla family had exerted a lot of influence in the Berber region of Morocco during the last centuries, when they had dominated large tracts of the upper Atlas Mountains. Although the family wealth had diminished considerably due to wars and petty feuds, the clan was still a force to be reckoned with.

Mustafa Goulla had been the chief of police responsible for the Marrakech and Ouarzazate regions for the past eighteen years. His rapid ascension within the corps had no doubt been helped by his ancestry. Goulla sheikhs had ruled the Ouarzazate region of Morocco in recent centuries, which was the main reason he had been able to secure his career post and the lucrative opportunities that came with the position.

Once a slender, handsome man with a seductive tongue, a hunger for the best things on offer in life and a clear inclination for the benefits that come with power, Goulla had so far only lost his slenderness. His appetite for food, and sweet desserts in particular, had over the years obliged him to accept his life-long friend and personal tailor's constant insistence to expand the size of his white linen costumes.

Like so many among the wealthiest men in Marrakech, Mustafa lived behind a decrepit door in the *medina* that concealed the true sumptuous living quarters where he indulged a life of luxury. Mustafa, still a bachelor at forty-seven – large, overweight and invariably exuding the overpowering smell of some new, expensive perfume – couldn't restrain himself from being on constant lookout for female companionship. Beautiful women were his greatest weakness, and he relished his knowledge of the fact. He sighed as he thought of the previous evening's encounter with the Egyptian belly dancer touring Morocco, who he had made futile attempts to seduce.

There was a short, hard rap on his office door, which he immediately recognised as that of his small, wiry and energetic assistant Lamrani.

"Some local people found two dead bodies in the Merzouga sand dunes", Lamrani began. "It's near to the Algerian border, on the outskirts of the Sahara. It's within our administrative responsibilities."

"I know where it is, thank you very much", Mustafa replied dryly. "My family ruled the region for centuries."

"It looks worse than usual", Lamrani continued, used to his boss's proud comments about his ancestry. "One of them appears to be a European, and he's been shot in the back of his head. The other looks like a national. Neither carry any identification. We've been requested to go there immediately to take over the investigation, to avoid what may or may not become a diplomatic embarrassment."

"Do we have any other urgent matter to attend to, here or elsewhere?" the police chief asked.

"Nothing that can't wait, or that I can't delegate."

Goulla looked at his watch.

"It's still early, we can make it today with spare time for a banquet at my cousin's villa in Ouarzazate. While I call my cousin, you will contact my housekeeper and tell her to prepare a suitcase with everything I need for a three-day trip. By the way, tell the officer in charge in Merzouga not to move anything. I want to have a first-hand impression of the scene, which has the potential to become a mess."

Twenty minutes later, Goulla's chauffeur-driven white Mercedes stopped near the entrance to the medina to where his elderly housekeeper had lugged a large suitcase with more clothes than he would need. She was a 70-year-old woman who had been in his family's service since he was born, and, if one was to make an intent of describing her, she wasn't very different to Lamrani: small, wiry, energetic and a totally dedicated servant. Like the colour of the Mercedes, every piece of clothing in the suitcase was white because of yet another of Goulla's idiosyncrasies. Although he rightly claimed he preferred to dress in this colour because it attracted less heat, he secretly saw himself as the elegant reincarnation of the more prosperous past of his clan: even the *tarboosh* that he wore, the Moroccan version of the fez, was white.

With Lamrani sitting up front with the chauffeur, Goulla comfortably spread his voluminous presence, clad in one of his twenty identical white linen suits, in the back seat. Three hours later, after having crossed the High Atlas Mountain Range, they arrived at Ouarzazate. Despite the short advance notice given, the generous meal at his cousin's house didn't disappoint Goulla. For his part, Lamrani was left in awe by the abundance of the delicious food.

The sun was colouring the cloud-free sky orange as the Mercedes rolled into Merzouga, a small town at the edge of the Sahara Desert. Known as the gateway to Erg Chebbi, a huge expanse of sand dunes located north of the town, it was only a short distance from the border shared with Algeria.

From his comfortable back seat, Goulla directed his driver to take them to the so-called desert hotel next to where the sand dunes dominated the landscape. The owner – yet another of Goulla's innumerable cousins, Lamrani noted – came out with outstretched arms to welcome them in person, forewarned by their relative in common back in Ouarzazate.

The structure and the facilities were quite rustic, but it had cold and hot running water and served a surprisingly superb lamb *tagine* dish accompanied by disruptive grunts from the dromedaries resting outside.

They had just finished their dinner when the local police sub-prefect made his entrance. Goulla leaned back on his comfortable cushions with an extended sigh of content over the second meal of excellence he had savoured on that day. He signalled to the sub-prefect to sit down and enjoy a cup of tea with the rest of them.

"I'm most honoured to sit here with you, sir," the flushed sub-prefect shyly greeted his superior.

"Of course, but do not worry yourself. Please feel more than welcome", Goulla replied, a bit patronising since, after all, he was heir of the Goulla clan that had once ruled the territory.

"I thought it important to immediately report to you the findings I so far have in this extraordinary case", the sub-prefect began.

"Please proceed."

"The two bodies were discovered by a local goat shepherd. We have not moved them, advised that you want to personally conduct the investigation, sir. At this moment, I have four guards watching over the corpses – at a certain distance, it must be admitted, given the smell and the circumstances. Your inspection of the bodies is an urgent matter, because by now the corpses have been exposed to the sun for an estimated four or five days. To diminish the possibility of decomposition, I ordered the erection of a plastic shelter to protect the bodies from direct sunlight. I personally made a research of the area, as well as an inspection of the bodies, shortly after they were discovered, and unfortunately there's not much to tell. The corpses wear no jewellery or watches, and they carry no identification. Judging by his tattoos, we suspect the first victim to be a Moroccan citizen who has spent some time in jail. As for the other body, the one shot in the head, we found this in the jacket lying next to him."

He placed two photocopies on the table.

"The originals are kept at the station", he added.

Goulla studied them with interest before looking up at Lamrani with a thoughtful expression.

"These are the prison release documents, dated five days ago, for someone by the name of Matthias Callaghan. How he ended up here is perhaps still a mystery, but at least we now know he's a bad apple."

Goulla frowned as he tried to get to grips with the implications.

"Lamrani, I must admit that I felt sceptical when you alluded the possibility to me", he finally said, "but with this Englishman shot in the desert, it seems we now do have an uncomfortable diplomatic situation on our hands after all."

Lamrani slowly nodded his agreement. They were both thinking about the terrorist attack that had taken place in Marrakech on their watch four years earlier.

Friday April 28, 2011

The blast of a loud explosion could be heard across central Marrakech. It was still not yet noon, and people in the crowded medina with its narrow alleyways next to the Jemaa el-Fnaa square looked up in bewilderment. After a brief pause, the chatter started in earnest and screaming people hurried towards the exits.

The balcony of the Argana café was popular with tourists who wanted a front seat overlooking the picturesque activities the square offered. This included snake charmers, hawkers of any goods imaginable, overloaded donkey carts, musicians with homemade instruments, tribesmen in typical clothing and monkeys on leashes for a memorable photograph. Those on the balcony, sipping tea or an early beer, regretted their choice the moment the bag with its bomb exploded, instantly killing fourteen people.

Chief Mustafa Goulla, head of the Marrakech police department, arrived at the scene seven minutes later with his assistant Lamrani in tow. The sirens of ambulances had taken possession of the airwaves. As Goulla and Lamrani took two steps at a time to get to the balcony, they perceived the agonising whimpers of the dozens of injured who had survived the blast.

Standing in the debris, Goulla's eyes hardened as he took in the scene.

"We will get those responsible for this massacre, be it al-Qaeda or anyone else", he told Lamrani between clenched teeth. "And I don't care if I need to coerce the truth from them with a pair of pliers."

Friday May 1, 2015

With the aftermath of the Marrakech bombing on their minds, and the caution that was sure to come from the tourism ministry without delay once the news had been relayed, Goulla and Lamrani set out for the place where the two bodies had been found. The Marrakech bombing had left Canadian, British, Russian, Swiss, Dutch and Portuguese citizens dead. The price had been high for the Moroccan government and its tourist industry. Now, with another foreigner citizen apparently murdered up in the Atlas Mountains, there were justified fears from the concerned ministries that the discovery could blow out of proportion. "Avoid, at all costs, to scare off tourists by announcing that a deadly attack has been carried out on another foreigner", was, in brief, the message conveyed by the authorities.

Including a detour along a nearly invisible dirt road, the trip from the desert hotel took Goulla and Lamrani twenty minutes before any tracks besides those of dromedaries disappeared. The last stretch, which consisted of barren land announcing the beginning of the desert with its towering dunes, took them another ten minutes to cross in the four-wheel drive jeep that they had commissioned from the local police.

A makeshift tent had been raised over the bodies. As requested, to his satisfaction Goulla found that the scene had been left untouched. The stench was unbearable. Goulla wiped the sweat off his forehead with a handkerchief before putting it over his nose. Lamrani, who lived in constant admiration of his boss, followed Goulla's example.

Goulla studied the victims' positions, noted the bullet wound at the back of Callaghan's head and the numerous needle marks on the Moroccan's arms. He wondered why Callaghan was lying shirtless inside the half-opened body bag, and then he tried to comprehend why he was lying in a body bag while the other victim wasn't. Goulla also tried to fathom the unlikely relationship between a Moroccan drug addict and a foreigner who showed no signs of drug abuse.

Next to the bodies lay the jacket, from which the local police had extracted the crucial evidence to identify the Englishman. The documents had been found in its breast pocket. Goulla studied the jacket more closely. It was a woollen garment, hardly suited for the desert. Inside it, a tag announced it in small letters as being "made by Tailor Brent Scofield, London, for The Honourable Matthias Callaghan". *This, of course, confirms the papers earlier found in it,* Goulla deduced.

He walked twenty steps away from the tent containing the victims. He looked around, curious about why two, completely disparate, persons had been found dead together in the Sahara near the Algerian border. *Perhaps that's the clue,* Goulla thought. *They were dumped here after being killed in Algeria. Then again, how did this Matthias Callaghan get here upon his release in London in less than two days? Well, the forensic evidence will tell us more.*

He looked around. Facing north, on his left he could see the sand dunes of the Sahara. In the other three directions, there was nothing but flat, barren land: no buildings, no animals, no people. *How did the bodies get here? Why choose this place to get rid of them? Why were they killed in the first place?*

Goulla returned to the crime scene. Lamrani confirmed that the bodies had been fingerprinted and photographed. There was not much else they could do. Goulla announced that the crime scene should be closed and the bodies immediately transported to Marrakech for autopsy. He and Lamrani then left for the jeep that had taken them there.

In the car, Goulla wondered out loud why on earth anyone would leave two bodies half-covered by sand at the edge of the Great Desert. No berber would do it, for sure. Any reasoning person would have the dead men dragged into the desert, buried them with some care in a sand dune, and no one would have been any the wiser for a thousand years or more.

"In conclusion", he lectured Lamrani, "someone not berber, someone not familiar with the desert, someone who tries to hide two bodies in this amateurish way, is the guilty party here. I can only imagine a foreigner. I want you to check whatever activity there was in the region last week, Lamrani. If necessary – just tell me – I could perhaps get a high-resolution satellite view of the moment this took place. My advice to you is, as always: don't delay and do give me results."

"Yes, sir", Lamrani replied with his usual submissive attitude to avoid triggering his boss's temper.

*

Just before dawn broke, those of us crammed into the building were awakened by the calls from a distant *muezzin*. After two dreadful nights and the day in between locked up in the abandoned, dirty warehouse in Tripoli, we were a little later given orders barked in Arabic that we had to step outside. No breakfast was offered; instead, the pots and pans were rattled to get our attention. In all, we were probably a little over 400 persons waiting to get on board the ship, including a lot of women and children. We were herded onto the lorries, this time without anyone bothering to lower the tarpaulin overhead to prevent the authorities from observing us. There was only standing room for us since the crowd had swelled significantly. Less than an hour later, we reached the port and were yelled at to quickly get off the trucks. Next to one of the piers, a mid-sized ship was moored. A dozen people, well armed, started shouting at us to get off the lorries and walk towards the ship.

Moammar, the man I had given one of my cufflinks, came ambling through the crowd in obvious search for someone. It turned out that I was the one he was looking for. Despite Omar's homemade recipe to alleviate my problems with the sun, he grinned like a spider detecting a defenceless fly when he finally recognised me.

"*Quoi?*" he shouted to me in French, laughing. "Are you trying to pass off as an African going back to where you came from? I can't believe this. Now the world is going crazy."

I didn't offer him any explanations. He laughed again.

"Anyway", he said, turning serious when I didn't respond to his taunt, "I only agreed to bring you this far for what you paid me. From here on, you have to deal with the captain of the ship."

He pointed at the fishing vessel moored at the pier. It didn't have the look of being very secure travelling the high seas, with its peeling paint and rusted hull crying out for maintenance. I could only imagine the state of the ship that wasn't visible. Its appearance was such that no one concerned about safe voyage would climb on board.

"And all the others ...?" I asked in French while making

a sweeping gesture on the people who were now boarding it.

"They paid the full fee before they left Mauritania. You didn't. My best advice is that you talk to the captain. His name is Ahmed. I will take you to him."

A few minutes later, a short, wiry man in his early forties arrived. Haroun left without another word. I felt Ahmed's stare as he studied me, presumably to decide how much money he could possibly extract from his bonus passenger. From my appearance, I don't think he had high hopes. On the other hand, if I didn't pay him something, he would leave me behind in Libya.

"Moammar told me you want passage to Italy", Ahmed finally said, giving me a hard look. "There is no room for more passengers. You have to wait until next trip."

Meaning the bargaining over what price I should pay had begun. I sighed inwardly.

"What is your usual price for taking people across?" I asked him looking at the vessel docked at the pier behind him. "I imagine your ship will have room for another passenger".

"Three thousand euros", he said, attempting to cover his lie with a crooked smile.

"In that case, I wonder why Moammar told me you charge five hundred", I replied. "Is five hundred euros what you will charge me for an upcoming trip?"

"I've never charged less than fifteen hundred", Ahmed retorted heatedly. "I have no idea why Moammar told you such nonsense."

He looked at me suspiciously.

"Or maybe you're just making this up. Anyway, there's no room for more passengers."

"Even if I were to pay you five thousand euros in gold and precious stones? For that kind of money, you can eject one or two other passengers, although somehow I find it highly unlikely that you will. You'll just cram one more passenger on board."

My offer got him interested.

"Show me."

I bent down and recovered the remaining cufflink from my sock. I held it out to him, he accepted it and brought it close to his right eye. He peered at the cuff link, and, surprisingly, seemed to be quite knowledgeable about the stones. He kept ticking off the names and, one by one, his rough value estimate. It was no surprise that his estimates were ridiculously low. He was, after all, the one on the buyer's end.

"So, if I give this piece of jewellery, can you take me to Italy?"

His hesitation was more for show than out of conviction.

"All right, I'll give you passage."

Finally, some words of relief.

As luck had it, after having negotiated my passage with Ahmed, I was allowed on board the ship as one of its first passengers. This allowed me to grab one of the life vests that hung from the railings. Calling it a "ship" may sound as if it were an impressive, seaworthy vessel. Once I climbed aboard, it rapidly made me feel as helpless as if I were back in the desert. As far as I could tell, the crew consisted of five persons, including the captain. After the vessel had received its last passenger, on and below ship deck we easily numbered more than four hundred people. The ship was a rusted relic that looked as if had been rescued from some deep spot in the sea that we were now about to sail across. I imagined that most of those who had boarded didn't have a notion of what they were getting into. They had probably never seen the sea before, because they were people who had tended cattle in the heartland of Africa before some local war had obliged them to search for a better life in Europe.

It was afternoon when Ahmed steered his ship out of Tripoli's port. To everyone's relief, the heat had died down a bit because the sun was hidden behind clouds. The sea was calm, and everyone wore a smile on their faces because they were leaving their poverty in Africa behind, and in a question of hours we were all going to disembark on the continent of abundance.

Sitting across the deck from me, Omar smiled encouragingly, even triumphantly. Although I didn't feel the same optimism, I didn't let it on when I returned his smile in the same vein. A good man. I felt grateful.

It began to rain, gently at first, then relentlessly. Everyone felt miserable going through his or her personal hell to make it to the continent. Then, about three hours after leaving shore, the wind began to pick up.

Saturday May 2, 2015

I never imagined the Mediterranean could have such rough waters. Men and women alike were throwing up over the railing. Every wave that violently washed across the deck confirmed my presentiment that the vessel lacked the capacity to carry so many passengers, and especially so in extreme weather conditions.

By now, after twenty hours at sea going northwards in the never-ceasing rain, I estimated that we couldn't be far from either Sicily or Malta. It was of course impossible to judge the distance we had travelled without the right instruments, and I desperately hoped that the captain knew what he was doing.

Unfortunately, he didn't seem to, because the next huge wave hit us from the side. The vessel lurched violently, with seawater flooding the deck. A woman's shout pierced the high pitch of the wind. She tried to reach the railing, but other passengers held her back by force. Straining my neck, I could see an orange object being engulfed by the waters. For an instant, the brown face of a child could be seen inside the orange garment, screaming in silent fear as it was turned towards the raging sea. Seconds later, there were only the heaving black waters to be seen.

*

Through one of the lawyers at the firm Ludmila Jordan had hired for the sale of her deceased husband's yacht, she finally received a message about an interested customer. Sitting in her twelve-room flat in Paris's 8th arrondissement, recently decorated by the latest interior designer in fashion (*"all gold, green and Marie Antoinette accessories – before her decapitation, naturally"*, was the designer's attempt to sum up his effort), she called her broker.

"I understand that someone is interested in my boat?"

"Hardly a *boat*, madame. In my view, it's rather an eye-catching and exemplary vessel for the high seas."

"A description that gives me a considerable sense of euphoria that I'm not sailing, but selling. Now, what about this interested party ... how should this sale be executed?"

"Please let me remind you, madame, that few people in the world have the necessary liquidity to pay for a two-hundred-and-fifty-million-dollar yacht. I think it's important that you personally preside at the meeting with our potential customer. Should he show any last-minute hesitation about the sale, I'm certain that your personal charm will clinch the deal."

Ludmila let out a sigh and then put down the receiver. Still, she couldn't help feeling flattered by his words.

*

Deep down, Ahmed knew that the ship he had bought with the help of Ghalib Mahfouz's money wasn't in the best of shape if it were to face a storm of the magnitude that the Italian coastguard had announced a few hours earlier. But, as always, it was the profit that mattered. He had been inoculated with the concept by his former boss on countless occasions before his boss's unexpected death six years earlier. A keen disciple of Abdul Mahfouz's teachings, Ahmed had looked for ways to maximise his profit. He had hired people to rip out everything on the ship, originally constructed for fishing, to make more space available.

Ahmed had crossed the Mediterranean Sea in varying ways on many previous occasions, but this journey was distinctly different. On the two previous occasions he had made the run across from Libya to Italy, the weather had been fine. And going from Tangier in a speedboat to Málaga was child's play compared to the menacing waves he now saw wash across the deck.

A giant wave came crashing down on the top deck, where the people in the overcrowded ship sat huddled bracing themselves against the stormy sea. *Why am I doing this for a mere fifty per cent?* Ahmed thought, feeling miserable as the craft veered sideways into the trough between two waves. *I'm the one risking my life, while Ghalib is relaxing in her comfortable home counting the money I'm making for her.*

He decided he would have a talk with her when he got back to Marrakech. *If I get out of this alive, that is.*

Sunday May 3, 2015
So far, the voyage across the Mediterranean had been merely dreadful. Now the weather was worsening by the minute.

I was sitting on the deck in the life vest that I had put on the moment I had set foot on the dilapidated ship. Presumably, most of my fellow passengers had never seen a storm at sea before and had no idea of the force of rough waters. Moreover, I doubted they knew about the use or the function of a life vest. It was just as well at this point, since I had detected less than two dozen of them on board. Everyone on deck, including me, was clinging to whatever could be found as the ship kept rolling with the waves, and I couldn't even imagine the nightmare the migrants who had been assigned space below deck lived through.

*

According to the sea chart, Ahmed estimated, they were now close to the coast of Sicily. Their destination was the Italian mainland, which he hoped to reach by morning. It was pitch black and no lights from land could be seen through the squalls of driving rain.

Ahmed cursed himself for not having studied the weather forecast more closely. He had now been awake for forty-eight hours and was dead tired. Although his crew had taken turns at the wheel, he didn't trust any of them with reading the charts.

The passengers on deck were constantly soaked by the cold sea water. He could see that some migrants had tied themselves to the hull. From the hold, the ingrained stench of fish mixed with vomit and fear came wafting. The small ship had previously been used for fishing with a small crew, and Ahmed hadn't bothered with the purchase of additional life vests. He had requested money from Ghalib to cover the expense, but after she had given it to him, he had decided that it made more sense to make it line his own pockets.

Suddenly, there were desperate shouts coming as a particularly vicious, giant wave washed over the ship and made it career violently. The ship leaned over, dangerously close to foundering.

*

Shouts of distress could be heard over the squalls. Three, or perhaps four, people fell overboard and were swallowed by the sea. Then, when the ship violently righted itself, I saw how the rope that Omar had tied around his waist snapped. With arms flailing, he flew through the air screaming. The last I saw of him was his frightened face as he realised that he had no way of climbing aboard again. Seconds later, the only one I had befriended since waking up in the desert was swallowed by the violent sea.

Another hour or so passed. The stormy weather began to calm down somewhat, but the fluttering fear in the hearts of those of us on board weren't. Then, abruptly, several strong search lights were trained onto our ship. They later turned out to belong to the Italian coastguard that had come to the rescue of our leaky fishing boat with the remaining 400 or so illegal immigrants that still remained on board.

*

Ludmila Jordan was waiting in the presidential suite at the Georges V Hotel in Paris together with two of the lawyers from the firm that she had hired to supervise the legal aspects of the sale of her yacht. She was dressed in an electric green dress made exclusively for her by her favourite Italian designer. Around her neck hung an emerald necklace that her late husband had paid 800,000 dollars for. The decision over what shoes to wear had been her morning headache. She had finally decided upon a pair with green and gold leather strips interlaced that she never previously had put on and couldn't remember having bought.

The phone rang, and one of her lawyers picked it up. The party they were waiting for had arrived. He gave his consent to let them access the suite.

A couple of minutes later, there was a knock on the door. After being allowed inside, Ludmila studied the five men who had entered the suite. Two of them had been made in the same mould as her own legal counsel; there was no mistake to be made about them. The remaining three men made her confused as to who the man was who had expressed interest in buying her yacht. One was taller than anyone else present, dressed in a black suit and sporting a demure grimace that she perceived would possibly be a sign that he wanted to drastically negotiate the final price, which she had set her mind not to do. Next to him was a slightly overweight man with a gold-capped tooth that showed because he smiled at her as if she were his oldest friend – another obvious trick, no doubt, in Ludmila's mind. The third man who had entered was smaller than the rest. He looked somewhat apologetic for his presence. Ludmila immediately dismissed him as inconsequential.

Introductions followed and they all sat down on the comfortable sofas. Ludmila offered them to feel free to serve themselves anything of their choice from the bar behind her, after excusing herself for not having a butler present due to the sensitive topic about to be discussed. The man with the gold-capped tooth got up to serve himself a glass of chilled vodka and a large cup of tea, the latter handed to the diminutive man Ludmila had previously discarded as irrelevant.

"We are here to discuss practical and financial matters regarding the transfer of a premium yacht that Mrs Jordan here has decided to sell after her husband's recent, unfortunate decease."

"It's very simple, really", the diminutive man in the sofa across replied in a soft voice. "We are willing to pay one hundred and fifty million dollars against access not later than by this weekend. Besides, there should be no public announcement of the sale. Are those conditions something you can agree to?"

Ludmila's attorney shot a glance her way, without responding. Ludmila inhaled the smoke of her cigarette while she deliberated. *He is the buyer, the small guy is the boss. He had me fooled. Now he wants to take the price down 100 million dollars –*

I can't accept that!

She took another drag on her cigarette while she kept studying the smaller man on the other side.

"Why on earth should I agree to these absurd conditions that –"

"So sorry to interrupt you, Madame Jordan", Vasily rudely cut her short, "but the price you have listed isn't the market price. Perhaps you can appreciate that for an amount as large as the one you're quoting, any serious buyer would surely make a market study. At least we have, and I'm sorry to say that the comparison hasn't turned out in your favour, madame."

With this he pushed a large envelope across the table.

"Please have a look at the information I have gathered. You will see that, in the best of circumstances, your yacht would fetch one hundred and eighty million dollars. I'm offering you thirty million less, but that is because my offer comes with a great incentive."

Ludmila puffed on her cigarette without replying, reaching for the envelope or taking her eyes off him.

"The one hundred and fifty million we are willing to pay you come free of taxes", Vasily finally added, "anywhere and anyhow you want the money. Would that be satisfactory for you?"

After four more hours of negotiation, they finally settled on the final price of 165 million dollars. The buyer was an offshore company Vasily had previously registered in Panama, which would buy the shares in the company Harry Jordan had created as the owner of the yacht. The official purchase sum would be 20 million dollars, and the remainder would be transferred to a shell company in the same country that in its entirety was owned by his widow.

For Vasily, the advantage of buying the company shares instead of a direct ownership of the yacht was that the yacht would remain registered to Harry Jordan's Panamanian company. Thus, its true owner was guaranteed to remain anonymous, should anyone too inquisitive decide to investigate the true ownership.

What Vasily didn't know, in spite of his in-depth research before purchasing the yacht, was that Harry Jordan had bought it with money stolen from the New York mob.

*

"The fishing boat was taking in water", the Italian interior minister stated as he gave a televised press conference, "when it was spotted about twenty-one nautical miles east of Sicily. We are still not certain how many victims drowned during the passage, but so far the rescuers have pulled ten out of the sea. The commander of the naval vessel involved in the rescue also encountered a dozen dead bodies in the hold floating in water, fuel and human waste. Three hundred and seventy people have been rescued, including thirty women and six children, and they have been taken to the Sant'Anna Cara migrant centre at Isola di Capo Rizzuto."

*

Ludmila felt pleased with herself. She had personally never negotiated anything in her life before selling the yacht on which her late husband had preferred to spend his last years.

Now she was truly free to do anything after her husband's death. Fortunately, Harry had never known about her occasional lovers, and now, barely 42, she had the money to do anything she put her mind to. What a thrilling idea.

Harry had lived his last years on board the yacht of his that she had just sold. During those twelve years, he had rarely left the yacht except to go to the casino. It had always been she who had travelled to Monaco when they needed to have a discussion about money. Yes, she had been impressed by its size the first time she had been invited to board it. Since then, she had learnt to hate the yacht. She couldn't stand to be on anything that floated. Ludmila even disliked the thought of swimming in a pool.

Well, she thought, pleased with herself, *now that little problem has been taken care of.*

*

After everyone on board the fishing boat had been safely transferred to the large naval vessel, we sailed at a steady speed through the choppy waters with Ahmed's ship in tow. The officers began asking questions. One of them spoke French, and he wanted the people to point out those responsible for the trafficking. More than a few were willing to do so and started signalling the ship's crew. It didn't take long before Ahmed and his crew were handcuffed and placed under arrest.

A few hours later, we were motioned to disembark. Armed, uniformed men waited on the quay and led us to waiting buses. When we arrived at a centre surrounded by a high green fence, we were met by more immigrants who lived in shipping containers with clotheslines hanging in between. We were a sorry lot, still wet, coughing and very few with any possessions to speak of after having lost them to the sea.

The centre had several barracks with beds lined up. Empathetic nurses in neat white uniforms welcomed us and indicated that we could choose from dry clothing stacked on tables lined up along a wall. We were also handed necessities like soap, shampoo and toothpaste along with a towel. A long queue formed to enter the shower stalls. I chose to be the last one.

The hot water felt delicious after one week of absence. I carefully scrubbed off the tarred diesel that Omar had used to dye my skin. It took me a good half hour before most of it had come off. In the mirror I saw my face, which appeared to me to have aged years since I had been abducted in London. There were bags under my eyes, and the skin sagging over my cheekbones hurt when I touched it. My hands felt even worse. I was very tired and felt an urgency to catch up on my sleep, but if my sketchy plan to get out of the camp was to work, I needed to act right away.

I had entered the facility as a dark-skinned individual in the middle of a crowd of lookalikes. After I had cleaned up, I knew I looked more Italian than any African immigrant. As I emerged from the showers, dressed in second-hand baggy white pants and a white threadbare shirt that I had grabbed off one of the tables, there were several activities going on in the barracks. Uniformed officials were sitting behind tables where they were taking names and statements with the help of interpreters. Doctors and nurses kept making medical exams. I walked steadily but not too quickly across the room towards the exit door. The officials were busy typing information on their laptops and didn't react to my presence. Or perhaps they didn't feel it was an issue, because as soon as I walked outside, I discovered that it was impossible to get beyond the guarded entrance and the fence surrounding the centre's perimeter.

No one shouted or came running after me. Judging by the sun's position, it would soon be noon. The heat could be felt under the cloudless sky. I walked up close to the gate where we had come through on the buses and waited behind a tree.

Next to the entrance was a gatehouse, and I counted at least six guards inside. The immigrants held at the centre were apparently allowed to move around the compound without restrictions. Several men and women strolled by as I waited. Some of my fellow passengers began exiting the barracks accompanied by officials who took them to another building that apparently was the canteen.

I sat in the shade of the tree and studied the movements around me. Three hours passed and I began to despair. I still hadn't come up with some way to get past the guards at the entrance. A couple of cars went through, the drivers' papers were checked and the number plates noted. I studied the green fence, about three meters high, and wondered if I would be able to climb it with my aching fingers. To try it, it would be necessary to wait until after nightfall before I did. Perhaps guards with dogs patrolled outside? I would have to find out.

The most obvious option available to me was out of the question. I could go to the officials and tell my story about how I had ended up on the leaking ship. But how could they believe me? Kidnapped in London and dropped in the Sahara Desert next to two corpses? Smuggled by traffickers to Tripoli and on board a ship, paid for by a pair of cufflinks? If I told them, they would check my record with Interpol, and they would see that I had been arrested for murder and extradited to the UK by the Italian police. They would also discover that the British police had a warrant out for me because I had jumped bail. I would be arrested before getting extradited again, which at best would take a week or two, after the paper work had been done with. I urgently needed to either get in touch with Dr Sternmacher or Samantha to get my medication, and for this I needed a phone. How much longer could my body fight the rejection of my transplants? Certainly not another week?

A group of doctors and nurses came strolling out of one of the barracks carrying their bags and instruments, heading for the gate. Their white uniforms looked clean and bright in the sunlight. This would be the opportunity I had hoped for. There were ten of them walking together, chatting. As the medics passed the tree where I was waiting, I stepped out from the shade and joined the group as a straggler.

When we came to the gate, I walked closer to them, hoping that my white clothes looked sufficiently like those the medics wore. Two guards stepped out from the gatehouse and nodded, smiling as they unlocked the door leading out to the street.

I was the last one to pass while the guards kept talking animatedly about some sports event judging by a word or two that I understood. They didn't glance in my direction. I followed the medics a little further and then crossed the street. My ruse had worked.

Half an hour later, I was walking on the main road with the village behind me. A lorry driver picked me up when I held out my thumb. He chatted incessantly in his impenetrable local accent about things I didn't understand, but he seemed happy enough to hear me grunt every now and then. A nice man who, when he stopped for a break, shared his homemade bread, cheese and sausages with me. I was starving and couldn't thank him enough.

I was in luck, because he was going all the way to Naples. Some five hours later, I expressed my gratitude with a repeated *grazie* and was let off near the port. My next stop would be Rome, and what better way to get there than by train? I walked through the city, tired, until I no longer could resist lying down in the grass behind a bench in a park.

The night air was warm. The stars twinkled above as I made myself comfortable. I shut my eyes and immediately went asleep.

Monday May 4, 2015

When I woke up in the park, the sun had been up for several hours. Traffic buzzed on nearby streets with an occasional horn honking. My limbs stiff, I got up and stretched.

I left the park, and when I met an elderly lady walking her dog, I asked her for the *stazione ferroviaria*. Although I didn't understand much of her animated explanation, I thanked her and continued in the direction she had pointed.

By asking people for directions, I eventually arrived at the railway station. There were passenger trains to Rome, of course, but to get on the platform I would have to pass through a metal detector after showing my ticket and an ID card.

How could I possibly get on the train without these requisites? By now, my stomach kept shouting to be serviced. There were other shouts, too, outside the railway station, from a large crowd with flags and assorted placards. A strike against the railway company, no less. The various entrances to the station were blocked by angry-looking people. A red-faced, heavyset man with bushy eyebrows shouted slogans through a megaphone, demanding higher pay for the workers. He seemed very much to be a union representative. All passengers were barred access to the trains, which in turn made people mad at the picket. The tumult threatened to become violent.

I obviously had to find some alternative transportation to get to Rome. Stealthily getting onboard a train in Naples was definitely out of the question. I racked my mind for options, but with no money and no phone – what could I do?

The only option I could think of was to once again start walking, heading north and hoping that Lady Luck once more would be on my side.

Tuesday May 5, 2015

When Detective Inspector Blackmoore entered his office a couple of minutes before nine, he immediately noticed that a new folder had been placed on top of the others. It had a Foreign Office seal stamped on it, which meant it contained a report related to something that had happened overseas.

He read the report as he sipped his morning coffee. It concerned two bodies found without any identifying documents in a Moroccan desert. However, in the breast pocket of a jacket lying on the ground next to them, receipts made out by HM Prison Wormwood Scrubs had been found. They had been issued to Matthias Callaghan on April 27, 2017. Blackmoore was informed of the situation in his capacity as the officer in charge of the investigation into the murder Callaghan was being accused of, and the bail Callaghan had skipped.

Blackmoore realised he needed to send someone to Morocco to meet with his counterpart in charge of the murder investigation, Mustafa Goulla, who was headquartered in Marrakech. Marrakech was also where the bodies had been taken for autopsy. It occurred to Blackmoore that George Jones might be just the ticket before he was due to leave the force in three weeks' time. He asked his secretary to send for Jones.

Ten minutes later, Georgie entered Blackmoore's ample office with its nice city view, something that had been denied himself during his years with the Metropolitan Police. He was curious about why he had been summoned. Blackmoore tended to be very distant with him, and rare was the occasion that he personally assigned Georgie any special work.

"Take a seat, Jones, this will take a while to explain", Blackmoore began. Georgie obeyed. "I received a report this morning that implies, although it doesn't ascertain, that our fugitive Matthias Callaghan has been found."

Georgie's interest was immediately peaked.

"Where was he hiding, sir?"

"Not hiding as much as being dead."

"Dead, sir?"

"Yes, and in the strangest of places – the Sahara Desert."

"The Sahara Desert?" Georgie looked at him non-plussed. "How in the world could he have travelled out of the country without a passport? And, on top of that, wind up dead in a desert?"

"That's what I need you to find out, Jones. I want you to get on a flight to Marrakech, where you will meet with the local chief of police. He will take you to the morgue. Besides the body that we're assuming is Callaghan's, there was one more found at the same time and site. Make sure to identify both and try to determine how they ended up in the desert. Should either, or both, be a British citizen, I need you to file the proper paperwork at our embassy there to get their bodies repatriated. When confirmed that a British subject is among the victims, you must also find out what you can about the events leading up to the death in question."

"That's certainly a handful, sir", Georgie said, his mind churning over the possibilities that now opened up to him. *Maybe I can make this surprising development work to my advantage?* "I will certainly make my utmost effort to not disappoint your expectations."

"Jenny is booking the necessary travel arrangements", Blackmoore continued, distractedly, as if he hadn't heard him. "I've also made you a copy of the Foreign Office's briefing. Anything else on Callaghan, you either already know or can dig up on the computer, of course. I expect you back in less than a week, with a report on my desk as soon as you land. Good luck."

Georgie knew from past encounters that this was how Blackmoore dismissed his subordinates when he had nothing more to add. He took his cue and left the office after collecting his copy of the file.

*

I woke up in another park at first light. It seemed to me that I had walked in endless circles the day before, because I was still surrounded by Naples' high-rise buildings.

After walking for two hours unsuccessfully holding out my thumb at passing cars, I arrived at a petrol station on the outskirts of Naples. The day was heating up and I was thirsty. I entered the restroom and drank from the faucet. In the shop next door I looked at a roadmap of Italy to gauge the distance to Rome, should it be necessary for me to walk all the way. The distance indicated was 220 kilometres which meant, unless I was lucky enough to catch a ride with someone, that it would take me four days to get there on foot. I doubted that my face and the cravings of my stomach would be able to last me that long.

There was a queue of four people in front of the cash register waiting to pay for their purchases. Outside I saw an elderly little lady with bluish hair finishing filling the tank of a Fiat with a colour that almost perfectly matched her hair. I held up the door for her as she stepped inside to pay. I walked over to her car and cast a glance inside. She had left the keys in the ignition. I got into the car and turned on the engine. Nobody shouted or came running after me as I left the station driving at a moderate speed.

*

Georgie spent two hours going over the briefing that Blackmoore had shared with him, checking some background details on the computer and thinking through his options. Then he picked up the flight tickets – economy class, to Georgie's dismay – and the details of his hotel booking by calling on Jenny, the department's head of the secretary pool. His flight to Marrakech was scheduled for the afternoon the following day. Efficient as always, Jenny had already confirmed Georgie's impending arrival to the local Moroccan police.

Instead of going home after lunch to pack, Georgie hailed a cab to go to the Savoy on the Strand. He asked for Samantha Callaghan at the reception. She was having afternoon tea in the Thames Foyer, he was informed by a courteous but very aloof desk clerk. *Why is it that these poorly paid employees at fancy hotels and restaurants always put on airs once they dress up in a uniform?* Georgie wondered to himself as he strode into the Thames Foyer.

Samantha was sitting by herself at a table ladened with the paraphernalia of the afternoon tea that the Savoy prided themselves to be the masters of. At 52 quid per person, Georgie considered the pot of tea with a few biscuits outrageously expensive, no matter how much he of late could afford it. He stopped near her table as she looked up.

"Missis Callaghan, I'm sorry to bother you in this inappropriate way", he said using a sombre tone. "I'm Detective Sergeant George Jones with the Metropolitan Police here in London. We met at New Scotland Yard a few days ago."

He showed her his identification. Samantha rapidly

studied it and then his face, before offering Georgie a sad smile.

"Please have a seat, Sergeant. Don't think for a minute I have forgotten our previous meeting."

Georgie accepted her invitation and sat down opposite her. In this new, more luxurious setting, he found the woman more ravishing than during their first encounter. A waiter appeared and wanted to know if he would take the complete afternoon service. He declined the offer.

"I'm sorry to be the messenger of some disturbing news", Georgie went on when the waiter was out of earshot. "I'm here because today Scotland Yard received news of your husband's fate."

He told her what he had learnt through Blackmoore, and that he had now been put in charge of the investigation of her husband's disappearance, which was an unabashed lie. During his explanation, Georgie couldn't help admiring her frank open look, her hair, her appearance; in short, her presence. He felt quite taken with the beautiful woman sitting in front of him.

"I'm flying to Morocco tomorrow for further investigation", he said at the end of his rehearsed discourse. "I was asking myself whether it wouldn't be best if you should accompany me – however difficult the result may turn out to be – just to make sure it's really your husband who was discovered in the desert?"

Tears welled in Samantha's eyes, and Georgie found her more attractive than ever. *I must play my cards right on this one,* he thought, *she's a prize worth waiting for.*

"Of course I must go with you", she croaked and waved to a waiter that she wanted the bill. "Will you accompany me to the front desk to get the flight ticket right?"

"Certainly."

After she had signed the bill to her room, they walked to the front desk, where they were told to consult the in-house travel agency. At the agency, Georgie explained to the young girl the details of the flight that had been reserved for him, and to his disappointment Samantha asked her to book a business class seat. He had wanted the opportunity to get her to know him better on the near four-hour trip. Still, he restrained himself from changing the economy-class ticket paid for by the Yard, because if his expenditure was checked later, it could make someone suspicious about why he had purchased an upgrade paid for by his own restricted salary. *The hotel in Marrakech is a different issue, though,* he thought. *Surely Samantha will wrinkle her nose at the one the Yard has chosen for me because of its tight money policies in place. But I can check in at the same one that she chooses while I keep the one booked by Jenny. No one will know.*

The return flight was for Sunday May 10. There was no British Airways flight from Marrakech to London on Fridays or Saturdays, and Georgie argued that she anyway would need the extra time to arrange for practical matters. Samantha was too distraught to give the issue her full attention. *It will give me three full days to take care of the paperwork at the embassy for the return of the bodies and console the bereaved widow,* Georgie thought contentedly. He asked her to be ready at 11 a.m. the next morning, when he would pick her up at the Savoy. Their British Airways flight to Morocco was scheduled for 3:05 p.m.

*

I quickly decided that I better get off the autostrada, where I assumed that there was a higher likelihood that the police would be on the lookout for the stolen vehicle, and take the smaller roads. Besides, I didn't have any money to pay for the tolls. At the first available exit, I turned off the autostrada at a place called Mugnano. I continued north for twenty minutes and arrived at a town named Capua, according to a road sign.

Here, I stopped at the parking lot outside a supermarket and rummaged through the glove compartment. I was in luck. Inside I found a torn map among some trash and the car's documents. The map indicated that the Mediterranean wasn't too far away, and a good option would be to follow the coast north. I turned west on a minor, tree-lined road, and thirty minutes later I could see the sea.

I glanced at the petrol gauge, and to my surprise it showed less than half full. The blue-haired lady hadn't bought a full tank. I wondered how far the petrol would take me, and how much time I had before I had to get rid of the car. After stealing it, surely some five minutes, or perhaps ten, must have gone by before its owner had managed to call the police and report the theft. She would probably have to go to a police station and report all the details, but I couldn't be sure whether patrolling police hadn't been advised of the colour, make and registration number of the stolen vehicle.

From Capua, I headed west until I reached Mondragone on the coast and continued north. With the windows down, the breeze from the sea felt like a blessing in the sweltering heat. I zipped through Gaeta and later entered a small town announced as Borgo Vodice. There the car suddenly died; it had run out of petrol. The clock on the dashboard showed 13:43.

What can I do? I wondered and sighed. *Nothing, except start walking again.*

With a rag smeared with oil that I found under the spare wheel, I made sure I wiped off the fingerprints I had left in the car. I then pushed it to one side into a parking space, rolled up the windows, wiped it clean of prints again, threw the keys under the front seat and left with the map tucked into my trouser pocket. I also kept a cheap BIC pen that I had used to copy down the owner's name and address from her insurance policy. It was only fair to the blue-haired lady to let her know where she could recover her stolen car.

Not quite like the Sahara, although I felt the Italian sunshine come in a close second. The sun was beating down, and after an hour I knew I wouldn't be able to continue before it became evening. On the lawn of a house someone had left a hose, and, after making sure that no one was watching me, I followed the hose around the corner, unscrewed it from the faucet and drank as much water as I could.

Later, I came to a glen next to the road and decided to

rest there in the shade until it became dark. I soon fell asleep, hungrier than I'd ever been before. I hadn't eaten since the lorry driver had shared his meal with me two days earlier.

I woke up a couple of hours later. The improvised siesta had restored some of my energy. Since the heat of the day had gone down considerably, I trudged on along the road for another two hours. It became dark. The headlights of occasional cars lit up the countryside, but I no longer bothered to put my thumb up. Nobody wanted to risk picking up a solitary man in his forties dressed in once white, now soiled clothes, and I could understand them. I wouldn't have picked me up.

For two more hours I walked north, consulting the map every time I came to a new village along the road. Finally, I realised I just couldn't continue any longer. It had been a long day, to say the least. I needed to sleep.

I found a ditch near a farm where I reaped sufficient long grass to make myself an improvised pillow. Exhausted I fell asleep covered by the starlight blinking from a cloud-free night sky.

Wednesday May 6, 2015

Bird twitter woke me up at dawn. The air felt fresh and carried the smell of dew and growing plants. I felt restored, in spite of my growling stomach.

I began walking again, towards a town the map claimed carried the name Latina. As on the day before, I walked through villages every so often. Crossing one of them, there was an irresistible, delicious smell of newly baked bread. I studied the bakery from the other side of the street, unable to move unless I could set my teeth into a piece of the bread they offered. Outside the bakery, there was a cart from where a young lady sold the bread to passers-by. At one point she went inside the bakery, when there were no customers in sight, presumably to fetch more bread. I ran across the street, looking right and left. No cars, no people nearby. I grabbed the largest loaf I could find, stuffed it inside my shirt and quickly walked away. The same moment, the woman came out with a new batch. Apparently she didn't notice my theft – the second that week, to my disgrace – since she didn't call out.

As soon as I was alone beyond the village limits, I sat down on a tree trunk and devoured the bread, the most fabulous I've ever tasted. I saved a third for later, just in case.

Reinvigorated, I continued towards Latina. When I felt tired, I slept beneath the stars again until the daylight woke me up. I finished the last of my bread before I started walking northwards again.

A few hours later, I reached Latina. It was 8:45 according to the station clock on the large brick station building. I entered. Inside, a lot of people were moving about: buying tickets, standing in throngs on the platform, incessantly chatting. A digital board showed that there was a train leaving for Rome every fifteen minutes or so, and that the next one was scheduled for 9:12.

The train arrived and stopped at the platform. I got on and immediately went to one of the lavatories located more or less at the middle of the train. I anticipated that I would have to move from it at some point, and I didn't want to be cornered if the conductor walked down the train from either the left or the right side. There could of course be several conductors on board, but what could they do with a tramp like me, with no ID card and no money? Throw me off the train? Hand me over to the police?

The train started moving. I began thinking what my next move should be, once I got to Rome. It occurred to me that I should look up Andrew, who years ago had been my butler. I did my best to recall where he had set up the restaurant. I remembered he had done so with the woman he had married some five years after I had sent him to Italy when things had got tangled up while travelling in the USA. What was her name, again ... yes, I remembered – Sofia! After some initial flurry of contact over the Internet, I had gradually lost contact with Andrew. He had told me he was very pleased with the new life he had found with his wife, and he had also expressed his gratitude to my generous attitude towards him. Whether true or not really didn't matter any longer. I needed to get cleaned up, I needed money, I needed a phone and I needed to get back to London. I didn't doubt Andrew would help me, if I could only locate him. He had the essence of a noble soul, something that had become clear to me on more than one occasion in the past. The problem was: where could I find him? Rome is a large city, and a trattoria with homemade meals can be found on every corner. However, I distinctly remembered that Andrew had mentioned a place somewhere in or near the historic centre, where Sofia had taken over a place her parents had previously run. What was the name they had given the place? It had something to do with a flower.

Someone tried the handle to the door, and when I didn't respond, angrily pummelled the door. I flushed the toilet and opened the door. A large madonna whose face looked as flushed as the facility I had deceptively let her know I'd just used, snorted before she entered the cubicle. I looked both ways. On my right-hand side, a conductor was working his way towards me, checking tickets and passes on his way. I immediately took a left turn. Three wagons down, I found a new lavatory that no one was occupying.

I could see how the countryside outside the dirty train window rapidly got replaced by city dwellings. The poorer constructions were exchanged for middle-class housing suburbs, then high-rise buildings coming into sight as the train began to slow down.

The moment came when I had to leave the cubicle and somehow get past the conductor. I exited, and almost immediately ran into the one man I wanted to avoid.

"Show me your ticket, please", he said in Italian.

"Right away", I told him in English. "I have it in the bag that I left on my seat."

Perhaps he believed me because I didn't carry any luggage. I rudely passed him and quickly made my way through not only that carriage but another three. I found an unoccupied lavatory where I hid, this time without locking the door in the hope I could fool the conductor in case he came looking for me. Ten minutes later, the train slowed down as it pulled into Rome's central station, Stazione Termini.

Immediately after the train had come to a stop, I opened the door and looked both ways. In the passenger wagons up ahead, the travellers were pouring out, struggling with their luggage. A huge clock indicated the time to be 9:51. Hungry, hurting, in need of a three-hour bath, anxious about my missing ciclosporin pills and having a general feeling of desperation about myself and my situation, I lumbered along the platform.

On the train, I had jotted down names and suggestions to my best recall of what Andrew had mentioned to me in the past. Now, inside the train station, I queued at the tourist information desk, where they gave me a map. Not even in possession of a few coins for a cup of coffee, I sat on a public bench doing my best effort to understand where I was, and where I should start looking for Andrew and Sofia's restaurant. Again, I tried to recall the flowery name of their restaurant, but to no avail.

I drew an imaginary circle on the map and memorised the names of the neighbourhoods. Suddenly, a recognition flashed in my mind – Trastevere. I returned to the tourist information desk, and asked them to help me find any restaurant serving meals in the Trastevere area that carried a name resembling a flower. The lady – who spoke good

English, had a great laugh and seemed genuinely interested in my unusual request – took delight in looking it up on her computer. After five minutes of searching, she came up with four names with references to a flower, but I didn't recognise any of them. Starting to read all the names of restaurants in that particular area, I shouted "Yes, that's it!" when she came to "Bella Donna". She offered me one of her pleasant laughs and told me it meant "beautiful woman". *Surely Andrew had named it after Sofia,* I thought. I told her that it was the name of a flower in English, hence the confusion. We both agreed it was fortunate she had ticked off the eateries in alphabetical order. The nice lady printed a map indicating the way to get there, and off I went.

It took me almost three hours walking on the shaded side of the streets, which meant constantly crossing them as they curved uphill and downhill, before I reached the small, sun-drenched piazza where at least a dozen restaurants served their customers in the shade of the trees. I happened to arrive a little after noon, and all the tables were taken to the last chair. The incessant talk must have reached the upper noise limit of the decibels permitted, but I couldn't see anyone complaining. In fact, two policemen sitting at a small table sounded louder than the rest.

Suddenly, I caught a glance of Andrew in one of the restaurants across the piazza. Fitted with a long white apron, he didn't seem to have grown a day older, although he had put on some weight. I decided to wait on a bench under a tree until lunch was over before making contact.

*

Samantha was packing her bags when she checked her phone for any messages. Dismayed, she noticed that the battery of her mobile was nearly empty and connected it to an outlet in the bathroom. As soon as she had finished packing, she went downstairs to have breakfast. She looked at her watch, which showed 10:05. It was a beautiful watch, one that Matthias had given her for her birthday a few years ago. Her eyes filled with tears as she thought of him. *How could he have turned up dead in the Sahara Desert?* she wondered for the umpteenth time since Detective Sergeant Jones had given her the news the day before. She was absolutely convinced that Matthias never would have left her of his free will, which meant that he had either had some accident or been abducted. *Did his disappearance and death have something to do with those past events he told me? Or was it in connection with his recent arrest over that ludicrous accusation that he had killed his former lawyer?* There were many question marks, and all of them were as inexplicable as the fact that he had been found in Africa.

Samantha went to the reception desk to check out, and found a queue of three before it was her turn. She looked at her watch, which showed the time to be 10:45. George Jones would come to pick her up shortly. She crossed the room to the concierge and asked him to send someone to her room to pick up her bags. After handing over her key card, she returned to the reception desk. A loud-voiced American was still arguing about some charges made to his account: "Three

304

slices of toast, eight pounds?! That's ridiculous! That's indefensible!" Impatiently, she waited her turn. The bellboy arrived with her bags. The American finally left, and she had just settled her bill when Detective Sergeant Jones appeared by her side.

"Are you ready to leave?" he asked her with a shy smile. Jones had a timid quality about him with his brown eyes and tousled hair that she found likeable.

"I'm as ready as I can possibly be", she said grimly. "I merely need to check my bags with the concierge before we leave."

*

I was famished, and getting the wonderful smell of garlic floating from food being carried outside from the kitchens, only made things worse. I kept salivating worse than Pavlov's dog. Finally, at 2:30, people began to return to work, and things were quieting down.

Andrew was cleaning the dishes off one of the tables when I walked up to him.

"Andrew", I called out. He turned around and looked surprised.

"Who are you?" he asked, and his eyes narrowed to suspicious slits.

"Matthias Callaghan … your former employer", I told him, taken aback over the tone he had used addressing me. Then I realised he never had seen me the way I now appeared to him: unshaven, dirty, with unkempt hair and dressed in strange secondhand clothes a size too large. Moreover, the last time we had seen each other had been six years ago in Arizona.

"Master Callaghan!" he cried out and almost dropped the plates when he finally recognised me. "What on earth has come to you?"

"To cut a very long and complicated story short, Andrew, I had all my things stolen after being kidnapped a fortnight ago." Since I hardly could tell the true story of events, I had come prepared with one for him and Sofia. He never would have believed me, anyway, if I had given him the true version.

"Kidnapped, sir?"

"Yes, Andrew, I was travelling here in Italy, and somehow the 'Ndrangheta Mafia thought of me as a target worthwhile to pursue. I was released somewhere in southern Italy, penniless and without my phone. The nearest persons that I could think of who could help me were you and your wife. Am I right in assuming so?"

"Why, yes of course, Master Callaghan! But you must be starving after such a horrifying experience –"

"I must admit that I am."

"Please, do have a seat, while I tell Sofia to prepare her signature dish."

He ran indoors with the cutlery clattering on the dishes he carried. I sat down in the shade of a tree, feeling much better. Now, with Andrew's help, the most difficult part was over. After a meal, a hot shower and a welcome shave, I would give Samantha a call. She would catch a flight to Rome and bring me my ciclosporin prescription.

Andrew returned with a fresh tablecloth and quickly set the table.

"It's so good to see you again, Master Callaghan, notwithstanding the circumstances", he smiled broadly. "You will meet Sofia in a minute, as soon as she is finished with your *lasagna alla gamba*. It's really delicious, you will see. Meanwhile, I will bring you a bottle of our best wine that is perfect with the lasagne."

Without giving me a chance to reply, he hurried inside again and moments later returned with a bottle of Chianti and a corkscrew. The wine he poured tasted delicious.

A woman, energetic and positively twice the size of Andrew, came rushing out of the trattoria towards me holding a large steaming platter high while beaming a smile.

"Mister Caallaghan! My Aandrew tell me aall aboout you!"

Her loud statement made Andrew blush and wonder on which foot to stand. It was a strange situation. Years ago, he had been in my service for an extended period. Now, despite having become his own man for the past five years, Andrew returned to his subservient attitude instead of proudly showing off that he was the owner of a successful restaurant togcther with his wife. Some things will never change.

Sofia threw down the steaming platter in front of me.

"You don't-ah touch-ah yet!" she almost yelled, wagging her finger. Her ebullient presence immediately made me

307

understand why Andrew would never return to his former employment as a butler – surely his wife was absorbing all his energy. "Still is too hot-ah for you!"

I didn't touch it until Sofia had returned to the kitchen inside, only to discover that she had exaggerated somewhat about how hot it was. After gorging on a truly fantastic meal after starving for days, I asked Andrew to sit down with me instead of acting as a busybody arranging tables and straightening tablecloths for the evening crowd.

"Andrew, that was the best meal I've had in ages. I will thank Sofia personally in a little while, but first there are a few things I need to discuss with you."

"I'm all ears, sir", he said after hesitating about taking the chair opposite me. He still reacted to me as if I were his employer.

"Please, Andrew, do call me Matthias – you're no longer in my service. It is I who am in your debt for helping me in my difficult situation. Now I need to get back to my wife … you do remember lady Samantha, don't you?"

"Of course, sir. With the most pleasurable memories, sir."

I realised that I would never be able to change his servant's attitude to me after all the years as my butler. *It's just as well*, I sighed inwardly.

"I need to call her. Do you have a phone?"

"Yes, I'll get it for you right –"

I held up my hand as he rose from the table.

"Hold on for a second, Andrew. There are a few other things I need to talk to you about before you do. As you know,

308

I have no money, since it was all stolen. This means I don't have anywhere to sleep for one night, assuming that my wife can get here by tomorrow. I really hate to ask the question, but I was hoping you could lend me a few hundred euros to tide me over until my wife gets here, which is when I will pay you back."

Andrew smiled mysteriously.

"Please excuse me, sir, I'll be back in a minute with, I hope, the appropriate solution to your problem."

Andrew got up and once again hurried inside. Two minutes later, he was back.

"I've kept these for the day I would be able to return them to you, Master Callaghan." There was pride in his voice over fulfilling a last duty after having been let go by me years earlier. "Perhaps these will be of help to you in your present quandary?"

He put down a bank card and a set of keys on the tablecloth. I didn't understand what he was getting at and looked up at him asking. Andrew looked triumphant.

"These are the keys to your flat on Park Lane, which I never found the opportunity to return to you when we left for America. And the debit card is the one you asked me to acquire before we travelled there, and then, in Arizona, asked me not to use again."

I stared at the man in wonder, and then gave him a toothy smile. Of course – now I remembered. Before we left for the US, I had asked Andrew to open a bank account with Barclays that came with a debit card. A fair amount of the balance had been spent on our trip across North America, but I was certain that a fair amount remained in the account. Then I studied the card. It showed its expiry date to be three years ago.

"I do appreciate it, Andrew, but the card is useless since it has expired."

"Then perhaps I could ask for a replacement, sir?"

"You're right, at least we could give it a try. Now, since you're the one who opened the account, you should be the one who calls the bank. Will you do that for me?"

"Of course, sir."

Inside, after ten minutes on the phone being forwarded a dozen times to different so-called customer service personnel, Andrew finally got through to a lady who seemed to know what she was supposed to do – i.e., to solve customers' issues with the bank. After a brief and polite conversation, Andrew hung up and turned to me.

"I can pick up the card tomorrow at the VISA office in Central Rome", he beamed.

"That's excellent news, Andrew", I replied.

"I'll be happy to pick up the replacement card first thing in the morning, Master Callaghan. Meanwhile, please make yourself comfortable in our humble guest room. It's in the flat right above our restaurant."

"I appreciate your generosity, Andrew. If your wife agrees to this arrangement, which I promise will be for one night only before I'm on my way, I accept your invitation with my sincere gratitude."

"Speak no further, sir", Andrew replied with his most subtle smile. "It's a done thing."

*

Special Agent Solomon Vaughn's phone rang while he was going through a particularly tricky passage in preparation for a courtroom hearing. With a sigh, he reluctantly took the call. His nameless secretary, who seemed to get changed twice a week for someone new, informed him that the call was from the credit card organisation VISA, and that the caller had specifically asked to speak with him.

"Put him on the line, then", he told her, vaguely curious about why the credit card company would call him.

"Sir, my name is Michael McDougherty. I'm with the legal department at VISA Incorporated, and I've been instructed to be your liaison concerning a past request made by the FBI. It was done six years ago about an account belonging to a British citizen by the name of Andrew Reese, and this request of yours has been dormant since."

"It doesn't sound like a very exciting lead, Mr McDougherty", Vaughn replied sourly. He had better things to do with this headache of a trial that he needed to prepare for.

"It's just that, after six years of non-activity, something has suddenly happened", Vaughn heard, just as he was about to put the receiver down.

"And what is that something, if I may ask?" he said, raising the auricular back to his ear.

"A replacement debit card has been requested for collection at our offices in Rome."

Vaughn had a vague memory of having heard or seen Reese's name recently, but he couldn't recall the circumstance.

"So the use of the card was flagged by the FBI, was it?"

"It was, sir, and your name was recently indicated as our contact in charge. But perhaps I'm speaking to the wrong supervisor of this particular case?"

"No, I'm the person you should talk to", Vaughn replied, trying his best to recall the details about why Andrew Reese was wanted for interrogation in the first place. "I appreciate your call, Mr McDougherty, and even more so if you could take the trouble to confirm the details in writing."

"Of course, I'd be happy to. But, tell me, should we release the replacement card or not?"

"I assume that it's linked to a bank account?"

"It is. Barclays, London. Since it's a debit card, I took the precaution of checking the account status – no movements whatsoever for six years, and the balance is slightly over ten thousand pounds."

Vaughn, very briefly, then smiled.

"Go ahead, release it", he agreed. "But make sure to keep me updated at all times regarding any use of the debit card."

*

Accepting the generosity of my hosts, I soaked in a long, hot bath for a good hour. Andrew had laid out a set of toiletries in the little guest room's bathroom, and after the bath and a shave I felt much better. However, looking into the mirror shaving, I was disturbed by the image looking back at me. My shaved face had taken on a greyish tone and the skin was drooping. No wonder that Andrew had looked at me with pity after he had confirmed who I was.

Dr Sternmacher's words kept ringing in my ears. I urgently needed to get ciclosporin to stop the rejection process.

Using Andrew's house phone, I called Samantha's mobile a dozen times over the next two hours, but I only got her voicemail. I gave up and dialled her brother Jack's number in Sydney. The time difference was nine hours. After prolonged ringing, his sleepy voice finally came on the line.

"Jack, this is Matthias. I'm sorry to wake you up at this hour, but I'm terribly worried about Samantha. I haven't been able to contact her for about two weeks, and now she doesn't answer her mobile."

That woke him up, all right.

"Hold on, hold on, I'm not sure I'm getting this straight, mate. The last I knew you were in jail, and Samantha asked me to fly to London to take your kids home. Which I did. Since then I've heard from her a dozen times, as recently as three days ago. She told me that you had been released, but she was worried sick because you had disappeared the minute you walked out. Then, here you are, telling me that it's Samantha who has disappeared?"

"It's a confusing story, Jack, and I'll tell you all about it

313

over a cold beer once we're back in Australia. The long and the short of it is that I've been held incommunicado for twelve days, and now that I finally have access to a phone, I can't find Samantha. What did she tell you the last time the two of you spoke?"

"As I said, it was three days ago. She told me she had a bad feeling about your disappearance, and that you never would skip bail and leave her without any news about your whereabouts."

"She was right, Jack. I was abducted."

"Abducted? You can't be serious, mate!"

"I am, Jack. I can't go into the details now. My priority is to find Samantha." I thought for a moment. "Look, I'm calling you from a borrowed phone. I'll get a mobile tomorrow and I'll let you know my new number, OK? Any news, please let me know.

"No worries, mate."

"How are the kids?"

"They're fine, and so far they have no knowledge of any trouble that their parents are in."

"Good. Please keep it that way, Jack."

*

Georgie and Samantha checked in late at the *riad*, because the flight from London had been delayed for two hours due to technical issues. The riad, one that Georgie had looked up before their departure, was a traditional ten-room house built around a courtyard converted into a small – as Europeans would describe it – quaint boutique hotel. Samantha's room was directly above the one given to Georgie.

Georgie made a mental note that he had to pay a visit next day to the uninspired reservation Jenny had made for him at the Holiday Inn on the outskirts of Marrakech. He needed to pay for the four nights that had been reserved for him, in case anyone checked his travel expenses.

Thursday May 7, 2015

Georgie had been informed that the morgue opened at seven. However, to be allowed to enter the facility, they first needed to meet with the Marrakech chief of police, Mustafa Goulla, who Georgie had been told was personally reviewing the case. Goulla would be available around nine. They should present themselves at his office at that hour, and after his short interview with the widow accompanying Georgie, they would go together to the morgue for a formal identification of her deceased husband. All this was reported to Samantha by Georgie over breakfast, for which she demonstrated little appetite. She had just discovered she had lost her phone somewhere. *Did I forget it on the flight?* she wondered as she distractedly listened to Georgie's explanation.

Ten minutes before nine, they were sitting in the antechamber to the police chief's office. Forty minutes later, Mustafa Goulla appeared, dressed in an impeccable, white linen suit that managed to give his portly figure a semblance of elegance. His eyes lit up when he set them upon Samantha, relishing her fresh appearance. He strode forward and kissed her hand. Then he turned to Georgie.

"I understand that you have come to confirm the identities of the men found in the desert. I'm so sorry to be the harbinger of bad news, of course, but surely you both know I'm only doing my job at the best of my abilities given my restricted resources."

It was a quick speech that Goulla had given dozens of times over the years during similar encounters and when it served his purposes. Without letting it show, he was particularly taken with the young, blonde woman – a rare beauty in the realm he overlooked. He wondered what it would take to get her into his bed, with the full understanding that a suitable period of grief must first be allowed to elapse. Encouraged by this last observation, he clapped his hands.

"Come, my dear friends, we must immediately go to the morgue to get this unpleasant business over and done with."

Twenty minutes before noon, they were ushered inside said sanctuary by the chief of police. An assistant led them to a wall fitted with dozens of metal doors. He extracted a wheeled stretcher after having opened one of them. Only the feet were visible, while the remainder of the body was covered with a sheet. Samantha held her fists against her mouth while the morgue assistant slowly revealed the face of the deceased.

"No. No, no!" she exclaimed, hoarsely.

The assistant returned the stretcher into the wall, closed the door and led them to another one nearby. After

316

uncovering the second body, Samantha let out a heavy breath.

"These two men, are they the ones found in the desert?" she asked.

The assistant looked askingly at the police chief.

"Yes, they are. Do you recognise them?" Goulla confirmed.

"I've never seen either of them before, ever!" she blurted with a gasp of relief. "I can't understand why you thought my husband was among them!"

Both Georgie and Goulla looked at her with surprise.

"Among the objects found with the victims was a jacket that carries your husband's name on the tailor's label", Georgie explained. "In the breast pocket of the jacket were two receipts that your husband was handed on the day of his release, that is, on April the twenty-fifth. The police could only assume that the jacket and the receipt belonged to either of these men. Otherwise, how would you explain two dead men and a jacket neither of them owned turning up in the Sahara, with nothing else for miles around?"

"I don't know, and I don't care!" Samantha cried, still euphoric with relief that neither of the bodies belonged to Matthias. "You thought you followed a lead that would prove that my husband skipped jail, and now I know someone pulled wool over your eyes."

Georgie decided it was best to not insist. Perhaps Callaghan would turn up dead somewhere else, and anyway, he should try to avoid annoying Samantha if he wanted to gain her affection.

"Do you know the identity of the other man yet?" he asked the chief of police.

"My men have been looking into it after taking his fingerprints", Goulla replied. "Please allow me to ask if they have got any results."

"Lamrani, have you found anything new about the bodies found in the desert?" he asked in English after dialling a number and activating the loudspeaker on his mobile.

"The one with the tattoos is a small-time thief already known to the police", Lamrani reported in the same language. "He is Hamza Khalis, a Moroccan citizen who is on our files convicted for larceny. The other one we still haven't been able to identify, but we're working on it."

"It would be helpful if you could share his fingerprints and a photograph of his face with New Scotland Yard", Georgie told Goulla. "That way I could quickly determine if he's a British subject or not."

"Of course. Please give the contact details to Lamrani, and he will make sure that you get the information at once." Goulla handed over his mobile to Georgie. "I do of course expect the courtesy to be returned: should Scotland Yard determine who the second victim is, I'd like to know without delay. Is that acceptable?"

"Of course it is. Thank you."

After Georgie had informed Goulla's deputy where to send the result of the request, he and Samantha exited the morgue and got a cab at a stand.

"I need to take care of a minor issue at the Holiday Inn

before we have lunch", he said. "I hope you don't mind?"

"Of course not", Samantha replied, elated that none of the dead men had been Matthias.

After the quick detour to Holiday Inn, where Georgie settled his bill for the four nights while Samantha waited in the cab, he took her to lunch. The place was simple, one that fitted a policeman with his salary, and the food was surprisingly good. They both opted for a lamb *tagine* earthenware dish since it was the recommended local food.

During the meal they discussed the events of the morning. Georgie took note of her great relief that her husband wasn't among the victims they had faced in the morning. His mobile vibrated to announce an incoming communication. When he glanced at it, he saw that it was something texted from the Metropolitan Police.

"Excuse me", he said to Samantha, "I think this may be some important information concerning our case at hand."

"Of course", Samantha told him. "You should make it a priority to do your job."

"It turns out that the second victim is indeed a British citizen", Georgie said, squinting at the small text on his mobile. "He's been identified as Allan Gould." Georgie looked up. "Have you ever heard of this man?"

It was an innocent question, but he noticed that Samantha's face became flushed as she responded.

"No, I can't recall I have", she lied, remembering perfectly everything that Matthias had told her about Allan when they had sailed to Bali.

Georgie chose not to confront her and switched the conversation to his impressions of Morocco. After lunch, he took her back to the riad where they were staying and excused himself since he had to go to the British consulate to arrange for the return of the deceased Brit to the UK.

Once inside the riad, the courteous woman who managed the place, and who truly worried about her guests' well-being, handed Samantha an envelope with the seal of the Marrakech Police printed on it. Samantha opened it. Inside, she found a formal invitation addressed to herself and Detective Sergeant Jones to join Chief-of-Police Mustafa Goulla for an informal dinner in his humble abode that same evening, at eight o'clock sharp.

*

First thing in the morning, Andrew left to pick up the VISA card at the company's office in central Rome. He returned just before lunchtime, sweating but triumphant, waving the card at me.

"There was some trouble at first, sir, but I finally got it!"

He seemed as pleased with himself as I was to finally have the means to continue my journey. During the morning, I had repeatedly called Samantha's mobile with the same lacklustre result as the day before. My number one priority now was to get more ciclosporin to avoid further rejections of my transplants. I urgently needed to get the medicine, but I was also worried about whatever effects my involuntary abstinence may cause me long-term. By now, I felt so awful that I couldn't concentrate on anything beyond my face and fingers. What would happen if they were rejected by my body, as Sternmacher had warned? What if I dropped my fingers, or lost my face for lack of my prescribed medicine?

I had three options. I could continue to hope that I would soon be able to talk with Samantha, and that she could hop onto the first available flight to Rome. For every hour that had passed since I first tried to reach her, this seemed less and less likely. My second option was to somehow break into a pharmacy where they kept the ciclosporin. I hated the idea, partly because I didn't feel physically up to breaking into a pharmacy, and partly because I feared the possibility of getting caught.

My third option seemed to me to be the only viable solution. I had to go to Dr Sternmacher's hospital in Switzerland. The question was: how could I get there?

*

When the, quite frankly, delicious lunch was over, Andrew drove me in his and Sofia's somewhat run-down Fiat to a nearby shopping centre. The car had been promoted as the smallest in the world to accommodate four persons. Andrew apologised to me, but I couldn't help feeling uncomfortable although there were only two of us in the vehicle.

I obviously didn't spell out any of my discomfort to Andrew. We had entered a curious relationship by now. He couldn't help acting or responding to anything I said or did unless addressing me formally me with a "sir", as if he still were my employee. It did make me feel uncomfortable, what with all the help he and Sofia had so generously offered me. However, there was nothing I could do to change his attitude, even though I had tried to tell him so on two or three occasions. The ingrained reaction from his perspective of class difference was now, at his age and experience, impossible to alter. It made me all the more pleased that Andrew had found a new life with Sofia in Rome.

I asked him about life in Rome and being a foreigner in Italy.

"I've never felt better my whole life, sir", he replied. "Not even when I was in your service", he graciously added. "Every day I'm improving my Italian with another couple of words; the Italians appreciate my efforts; the weather is certainly much nicer than in the UK; the history and the surroundings never cease to amaze me; and my wife is a wonderful cook. What more can I possibly ask for?"

"I'm glad for you, Andrew. I can't think of anyone who deserves it more."

"Thank you, sir."

"Once I'm out of my present predicament, please don't hesitate to contact me should Sofia and you require any financial assistance –"

"Oh no, sir, thank you all the same, but we're getting along just marvellous. I don't even have a bank account or any credit cards, because I no longer need them. Sofia manages everything, and anyway, most Italians pay cash when they come to our little trattoria."

"I'm very pleased to hear it, Andrew. Still, just in case, should you ever encounter some difficulties, I'm counting on you to tell me."

"I do appreciate your offer, sir."

I bought a mobile that came with a prepaid card. Since proof of identification was needed, Andrew did me yet another favour by making the purchase for me. In a nearby bookshop, I found a map of Europe. I picked up a carry-on and clothes to cover me for a couple of days, along with some toiletries.

Once again feeling hungry, I asked Andrew to join me for something to eat at a pizzeria. He only ordered a beer to keep me company while I devoured a thin pizza with the most toppings on the menu.

"Sir, may I take the opportunity to inquire about something that I've wondered about for a long time?" Andrew, embarrassed, suddenly asked.

"Of course, Andrew", I replied, not knowing what to expect.

"Back in London, while still in my first employment with you, there was this incident that I never got the chance to talk to you about. You see, I went down to the garage to leave some of milady's suitcases in the appropriate space. Neither she nor you, sir, were in the flat at the time, and there were none of the usual notes you used to leave for me."

I could only anticipate the worst from his introductory

323

words. It had been long in coming, and I knew I had to come up with an answer that was both plausible and convincing.

"Well, sir ... I went over to your Aston Martin", Andrew hesitated, before suddenly letting the words pour forth without restraint. "The back-seat door was slightly ajar, which I found very strange. I pushed it open, and the view filled me with dread; honestly, it was the most horrifying thing I've ever been subject to when I think back on it. There was blood all over the upholstery. When I opened the driver's door, I found a large, bloodstained Manila envelope on the seat. I pulled it open and ten fingers fell out."

As I listened to Andrew, as I needed to, I was revolted by hearing the story of my life described to me once again. Simultaneously, the back of my mind searched frantically for something that could explain to Andrew what he had seen all those years ago. His sudden investigation into my past complicated things to a point where I felt an urge to scream out loud. I couldn't start an explanatory, truthful session with Andrew. The issues were far more complex than I suspected he would either be interested in or to be able to profoundly analyse, because, to be honest, Andrew wasn't the brightest of fellows. A lot of other qualities, to be sure, but being bright wasn't one of them.

I still didn't tell him a word.

"You see, sir", he continued, after hesitating slightly as his eyes brimmed with tears, "I didn't know what to do next. I remember thinking I wanted to be as clear-headed as you, sir, so I thought the best thing was to conserve the fingers I'd found, some of which were still dripping with blood. In the confusion, I couldn't think of a better solution than to place them in one of the freezers, as a temporary solution until I'd have a chance to talk to you."

He paused.

"Shortly afterwards, lady Julia told me that I had been suspended from my position –."

"Thank you, Andrew, I think I'm familiar with the story from here on." During my silence, I had racked my brain for some plausible explanation that I felt obliged to give him. "As you know, I was hospitalised at the time due to a car accident on the continent. An acquaintance of mine, a Moroccan by the name Abdul Mahfouz, visited me in the hospital, and promised to help me out with some urgent business of mine that I couldn't handle while I was incapacitated. For that purpose, I gave him access to my flat and the use of my car. What I didn't know at the time was that he had some unresolved dealings with a crime syndicate, who apparently found him at his disadvantage in the garage on Park Lane, and cut off his fingers. I'm sure you can imagine the rest of the sordid details."

No need to be too explicit, or Andrew might catch me in a lie.

"I see, sir. Thank you for telling me." Andrew sounded apologetic, and hesitated a bit before he continued. "I've never told you this, sir, but I was in Mister Mahfouz's employ for a brief time after lady Julia dismissed me. During that time, I once or twice had the opportunity to see that all his fingers were artificial. Poor man. Well, I suppose that clears up the

325

doubts I've had all these years regarding this bizarre and tragic affair."

A bizarre and tragic affair, indeed. If Andrew had only learnt half of it, I couldn't help thinking.

Later Andrew drove me to the train station. After thanking him for all the help and promising to keep in touch, I used Andrew's debit card to buy a single first-class ticket to Milan. I asked the elderly man at the ticket counter how I could go from there to Switzerland, and was given a timetable with the appearance as if it had been printed the year he was born. Before I got on the train, I made a 400-euro withdrawal from a cash machine.

Forty-five minutes later, the train left the platform heading north.

*

When Special Agent Solomon Vaughn arrived at his office in the morning, he found a note that his secretary had left on his desk. It asked him to call Michael McDougherty at VISA followed by the number where he could be reached. McDougherty picked up his phone on the third ring.

"After six years, today there have been quite a few transactions with the card that Andrew Reese picked up this morning", he began.

"Are you sure it was Reese?" Vaughn, who now had read up on the case and knew who McDougherty was referring to, asked.

"Absolutely. He identified himself with his British passport when he picked up the replacement card. I'll be happy to mail you a copy."

"Please do."

"He then went to a shopping centre, where he bought a mobile phone, some article in a book shop, a piece of luggage and several items of clothing. Then he paid for a train ticket at the Rome terminal and –"

"Can you tell me the destination?" Vaughn interrupted him. "Was it a single or return ticket?"

"He bought a single first-class ticket to Milan", McDougherty replied. "He also withdrew four hundred euros from a cash machine. I will send you a detailed report of the transactions."

"It will be appreciated."

After hanging up, Vaughn chewed for a while on the information he had just learnt. *It sounds like a perfect moment to grab Reese for questioning about the death of Thompson and the ensuing disappearance of Callaghan,* he thought. *I should get in touch with the Italian police through Interpol and have them pick him up when he arrives in Milan.*

He went through his incoming mail and found McDougherty's. The ticket had been bought at 12:35 p.m. A web search showed him that the first train to Milan after the purchase was made had left Rome at 1:20 p.m. and would arrive at the destination at 4:40 p.m. The price Reese had paid confirmed it to be a first-class executive ticket. Vaughn looked at his watch. It showed 8:27. Considering the time difference between Washington and Italy, he had a little over two hours to arrange everything. *A good thing McDougherty had attached a copy of Reese's passport,* he smiled to himself. *That saves me the time and the trouble to find one elsewhere.*

*

Once the train had departed, I tried to call Samantha again. After a dozen attempts, I gave up. Her silence worried me. My face and fingers falling apart worried me. Having no ID or passport worried me. And if I could get back to London, should I worry about the police? I was supposed to report to them daily and not leave the country as part of the conditions for my release on bail. How could I possibly explain that I had been anaesthetised in a taxi that had picked me up upon leaving prison, only to come to my senses as an airplane took off in the Sahara? Surely they would find me either delirious or lying, trying to explain away that I hadn't complied with my bail conditions. Either way, I would likely be put away, either back in jail or in a madhouse.

I studied the map I had bought. The first city upon entering Switzerland from Italy was Locarno, located on the northern tip of Lago Maggiore. From there, it was perhaps a four-hour train ride to Zürich and another hour and a half to St Puys. To get to Locarno, I had two options: by train all the way from Milan, or by getting off in Stresa and taking the ferry. Somehow, I felt it easier to slip through a possible immigration control if I took the train all the way. According to the timetable, a train was leaving the Milano Centrale railway station every half hour or so.

So far, so good. Now I had to make contact with Dr Sternmacher. A search on the web revealed the phone number to the clinic in St Puys. A woman answered in German, and I asked for Dr Sternmacher in the same language.

"I'm sorry, the doctor is not available this afternoon", she said. "May I ask who's calling?"

"This is Matthias Callaghan calling him about an emergency", I replied. "Can you please indicate how I can reach him on his mobile?"

"We are not allowed to give out his private number", she told me, icily. "You must call back tomorrow to see if he can take your call."

"No", I retorted, vexed and desperate. "You can call Doctor Sternmacher yourself, and tell him he must call me! He knows who I am, and I doubt very much that you will keep your job unless you comply."

Not giving her a chance to protest, I spelled out my phone number twice.

"I will see if I can get Doctor Sternmacher", she said sourly, "but I don't promise you anything."

*

Henrik Sternmacher had taken the afternoon off to put a tracker chip on his young Belgian Shepherd. The dog had kept escaping the premises of his home to his 11-year-old daughter

Hilde's constant grief. He had bought Hilde the dog shortly after her mother, his wife, two years earlier had succumbed to cancer. The dog, he had thought, would serve as company for her during the long shifts when he needed to operate. She loved the dog, but when the dog was a year old, it had begun to show tendencies of exploring the world beyond their home. The dog's escapades escalated into a problem when neighbours and strangers called to say her dog had been identified by its collar after days roaming far from home. The tenth time he had to send someone to pick up the pet, Sternmacher was repenting his choice. Still, there was nothing he could do about it now. The girl cried every time her dog got lost, and he had had to accept that it had become a part of the family.

The solution, he had discovered, was to insert a GPS tracker implant underneath the pet's skin. After some research, he found one that suited his needs: a GPS microchip the size of a small coin that could be tracked by satellite through a commercial application. It was powered by an advanced micro-battery that used the animal's body heat to recharge itself.

He was watching the veterinarian anaesthetise the dog when his mobile rang. Excusing himself, he stepped outside to take the call from his secretary.

"A Matthias Callaghan called, claiming that he's in an emergency situation. I didn't give him your number, of course, but he insisted that I should tell you he must talk to you immediately."

Matthias Callaghan? As Dr Sternmacher wrote down the number he should call, he felt his curiosity challenged by the urgency.

*

Dr Sternmacher called me back ten minutes later. He sounded distant, as if I didn't have his undivided attention.

"I'm experiencing a severe rejection of my transplants", I implored. "I feel awful. I need to see you without delay."

"Are you still taking the prescribed dose of ciclosporin?" he asked.

"Not exactly, due to circumstances I can only explain in person", I replied. "I need to see you tomorrow. Can you pick me up in Zürich?"

He thought for a moment.

"At the airport?"

"No, outside the main train station."

"You sound upset."

"I am. You have no idea how upset and awful I feel, but you will know tomorrow. Please pick me up at eight."

"Will you need an ambulance?"

"Medical attendance while travelling to St Puys is a good precaution."

Feeling slightly better after having established contact with Dr Sternmacher, I disconnected. I went to the restaurant car to have lunch, where I found a free table for four. While I was studying the menu, someone sat down opposite me after throwing down his jacket on the seat next to him.

"You don't mind, do you?" a man my age asked me in a Liverpudlian accent after the fact. "All other tables are taken."

"No, you're welcome."

I went back to read the menu. The waitress handed my table companion another one. I ordered a salmon carpaccio for starters, *osso buco alla milanese* for main course and a bottle of Chianti.

"Sounds good. I'll have the same", the Liverpudlian said after the briefest glance at the menu. "I'm Nathan."

"I'm Sidney." I don't know why I made that name up; perhaps because I wasn't in a mood for conversation with this stranger.

He insisted on chatting.

"Rough night? You look like you've been through some good time, Sidney." His tone was suggestive and overbearing.

Nathan was tall and flabby, loud-voiced and rosy-cheeked. His chatter went on, although I ignored him most of the time. The food arrived. I tried to shut out his constant small talk and concentrate on what I could expect during the coming days. I had to risk crossing the Italian border with Switzerland without an ID card. I thought I knew how I could make Dr Sternmacher cooperate and send me on to London. I had to convince him of the urgency, of course. Then there was the little detail of entering the UK without some identification, I still hadn't solved.

"Great food, good choice", Nathan sighed as he licked his knife clean. I merely gave him a lopsided smile before waving to the waitress to bring me the bill.

"Bring mine, too, will you, darling?" Nathan said and changed his smile into a seductive one. "I need to go to the loo, but I'll be back in two seconds."

The train had just left its last stop before our arrival in Milan scheduled to be in less than forty-five minutes. I showed the waitress my newly acquired debit card. She said that she needed to fetch the terminal. Nathan rushed off to the lavatory.

Nathan had left his jacket behind. In a flash, it occurred to me that his wallet might be in it. I leaned over, grabbed the jacket and quickly searched the inner pockets. His wallet was brimming with odd papers and credit cards. Behind one of them I found his driver's licence, which I stuffed into the breast pocket of my shirt. I managed to return the jacket with the wallet to where Nathan had left it just before the waitress appeared with the terminal for my digital signature. I punched in the four digits after adding a 20 per cent tip. She looked pleased.

I decided to wait until Nathan had paid his bill to see whether he would discover my theft. The waitress had left his bill on the table and he searched for his wallet. Without hesitation, he brought out a corporate VISA card.

"Company business, so I've got all expenses covered", he winked at me triumphantly. "That's why I'm going to Milan now to catch a flight back to jolly good England."

He handed the card over to the waitress, who repeated the procedure with the terminal. Nathan didn't notice that his driver's licence was missing. I smiled at him as he returned the wallet to his jacket and told him goodbye.

I returned to my seat and tried Samantha's mobile again. An automated voice advised me that her voice mailbox wouldn't allow any more messages to be recorded since it had run out of space.

No wonder. I had left her at least thirty voice mails.

*

A ping alerted Vaughn to a new mail from McDougherty. It showed that Reese's debit card had been used on the Rome–Milan train at 3:31 p.m. *Good,* Vaughn thought, *it confirms he's actually on it.*

He dialled the number Interpol had given him for direct contact with the Italian officer in charge of the apprehension of Reese for questioning.

"Commandante Rossi, this is Special FBI Agent Solomon Vaughn again. I just got renewed confirmation that the person of interest is on the train that will arrive in Milan at 4:20. I assume you have your men in place?"

"Of course. We Italians can be as efficient as the Americans when we really set our minds to it." Vaughn thought he sounded a little put off.

"I do appreciate your collaboration. Please, do give me a call when he's been apprehended. I'm arranging for one of our interrogators in Europe to go to Milan on the next available flight. I'm expecting him to arrive tomorrow morning."

*

The train arrived Milan's Central Station exactly on time. A sign outside the train window indicated that it had done so on platform eight. People bustled to get off the train with their luggage.

My wagon was one of those furthest away from the platform exit. With plenty of time to purchase a ticket for Zürich, I didn't mind being among the last walking toward the exit. As I reached the end of the platform, just before entering the main building, a crowd blocked the entrance talking loudly in Italian. They were waiting impatiently for their turn to get access to the station building, but they were being held up. As the crowd thinned, I could see two policemen carefully comparing the face of each passenger with a document that one of them held. I was among the last to be allowed to pass, and as I did so, I managed to catch a glimpse of the document they checked the passengers against.

I felt the hair stand on my neck as I with horror recognised an enlarged photograph of Andrew's face. *Why should the Italian police be looking for Andrew arriving in Milan by train?* I wondered as I hurried inside the huge, high-ceilinged terminal where thousands of people were milling about. *Why now, after all his time in Italy? Why now, checking the very train I had just disembarked?* My heart was beating faster from the sudden realisation that something was terribly wrong.

With my head full of questions, I made my way to the ticket counter. There was a queue of fifteen people waiting their turn. I used the time to think about why the police were looking for Andrew.

Having known him for years, I was convinced I understood his character to the last detail. Andrew was incapable of any crime or manipulation, I was sure. Then the fact that the police were looking for him getting off the very train I had taken from Rome made me realise that the only way they could have known this was because I had used a debit card issued to him in order to buy the train ticket. Yes, that was it! But did it mean that the police wanted me or Andrew? Well, they had *his* photo, not mine.

It became my turn at the ticket counter. By now, I understood that I couldn't use the debit card any longer. I still had the four hundred euros that I had cashed in Rome, and used thirty-two of these to purchase a second-class ticket to Zürich.

The train I was taking would take three hours and twenty-eight minutes to reach Locarno, I was informed upon asking. It would arrive in Locarno at 20:43.

*

Samantha was watching the city lights from the riad's roof terrace when Georgie returned from the consulate moments before dusk was settling.

"It's been a frustrating afternoon", he said, obviously angered. "It turns out that the matter of shipping back the corpse can't be handled from the consulate here in Marrakech, the paperwork can only be done from the embassy in Rabat. This means I have to catch the first flight in the morning to go there. I'm sorry, but it implies you'll have to spend the day tomorrow on your own."

"Please don't worry about me", Samantha replied, "I can take care of myself. By the way, we've received an invitation for dinner tonight from the police chief, what do you think about that?"

Georgie looked at her surprised as she handed him the invitation.

"We're both invited", she said, "but I'm not up to it and, besides, I don't think it would be appropriate for me to go. You should go, though, it would probably be good for your career to have Goulla as a personal contact."

Georgie quickly read the invitation.

"I doubt that I'm the guest he's interested in", he replied, smiling at her. "If I'm reading this correctly between the lines, combined with the attention I saw Goulla give you earlier today, I've only been invited as your chaperone. Now, look, we have to spend time here until the flight back to London on Sunday, so why not make the best of the time we still have left in Morocco?"

"You're saying we both should accept?"

"I am. Actually, I think it'll be damn interesting to see the inside of a local house, observe local customs, eat local food … and on top that, it's the local chief of police who's inviting us. What can be bad about that?"

After some additional arguments, Samantha, still

reluctant, accepted that Georgie would take her to Goulla's dinner, set for an hour later.

*

"This Andrew Reese that you're looking for, he was not on the train from Rome", Solomon Vaughn heard Commandante Rossi's accusing voice inform him, "despite your reassurance that he would be."

"It makes me quite disappointed to hear that, Commandante Rossi", Vaughn said slowly, wondering what could possibly have gone wrong. *He used the card on the train, so it means he must have disembarked on some station before arriving in Milan,* Blackmoore concluded. *Did it imply that Reese knew the police were onto him? No – impossible. Had he got off the train before arriving in Milan, although he had bought a ticket for the whole distance?* So many questions and no clear answer.

"I'm terribly sorry for having made your people go through all the trouble. I'll keep you posted if any new information comes along."

*

Mustafa Goulla had ordered a feast for twenty despite there being merely six for dinner, including himself. After knocking on the discouraging door of rotting wood facing the street, Samantha marvelled at the sumptuous interior when she and Georgie had been let inside. In her imagination, the closest she could think of if she one day would have to describe it, was something out of *One Thousand and One Nights*. Rich carpets upon carpets covering the floors; tapestries hiding the walls; indescribable, even mystical, objects seemingly cast aside in the corners at random; mysterious servants silently appearing and disappearing from behind curtains ... and then there was the banquet room. The floor was covered with hundreds of multi-coloured cushions around a magnificently inlaid table that could seat at least sixteen should the guests sit upright in the European fashion. Encouraged to recline on the pillows, a servant immediately hovered over Samantha and offered her a choice of beverages, among which she chose mint tea.

The other three invitees were friends of Goulla, working in the government. They all spoke fluent English and from the beginning the conversation was both interesting and sophisticated. Samantha was impressed with their eclectic knowledge.

Then the platters with food arrived, with one eye-pleasing dish after another, exquisitely arranged with colours and aromas that filled the dining room. Samantha relished the food with flavours she had never tasted before.

"It's delicious!" she exclaimed when platter number nine arrived. "But if I take another bite I will explode."

Goulla and his cronies laughed. A servant filled her empty cup after she had refused one of the water pipes that were brought before each guest. After they had begun sucking on their water pipes, Goulla – who this evening was in an excellent mood – began to tell stories about his ancestors. He had the natural gift of a storyteller, knew when to pause for effect and when to raise an inquisitive eyebrow to make a point. Soon all present were roaring with laughter.

Between laughs, Georgie watched Samantha enjoy herself. With the chief of police paying her particular attention, she looked radiant. *It's a good sign that she momentarily has forgotten her vanished husband,* Georgie mused.

Around midnight, Samantha rose and said it had been a delightful evening, but the time had come to return to the hotel. A servant led them through the narrow streets to an open space, where they found Goulla's private car waiting. They were dropped off at a different entrance to the medina.

"The man is charming", Samantha said as she took Georgie's arm walking the last distance into the medina, where cars couldn't enter the narrow alleyways", although I doubt that you can become chief of police here by merely being delightful."

*

As I had expected, there were no border immigration checks after the train pulled into the station in Locarno. Since I had two hours before the next one left for Zürich, I went to an Internet café that stayed open late. Ever since I had returned to life in the Sahara, at the back of my mind I had been turning over the largest question mark of all – why had I been abducted and left alive in the desert with Allan and another, unknown man? Was it meant to be a warning? Or was I

340

supposed to have died, too?

Whatever the intention – who was behind my abduction? After so many years away from the UK, I didn't think I had any enemies and even less someone who was both ruthless and able to carry out an obviously sophisticated operation.

The only possible answer I could come up with was Mikhail Berlosky and the Russian Mafia. Excluding the British counterintelligence, I couldn't think of anyone else in the UK with the means and the resources to plan and execute what they had done to me within such a short space of time. It would fit in with the killing of Allan, too, if the Russians had decided he was no longer useful and wanted to get rid of him. I needed to know more to be able to protect myself and my family, and the only thing that occurred to me was to contact the private detective I had used with such good results in the past: Clemens Porter.

I continued to worry about the recording that Flint had made when I had challenged him to kill Rathbone. Flint had died years ago, I knew. To whom could he possibly have left his recording of our conversation? Despite the motorcycle that I had kept running, my Mahfouz voice impersonation had, incredibly, been made clear enough to recently make it into a transcript of our conversation. On the other hand, as far as I could understand, Flint had never had the opportunity or the information to connect my Mahfouz character with my true self. Which meant that someone else must have made the connection – and had done so many years later.

Who was that someone else?

*

With all this in mind I looked up past e-mails from Porter saved in my inbox until I found his number. It took him six rings to pick up the phone. He grunted something unintelligible, as if he had been woken from a profound sleep. The computer showed 9:11 p.m. With the one-hour time difference, it told me that Porter went to bed early.

"I'm terribly sorry to bother you at this hour, Mister Porter", I greeted him using my raspy Dr Ibrahim voice. "This is Doctor Ibrahim, for whom, I hope you remember, you've done some profitable work in the past. I'm once again in dire need of your most qualified services, for which – it really goes without saying – I'm willing to pay most handsomely."

The flourishes of my speech seemed to revive both him and his interest.

"I remember you well, Doctor Ibrahim", he replied, "although we've only had the pleasure of meeting in person once. Actually –"

I stopped him cold, because I wasn't interested in his speculation about whether I could be somebody other than Dr Ibrahim.

"To come to the point, I urgently need the following information, for which you may charge me your usual fees. It concerns a man you investigated on my behalf back in two thousand and twelve. I need to get an update on the who and the why of Allan Gould's recent killing in London. I'm not sure, but I suspect some other people you investigated in the past may be behind it; namely Mikhail Berlosky and his associates at Arexim."

I could hear Porter mutter as he took notes.

"Your second task is finding out everything about the deceased Jeremiah Flint. He used to be the employer of someone else you once successfully investigated for me. Perhaps you recall him: Richard Thompson?"

"I do have a vivid recollection of your past request."

"Flint used to be the owner of a pub called The Lion's Head in Islington. I want all details of interest that you can find about him from March two thousand and nine up to his death later that year. Still more important, though, will be your investigation concerning his inheritance: who were his heirs; has the pub been sold since; and if that were the case, who were the sellers and the buyers since Flint's death? Who is the owner of the pub today? That sort of thing."

I imagined hearing the scratching sounds as Porter wrote everything down.

"I want every possible name linked to him, be it a professional, a relative or a personal acquaintance, together with a brief explanation about the relationship. Is this something you can do, and how long do you need?"

"Apart from Berlosky and the killing of Allan Gould, where I would have to tread carefully, it doesn't sound too complicated. I'll see what I can come up with and will get back to you in a week or two. As for Berlosky and his friends, I'll tell you then whether I need more time – I remember that particular set-up to be a hornets' nest. Now, as always, you know I need a down payment before I start working, let's say … two thousand pounds, in this case."

"Of course – the money will be in your account tomorrow. Can I use the same one as I've done on previous occasions?"

"You may."

My next call was to Jack, who at this hour was up and running. After asking him about Samantha and our children, I told him about the transfer that I wanted him to make to Porter. There was still no news about his sister, he said, otherwise everything was hunky-dory in Australia. He did express his deep concern over the lack of information regarding myself and Samantha. I ended the call by ordering him not to worry, and, within a day or two, he was certain to hear from both of us with lengthy explanations about everything. However, I claimed that at the moment I simply didn't have the time to chat with him since I had a train to catch.

The train I was to catch wasn't due to leave until an hour later, which gave me time to buy some inexpensive sandwiches that didn't make too much of a dent in my remaining funds. The last train out of Locarno that evening wasn't even half full, which allowed me to stretch out in a compartment that I had all to myself. The steady rhythm of the train travelling over the tracks quickly made me fall asleep. Two hours later, I was awakened by a ghastly loudspeaker voice announcing that we had arrived at our final destination. The booming, metallic Big Brother voice sounded portentous and the announcement downright ominous.

Weary to the bones, I got off the train and found a bench discreetly located in a corner of the terminal where the lights weren't too glaring. Using my carry-on as a pillow, I managed to go to sleep again. It wasn't too difficult. I was exhausted from the day's long journey.

Friday May 8, 2015

When the time had come, with my face hurting as much as the rest of my body from the uncomfortable bench, I crossed the Hauptbahnhof to the exit where I had agreed with Dr Sternmacher that his ambulance would pick me up. And there it was. Although I was ten minutes early, the ambulance had already arrived. Feeling truly terrible, I knocked on the window to the passenger seat and the two orderlies immediately stepped outside. I must have looked as awful as I felt, because they hurriedly opened the back and pulled out a stretcher instead of asking me to step inside. I climbed onto it, closed my eyes and lay my aching hands across my chest.

*

Georgie left the riad at six in the morning to catch the flight to Rabat two hours later. He was received at the embassy by the ambassador's personal secretary, with whom he discussed what was known in the case concerning the British citizen who had been found in the Sahara with a bullet in his head.

After they had agreed on the arrangements necessary to transport Allan Gould's remains to London, Georgie asked for a computer to inform his superiors. He wrote a lengthy report and sent it as an e-mail to Blackmoore. He just about managed to get on a return flight to Marrakech that left at 5:35 p.m.

*

Samantha, tired after the late-night dining at Goulla's house, rose late. She managed to get an improvised breakfast on the rooftop terrace despite having arrived past the breakfast hour. After asking at the reception for recommendations what she should get to know in Marrakech, she received an extensive list of suggestions. She chose to go to Jardín Majorelle, the property of a deceased French fashion designer that had been turned into a museum. Her impression after walking out from the establishment was at best lukewarm. In one of the shops outside, she bought a handmade white dress with an intricate design that, if you looked closely, depicted hundreds of different animals delicately interwoven.

A taxi took her to Jemaa el-Fnaa, the principal open space in Marrakech. She walked past the snake charmers and men with monkeys who urged that she'd pose with their animals for a few coins. The multitude overwhelmed her, with the vendors' insistence that she must buy their goods at a special price that they almost immediately offered to lower. She escaped into a restaurant, where she was shown how to get to the roof terrace. Ordering a bottle of Perrier, she watched the spectacle below.

Where is Matthias now? she wondered. *Is he still alive?*

*

Solomon Vaughn couldn't stop chewing on Andrew Reese's mysterious disappearance from the train to Milan. Fuelling this obsession was his humiliating experience with the Italian police. After one of his assistants had made a comprehensive timetable of Reese's train trip, it turned out that the last charge to the debit card had been made *after* the last stop before arriving in Milan. Since he didn't get off the train in Milan, it meant that Reese must either successfully have hidden himself while the Italian police searched the train or somehow got off it before its arrival. But how would that be possible? Reese couldn't have had any knowledge that the police would be looking for him, and besides, Interpol had confirmed that he wasn't wanted for any crime. The train had been a high-speed bullet train, so how could he possibly have jumped off it? Added to the puzzling circumstances was Reese's complete disappearance after the purchase on board the train, and he hadn't used his debit card since.

*

More asleep than awake, I felt strangely secure travelling in the ambulance with the knowledge that within hours my ordeal would be over. Sirens blasted intermittently when

347

something obstructed the vehicle. It took the ambulance one hour and twenty minutes to come to a halt on the driveway of the St Puys clinic.

I was placed in a wheelchair despite my half-hearted protests, pushed into a room inside the clinic and placed on a bed. Dr Sternmacher appeared almost immediately after the orderlies had finished their task. He took a long look at my face and my hands and seemed suitably worried.

"Please", he began hesitantly as he took a chair next to my bed, "tell me what has caused this degradation after the most unique and successful transplants I've ever performed."

I began telling the story I had prepared for him during the long hours on the train.

"I was vacationing on my own in Naples, when I was abducted by one of the Mafia organisations in that region, the 'Ndrangheta. Unable to get a ransom for me, I was robbed of everything I owned – my clothes, my wallet, credit cards, my medicine, even the prescription you made out although I begged them to at least leave that for reasons of my health. They merely laughed, and after a fortnight as their captive, they kicked me out for being useless to them."

"Mister Callaghan", he asked after a pause, looking as if he didn't believe me, "I've come to know you as a wealthy man. How come they were satisfied with your wallet, clothes and the prescription for your ciclosporin pills?"

Of course he would ask that. He had, after all, charged me eight million dollars for my second face transplant.

"I suppose because they never knew who I was, and

obviously I never let on that I was wealthy. If I had, who knows how long they would have kept me in captivity and what they would have done to me. Chopping off an ear to press for ransom, perhaps, or even", and here I shuddered at the thought, "start cutting off my fingers one at a time."

I don't think my story was sufficiently convincing to dampen the intelligent Dr Sternmacher's curiosity, but, whether he believed it or not, he anyway dropped the subject.

"When was the last time you took your prescribed dose of ciclosporin?"

It had been the morning I was released from the detention centre in London, an eternity ago.

"On the twenty-fifth of April", I told him.

He made a quick calculation in his head and looked appalled.

"That was thirteen days ago. No wonder you look so … exhausted. Please excuse me, I'll be back in a minute."

When he came back, he brought with him the ciclosporin pills I needed so badly. In addition, he made me swallow two different pills.

"Now you must sleep for as long as you wish", Dr Sternmacher ordered me, "to let your body reverse the negative effects. I will allow you into one of the bedrooms, where I think you should remain for at least one week."

The effect of the pills I had swallowed was immediate. I felt drowsy and had difficulty speaking clearly. All I wanted was to go to sleep … but I had to get back to London … London …

As I drifted into sleep, I heard Dr Sternmacher talking in the distance to someone else who had entered the room.

"Take him to suite seven. He should be asleep for at least eighteen hours, possibly up to twenty-four. Let me know at once the moment he wakes up, and don't leave him alone for a second."

The last I remembered before becoming unconscious was that I needed to convince Dr Sternmacher that I urgently needed to travel to London.

*

Blackmoore went through the emails on his desktop computer and found one from George Jones, the detective sergeant he had ordered to deal with the problem in Morocco. *Finally some news about Callaghan,* he thought as he opened the mail.

Callaghan had not been one of the two victims found in the desert. However, Jones wrote, one was a British citizen identified by his fingerprints and his facial features as Allan Gould. The autopsy showed that he had been shot in the head with a nine-millimetre bullet at close range. According to the pathologist, he had likely been killed on or about April 27.

The same day that Callaghan disappeared after walking out from Wormwood Scrubs, Blackmoore reflected. *Then Gould ends up dead next to Callaghan's jacket. There's no coincidence here. The cases are related – but how?*

The other body had been identified as Hamza Khalis, a small-time Moroccan crook who had been in and out jail before disappearing off the Moroccan police's radar twenty months ago. The official autopsy report had not yet been issued, but the probable cause of death was an overdose of an opioid substance.

Besides his jacket and the two receipts bearing Matthias Callaghan's name, there was nothing to implicate that Callaghan had been at the murder scene. Unless there was some compelling evidence coming from Interpol or Scotland Yard to prove the contrary, the Moroccan police insisted that they would continue to investigate the murders as local homicides without any suggestions of international or political connection. Jones finished by saying that he would return to duty in London shortly.

Blackmoore sighed. He had never taken to Jones, a social climber he had increasingly found too brash for his liking, with a dash of unreliability thrown into the mix. Jones had never seemed to be struggling to make ends meet like all the others his age in the corps. Nevertheless, he couldn't help maintaining a certain respect for Jones's proven ability as a detective.

The report set Blackmoore's investigation of Callaghan's disappearance back to the day he had walked out of Wormwood Scrubs on April 27. It was from that moment that the many questions emerged. *If Callaghan hadn't died in the Sahara, how did the receipts made out at his release end up in Morocco? Where had Callaghan gone? Had he made contact with Allan Gould or Hamza Khalis before their deaths? Had he really skipped bail, or was there some other reason for his disappearance?*

Why had he removed the monitor around his ankle immediately upon leaving prison? Was the simple answer that Callaghan killed Gould and Khalis? If that was the case, had he done so with the help of others?

Blackmoore remained convinced that Matthias Callaghan was guilty of the murder of Charles Rathbone, and he had a strong suspicion that Callaghan was involved in other serious crimes. He knew that the only way that he could ascertain his hunches was to bring Callaghan in for questioning.

Saturday May 9, 2015

When I woke up from a deep, dreamless sleep, I felt surprisingly refreshed without the nauseous anxiety that I had experienced increasingly during the past weeks. The nurse made a call, and seconds later Dr Sternmacher entered.

"Please don't get up", he beamed, "although I'm pleased to observe that you look remarkably improved when compared to the person I received yesterday."

"I can only thank yo u for your efficient attentions, Doctor", I replied, "which, after all, is the very reason I looked you up in my hour of need."

"Please, Mister Callaghan", he proffered with a dishonest smile, "we are all professionals, aren't we?"

He was really lousy at making small talk, but, then again, I had no interest in it.

"Can I have a word with you alone for a minute, Doctor?" I asked, casting a meaningful glance in the direction of the nurses who stood grouped behind him listening to our conversation.

"Of course." He ordered everyone out of the room, before turning back to me. "Something's not what it should be, right?" he asked me. "And I'm not talking about the lost prescription and the ciclosporin pills."

So now the good doctor, employed by me for what surely must have been in the competition for the most expensive surgery in history, wanted to pick my brain for answers that suited his curiosity? The moment has come to show him his place.

"Do you remember signing a carefully drafted legal document before performing my second face transplant, in which it was specifically stipulated that neither you nor the clinic could divulge any details about my surgeries here?"

"I do", Dr Sternmacher confirmed, looking miserable.

"Because of your carelessness and lack of security, the videotapes of my transplants were stolen. I have since learnt who stole them, and you won't like it a bit when I tell you who did it or why it was done. Do I have your attention?"

He nodded reluctantly without offering a reply. I decided to change my approach to keep him confused.

"There are two reasons for my coming here. The first one is obviously that I need my ciclosporin pills and the prescription to be able to buy more. The second one is that I want you to arrange a MedicAir flight from here to London tomorrow morning, and I need to enter the UK as a patient. Do you understand?"

Dr Sternmacher looked taken aback by my blunt request.

"Are you suggesting that I should smuggle you into the UK without the proper paperwork? Why should I do that?"

"Let's put it this way. You can either do it as a friendly favour to me after all the money I paid you when you made my second transplant. Or, if you prefer, I can send copies of the money transferred to you for the surgery to your local tax office."

I could tell that he didn't like my blackmailing method one bit.

"You've had a near-rejection after one of the most complicated operations in history", he began, evading the point I was making. "As your doctor, I must seriously advise you that you should not leave this bed for at least a week, to allow us to balance –"

"It's out of the question, Doctor Sternmacher", I interrupted him in a cold voice. "I want you to get me out of here by tomorrow morning. The time has come for a serious talk about our past and present doctor-patient relationship. First the broad facts: unconscious, I was brought here six years ago by my wife, and under her instructions you performed a face transplant that didn't remotely remind of my old self."

I raised my hand to stop him from interrupting me.

"I don't blame you in any way for that particular surgery, the most traumatic experience in my life, even should I take into account all the unimaginable things that have happened to me since. The next phase in our relationship was when my father died and his dead body became a genetically extraordinary replacement for the previous failure ... yes –

failure, for me, because I loathed every moment of my time with my first transplant. Then you made the second one, a definite improvement; there's no doubt whatsoever about that. Nevertheless, I think it's important to tell you that now, after years of living the experience: I don't imagine that you can imagine what it's like looking into the mirror every day seeing your dead father shave your chin. That's what I have to live with nowadays. Once again, I don't blame you and you certainly did a professional job on me twice. Now I come to the second part."

Dr Sternmacher sat in his chair, leaning forward, his elbows resting on his thighs and his hands clasped in front of him. He no longer attempted to interrupt me.

"Then another thing happened that shouldn't have occurred. When it comes to the execution of my transplants, I can only applaud your, and your staff's, work. But – and this is a big 'but' – I was given your personal guarantee after paying you *eight million dollars* that you would maintain total secrecy of my second transplant. Yet, a short time afterwards, your primitive sense of security allowed the filming of my two face transplants to be copied by someone who broke into your hospital. Now, am I correct when I claim these facts, or is there some detail in my version of the flow of things that you'd like to argue?"

Dr Sternmacher slowly shook his head sideways and didn't answer, waiting for the conclusion of my angry speech.

"Fast forward to today, in May two thousand and fifteen. I have four issues that I can't solve unless I can count on your immediate assistance. The first one is obvious: I need the prescription and the pills to get well again and avoid a transplant rejection. It shouldn't be a problem – I actually feel significantly better now than when I arrived. I just need the prescription on paper, and while you're at it, why don't you sign three or four of them, in case I should lose one or two in unforeseen circumstances?

"The second one is that I can't stay here for a week, as you suggested. There are stakes at play that are of more concern than my health. I've been robbed of everything. I've lost contact with my wife. My life has been threatened, and I fear that hers has, too. Tomorrow morning I need to fly back to London, which is where I last saw her, and I need your help to do so.

"The third thing is how you should help me get to London. Since I've lost my passport, I can't travel in a secure manner from Switzerland to another country because of the risk of being detained. Neither can I go to the British embassy to apply for some emergency passport, because of circumstances that are of no consequence to my plea for help from you. To make it short, I need you to get me into the UK without the need for me to identify myself as Matthias Callaghan. I'm thinking that the way to do it is to hire a MedicAir plane to take me there. You can make up any kind of excuse for transporting me as a patient, for example as a patient with severe burns who needs specialist care somewhere not too far from London. That way I would travel unrecognisable wrapped in bandages. A friend of mine,

Nathan Ripley, has kindly loaned me his driver's licence and it's my intention to enter the UK under that name.

"The fourth and last item on my list is how to cover the costs incurred for your services here and the transport. I leave that up to you, but you have my word of honour that whatever the amount you feel appropriate to charge, I will cover it as soon as I have access to my financial assets again."

Having finished, I waited for him to respond to my request. I had chosen to be blunt, because I had always perceived Dr Sternmacher to be a no-nonsense person who wanted a straight opinion.

He thought for a long time before he replied.

"I understand what you're telling me, Mister Callaghan", he finally said. "I will make the necessary arrangements for your transfer to a UK hospital tomorrow morning. And, you don't need to worry about the cost – as our most celebrated client, it will be free of charge."

PART XII

Catching a viper by the neck
renders it unable to use its fangs.

Saturday May 9, 2015

"Tomorrow we go back to London", Georgie told Samantha, while they were having breakfast on the terrace overlooking a considerable number of rooftops in the medina, the majority adorned with rusted satellite antennae. "We should make the most of our last day here."

"Do you have anything particular in mind?" Samantha asked.

By now, their relationship was more relaxed, and Samantha considered herself fortunate to have someone within the Metropolitan Police as her friend.

"I feel curious about walking through the marketplace of

the medina", Georgie replied. "It's certainly not something one sees every day, and perhaps we could pick up an interesting souvenir or two while we're at it. Most important, of course, is to get a feel for the local folklore. Then I will use the rest of my travel allowance inviting you to dinner at a place I'm told is as spectacular for its surroundings as it is for its food."

"It certainly sounds tempting, George", Samantha acknowledged with a brief smile and her eyes fixed on the Atlas Mountains in the horizon.

Georgie had noticed that she was somewhat distant this morning, and he wasn't sure why.

The riad where they were staying was located in a part of the medina where the houses served as living quarters. Georgie asked the nice lady who was in charge of the guests' well-being how they could get to the market, and she gave him a map where she had circled the most important spots to visit.

They set out on foot following the 1,000-year-old winding alleyways. As they came closer to the market, they were increasingly surrounded by beggars, street vendors, women covered in veils and black cloth, and children playing and running around.

"If it weren't for the mobiles everyone is carrying", Samantha said to Georgie, "you'd think we were back in medieval times."

However, when they reached the market with its shops lining the narrow, crowded lanes, Georgie noticed that

Samantha began to pale. They were walking down endless lanes in the shade beneath awnings that protected them from the sun, constantly running into people. Seeing tourists from Europe, the shop owners inevitably ran outside to insist they should have a look inside at the marvels they had on offer. An unconcerned man with a donkey that carried two large bags forced all pedestrians to make a detour. The constant chatter came in waves as they zigzagged through the relentless crowd.

Georgie felt how Samantha gripped his upper arm with both hands. He could feel her nails digging into the flesh.

"George, get me out of here." There was panic in her voice. "I can't take this any more, I can't take it, I really can't."

Georgie was consternated over the effect the place had had on her. Crowded, yes, but nothing gross or inappropriate had taken place. It was merely a large bazaar with huge crowds brushing elbows, as they had done for millennia, as far as he understood it. But he immediately consulted his map for an exit, and fifteen minutes later they emerged on the sunlit Jemaa el -Fnaa.

Samantha breathed with relief.

"I'm sorry, I just can't handle crowds in narrow spaces like that", she told Georgie. "They provoke a sense of helplessness in me."

"Don't worry", Georgie answered. "Why don't we go to that café across the square to sit down and take a deep breath?"

It was the bazaar in Istanbul all over again, Samantha

recalled after reliving flashes of the day she was abducted, *the crowds, the hawkers, the beggars. Then, in a second, you're gone, but that's not something I can tell my protective detective sergeant.*

Samantha put on a brave face when they were seated at the café's balcony overlooking some snake charmers who offered tourists the opportunity to be pictured with their pets. Both ordered ice cream.

"George ... I've been thinking a great lot about my husband's disappearance", she began. "Despite not being among the victims at the morgue, I recognise the possibility that he's dead – although I'm not sure why that would have happened." Her eyes, downcast, made Georgie realise anew how she was overcome by the tragedy she was living. He placed his hand gently on top of hers, to comfort her. He felt electrified when she didn't withdraw it, but turned it around to grasp his in a gesture of gratitude.

Gradually, they both lost awareness of their colourful surroundings as Samantha began to talk in confidence of her misgivings about Matthias's disappearance. Georgie, by now infatuated with her, did his best to scatter her misgivings by inspiring hope. Eventually, because she now trusted him and her heart was overflowing with joy that she now had found her biological family, she couldn't resist telling Georgie the story of her abduction as a young girl.

"That's why I couldn't stand the crowded alleys in the medina", she finished her story with tears in her eyes, grasping one of his hands with both of hers. "It reminded me of the ..."

"I understand perfectly", Georgie said, moved by her story. "You're a remarkable woman."

Later, when her emotions had calmed down, Georgie suggested that they take a cab to La Mamounia, where he had reserved a table. After passing through the heavy security to enter the city's most fashionable hotel, they were escorted to a table in one of the gardens, next to an enormous buffet that outdid everything any of them previously had ever laid their eyes on.

Over dinner, Samantha felt she bonded with Georgie as he started telling her tidbits from his life struggling to become a police officer, most of which he made up as he went along.

*

On May 5, Mossack Fonseca had sent a cease-and-desist letter to the International Consortium of Investigative Journalists (ICIJ) in an attempt to prevent further publication of the leaked documents hacked from their computers. After four days of contemplation, ICIJ chose to ignore the threatening letter and instead released a large number of additional leaked documents. Among those mentioned figured various companies, registered in Panama and other fiscal paradises, that clearly stated Harry Jordan as its chief shareholder.

Luigi Monticalli's grand-nephew, known to those close to him as Benny Botana, read the article in *The New York Times* with interest. His great-uncle had more than a decade ago closed his eyes for the last time at the age of 95, but not before he had extracted a promise from Benny and his siblings that they'd exact revenge on the lowliest of all the low traitors in the business: Harry Jordan. And now, all of a sudden, there was finally a promising clue where to find the traitor and the ill-gotten riches that in Benny Botana's opinion should rightly benefit himself and a few other associates in the business they'd taken over from the old-timers.

Sunday May 10, 2015

The MedicAir airplane touched ground at London Luton Airport at half past noon local time. As the plane taxied to its slot after landing, an ambulance with its lights flashing followed the established driveway marked on the tarmac. The sedated and heavily bandaged patient was immediately transferred from the airplane to the ambulance according to the established protocol. An immigration officer made his presence and took a picture of the identity card of the newly arrived. Shortly afterwards, the emergency vehicle left for the University Hospital in Milton Keynes with blaring sirens, where it arrived setting a new record driving the distance. The patient, with severe burns according to his accompanying medical chart, was taken to the hospital wing where emergencies were treated. When the clock showed 1:25 p.m., he was left in the solitary room as per the request of the Swiss hospital that had solicited his transfer. The shift of the doctor specialised in skin burns was scheduled to begin thirty-five minutes later.

363

When the doctor arrived at 2:02 p.m., the room was empty.

*

As soon as the nurses left the room in belief that my immobility combined with my heavy breathing meant that I was asleep under sedation, I jumped into action. I unwound the bandages and quickly changed into regular clothes packed in my carryall and left the room. Carrying my bag, I calmly walked out of the hospital without being challenged by anyone.

The hospital Dr Sternmacher had found was located in Milton Keynes, a town an hour or two away from central London, depending on the travel mode. There was a train leaving for the capital every hour. I nevertheless chose to take the bus, which was nearly as fast.

I was in luck – a direct bus, making no stops, left Milton Keynes twenty-five minutes later. I got off the bus not far from Trafalgar Square just over an hour later.

It was now late afternoon. Samantha stayed at the Savoy Hotel, on the Strand. It took me a mere twenty-five minutes to walk there.

The man at the front desk, with his left eyebrow apparently raised in perpetual disapproval, made a badly executed cover-up of his unfavourable grimace when I walked up to him. After weeks of hardships to get back, wearing clothes that would look better on a professional beggar, I could understand his reaction, but I couldn't permit it. Although I was there for the sole purpose of finding some hint of Samantha's whereabouts, something inside me snapped. Using my poshest upper-class accent, I addressed him as an employee who was at my service.

"Good afternoon to you, too", I greeted him sarcastically. "I wish to speak to a guest at your hotel, a certain Samantha Callaghan. I'd appreciate if you could provide me with her room number."

"The policy at the Savoy is to never reveal such information", he replied, insolently. "For security reasons, of course."

"Then kindly call her room to inform her that her husband is waiting in the lobby, and we shall both soon know whether she will take my call or not, shan't we?"

That at least got him tapping away on his computer.

"The guest in question checked out on May sixth. I'm sorry, but I can't help you with any further information." He didn't sound sorry at all, but instead studied me sceptically beneath his raised eyebrow.

"She didn't leave any messages for me?"

"No, she did not leave a message for anyone." He made 'anyone' sound like a disease.

I walked out of the hotel in confusion. Where had Samantha gone? When I had spoken to Jack two days earlier, he had no news of her. *He must surely know by now,* I thought and made a mental note to call him again.

I happened upon a cybercafé not far from Charing Cross

and went inside to catch up on my e-mails, thinking that Samantha had perhaps written me. She hadn't, but there was a mail from Clemens Porter in my Abdul Mahfouz inbox. Porter wrote that, although he still had the more "complex work" ahead of him, should I be interested in a partial report, he had some information he could provide. His mail had been sent a few hours earlier.

I called him using my disposable Italian mobile.

"Thank you for getting back with a response to my urgent request so quickly", I told him, not forgetting to pose as Dr Ibrahim. "I just got back from some minor business in Morocco."

"You have me intrigued, Doctor Ibrahim. You do have a lot of information about things few other people have. I think you'd make a great investigator."

"I thank you kindly for the compliment, Mister Porter. I can only say that I'm not interested in taking a position different from my present one, so, if you don't mind, could we get down to your report?"

"I don't have much yet, but since you advised me it was urgent, I thought that this time you'd like to get the information piecemeal."

"I do appreciate your concern, Mister Porter. It won't be forgotten when I settle the bill."

"What I have so far isn't too exciting, I believe, but I checked the public records concerning the information you're seeking. After Jeremiah Flint's death in two thousand and nine, Flint's property *The Lion's Head*, was left to his sole heir

Philip Jones. When Philip Jones died five years later, the pub was inherited by his son, George Jones. George Jones sold the pub six months later to a corporation named Hidalgo Limited, one that has aggressively acquired drinking establishments across the country over the past fifteen years.

This information doesn't give me much to go on, I brooded. *Who are Philip and George Jones? What relationship did they have to Flint? Had any of them got their hands on the recording Flint had made of my pitch to Flint to kill Rathbone? If so, how did that recording end up at Scotland Yard years later?*

"While I was checking out the public records, I also made research concerning the properties – not rented, mind you, but owned – that Arexim, headed by this Mikhail Berlosky, have in the UK", Porter continued. "It turns out there are three: the building on Saint Katharine's Way, a warehouse on Wapping High Street and a flat on Park Lane –"

"On Park Lane, you say?" I had a hard time believing the coincidence that I had once been the Russians' neighbour.

"Yes, it was purchased by Arexim in two thousand and nine. The previous owner was Matthias Callaghan, whose name you may recall from one of my past reports …"

Porter let the words hang in the silence between us, to see if he could elicit some clue in my response. Although I didn't give him the pleasure, I once again had that horrible sensation of being caught up by the inexorable past.

"Anything else?" I finally asked him.

"No, I'll get back to you later on the rest of the stuff", Porter said.

"There's one more task I want you to consider, Mister Porter", I told him. "This George Jones who inherited the pub and then sold it – I want you to find everything you can about him. His background, what he does for a living, the company he keeps, what else he inherited from his father, if he sings in the shower – everything."

"It will cost you an extra –"

"Yes, it will. Just send me the bill, which, as usual, I trust you will do before it's followed by the requested information."

I disconnected the call, angrily. That was both stupid and unjust of me, because it wasn't Porter's fault that the Russians who had tortured me were now in possession of my beautiful flat. I really should be angry with myself, not with him.

How did the Russians come to acquire my flat? I pondered after finishing the call with Porter. *Well, perhaps it isn't too incredulous when you think about it. Since Berlosky has his nice house outside London near a golf course, where his son was born and goes to school, it's more than likely that my old flat now is Vasily's living quarters. My departure from London took place a couple of months after Vasily had arrived, and there could be no surprise if he had been searching for something upscale. Something attractive like my flat doesn't often come on the market. When Vince told me my broker had made the sale but the money for it had ended up out of my reach because Allan had managed to get my bank account impounded, I hadn't bothered asking who the buyer was.*

I counted the money I still had on me. Fifty-odd euros that I needed to change into pounds plus some change that the cashier had given me at a lousy rate when I had bought the bus ticket in Milton Keynes. I paid for the time I had used at the cybercafé and ventured out into the evening, now dark and overcast with a wind picking up. There was rain in the air. I aimlessly wandered about central London, going over everything I had learnt during the past few days. I had no clue what to do next, except that I knew I had to call Jack to transfer me some money. A fugitive from the police, Samantha vanished, the Russians always one step ahead of me … there was no end to the odds stacked against me.

*

The BA flight from Marrakech landed on Gatwick seven minutes ahead of schedule. Since they travelled with carry-on bags only, Samantha and Georgie quickly made it through immigration and navigated through the throngs of people to the exit, where they caught a cab. Arriving at the Savoy, Samantha got out of the car after thanking him for everything with a peck on the cheek.

Feeling thus rewarded in his most difficult of conquests to date, but quite assured that things were working in his favour, Georgie ordered the cabbie to take him to his home address.

*

Samantha checked into the Savoy again. She now waited impatiently in her room for the concierge to come up with the bags that she had left when going to Morocco. She felt tired. The initial relief that Matthias wasn't one of the men in the morgue had given way to renewed uncertainty about his fate and whereabouts. Samantha longed for a hot shower. There was a knock on the door.

"Here you are, ma'am", the porter said upon entering the room with the three bags, two that were hers and one belonging to Matthias. "There's also an envelope for you. It seems you left your mobile behind during your last stay. It was found charging in the bathroom by the maid."

"Oh, that's where I left it!" Samantha exclaimed, relieved. "Thank you so much!"

The porter disappeared after receiving his tip. She turned on the mobile and saw that she had three missed calls from Jack and another two dozen calls from an unknown number. Her voicemail inbox was full.

Samantha, this is Jack, she heard her brother say. *I just got a call from Matthias, who says he's in Italy and doing well. Call me!*

Her heart beat faster. Matthias was alive! *But how had he gone to Italy without a passport? Had he skipped bail, after all?*

She checked the voicemails from the unknown number. *Samantha, love,* she heard Matthias's tired voice say, *just to let you know I'm alive and kicking after the most horrendous experience. I'm in Rome, where Andrew is helping me. Call me at this number, will you?*

There were more messages from him with the same plea, but Matthias didn't explain what his horrendous experience had been. Then he said he was becoming worried that she didn't answer or call him back. *If he only knew*, she thought and felt awful about having been so careless leaving her mobile behind.

In the last voicemail from him, Matthias managed to say he was on a train to Milano before he was cut off. Her messaging service had run out of space.

She dialled his number. There was no answer or voicemail service.

Where is he now? Samantha wondered, feeling less worried but still concerned about Matthias's whereabouts. *Where can I find him?*

*

As promised by the dark skies, a drizzle began and soon turned into showers. I ventured into a pub near Leicester Square, where I ordered a pint and the largest hot sandwich on offer. I was allowed to pay for it at the lousy exchange rate of a euro for a pound.

Being Sunday, the pub was full. Or maybe it was the rain. A couple left and I managed to get a seat in the corner. I needed to put my thoughts in order, to determine my objectives and to find a way out of my maze of a mess. According to the clock behind the counter, the time was 6:05 p.m.

I tuned out the noise from the crowd in the pub as I devoured the sandwich and concentrated on what to do next. I didn't have enough money to stay at a hotel, so where to sleep was my most urgent concern. I could call Vince or some other friend from my past in London, but it didn't appeal to me to ring them up like a beggar in shabby clothes and ask for a charitable act. Besides, their obvious questions, all considered, about how I ended up in this situation wasn't one I was prepared to explain in exchange for a night or two in their guest room.

The time difference with Sydney was nine hours, so surely Jack must be up by now. I dialled his number and heard the phone ring once. Then I was informed by an automated voice that my pre-charged phone required additional funds. *Isn't life a gas,* I thought, gloomily. *No phone, no money, nowhere to sleep, no change of clothes, no Samantha and my kids halfway around the world.*

The bell for last orders sounded 10:45, and twenty minutes later I was out on the street with the rest of the lingering pub guests. The rain had let up, but the air was chilly and humid. I needed to find some shelter to keep warm during the rest of the night.

In the nearby theatre district, I found a café with a promise that it stayed open 24 hours. I went inside and ordered a large cup of coffee that had the benefit of expelling the chill out of my bones. I nursed it in a corner, trying to look as invisible as possible as people came and went. When one of the youngsters behind the counter looked disapprovingly at me, as if I had overstayed my visit, I ordered another coffee. This one I sipped once before placing it on the table in front of me and promptly fall asleep.

Monday May 11, 2017

A few hours later, the barista decided he had had enough of the homeless man and his pitiful bag, punched me in the chest and ordered that it was time for me to leave. As I obeyed, I was told that I could take with me the coffee I had barely touched. I graciously declined, arguing that I never drank my coffee cold.

I guessed it was about five in the morning as I wandered aimlessly along the still dark and empty streets of London. Samantha was missing. I was down to 25 euros and some change jingling in my pockets. On top of that, there was a drizzle to cheer me up.

I rummaged through my holdall to find something to protect me from the rain. At the bottom, I found a set of keys. *What are these keys for?* Then I remembered. They were the keys that Andrew had returned to me in Rome, some six years after I had sold the flat.

Suddenly it hit me. *What if the lock to take the elevator to the penthouse hasn't been changed?* Since I had a hard time believing that anyone besides Vasily and Berlosky would have the motivation, the capacity and the money to leave me for dead in the Sahara Desert twenty-four hours after my release. I was convinced that it must have been the Russians who had organised it. *Did Vasily believe that I was dead? Surely he must have received some report after Allan, I and the other unknown victim had been left in the desert?*

With nothing better occurring to me, I decided I'd take a chance revisiting my former flat. It took me a little less than an hour to walk there in the light rain and with my Italian summer clothes wrapped tight against the morning chill. When I finally reached Park Lane, I let myself into the garage and hid in the corner behind a dust-covered Rolls-Royce. It belonged to my former neighbour Mr Baker, who hadn't made use of it his since his stroke ten years earlier.

There was a large, black Mercedes in the parking space I used to occupy. More interesting, in the other parking space that came with the flat, was a two-tone Bugatti Veyron that I knew came with a price tag that easily surpassed the cost of five Rolls-Royces.

At eight o'clock sharp a sturdy man dressed in a black suit used the stairway from the reception desk to enter the garage. He used a remote control to enter the Mercedes.

Not until 9:25 did Vasily and another man, unknown to me, emerge from the elevator. Vasily didn't look a day older since we had last met. With the mobile's flash turned off, I managed to take two quick close-up pictures of Vasily just before he entered the back seat and the door was closed. The chauffeur started the car, and, thirty seconds later, it was gone.

After hiding my bag behind the dusty Rolls Royce, I went to the elevator and inserted the key to ride it to my former flat. To my satisfaction, the key still fitted, and the elevator started its journey through the building. The advantage of a private elevator, a perk that only the penthouse enjoyed, was that the people at the reception couldn't notice your comings and goings. On all landings below, there were security cameras recording any movement. When I got to the top floor, I held my breath after the elevator opened up inside the sitting room. The conversion of my former living space was overwhelming. I stood outside the elevator for a good minute just to take in the tremendous changes made.

There were exquisite pieces of furniture from three different centuries: an enormous glass sculpture replica of Botticelli's painting of *Birth of Venus*; overlapping thick Middle Eastern carpets; an Alexander Calder mobile in bright colours; and an enormous home movie theatre that could be watched from two ostrich leather-clad rotating chairs. Most impressive of all, however, were the paintings hanging on the walls: Picasso, Klimt, Freud, El Greco, Kandinsky, Turner, Zorn and many others.

The effect, of course, was quite eclectic. An impressive show of wealth and independent pieces of great beauty, but the overall impact was nevertheless one of poor taste. The owner had over a short space of time jammed the flat with things he had spent huge money on. In my own experience, a living space needs to grow over time, adding things of special interest from journeys, experience and chance encounters that fit into the general culture of you and your family.

But I hadn't arrived there to judge the taste of a man who had made a fortune creating a drug empire. I didn't know how much time I had, but, before the flat's present owner returned, I needed to cover its eight rooms in search of anything that might incriminate him. Before doing so, I found it wise to set up an alternative escape route, just in case. I went into the kitchen, which to my surprise looked both unused and very much the way I had left it, and unlocked the door leading out to the building's main staircase. This was the entrance that Andrew had used in the past when he still worked for me.

I returned to the sitting room, by far the largest room in the flat, and started looking for information in all drawers and all other possible hiding places. Five minutes later, I had found a lot more than I had bargained for. It shocked me to the bones. Lying openly on the counter of the ostentatious bar was a set of printed pictures taken in the Sahara Desert, showing Allan, me and the third man without signs of life.

I felt the anger well up inside me. Here I had indisputable proof that Vasily had executed the operation to kill me and Allan. I didn't understand why he had decided to have Allan killed and leave me alive. Perhaps he hadn't intended to, and some mistake had been committed. I should be grateful for the fact, I knew, but the only thing I felt was tremendous rage.

Putting the pictures in the inside pocket of my jacket, I continued into the next room, where another surprise awaited me. Hanging on the wall was *La femme à l'éventail*, a painting by Amedeo Modigliani stolen in 2010, which I had read about on the flight coming from Australia. After my initial incredulity, I snapped some pictures of the painting with my mobile. I then took pictures of all other paintings in the flat, unsure if there were additional ones that had been stolen.

With stolen artworks on your walls, Vasily, I've got you painted in a corner, I thought, just as the door opened. A woman with a pistol, which she professionally held with both hands and pointed at me with her arms extended, entered the room.

"And who are you, I wonder?" she asked, looking as if she didn't need an excuse to fire her weapon.

*

It occurred to Samantha that her new friend Georgie could help her find Matthias now that she had news about him. The police should by now know something if he had left the country and ended up in Rome, and surely Georgie could help her find out. She dialled the number he had given her, but there was neither a reply nor an answering service.

She called Jack in Sydney, who was relieved to hear from her. He confirmed that Matthias had called him twice from Italy, the last time when he was about to take a train to Switzerland.

He went back to the hospital and Dr Sternmacher, Samantha thought with a sinking heart. *He's suffering rejections from his transplants. Something bad happened to him.*

*

The woman who pointed her gun at me was unknown to me. Her blond hair was cropped short, she was clad in a short-sleeved pyjamas that revealed some tattooed skin and she looked as serious as the weapon she held in her hands.

"Who are you?" she repeated. "How did you enter?"

From this short sentence in English, and from her hard accent, I judged her to be Russian, or at least from some country behind the former Iron Curtain. Thinking fast, I hoped an approach projecting innocence might convince her.

"Why do you point a gun at me?" I scolded her in a pitched voice, that for some subconscious reason came out sounding French. "How rude of you! I was asked by Monsieur Vasily to make an appraisal of his art collection, and here I am. I repeat: not to steal it, but to appraise it, ha ha. See for yourself – here are the keys he gave me to let myself in."

I took the keys out my pocket. She didn't appreciate my attempt to joke away her concern about my presence.

"I will call Vasily, and we will see if he confirms what you're telling me. Go back into the sitting room."

She waved her pistol in the direction of the flat's main room. I obeyed her, clicking my tongue in disapproval. When we reached the door, I pretended to stumble on the threshold and crouched in the process. This made her involuntarily lower the weapon. I slammed the door shut before she had a chance to follow me. The impact of the door caught her by the wrists. She cried out and dropped the gun.

I rushed to the kitchen and opened the door to the staircase. The woman who had threatened me called out from behind. *My problem now is downstairs, not behind me: how will I be able to get past the people in the reception?* I wondered. I shut the door behind me with a bang and rushed down the stairs while pulling my jacket over my head to prevent the cameras on each landing from recording my face. When I got to the landing just above the reception, I heard the reception clerk responding to a call that I had to assume was from the woman in the flat I had broken into.

I stopped, hesitating briefly as I listened to his response. I recognised the porter's voice as that of Henry "the Hoarse", recalling his nickname. He would inevitably recognise me, something I couldn't afford. Holding the prints I had found on the bar counter in front of my face and my key ready, I ran down to the last steps. I quickly unlocked the door leading to the garage, and escaped down the last pair of stairs before Henry got the opportunity to gasp.

Seconds later, I had picked up my carryall and emerged from the garage, quickly getting lost in the crowd on a neighbouring street.

*

Furious, Sonia speed-dialled Vasily's mobile.

"There's been an intruder here at Park Lane", she fumed. "I woke up hearing strange noises after you left, and there he was, claiming that you had hired him to make an appraisal of your paintings! An unshaven man in his forties in rumpled clothes that looked as if he had slept in them. I didn't believe it and held him at gunpoint. He tricked me and managed to escape."

Sonia's report made Vasily sit up straight in his office chair. He felt aghast that some delinquent had made his way into his inner sanctum, the place that only a handful of his most trusted people were allowed to visit.

"Rest assured that I haven't authorised any such appraisal", Vasily responded heatedly. "Who was he? How did he get in? Did he remove any of –"

"He dangled the keys to the flat in front of me", Sonia interrupted him, "that's how he got in."

The information made Vasily calculate the possibilities for nearly a minute. *Apart from the audacity, who could possibly have keys to my flat?*

"Don't do anything. Wait for me, I'll be right over."

Disconnecting, he ordered his car to be ready immediately. The same moment he received a call from Mikhail Berlosky.

"Look, I don't have the time to talk to you right now, Mikhail. Something important has come up and –"

"Not more important than what I'm about to tell you, Vasily", Berlosky retorted. "The ship with the latest cargo from Afghanistan has been detained in a Spanish port."

Suddenly, Vasily realised that there seemed to be no end to his troubles.

"I don't want to give you the details, or the solution, over the phone, as I'm sure you can appreciate", Berlosky continued in a sombre voice. "I'll see you in ten minutes."

*

Out of breath, but satisfied that I had outrun any follower, I entered a small coffee shop full of noisy people on their way to work. The best way to hide, I suppose, is in the middle of a crowd.

What should I do now? I asked myself, realising that I had the perfect weapon to bring down Vasily and his drug empire. My pictures of a stolen painting worth millions in his home would surely get the police interested. Sipping on a cup of hot coffee, I thought through my situation. *Will Vasily understand that I was the person who had broken into his flat? If I go to the police, what will they think about the device that was removed from my ankle? Will I be able or not to continue my freedom on bail, despite not having reported regularly to the local police station?*

Sooner or later I had to face the police, I reasoned, and I did have the pictures of me lying in the desert with Allan and the other man. Surely the police would be able to corroborate their deaths with the authorities in Morocco. I decided to call Scotland Yard and turn myself in.

The woman in charge of the switchboard corrected me when I asked for Detective Sergeant John Blackmoore.

"It's 'Detective Inspector', sir", she rebuked me before connecting the call.

It took three beeps before I heard a voice say "Blackmoore."

I recognised his voice from a few years back when I had made my "confession" speech to get my true identity back.

"Good morning, Detective Inspector", I greeted him. "This is Matthias Callaghan calling you, because it occurred to me that you might be interested in listening to yet another fascinating story I'm ready to share with you."

There was a prolonged silence – as if he couldn't quite believe who the caller was – before he replied.

"Good morning, Mister Callaghan. It's certainly a surprise to hear from you."

"I've been in a bit of a pickle this morning, and it would be convenient if I could have a chat with you without delay. Would you be so kind to send me one of your cars?"

He snorted a little at my cheekiness for a free ride, but I suppose he found me too important not to interview, so he acceded. I gave him the address. He promised me a patrol car would be there within a few minutes.

While I was waiting, I asked one of the personnel for their Wi-Fi connection. He gave me the password and I managed to get my phone operational via their modem. With the likelihood that I'd be arrested again, as a precaution I forwarded the pictures I had taken of Vasily in the garage to Samantha's email address.

*

Berlosky rushed into the office where Vasily was waiting impatiently.

"Be brief, Mikhail", Vasily cautioned him, "I have another urgency that can't wait. Sonia called me to say that someone broke into my flat this morning, possibly to steal some of my paintings."

Berlosky blinked repeatedly at him in surprise. He found it unimaginable that somebody would attempt to rob something from Europe's most important drug baron. *Severe punishment awaits whoever tried to*, Berlosky thought, not doubting for a second that the perpetrator would be caught.

"The Spanish police officer we bribed in Málaga let us down. He was supposed to look the other way when we brought in five hundred kilos, and to make him look good, we allowed him to find thirty kilos that we would tip him anonymously where to encounter. Somehow he found out about the larger shipment, and impounded both."

"So, shoot him and bribe someone else to get our shipment back", Vasily shrugged.

"Don't think I haven't thought of it, but the problem is more complex. It turns out this officer was an undercover agent for Interpol, and now he can't be found. Nor do we know where the cargo is. It's been flown under heavily armed protection from Málaga to somewhere in France."

Vasily began to show irritation, Berlosky noticed. It was never a good sign.

"The number of people we have on our payroll is larger than the population of Iceland – so find someone who knows where it has been taken!"

Vasily rose to show the interview was over.

"Look, one solution would be to just forget about this one … Why, it only cost us twelve million and –

"Absolutely out of the question!" Vasily raised his voice until it trembled, which was very unusual for him. "It's not about the cost. The street value is three hundred million. Find my heroin, or someone will pay me what it's worth!"

With this instruction, Vasily stomped out of the office to find his waiting car.

*

Blackmoore studied me with his no-nonsense eyes as I, wearing handcuffs, was shown into the conference room where he had agreed to meet with me. We had only met in person on one previous occasion, three years earlier. His face disclosed what he thought as I sat down: *A man in his early forties. Green eyes. Sandy hair. An intelligent glint in his eyes. Looks undernourished. Definitely not a crook of the common type, but still a crook.* I think I wasn't too off the mark trying to read his assessment of me.

Blackmoore ordered my handcuffs to be removed and nodded at me to take a seat. The clock on the wall behind him showed 10:52. I heeded his nod and took a chair opposite him. The warder who had brought me remained standing behind my chair.

"I'm told that you've been scarce lately, Callaghan", he challenged me in a brusque tone.

"Well, I've been kept busy, but through no fault of my own", I retorted and began to tick off my mental list. "I've been kidnapped, drugged and illegally smuggled out of the country. I've risen from the dead in a sandbox where my two companions didn't make it. I've crossed six countries to sit here and give you a full report. I've even found a stolen painting with a worth of, what, some fifty million pounds,

384

that the real owner no doubt will be interested in having returned. Oh, and by the way, I think I do have the answer, should you be keen on dismantling the number one drug cartel in Europe."

There was a long pause while Blackmoore chewed on what I had said.

"That's quite a mouthful, Mister Callaghan", Blackmoore finally replied with a mystified look. At least he had moved me a rung up the ladder of respect by adding a "mister" to my name for the first time. "Do you have anything to back up all these Hollywood plots?"

"I certainly do, sir", I said and brought out the photos of me and the dead men in the desert that I had found in Vasily's flat. I shoved them across the table.

As he studied them, Blackmoore immediately became more serious and less overbearing.

"That's Allan Gould, my former business partner", I said. "The other victim is unknown to me."

"I'm aware of the identity of both men", Blackmoore said as he shuffled through the prints. "We've had extensive contact with the police in Marrakech about the situation. One of our detectives is returning from Morocco as we speak."

"I'm glad to have given you evidence that my whereabouts of late were involuntary", I said, unable to avoid a bit of sarcasm. "I am, of course, willing to give you the full account for the record. However, I think it's more urgent dealing with the stolen painting and bringing down the drug cartel. Do you agree?"

I'm sure he didn't like my tone, but he kept his poker face.

"Don't be shy. Tell me all about it."

"By sheer coincidence a set of keys to my former flat on Park Lane was returned to me the other day. A couple of days later I was back in London, and I was curious about what state it was in, now that I'd sold it. I rang the doorbell, of course, but no one answered. So I let myself in using my keys."

"That has a severe implication of confessing to illegal entry", Blackmoore said.

"It does, doesn't it?" I replied. "But then again, I wouldn't tell you this if it weren't for some odd things I discovered while making that very same illegal entry. First of all, in this flat is where I found the set of photographs you're now holding. Secondly, I took this picture of a very famous, albeit stolen, portrait."

I held out my mobile to show him the photo I'd taken of Modigliani's painting. It took Blackmoore three seconds to grasp the situation. He picked up the phone next to him.

"Is Anne Slater in?" I couldn't hear the response, but he was apparently given an affirmative reply. "Please ask her to urgently come to conference room fourteen on the seventh floor. I have something important that will interest her."

After hanging up, he turned to me again – for the first time with the hint of a smile.

"You're certainly full of both surprises and entertaining stories, Mister Callaghan. While we wait for my colleague from the art fraud division to arrive, why don't you expand a bit on the claim that you know how to bring down this drug empire you've been telling me about?"

"I'd be more than happy to do so, Detective Inspector, but there's one thing we must agree on before I give you the full picture."'

"And that is …?"

"The man you want to apprehend is head of the organisation that has hounded me for years. Surely you remember when I was last here and told you –"

"I remember."

"The name of the head of the Russian Mafia in London is Vasily Ivanovich. Unbeknown to me, circumstance had it that he bought my flat on Park Lane after I had decided to move from this country. His number one employee, who in practice runs the day-to-day details of the illegal operation, is Mikhail Berlosky – a Russian with whom I've had some run-ins a couple of times in the past. Since you haven't grabbed Vasily or Berlosky after all these years, it must be because they enjoy a perfect cover, or even protection from higher up in the police echelons … who knows. It struck me that perhaps you could nail him for something else, like the FBI jailed Al Capone over tax evasion instead of his other, more serious crimes. Wouldn't finding a stolen painting worth millions of pounds provide you with that opportunity?"

The door opened and an attractive woman with auburn hair in her early forties entered.

"You wanted me, John? Something urgent, I was told?"

"Hello Anne. This is Matthias Callaghan", he said and

nodded in my direction before he explained to me who the newcomer was. "Detective Inspector Anne Slater is the head of the division here at the Yard that investigates fraud, theft and illegal exports of art works."

She nodded at me. I nodded back, politely.

"Please show her the picture of the painting", Blackmoore asked me.

I did as I was asked.

"It's the Modigliani stolen from –"

"I know exactly *what* it is", she cut me off. "I'd be more interested in knowing *where* it can be found."

I gave her the address on Park Lane. "It's the penthouse flat", I added.

Slater looked at Blackmoore.

"What do you think of this? Is it real?" Between the lines, I understood that she was asking whether I was to be trusted or not.

"I do believe it is", he replied slowly.

"If you want the stolen painting back, I suggest that you hurry, because …", I looked at the clock on the wall, "… I took this picture about an hour and a half ago and had to flee when I was seen doing it. There's always the possibility that its present owner has removed it."

Anne Slater gave me the impression of being a woman who was both intelligent and decisive.

"John, I will take some men to the address given and block the exits to prevent the possible removal of the painting. Meanwhile, I implore you to help me process the court order for a search of the flat."

She turned and looked at me sternly.

"I sincerely hope you're not sending me on a fool's errand, Mister Callaghan."

"You may rest assured it's the other way around", I told her, unruffled.

*

Sonia was getting increasingly nervous when Vasily didn't turn up. She knew better, though, than to call him again. She had learnt the lesson in the past: "call me once to inform me, but if you call me twice, it's nagging. I don't like nagging. It reminds me of my mother". The giggle that followed didn't fool her, and she had adhered to his advice ever since.

When an hour had passed, she couldn't stand being alone in the flat. As a precaution, she dressed in neutral clothes and put on the red wig that Vasily liked her to wear in bed. *Who was the man she had held at gunpoint?* she wondered. *Had he come to intimidate Vasily, to gather evidence of the drug business, or was he merely a simple thief out to steal valuables? What nerve – standing there as cool as a penguin, facing a muzzle and telling her that he had been sent by Vasily to inspect his paintings!*

Nervous about receiving no news at all, she left the flat using the elevator. In the garage, she went to the Bugatti, which she had always found a very striking choice for someone who preferred to go as unnoticed as possible. She

389

had never seen Vasily drive it, though; perhaps he had merely bought it as the lucrative investment it was certain to become. She gunned the car out of the garage and didn't stop until she found an empty parking space in the Belgrave area. *Here the car would be less noticeable among its equals*, she thought, since Rolls-Royces, Bentleys and a variety of high-end sports cars abounded in the vicinity. Two streets away, she hailed a cab that took her to the Ritz Hotel on Arlington Street.

The moment she registered for a room using a forged passport as identification, four police cars arrived on Park Lane to bar entrance to, and exit from, the building she had left a quarter of an hour earlier.

*

After Slater had left, Blackmoore continued to interrogate me. From his questions, I could deduce that he wasn't entirely convinced of my innocence regarding my immediate disappearance after being released on bail. He twice went over all aspects of what I had told him, after declaring that it was his duty to verify the facts. Meanwhile I would have to spend the night in detention. Not that I was completely opposed to the idea of free accommodation since I was both penniless and very tired, but it did hurt my self-esteem that my account hadn't persuaded him that what had happened had been no fault of mine.

*

Detective Inspector Anne Slater's mobile sounded with a resolute sound of broken glass. Someone in Blackmoore's office had just sent her a scanned copy of the judge's warrant to search the premises, she noted, contented.

"All right, everybody", she shouted to shut down the chatter among the idle policemen. "I just received thumbs up from the court that we're allowed to enter. Unit two and three, follow me, unit one, remain outside and vigilant, should anyone try to leave by the main entrance or the garage."

Followed by six uniformed policemen, she walked in through the main entrance. The doorman in service had been craning his neck for the last half hour to understand what the flashing lights outside the building were all about. His curiosity yet to be sated, he perked up as the police entered.

"I have a warrant to search the penthouse flat owned by Arexim Limited", Slater announced, using her most authoritative voice while showing him her credentials. "I need to know all its entrances and exits, and I also need to know if there is anyone in the flat at this moment."

"I always wondered whether there wasn't something fishy –", Henry the Hoarse began.

"I'm not interested in your speculations", Slater interrupted him. "Just answer the questions."

"Well, it's difficult to know if someone's in or not, you see, the elevator goes straight to the garage and –"

"For heaven's sake, man, get to the point!" Slater shouted, slamming her fist on the counter.

"Which I am, of course", Henry snorted, offended,

"given the right amount of time. You see, the penthouse is on the only floor where the elevator opens up inside the flat. You need a special key to get there, of course. And should anyone in the building want to take the elevator straight down to the garage, there's no way for us here at the entrance to know this. Except that we can hear the sound of the elevator moving", he added as an afterthought.

"I see a staircase next to the elevator shaft", Slater stated. "I assume you can go to the top floor using it?"

"Yes, that's right, and –"

"Unit two, take the elevator with me. Unit three, walk up the staircase. Detain anyone coming down."

Slater walked over to the elevator conveniently waiting on the ground floor. She held up the door for her men and was the last to enter. They had to get off at the second but last landing and walk up to the penthouse floor. Two minutes later, they were joined by unit three.

Slater nodded to the policemen to draw their weapons and then rapped hard on the main entrance door. There was complete silence for thirty seconds. She then tried the handle to open it. The door was locked. She nodded to the policeman who had brought a demolition bar to break open the door. Before it was done, one of the policemen pointed in silence at a more inconspicuous door further down the same landing. Slater walked over to it and tried the handle. The door was unlocked.

With weapons drawn, they entered the flat maintaining the silence, with Slater taking the lead. They found themselves inside a large kitchen. Holding up her hand to refrain her teams to make any sounds, she strained her ears to catch the sound of anyone present. There wasn't any.

She pointed at her task force to indicate that they should spread and search the flat. With their guns drawn, the policemen searched the interior. After having gone through all the rooms in order to secure the flat, Slater declared that it had been cleared.

"For bad or for good, there's no one here. Let's make an orderly search to see what we will find."

*

That instant Vasily's elongated Mercedes arrived outside the building. When he saw the flashing lights from the police vehicles, he ordered his chauffeur to return to Arexim.

So now the British police have moved into my home, he thought with a mix of fury and alarm. *They are likely to find a lot things that will put me in a bad light, but surely there's nothing a sharp lawyer won't be able to sort out. I've never kept any records of drug shipments in my flat. Mikhail is the one who keeps track of the logistics and the documents involved. And, if necessary, I can always sacrifice Mikhail.*

His thoughts kept grinding the threats and his options until he was back again at Arexim. Anticipating a major police raid also at his offices, he hurried to his luxurious office space. Vasily thought quickly. *What documents do I have to destroy?* Quickly, he leafed through the files locked away in his desk drawer. He pushed a dozen sheets through the shredder, in essence his own business projections, although they would most likely be incomprehensible to any outsider.

Vasily tried to think of anything else that could incriminate him. Documents ... no – only people. People like Berlosky, but Berlosky knew the business and that was worth something. His loyalty also counted.

Then his thoughts went back to the flat. His knees felt weak when he suddenly remembered the pictures of the dead men in the desert that Berlosky had shown him. *How can I explain away that?* he wondered. Then another thought hit him. *The stolen paintings. But surely I can say I bought them in good faith ... they will ask for invoices and how I could pay for the artworks, stolen or not. I must have more than a hundred million pounds of investment in my home. There will be digging into my finances, my cash flow, the source of my fortune ...*

Vasily had no idea how to explain the fortune he had amassed and that now had turned against him.

His phone lit up to indicate an incoming call. It was Sonia, who had decided to call him despite the risk of being punished for nagging him.

"My flat is crawling with the British police!" he shouted angrily in Russian.

"Yes, I guessed as much", she replied laconically. "Fortunately, I left it before they arrived. What do you want me to do?"

Her seemingly disinterested reply had a calming effect on him, and Vasily began to see the events in a different light.

It's a challenge, yes – but, if I look at the situation from the bright side, perhaps also an interesting way to measure my wits and resources against those who work to obstruct me. Loss of money meant nothing to Vasily, because he had more of it stashed away than he knew what to do with, in addition to expectations of enormous windfalls in the coming future. Now that he began to see the troubling events in a different light, he giggled, much to Sonia's surprise.

"Thank you for your wise advice, my dear redhead", he told her. "Your calm words have made me see our new situation in its true light. There's nothing to worry about, but we do need to take some precautionary steps."

"So, what do you want me to do?" Sonia repeated, wondering about the advice he perceived she had given him.

Vasily thought for a moment.

"I think it's time for a chat with the Irish boy. I want him to take us to Auntie Alina until things calm down." He spoke in riddles because he was confident Sonia understood perfectly what he meant, and at all costs he wanted to avoid anyone who might be listening in to understand the exact location he referred to. "Meanwhile, you should think of the best way to make it to King Henry's place."

*

Anne Slater dialled Blackmoore's number.

"John, we've found more than we could ever have bargained for here at Park Lane", she began after he had picked up his phone. "There's not only the stolen Modigliani painting, there are at least three more of the kind. Besides, this pad is made for a modern-day Croesus, which sort of contradicts his need for buying stolen artwork on the cheap, doesn't it?"

"What do you need, Anne?"

"Believe it or not, I think we've found the drug dragon himself after he has eluded us for so many years. I require at least another six men to conclude the investigation here at the flat. I also want you to check up on a man by the name of ..." she peered down on the paper she held, "Mikhail Berlosky. On top of that, I need to talk to the people at Drugs, because they'll be very interested."

"If it's high-level, that would be Chief Detective Inspector Ralph Ramsey. He's head of the narcotics division."

"Then he's the very person I'll call. Believe me, this will be the catch of the decade."

"I do", Blackmoore said, "but, just because the owner of the flat has some stolen artworks, why does it make him a drug dealer?"

"I'll explain the details when I see you", Slater replied mysteriously before disconnecting the call. *If my hunch is right,* she thought, clutching the real estate prospect with a copy of the contract interleaved. She dialled Scotland Yard's switchboard number and asked for CDI Ramsey.

"Chief Detective Inspector Ramsey, this is Detective Inspector Anne Slater", she began when he came on the line. "I have reasons to believe that we have found the big barracuda's private lair." She explained the details to him.

"To not allow these people to escape, it's of utmost urgency that you send all patrol cars you can spare to shut off the exits to the building on one twenty-eight Moorgate, including the one from South Place Mews."

*

By now, Vasily had come to the full insight that his British network was falling apart. Since he operated in cells across Europe and Russia, and to some extent in the United States where he had made recent inroads, he wasn't too worried despite the UK so far being the most lucrative market. *I can always lie low for a while and then make a comeback*, he reasoned. The most urgent matter now was to salvage the cash being processed through the bogus lender operation. Vasily remembered that the last number Mikhail had mentioned to him less than a week ago was a cash pile equivalent to 250 million pounds. *How can we move this money before the police unveil my flat's connection to Arexim, and that Arexim is connected to the lending scheme in the old bank locale?*

He called Berlosky.

"Mikhail, the situation is getting worse by the minute. The cops are in my flat as of this moment, and it won't take them long before they will ransack Arexim's offices."

"So, what shall we do?" an audibly shaken Berlosky asked.

"We need to put everything on hold until things quieten

down again. The important thing right now is to salvage whatever money we have in the vault at Moorgate. Do you have the number?"

"It … it should be somewhere around two hundred and eighty-five million pounds, last time I looked", Berlosky replied hesitantly. "The cash has been flowing in faster than our new financial operation has been able to displace it. It will likely take at least ten trailers to move all that cash, but I can't think of somewhere safe off the top of my head."

"Get whatever transportation you need and move it out of there quickly. If necessary, buy the trailers and leave them parked with the cash somewhere where they won't draw attention."

"What about Frank and the operation?"

"What about it? Don't you understand? The game is up and we need to salvage what we can!" Vasily momentarily removed the mobile from his ear and looked at it, shaking his head. After mumbling something inaudible in Russian, he raised it again to his head.

"Mikhail, it's not your job to think. Now act as you're told. One: find the means to remove the money from Moorgate. Two: stop the meth from being shipped from Holland. Three: put the investigation into the Málaga disaster on hold. Four: delay all shipments from Afghanistan, and also from the Mexicans. Do you understand?"

"Yes, Vasily."

"Don't call me until you've finished your tasks", Vasily warned him before hanging up.

*

Upon entering the detention centre, my picture was once again taken, along with my fingerprints, my clothes and my mobile. I really resented the experience, with the police officer in charge who sneered at me revealing his years of practice on how to best humiliate new internees. The soles of my feet were inspected for hidden razor blades, and I had to demonstrate that I didn't conceal anything underneath my tongue. After showing Dr Sternmacher's prescription, I was after some deliberation allowed to keep my pills.

At least it had its advantages to be incarcerated. To be sure, I didn't have the freedom to roam around the city or travel long-distance and things of the sort. But, short-term, I didn't mind being locked up with no concern where to sleep the next night, or worries about food or any other practical issues.

I felt immensely tired after the past weeks' travels. Although I felt much better having my pills again, the constant worries and the lack of communication with Samantha were doubtlessly wearing me down. I spent my day in the holding cell sleeping on and off, and I didn't even bother to get up when I was told that food was served.

I wondered where Samantha was. Then I wondered if they would ever let me out again. I felt so tired. Exhausted, I wondered whether I could dare to go to sleep again – which was all that my body begged and begged. If I did, would I ever wake up to see my wife and children again?

Berlosky sped as fast as possible through the streets of London in the blessedly light traffic. He stopped his Audi at the corner before entering Moorgate where, nearly two years ago, he had suggested to Vasily that they should establish the financial service to launder their income. Now he had to rescue what could be saved from the ashes. Berlosky was sweating profusely, because for Vasily it was easy to say "move the money". To move several hundred cubic metres or more of cash, he first needed to cover up the pallets with something that made it impossible to identify the contents. Rolls of black plastic probably would do it – but where could he get this in a hurry? Then he needed to call some movers to load the pallets onto their lorries and give them some false, faraway address where they should make the delivery. Once there, Berlosky would have to reverse the instructions, and send the lorries somewhere else. *It will be a tricky challenge to put together,* Berlosky thought. *Vasily's right, the best option would be to outright buy a couple of lorries, load them and then park them somewhere until this whole thing blows over. But how long will it take me to buy a couple of lorries? And where can I find the drivers needed to drive them in a hurry?*

Berlosky was rich beyond anyone's wildest dreams – at his most recent count he considered himself worth at least 112 million pounds. The amount didn't give him satisfaction in the sense that it was enough, but it gave him the pleasure that he had done more than well. His fortune amounted to more than what only a few thousand people in the world could claim to be worth. This made Berlosky proud, but it wasn't enough. He wanted to belong to the exclusive billionaire club.

Now he had been tasked with moving and hiding a fortune that was more than twice as large as his own. He had no idea how to do it, and he didn't know how violent Vasily's reaction would be if he didn't succeed.

That moment, six police cars came gunning through the streets and stopped on Moorgate, South Place and also blocked the access to the building from South Place Mews. Berlosky, who had just opened the door to his car to step outside, felt stunned. *The cops are everywhere,* he thought with alarm. *Vasily's flat raided, Arexim no doubt investigated, and now a raid at the Moorgate operation. I need to consider my own safety.*

Berlosky quickly went over his options. He needed to get his wife and son to a safe place. Where? Then it hit him, and he turned his Audi around and headed for his home in Kent.

As he raced away from Moorgate, he speed-dialled Pyotr.

"Pyotr? The police are all over Moorgate. Get you and your people out of there as quickly as possible, and make sure you don't let any of our numbers fall into the hands of the police."

*

Alarmed by Berlosky's abrupt and unexpected call, Pyotr immediately ordered his team to delete everything on their computers, reboot them and disconnect the two external discs with the backup. After a quick glance from behind the curtains to confirm the presence of multiple police cars with his own eyes, he rushed over to the space outside the vault that served as a counting room.

"Everything inside the vault, at once!" he hissed to the guards. "The police are outside, in large numbers."

Pyotr studied the security cameras and could see how the policemen, more than fifty of them, were closing in to secure the exits. To his relief, the door to the adjacent building hadn't been covered. Since the protection of the cash in the vault wasn't his responsibility, and knowing that the guards could compromise his own escape, he chose to not tell them about the secret side door. It would still be possible for him and his team of accountants to make their escape.

Three minutes later, just as the Metropolitan Police was making a coordinated effort to enter Moorgate 128 from its various known entrance points, Pyotr and five of his accountants slipped out of the building using the side door that wasn't marked on any plan in the public domain. In his pockets Pyotr carried the two five-terabyte external drives where the numbers concerning Vasily's business had been backed up.

*

After travelling back to the UK over the weekend, Georgie allowed himself to sleep late and enjoy a long lunch at his favourite sushi restaurant. He needed the time, he felt, to think through everything that had happened during his trip to Morocco, and how he best should present it to his superiors.

Hence Georgie didn't appear for duty until a couple of minutes after two in the afternoon.

Blackmoore, his office door ajar, was sitting behind his desk reading a document.

"Come in, Jones", Georgie was told after having rapped twice. "We have a few things to discuss."

"You got my report, I'm sure", Georgie said as he sat down in front of his boss.

"I did, Jones", Blackmoore replied and looked up over his reading glasses. "You're late."

"That's because I came in late last night, sir, flying all the way from Africa", Georgie retorted in a hurt voice, tweaking the truth.

"Well, with that you missed all the excitement we've had this morning, no less."

"Excitement, sir?"

"Yes, some very interesting development has occurred here in London. You see, the victims in the Sahara were apparently killed on the order of a Russian drug kingpin, and the order was to include Callaghan. Somehow, he made it out alive."

Georgie felt confused.

"Callaghan made it out alive from the Sahara, where a drug trafficker tried to kill him? I'm not sure I follow you, sir."

"Of course you don't", Blackmoore returned to the report

he had been reading when Georgie had entered, "because you chose to come in late today."

"I've travelled back and forth to Morocco on your orders, sir", Georgie, irritated, challenged him in a loud voice, "and I need to add that the experience was neither comfortable nor agreeable. Should you have information regarding the case I was investigating, I would certainly appreciate if you could share said information with me."

"There's no need to shout, Jones", Blackmoore said as he looked up from his report. "You see, we have identified the man who ordered the deaths of the victims found in the desert, and in the process we have discovered a huge narcotics network."

Georgie paled at the news.

"You don't look well, Jones … have some water." Blackmoore pointed at a dispenser in the office corner. Georgie didn't pay Blackmoore's concern any attention. "Anyway, you'll be pleased to learn that the very same person I sent you to confirm whether he was a victim is back in London and, frankly speaking, Matthias Callaghan was the one who tipped us off about the whole thing."

"Callaghan did?"

"Yes, and now that you're here, I want you to immediately order a team of four units to Anglo-Russian Export & Import Limited, which this Russian named Berlosky is heading. The name is Arexim, for short, and it's located on Saint Katharine's Way. There's also a warehouse in Wapping that needs to be checked out. All the details are in this report I received ten minutes ago about Berlosky's activities in the UK." He handed over a printout of the report to Georgie.

That moment, Georgie felt the mobile Berlosky had given him start to vibrate in his pocket.

*

After obeying Blackmoore's instructions, Georgie was finally able to leave the Metropolitan Police building. He was severely shaken, because he was uncertain about the consequences the latest development would have on him. When he was outside, Berlosky called him for the fourth time. This time Georgie answered.

"Why don't you pick up the phone when I'm calling, Minnow?!" Georgie could hear that Berlosky was more upset than he had ever heard him before.

"I couldn't. I was in my boss's office receiving some disturbing news."

"It can't be more disturbing than what I learnt this morning", Berlosky growled. "I want you to find out the details about a police raid on one twenty-eight Moorgate."

"I'll certainly try –"

"You'd better bloody do it, and right away!" Berlosky exploded. "There's another raid taking place on Park Lane – now, what's the reason for that one, what do they expect to find and who was the intruder in the flat before the police arrived?"

"That information I can give you off the top of my head,

because that's why I was with my boss a quarter of an hour ago. There's been a trustworthy tip about stolen paintings in the penthouse on Park Lane."

"Stolen paintings?" Berlosky sounded confused. *Had Vasily kept stolen art at home?*

"Yes, and there's more", Georgie continued. "Some photos were found there, too, of some dead men in the Sahara."

Berlosky was not a man usually given to nervousness, but now he felt his forehead breaking out in sweat. He had forgotten about the photos … how could Vasily have been so careless not to destroy them? Was it the intruder who had found them?

"As for the man in the flat who gave the information to the police, you're in for a surprise."

"Who?"

"Matthias Callaghan."

"Callaghan?" Berlosky was incredulous. "Impossible!"

"I assure you, he made it back from Morocco somehow, and he's now in police custody."

"I don't believe you. He's dead."

"Give me a couple of minutes and I'll send you a picture that was taken of him when he was detained this morning."

*

Georgie returned to New Scotland Yard and went to the office he shared with three other officers. On his computer, he

406

looked up Matthias Callaghan and found the picture taken of him that same day. He copied it onto a USB drive and then left the building again.

He transmitted the photo to Berlosky's phone in a nearby Internet café. Georgie looked more closely at the picture. *Callaghan looks thin and haggard and a lot older than I remember him,* he mused. *With patience, it won't be too difficult to make Samantha give up on this poor bastard.*

Moments later, Berlosky, who was driving at excess speed towards his home in Sevenoaks, heard a sound that indicated an incoming WhatsApp message. He was on the phone giving instructions to his wife Tania to urgently pack their suitcases with necessities and clothes for two weeks. He would pick up their son Sasha at school, he explained. Tania knew better than to ask what the rush was all about.

Berlosky looked at the photo Georgie had sent him. *It's Callaghan all right,* he thought grimly, *risen from the dead.* The date in the corner confirmed it had been taken the same day. Without slowing down, he managed to forward the photo to Vasily, before calling him.

"Take a look at the picture I just sent you, Vasily", Berlosky said between clenched teeth. "It appears that Callaghan didn't die in the desert after all. Look at the date. It was taken today when he was returned into custody by the police."

"I'm surprised."

"You'll be even more surprised to learn that the intruder Sonia saw in your flat was the very same Callaghan. Besides keeping the photos Paddy gave me to prove he and the others were dead, Callaghan also took pictures of your paintings. It appears some of them are stolen. That's why the police raided your flat this morning."

"I see."

Vasily sounds unusually muted, Berlosky noted. *All of a sudden, it seems giggling has gone out of fashion.*

"However, that's nothing compared to today's real disaster", he continued. "I went to Moorgate, and the moment I arrived, half a dozen patrol cars surrounded the building. I'm checking with my contact in the police what happened, but I doubt very much there's anything we can do to recover the money or keep up the operation here in the UK."

Vasily, who never was in want of words, was silent for once.

"Vasily?"

"I'm still here. What are you going to do?"

"I'm going underground with my family until the worst blows over. Then I'll think of something. I hope you have some contingency plan, too."

"I do. This is not good for business. I have to think things through. I'll be in touch, Mikhail."

Berlosky's mobile went dead.

*

Vasily, usually so cool and collected, was boiling with rage as he in his mind went over the information that Berlosky had shared with him.

They're going to confiscate my money, he thought. *My money! And all this havoc that Callaghan has caused will disrupt business as usual, and oblige me to rearrange everything. My flat – my flat! – was supposed to be untouchable. Well, you learn from your carelessness, and there are two people who will pay for the disruption, with Callaghan at the top of the list.*

He was sitting in the plush back seat of a black van that one of his bodyguards had brought around. Vasily didn't want to travel in his usual Mercedes, which was registered to Arexim, in case the police were looking for it. Apart from Ilya, who was driving, Oleg, Boris, and Vladimir were also in the van. Vasily had ordered Ilya to take them to his mock-Tudor country estate in Hertfordshire, which had one of his Panama companies, managed by Mossack Fonseca, as its listed owner.

As they rode in silence, Vasily mulled about what his next move should be. He obviously couldn't go back to London, and he probably wasn't secure in the UK at all. The British police were sure to contact Europol if they suspected him of having travelled to the continent. *But why so pessimistic?* he thought, trying to cheer himself up. *My name is not in any official Arexim documents; the flat is in the name of Arexim, as are most of the official properties and leases like the Moorgate one. Mikhail Berlosky is the CEO of Arexim – and it's a good thing he has gone into hiding. I entered the country on a forged passport under the name Benyamin Bogdanovich. The police have no pictures of Vasily Ivanovich beyond grainy security camera footage of an unknown man and the passport picture they scanned when I entered the country. So, what I need to do, is to create a completely different identity. That's easy. I can do it. Mikhail is the one who should worry, not I.*

Feeling better, Vasily called Sonia, who was waiting for his instructions at the Ritz Hotel.

"Yes?"

She sounds calm. Good.

"It gives me a lot of reassurance to know that I can always rely on you, Sonia. Have you found some way to travel to Henry's place? Tomorrow at dawn we will take to the skies."

"Yes, I'll go some of the distance by train, some by bus, some by cab. Don't worry about me. I'll get there in time."

"I know you will. I'm switching phones according to plan, if you need to call me. See you tonight."

Using a different mobile, his next call was to Paddy O'Hare. Although he insisted on having the contact information of all the people he employed as a backup, he had never before spoken to Paddy. Orders for Paddy's missions were usually relayed by Oleg, Berlosky's lieutenant, or on rare occasions by Berlosky himself.

"This here is Paddy speaking." His Irish brogue was hard on Vasily's ears, who had to strain to understand the words.

"You've undertaken a few missions for us, Oleg tells me. You recently made a successful one to a desert, remember?"

"Who's calling?" Paddy replied, suspicious.

Vasily passed the mobile to Oleg and encouraged him to

identify himself to Paddy. After a brief exchange, Oleg handed the phone back to Vasily.

"To facilitate communication, you can call me Ben. And now that we've cleared up the mistrust between us", he giggled, "I want you to undertake a new mission with a special cargo to a place where you've never been before."

"OK, Ben. Where to?"

"Tomorrow morning at five I'll send you the coordinates where you can pick up the goods. This time you should use the helicopter, fully fuelled. You must leave immediately when you receive the coordinates on your phone, so you better stay sober and get an early night, OK? You will only have twenty-five minutes to reach the pickup target."

"It sounds a lot more complicated than usual. Oleg never had me –"

"It *is* more complicated than usual", Vasily cut him short, "and we're also aware of the quality of your work of late. That's why your pay will be twice as much compared to what we usually pay for such work."

Paddy whistled silently to himself. *Fifty grand!*

"I'll be there, Ben, count on me."

*

It was dark when Berlosky and his family arrived at the suburban house that had been bought to be used as a safe house if needed. He couldn't recall that it had actually been used with that particular intention before, but it was here that

Callaghan had been tortured and Allan had been held captive. There were a few other similar incidents with people who hadn't paid up in time, but, no, this was the first time it would be used for its original purpose.

Sheltered by the dark, Berlosky carried two of the suitcases up the gravelled driveway and unlocked the front door. No one had inhabited the house for quite some time, and there was a pungent, musky odour emanating from the interior. He was followed inside by Tania and their 12-year-old son who carried his own suitcase. Tania wore her usual weary, neutral face, he noticed, but Sasha pouted and looked more prone to protest than ever. *It's only natural,* Berlosky convinced himself, *he's entering puberty. That's how teenagers behave.*

The first thing he did before settling in was to make sure that the door leading to the cellar was locked.

Tuesday May 12, 2015

At five o'clock sharp, Oleg sent Paddy the coordinates of a soccer field close to the estate where they had spent the night. Paddy immediately replied with a thumbs-up emoji followed by one of a whirling helicopter.

After having made elaborate diversions to reach the property, Sonia had arrived by cab close to midnight. She and Vasily had discussed the situation in privacy until one in the morning, and both now appeared with dark rings under their eyes from lack of sleep. Everybody appeared to be on edge as they left for the soccer field.

At 5:20, they heard the helicopter in the distance. The rising sun was already colouring an unclouded sky, with the promise of a beautiful day. As soon as Paddy had landed, he was surprised to see how Oleg ushered in five other persons before getting inside as the last passenger. Paddy had been expecting a drugs cargo.

Wisely, he held his tongue and didn't ask questions. Unless he shouted, it was anyway too noisy in the cockpit to make himself heard by his passengers.

"This is where you will fly." Oleg showed him their destination on a map of Europe, where he had written down the coordinates. "Just make sure you fly very low. We don't want to be detected by radar."

Paddy studied the map. The destination he had been assigned looked like an uninhabited region east of Munich in southern Germany.

*

The police had kept up their vigilance on Moorgate and the adjacent streets all night. At eight o'clock in the morning, the firm that had installed the vault in the bank twenty-one years earlier pulled up. Followed by three workers in overalls, a small, tidy man wearing an impeccable three-piece suit presented himself to the officer in charge, Sergeant Craig Williams.

"We have been asked to open up a steel-reinforced concrete 1994 Beckingshire vault, which has a –"

"Please spare me the details, Mister Cairn", the sergeant sighed. "You can make the pitch in your report later. Now, tell me, how much time will you need to open the vault?"

Mr Cairn looked hurt that Sergeant Williams wasn't interested in knowing more about his highly specialised field.

"Because of the *high quality* that this class-three vault represents", he said, stressing the words, "I estimate it will take us four hours. At least. And this will be paid for by the police, I presume?"

"With the tax payers' money", Sergeant Williams said and made a grimace. "That is, yours and mine, no less."

*

It was around 10:30 local time when Paddy, still flying barely above the treetops, visually located the place where he had been told to take his passengers. He checked the fuel level. There was about a quarter left, which afterwards would enable him to reach Cologne where he could get the helicopter refuelled.

He settled down the oversized helicopter on the meadow, where not a single house could be seen. *That also works the other way around,* he thought, as the rotor blades were coming to a standstill. *No one has detected our landing.*

His six passengers got out, and he followed them to stretch his legs and with the expectancy to get paid. Vasily walked up to him. Paddy didn't know what to make of the short, giggling man, but he assumed he was a secretary or

414

something to Oleg, who was the guy who handled the usual business.

Vasily, his usual dapper self, looked at the scruffy pilot and smiled.

"I congratulate you, Paddy", Vasily said with plenty of bonhomie, "you're a good pilot, and your pilot's skills are no doubt worth what we've been paying you."

"And that's why you're doubling my salary, right?" Paddy said in the Irish brogue that cost Vasily so much to understand, in an attempt to make a humorous comment to one more satisfied customer.

"I told you that your pay would be twice as much as what we usually pay for what you've done." Vasily looked him squarely in the eye before he giggled ominously. "Don't worry, I will keep my word."

Paddy's mouth suddenly felt dry. He knew these were dangerous people. He looked around at the others and only saw their stone-faced, non-committal expressions. That instant, he realised that the real boss was the man addressing him.

"I haven't the slightest idea why you're talking to me that way. Didn't I get you here safely, on my word of honour? Haven't I always done right by myself, delivering the goods without a single bag missing? By my mother's early grave, what is it you claim that I've done to upset you?"

Vasily giggled helplessly. Paddy looked at him in astonishment.

"You see, you didn't kill Matthias Callaghan, as you

were ordered to. That's why you will now be paid twice as much – this time in lead."

Paddy looked at Vasily dumbfounded. Vasily nodded at Oleg, who was standing behind Paddy.

Two shots immediately rang out, and Paddy toppled to the ground.

"Leave him in the chopper before you set it on fire", Vasily ordered Oleg.

He led the way for the remaining passengers to two waiting Mercedes that would take them to a chalet overlooking a small lake not far from the Swiss border.

*

At 12:15 a.m., the team hired to open the vault finally accomplished what they had come for. Mr Cairn went to look for Sergeant Williams to inform him of the breakthrough. He found him outside in the pleasant sunlight, munching on a sandwich.

"The missus sent me one of our young ones with some breakfast." Williams smiled sheepishly, as if Mr Cairns had caught him doing something inappropriate.

"Whatever you say, Sergeant Williams. I just wanted you to know that we have now succeeded in unlocking the vault. Perhaps you'd like to be the one to open it. Maybe we should have some press here to make more noise about this historic event? What do you say? Or should we call the commissioner to ask his opinion?"

Sergeant Williams, who wasn't a very bright person, seemed confused by the rapid questions posed by Mr Cairns.

"Please hold it there for a second, Mister Cairns", he cautioned. "What we will do is that I, accompanied by my men, will enter the vault to see if there's anything compromising. If there is, then I'll contact my immediate superior, who will make a decision whether to call in the press." He snorted. "Hah! That's how things work with me."

He called the men in the units he had been assigned and ordered them to put on their bullet-proof vests and draw their weapons.

"You never know what to expect", he said to the fourteen men he commanded. "Better safe than sorry."

*

"Trudy, you've been handling the Callaghan story for the past months." Burns sounded excited over the fact, Trudy noted. "Well, it may be that your breakthrough has arrived. The story is developing fast. You'll probably secure the scope of the year if you hurry down to Moorgate where the police are raiding a former bank. It looks like organised crime has been using the facility to launder money."

"What does this have to do with Callaghan?" Trudy asked.

"I got a tip from an insider that it was Callaghan, suddenly back after skipping bail, who put the police on track to uncover a money-laundering scheme, possibly the biggest in the UK's history."

"All right, I'll get on it", Trudy replied, not sounding too enthusiastic.

"I forgot to tell you: the same building also has an entrance from South Place Mews around the corner. Inside, with the help of some experts, the police just opened the vault that belongs to the baddies."

*

Sergeant Williams took the lead as he and his men entered the vault that Mr Cairn's team had so expertly opened, followed by Mr Cairn himself.

Somebody found the light switch, and all of a sudden the vault was flooded with light. The place looked like an overbooked warehouse.

As their eyes became adjusted to the light, Sergeant Williams sniffed the air tentatively in an attempt to determine whatever it was that made its smell so unusual. Then, as he connected what he was watching with the peculiar odour that was lingering in the air, it dawned on him.

"Blimey! They say that money doesn't smell, but now we have the final bloody proof that it bloody well isn't true. It smells of dirt and decay, right? Or would 'pungent and musky' be a more fitting expression?"

The men gasped when they realised that, in front of them, were hundreds of pallets neatly stacked with banknotes and wrapped in stretch film. On tables between the pallets stood rows of cash-counting machines.

Hundreds of pallets with hundreds of millions. *If I could just have a fistful of these banknotes that no one will miss, it would be a welcome blessing,* more than one of them thought. Fortunately for the British tax payers, Sergeant Williams was not one of them.

*

A call from a conscientious citizen who from a distance had noticed a large, burning object in a meadow alerted the local authorities in Baden-Württemberg. The German police arrived with firefighters, who put out the last of the fire that had by now consumed most of the flammable materials of what turned out to be a helicopter. An alert was sent to the state's criminal investigators when a dead body was found inside.

*

Yuliana had finished her Tuesday evening performance in the West End and had, against her normal routine, gone out for a nightcap with some fellow performers. As a consequence, she hadn't got into bed until two in the morning.

At the time, she wasn't worried about her husband Frank's absence since he had mentioned he would entertain some American investors that same evening. His business meeting had been the main reason for her to stay up late and go out for drinks with her friends.

Wednesday May 13, 2017

When Yuliana woke up at ten in the morning, she was surprised to find that Frank had not yet come home. Since he had never been a party person, it made her worry. Yuliana tried calling his mobile, but there was no reply.

By now, she was getting distraught and jumped out of bed. Out of habit, she turned on the television. There was a commercial on and she went into the shower. Because of this, she missed the breaking news story that followed the advertisement: the dismantling of a sophisticated drugs money-laundering operation on Moorgate, headed by its CEO Frank O'Hare.

*

"We've seen some astonishing developments since yesterday, Jones", an unusually enthusiastic Detective Inspector Blackmoore told Georgie as he entered the inspector's office. "I just got wind of the latest news on the drug cartel business: a vault with hundreds of pallets stacked with money. A preliminary estimate places the amount to be somewhere between two hundred and three hundred million pounds."

"Amazing, sir!" Georgie tried his best to sound as excited as his boss was.

"We've arrested sixteen people at work in the offices occupying the building rented by the so-called Full Sails Financial Limited. Outside the vault, we encountered three men presumably working the cash counting machines in the

420

vault, lorded over by heavily armed guards. Fortunately, the latter chose not to resist arrest when they realised the overwhelming force they were up against. On a sour note, however, it regrettably seems a handful of people escaped from the accounting area using a side door undetected by our teams."

"Besides the armed guards, who were the other people arrested?"

"Eight Russians, some secretaries, two office boys. and the managing director, a certain Frank O'Hare. However, I believe the secretaries and the office boys will be released as soon as they have been interviewed. Apparently, they were mere employees carrying out their work without any knowledge of the true business. The director is different ticket, though. What we've learnt so far indicates that he must have extensive knowledge about the money laundering operation."

"Any news from the raid on Park Lane?"

"Yes, various stolen paintings have been recovered. And, you'll never guess who was the previous owner of the property!"

Georgie frowned, trying to understand what Blackmoore was hinting at.

"Don't keep me in suspense, sir."

"Matthias Callaghan, no less!" Blackmoore triumphantly exclaimed and leaned forward. "How about that revelation? It makes for some interesting conjecture about Callaghan's participation in this iceberg enterprise that so far we've only seen the tip of."

"But Callaghan was the one who came forward and allowed us to uncover the whole affair –"

"There are many things that remain to be revealed and explained for, I'm sure", Blackmoore intervened. "Perhaps there has been some rivalry within the criminal group, and Callaghan wanted to settle scores with some perceived competitor."

"Would he have given himself up so easily, if that were the case?" Georgie asked, suddenly uneasy about the forces he had unleashed when he had mailed Flint's recording to the Metropolitan Police the previous year.

"Nothing is certain at this point", the contented Blackmoore replied and leaned back in his swivel chair to make a pyramid with his fingers. "Maybe Callaghan was close to the top of the organisation or perhaps he has plans to go all the way. He's quite a clever bloke, as you well know. Or maybe he just threw out the baby with the bathwater and got caught in his own scheme. One thing is certain though: if Callaghan hadn't pointed our way to the stolen artworks on Park Lane, we wouldn't have discovered the operation at the Moorgate address. Anne Slater found a prospect in the flat that led us there. And since the owner of the flat is Arexim, it wasn't hard to connect the dots and flush out the cockroaches into the light."

"Who's been sitting at the top of this pyramid of crime, then?" Georgie asked.

"I'm fairly certain that the kingpin is Mikhail Berlosky. He arrived here nineteen years ago and is listed as the CEO of

Arexim. None of the other Russians in this case has been here as long as he has. When we start digging, I'm sure we'll find more links between Arexim and Moorgate."

"I see. Well, sir, congratulations. You certainly look like the hero of the day."

"There is only one thing in this blasted vipers' nest that bothers me, Jones", Blackmoore said and knitted his eyebrows. "The Russians abducted Callaghan when he left the prison: how could they have known he was getting out? Callaghan told me that a policeman called his wife the day before to inform her that Callaghan had been transferred to Belmarsh before his release. If that's true, who was the officer who made it his purpose to lie to her? After his release, Allan Gould was hiding in a rented flat near his home in Wimbledon. How did the assassin know where to find him so his corpse could be flown to Africa together with Callaghan? It could only be through someone who had access to the log of Gould's ankle monitor."

Blackmoore looked up at the still standing Georgie from under his bushy eyebrows.

"I'm getting more convinced by the minute that the Russians had a source inside Scotland Yard, Jones. You still have fourteen days left before you're on leave. I want you to concentrate on finding the disgraceful informer who has sabotaged our work here by snitching to the Russians."

"That's an awful assumption, sir."

"Yes, it is, Jones. Hand over anything else you're handling to Jenny; she'll see to it that someone else is assigned. Instead, discreetly get in touch with internal affairs and give them the whole picture. I can't think of anyone more suited; you've been on Callaghan's case for some time and know the details. And, Jones – get this one solved before you leave, will you?"

Thus dismissing him, Blackmoore went back to study yet another report from his inbox. Feeling queasy, Georgie took his cue and left.

Back at his office, seated in his reclining chair with his hands clasped behind his neck, Georgie chewed on the information Blackmoore had given him. By now, it was clear to him that Mister Fisherman must have passed on his information to the man Blackmoore had pointed out as the top boss, Mikhail Berlosky. Georgie was unsure what to do next, and he wondered if his work as an informant would give him away before his official leave would start. Callaghan had mentioned Peter Scarborough's call to Samantha that had sent her to Belmarsh, but he hadn't known the officer's name or Blackmoore would have told him. Should Samantha recall the officer's name when interviewed, it would lead the investigators at internal affairs to Scarborough. Scarborough would tell them it was Georgie who had ordered him to call Callaghan's wife. The cards were about to tumble down. The trap was closing in.

A fortnight left, he thought, *and before I leave I'm supposed to come up with leads pointing to myself. I really should consider a plan B.*

His mobile rang. To his delight, it was Samantha calling

him, for the first time ever.

"So good of you to call me, Samantha. How can I be of any service?"

"I've got a huge problem, George, and I can't think of anybody except you to solve it for me."

"I'm at your disposal whenever you need me, you know that."

"I ... I need to find Matthias, and I've learnt that he's been jailed by the Metropolitan Police. Can you tell me where he is, and how I can meet with him? I'm desperate, you know, although of course it's a great relief to know that he's alive."

Georgie thought quickly. *Maybe I can make the situation work in my favour.*

"I just came out of a meeting where I learnt some discouraging news. A large drug-trafficking organisation has been discovered after years of investigations. Unfortunately, it seems that your husband has been involved in a deep way –"

"That's impossible!" Samantha heatedly refuted his implication. "I know him better than anyone alive, and, besides, he's been living in Australia for years. Australia certainly doesn't seem like the right place to be if you want to traffic drugs in London, now, does it? Anyway, it's beside the point. I would appreciate your friendship and the courtesy if you could find a way for me to meet with my husband."

"Of course. Just give me some time. I'll call you back as soon as I know something."

*

By noon, Yuliana was sick with worry about her husband. Nobody answered the switchboard at his work, and she only got his voicemail when dialling his mobile. His disappearance had her shaking, recalling the day that Matthias had been abducted. *Has someone kidnapped Frank?* she wondered, the uncertainty building up to hysteria. As most people in show business, Yuliana was highly emotional. She was not prone to reasoning when she was faced with difficulties; instead she acted on her feelings. It made her a successful actress on stage, but the very same trait made her prone to become hysterical under stress.

Matthias was taken by gangsters, she thought, *and look at the things he went through. I can't let that happen to Frank. I can't! Where is he? Who can I talk to? Should I call Samantha?*

Once the idea had occurred to her, Yuliana dialled the mobile number Samantha had given her. There was no answer.

*

To be able to enter the jail facility, the guards had obliged Samantha to be searched and leave behind several items, among them her mobile.

She had to wait more than ten minutes before Matthias finally appeared before her. Her heart sank when she took in the awful state he was in. Since she had last seen him, he looked as if he had aged a decade. Matthias was sunburnt, had more wrinkles near his eyes than she remembered, and

426

his skin sagged. However, she still saw that particular, amused spark in his eyes that she unconsciously always associated with the Matthias Callaghan she had fallen in love with.

They sat at a wide table, with the stern admonition that if they touched, the audience would be over. Two warders watching over them stood close enough to overhear their conversation, which made them both feel even more uncomfortable.

"Oh Matthias, dear, you're alive!" Samantha began, tears in her eyes.

*

Despite still being jailed, after weeks of not having seen her, it felt like a miracle to once again look into Samantha's fresh, honest face. She gave me a much-needed boost, as if I once again were returning to reality. The light of my life. The nightmare was finally over. It made me feel that dipping my toes into the River Styx had never happened.

Of course, the reality of life always insists on being unrelenting. We were not allowed to touch; two guards were leaning over to catch every word we whispered, and I felt shame sitting there with Samantha, jailed anew as a man wanted by the police.

"Please, tell me, what happened?" she asked me and leaned forward, putting out her hands towards me only to immediately retract them, heeding a warder's warning grunt.

"Before anything", I began, because it would be of such

significance for what I was planning, "I need to tell you that I've sent some photos by email to you. It's of the utmost importance that you don't share them with anyone – I repeat, not with anyone. When the time comes, I will ask you to make some high-quality prints of them. Please, don't lose these pictures."

"I get the message", she replied and narrowed her eyes. "I won't lose them and I will print them when you tell me. Now, what happened, where have you been, what have you done?"

"I'll tell you the short version of my story", I told her, signalling the warders with my eyebrows. "I took a cab outside the prison where I was supposed to see you pick me up. In the cab, the driver threw a canister into the back seat that contained a gas that after a few minutes made me unconscious. I woke up the next morning buried in sand, with one corpse across my chest and another lying next to me."

Samantha raised her fists to cover her mouth. She didn't lower them for an instant while I, in brief sentences, told her the rest of my story about arriving in Europe before finally ending up in London.

"There's obviously going to be a trial before I'll be able to regain my liberty", I finished my story, "and this time around I won't be let out on bail. Now, tell me, why couldn't I reach you? I must have called you thirty times or more."

"I forgot my phone at the hotel when I left for Morocco in a hurry", Samantha replied. "I was constantly worrying about you, and I simply didn't remember that I had left it charging in my hotel room. I have this contact at Scotland Yard, a very nice detective who's been assisting me to track you down since you disappeared. He helped me find you here."

I nodded for her to go on.

"I went to Morocco with him, because the police said you had been found dead in the Sahara. Fortunately, it wasn't true."

"Believe me, I'm just as relieved as you are."

"Stop joking, Matthias."

"I'm not joking … but that's for later. Please continue."

"Just like you, I'll tell you about the trip to Morocco when we can talk at a proper time in a suitable place. For now, I'll tell you something that the police know, and I was unaware of until very recently."

"What can that be?" I said, fearing the worst.

"The police officer who accompanied me to Morocco told me that a recording was recently received by the Metropolitan Police, in which Abdul Mahfouz, by then confirmed dead, asks a certain gangster, now deceased, to kill a certain solicitor, found dead immediately after Mahfouz bargains for his death. What do you make of that?"

I wondered if Samantha noticed that my forehead suddenly broke out in sweat. What could I tell her? What could I do?

"Yes, that recording is the flimsy evidence that the police claim as proof of my guilt", I finally said. "This recording is the reason I was arrested in Rome. It's sheer nonsense, of course."

"Yet I remember clearly that, when Mahfouz died, you took on his face and his identity."

"That sounds exactly like how the police are reasoning. It's not my voice on the recording. Anyone, for a variety of reasons, could have acted the role."

Samantha didn't look very convinced when the visiting hour was over and the warder approached to escort me back to my cell.

The warder shouted into his radio that my cell door should be closed. Seconds later, there was that menacing sound of the electronically controlled lock mechanism loudly announcing that the bolts had been secured. There was nothing for me to do except to lie down on the uncomfortable bed with sheets made of paper to, I suppose, prevent the prisoner from making a rope to be used either for escape or suicide. I locked my hands behind my neck and began digesting the things I had learnt during Samantha's visit.

It was all so overwhelming. I had been unable to talk to her about what had taken place because the warders listened in on us. Her comments on Flint's recording had caught me off guard. I was still a prisoner who, in Samantha's eyes, had been arrested upon entering Europe. How did all this information make me look to her?

When I had requested the meeting with Flint in Hyde Park, I remembered being concerned about the possibility that he would tape me. Years later, I had voluntarily confessed to the Metropolitan Police that I had undergone a transplant that had given me Mahfouz's face, to be able to get my true identity back. And now that recording, after being cleaned of all the motorcycle noise, had somehow mysteriously found its way to Scotland Yard.

How could this recording now be traced back to me? I wondered. *How come the recording had emerged so many – what, six? – years later? Who had submitted it to the police after all this time?*

The million questions swirling in my head made me want to talk to Porter again, but I had been told that I wasn't allowed to be in contact with anyone on the outside unless it was my lawyer or my spouse.

I had only one remaining card up my sleeve to play – the two pictures I had taken of Vasily getting into his car. What could I possibly get in exchange, if I traded them?

Thursday May 14, 2015

After spending two days and two nights in drizzling rain at his villa overlooking the Bodensee, Vasily suddenly announced they would all leave for a more pleasant place where the weather would cheer them all up. As usual, he didn't share the details of the plans he was making for everyone, and, as always, no one dared to ask.

Vasily is more skittish than usual, Sonia noticed. Among those who now stayed with him in the large, beautiful house overlooking the lake near the Swiss border, she was no doubt the one who was closest to him. Although he was for most of the time impenetrable, she did have insights into his personality that few others had.

*

Sonia, brought up as the sole child of a widowed Russian army career officer, had from a young age constantly been cautioned to keep order as well as obey any such given to her. She had been born south of Yekaterinburg in the Sverdlovsk province, not far from Kazakhstan when the Soviet Union still existed. Life in rural Sverdlovsk had not been easy for her mother. Sonia's father had been stationed far away and only came home on furlough for two weeks every four months. Sonia didn't have many memories before the Soviet Union collapsed in 1991, merely that food was scarce and that they mostly ate potatoes and whatever they grew in their little vegetable plot at the back of their small house.

The dramatic changes that followed the political events that year led to two important events in Sonia's life within the next eight months. Her father returned home with a war wound and a small pension, and her mother died shortly thereafter. Sonia never learnt the reason for her mother's death, and she never dared to ask her authoritative father who inspired fright with his bushy moustache and eyebrows, his stern gaze and absolute command.

Her father had been awarded a medal for bravery in the field and made captain two months before he had been shot in the abdomen by accident. A soldier had been cleaning his weapon and a bullet had gone off. Thus, in a matter of months Sonia's life changed from her almost exclusive dependence on her worrying, over-protective mother to the care of her stern father who demanded of her, at seven, to match his own hardship at the same age.

In her late teens Sonia had become as tough as her father, which, curiously, increased his respect for his daughter and even a certain envy, but there was no affection between them whatsoever. She rejected any attempt of his to share a family bond. After years of living in relative poverty, with no electricity and water from a pump in the yard, an unexpected opening presented itself for the 17-year-old girl.

A soldier friend to her father told him that his younger brother was looking for promising army material. For those who were accepted came the potential of working with counterintelligence in the FSB, the organisation that had replaced the Soviet Union's KGB intelligence and secret police agency. The negotiation of Sonia's future was made over her head. One day she was simply told that she needed to start earning her living. What better way to do so than by enlisting in the Russian army? Under the protective wings of her father's contacts in Moscow, she was ensured to make a career and reach a good position.

Sonia was still a country girl, whose only knowledge about life and the Russian army was what she had been inculcated since her father had taken over her life at seven. Obeying her father's instructions, she travelled on her own for two days on the Trans-Siberian train to the capital. No one met her at the station. She walked for three hours in the wind and the sleet of the usual Moscow March weather until she could announce herself at the quarters where she had been ordered to report for duty.

After two years of basic military physical training, she went through an evaluation like all the privates in her class. Found to excel in analysis and administrative tasks, she was recommended to the appropriate department with a low-level security clearance. The five years Sonia worked at the FSB desk for espionage on the West, she not only managed to rise in the ranks with the higher security clearance that came with each promotion. More importantly, she got a very good grasp of security issues in the decades after the Cold War, and insights in illegal transfers of goods and people and the inevitable corruption involved. She also acquired a taste for the luxuries available in the West.

One of her superior officers was friendly with a politician of the old guard, a former senior member of the politburo in Moscow who had fallen out of grace. Sonia's superior let her know that there might be a more rewarding job waiting for her if she accepted work from the politician's son, a successful businessman who was looking for able people like herself. Curious, she accepted to be interviewed.

The man who sauntered into the conference room was only a few years older than Sonia. He giggled as he sat down and studied her eyes, which made her feel awkward.

"My name is Vasily, yours is Sonia", he beamed at her. "Now, tell me everything about yourself."

She was interviewed by Vasily Ivanovich in February 2009, three weeks after his adoptive father had made his recommendation and two months after Vasily had arranged for Kiril to be blown up by terrorists on an airplane. Her father's daughter, she had done her best to truthfully recapitulate her first twenty-four years in the interview. Vasily's final impression was that Sonia excelled in a surprising amount of things, she had plenty of determination, and she put goals before people. In short, he found her character similar to his own.

On the spur of the moment, Vasily decided to hire her and, tripling her previous salary, assigned her to Bogdan Sokolov. Sokolov was the man he had decided would run the business in Moscow after he had moved to his new headquarters in London.

Then, years later, the business in Western Europe had grown ten times faster than it had in Russia. At Berlosky's request, Vasily had brought in more people from Russia to help out with the tremendous sales growth in the UK and on the continent.

Sonia had been one of those Vasily had decided to bring over from Moscow. The transfer had turned out to be mutually rewarding.

*

The helicopter landed noisily on the front lawn, its rotor blades devastating the carefully kept flower beds that meant nothing to Vasily. Three minutes later he, Sonia, Boris and his three bodyguards were in the air heading for the south of France.

After a two-hour flight over the Alps, the helicopter descended towards the Riviera. The beautiful waters were matched only by the mountain slopes that ended in the sea. The helicopter, rented from a company operating out of Nice, landed in Monte Carlo where it delivered its passengers.

Two dark red Rolls-Royce Phantom cars were waiting close to the helicopter tarmac to immediately whisk the passengers to the previously established address: Quai Rainier 1er in Port Hercule.

*

Pyotr, Vasily's chief accountant, had managed to make his way undetected from London to Monaco by taking a train to Dover, and from there a ferry to Calais. On Vasily's instructions, he got on a high-speed train when he reached Paris, and was waiting on board the yacht hours before Vasily arrived. As ordered, in the meantime he prepared an analysis of his boss's losses.

When Vasily summoned him after his arrival, Pyotr handed Vasily a spreadsheet with his assessment of what the police raids in London had cost him. All considered, Pyotr claimed that 460 million pounds had been wiped out thanks to the raids. Vasily couldn't help the anger building up inside him, although he was convinced that it would take him less than two years to recover the loss. But, again – it wasn't the money, it wasn't the loss. For Vasily it was about losing to some operator who had outsmarted him. He couldn't allow that. *It would be disastrous for my troops' morale,* he thought.

The immediate losses consisted of the cash stashed away in Moorgate vault; the dismantling of his money-laundering operation; the end of Arexim; the expropriation of his Park Lane flat and it's contents – the termination of his UK operation in every sense. Vasily felt like blowing up something, the way he had blown up Kiril to take over the flourishing organisation. This led Vasily to think about the appropriate way to get rid of the man with a singular record of obstructing him.

I will study Callaghan thoroughly, find his weaknesses, lure him into a trap and have him killed in a very appropriate, yes indeed, in the most spectacular way, he seethed.

*

Yuliana knew she had put on a miserable performance the previous night, but she had refused the notion of letting her understudy replace her. The thought of her husband's disappearance was constantly present, but she simply couldn't allow things still unknown to her to take over her life.

She hadn't been able to sleep, sure that something had happened to Frank. Calls to hospitals and local police stations had drawn blanks. Yuliana feared the worst: Frank must have been kidnapped.

Then, an hour before noon, she received two calls that later made her phone the theatre to finally request her understudy to cover for her. The first one was from the office of the Foreign Secretary.

"Ma'am, I've been advised that this is the number to call when there's an urgency regarding Mister O'Hare. Am I correct in assuming this?"

Yuliana felt her heart race to her throat.

"Yes … you are", she replied in a whisper, taking a seat. "What has happened?"

"I'm afraid that Paddy O'Hare had an accident while landing a helicopter in Germany. He didn't survive the crash."

Yuliana felt relief when the news wasn't about her husband, and then guilt to overcome her because she hadn't felt the proper grief over his brother.

"I'm … I'm devastated to learn this … how can I –"

"I would like to caution you that we've only received a preliminary report from the German authorities. I will be in touch with you again, not least because we have to go through the identification process."

Yuliana hung up without uttering another word. The grief settled on her, more than anything because the news added drama to Frank's disappearance. She had only met Paddy on two occasions, once before her and Frank's wedding, and then on the wedding day. Yuliana didn't have a favourable impression of him. Paddy had been very different from his half-brother: sloppy, wearing awful tattoos on his arms, badly dressed, and with a tendency to shout his opinions as he got drunk. The only good things she could recall about him was that he had been overly generous, and that he never had a bad word to say about anyone.

Her phone rang a second time. Again, her apprehension provoked nausea as she anticipated more bad news. It was.

"Am I speaking with Miss Julie Cross?"

"You are. Who is this?"

"My name is Wilclair Bartlett. I've accepted the assignment of representing your husband in a case concerning illicit trading, commonly known as 'money laundering'."

Horrified, Yuliana couldn't help letting out a noticeable gulp.

"Frank O'Hare has asked me to convey to you that at present he is responding to the authorities' questions without any restriction whatsoever, and that he believes he will shortly be released when the groundless accusations against him have been determined for what they are – that is, groundless."

"Where is Frank now?" Yuliana managed to put in.

"He's in custody, and the Metropolitan Police has made it clear he can't receive anyone except his solicitor, meaning myself, while he's being debriefed."

"But why has he been jailed in the first place? He –"

"I'm sure you'll be able to read about the details in the papers, Miss Cross, but the short of it is that your husband is accused of fronting a company that has laundered the illicit proceeds made by the Russian Mafia."

After hanging up, Yuliana sat down on a nearby sofa with tears welling. *It is the past revisited*, she thought.

Memories of Matthias and Allan and Jaime Hernandez crowded her mind. The hospital in Switzerland. The moment she found Matthias's fingers in the envelope. His silent rejection of her. So many years ago, yet so present. And now the horror was repeating itself with her new husband. Why was there never an end to it?

Debating with herself whether it was a wise thing to do, Yuliana finally found the courage to again make a call to Samantha. In the end, she called her because, although they had known one another only for a brief time, she couldn't think of anyone who could better understand her distress. Yuliana's intuition also told her that there was an understanding between them, like sisters, that gave her licence to call and commiserate.

The line was busy.

*

Blackmoore slit open the envelope retrieved from his physical mailbox and read the letter inside. In it, Matthias Callaghan requested an urgent interview with him that concerned additional information about the raided flat on Park Lane.

He felt hesitant about meeting Callaghan again during the ongoing investigation that kept growing by the hour. Blackmoore's father had been an old-school policeman who had repeatedly drummed into him, when he was a young boy, that there was a great moral difference between those behind bars, and the men who had put them there.

To Blackmoore, Callaghan was a shady character who he briefly had come to know during Callaghan's so-called Scotland Yard confession three years earlier. There were things he didn't understand about him, and that he wished his predecessor Herbert Barker had shared before his own untimely death. *Barker must have taken a lot of his knowledge about the Callaghan case to his grave,* Blackmoore had told himself more than once. The present request for him, and no one else, to see him had been conveyed through Callaghan's lawyer.

Blackmoore sighed, rose from his chair and straightened his uniform. *Duty – in the end, it all comes down to duty.*

Forty-five minutes later he sat down in front of the prisoner.

*

"I appreciate that you have taken the time to come here, and I assume that you're aware of not only the circumstances, but also the details, why I'm still being detained despite having done the police a great service?"

"I am, indeed, Mister Callaghan", Blackmoore replied disinterestedly, "and I wouldn't mind if you could explain exactly why you asked me to come here in the first place. I was told that you had some additional, perhaps even important, information to share?"

I leaned back in my uncomfortable chair, with the knowledge that he had swallowed the hook.

"I'm here to help you, Inspector – why the hostility?"

I let my question hang in the air for several seconds, but instead of an answer, Blackmoore chose to show me a non-committal face.

"You are, no doubt, interested in capturing the main villain, not just the small fry fleeing the Arexim scene", I continued.

For the first time since he had entered the interrogation room, I could see that I had caught Blackmoore's attention.

"I have two topics that I'm interested in discussing with you. One is my immediate release. The other is the identity of the leader of the drug cartel that you just busted, as you are perfectly aware, with significant help from me. I find it disgraceful that you still keep me in custody. Wouldn't you agree?"

"Come now, Callaghan, you can keep giving me all the nonsense you want, and it won't change your situation a bit."

Blackmoore made an attempt to stand up.

"Not even if I have a name and pictures of the man responsible for all this?"

He sat down again.

"What do you mean … pictures?"

"I'm in possession of two recent, clear, high-resolution photographs of the kingpin in charge of the drug operation you just learnt about, and I can back it up with his personal information … how's that for a major bargaining chip?"

"What do you want in exchange, Callaghan?"

"You've got nothing on me, and I don't want to spend

months locked up here because of your risible legal rules. In return for giving you the information about the man truly in charge of the drug operation, I merely want you to speed up my preliminary hearing in court. Today is Thursday. I want it to be held by Monday."

Blackmoore thought for a moment, one hand leaning on his thigh. *Callaghan might be bluffing, but if he is, where would it lead him? He won't be able to improve his situation unless he presents the intelligence he says he sits on. So far, he has come with valuable information that has allowed us to dismantle a major crime organisation. Perhaps it's worth a shot.*

"I can't see anything inappropriate with your proposition, Callaghan. Although I can't promise you it'll be on Monday. I'm willing to talk to the prosecutor's office to see if they agree to get you an early court hearing – with no promise regarding the outcome – if you're willing to share with me information that leads me to the main villain in the drug cartel."

"A deal, then. I expect my hearing to be early next week, and I stress that I won't share my information with you until it takes place. You don't want too much to time elapse, because that will allow him to elude you. Meanwhile, I need to call my lawyer."

*

Yuliana tried Samantha's number again. This time Samantha took the call.

"Dear Samantha, this is Julie, Julie Cross. I'm so sorry to bother you", Yuliana said over the phone while doing her best to keep up her composure. "I was … I was trying to … I'm suddenly finding myself in a situation that very much reminds me of the one you recently went through. I'm … I'm so sorry if I sound confused, but something terrible has occurred. Can we meet?"

"Of course, Julie. What about lunch tomorrow?"

*

I hadn't met with David Sandhurst since he had helped me get out on bail almost a month earlier. He looked a little taken aback at my weight loss. The ciclosporin hadn't yet worked its full wonder on my face, which still felt a bit stiff. Yet, always the gentleman, he chose not to mention my decay.

"You're once again in a jam, I believe", he said as we sat down. We were facing each other in an interrogation room after I had been brought there from my holding cell.

"Back in London and back in trouble", I replied. "I need you to help me find a barrister who can talk me out of this mess that's none of my own doing."

"Give me the background, and I'll see what I can come up with. Why didn't you come to me after I got you out on bail?"

"I was kidnapped the minute I was released from prison. I was going to see you. A cab picked me up and the driver threw a canister with some sedative into the back seat where I was sitting. I didn't wake up until the following morning, when I heard a plane take off. I had been dumped in the Sahara with two dead men on top of me."

"Unbelievable!" Sandhurst said, shaking his head. "You're certainly prone to mishaps, Matthias."

"That's the understatement of the decade, surely", I retorted. "Do you remember that I told the police back in two thousand and twelve that the Russians had kidnapped and tortured me, but that I had no idea about their identities?"

"I remember."

"Well, I do now. They also ran a drug operation headquartered in London, which I've recently helped the police to break up. I'm holding back one last trump card, though, and that's the identity of the real boss. I want to use that information in exchange for a court date in three days' time."

"That doesn't leave us with much time for preparation."

"You already have all the relevant information about the murder of Rathbone that I'm accused of. That's the first of the two important issues that will be at the core of the trial. The other is that a few days ago, I learnt that my old flat on Park Lane, incredibly, was sold to the very same Russians that cut me up. So now the police suspect that I'm somehow involved in their illegal activities … In other words, that I'm involved with the same people that tortured me!"

"I understand that you want to get out, Matthias. I'll see what I can do. But I also need to know every minute detail that took place from the moment you were out on bail up till the moment you went back inside."

In essence, I truthfully told him everything I had been through. The trip through the desert; the people smugglers; the ship that capsized off the coast of Italy. I hesitated whether I should mention Andrew's help, but decided that it was necessary. Otherwise, where had the travel money come from – I could hardly have hitchhiked across all of Europe to enter the UK. Besides, my mobile was registered to Andrew's name and could be checked for calls to Samantha. I didn't tell him that the police in Milan had been searching for Andrew, though, which was why I had hesitated to tell David in the first place. I hoped I wouldn't put Andrew in a spot, whatever the reason had been behind the Italian police looking for him.

He learnt about my visit to St Puys and the ciclosporin scare. Then the last leg, back to the UK, which I found difficult to tell him since it involved some illegalities. It was however inevitable and necessary.

"Technically I entered the UK without the necessary paperwork", I confessed. "I called on Doctor Sternmacher's good heart and past services rendered, and he basically felt obliged to ship me back here under the pretence that I was a badly burned patient. I arrived here using somebody else's driver's licence."

"Well, that can be a tricky one in court." He continued to make copious notes.

"On the other hand, what was I to do? I think there must be some mitigating circumstances in all this. I arrived penniless after a shipwreck in the Mediterranean, with my

446

body in rejection of my face and fingers. My premier thought was to reach Saint Puys in Switzerland. Could I have gone to the Italian police? They would never have understood the gravity of the situation. They had, after all, recently extradited me to the UK. I tried to reach my wife so she could fly to Rome with a new prescription, but she had lost her phone and gone to Morocco since she was told by the police that I was in a morgue in Marrakech. You see my dilemma."

"Taking on the role of the devil's advocate …", David began, before smiling sheepishly when he realised his choice of words wasn't the most appropriate. "Not that I mean that you're the devil, it's just an expression."

"Don't worry about it, I know what you mean."

"You could have gone to the police in Switzerland after visiting the clinic."

"Another country I had just entered illegally while still known to Interpol as a murder suspect? No, I preferred to take my chances in the country I'm a citizen of."

When Sandhurst had left, after four hours of discussing my case, I felt very tired as I was led back to my cell. Yet I was unable to sleep when I lay on my bunk with its paper sheets and a mattress padded with the most uncomfortable pebble-like stuffing imaginable.

Friday May 15, 2015

Having put in for a free day with the Met's human resources department, claiming his extended trip to Africa as the reason,

447

Georgie left his home just as dawn arrived. He threw the bag inside the cab he had ordered before entering it.

"To Saint Pancras", he replied, when the driver asked where he wanted to go.

"The EuroStar?"

"Yes."

Georgie longed for Nathalie's sensually gratifying company, but he couldn't push the much more vivacious and sophisticated Samantha out of his mind. Matthias Callaghan had somehow made it alive out of the Sahara, and now he was back in jail awaiting trial for murder. *We'll see how that one will turn out,* he thought, grimly. *What if I study the recordings left behind by Uncle Jeremiah more closely and perhaps come up with something that cripples Callaghan for good? I'll have time to do that as soon as I've permanently moved to Paris,* he decided. *For now, the upcoming weekends are to be dedicated to, and enjoyed with, Nathalie.*

Georgie looked forward to his three days with her before he would go back to London on Sunday evening. At Saint Pancras, he bought a first-class return ticket to Paris identifying himself with one of his forged passports. After he had paid for the ticket in cash, he left the counter and hurried up the stairs to catch the train. The next person in line, a plump bald man in his mid-fifties who could do with a shave, asked for a single first-class ticket to Paris.

"And, should it still be free, I'd very much like to have the seat next to the gentleman who just left", he added.

*

A warder came to fetch me and led me to an old-fashioned telephone secured to the wall in a corridor across a glass-walled room full of monitors.

"I have good news, Matthias", I heard Sandhurst's voice on the line. "I've been informed by the court that the preliminary hearing of your case will take place behind closed doors on Tuesday, starting at nine. That means we don't have much time to build your defence strategy. The recording, of course, is the prosecutor's strongest card."

So Blackmoore had managed to move the hearing forward, as promised, I thought, pleased.

"That *is* good news, David", I told him. "I assume that 'behind locked doors' means the general public, including the media, won't be allowed access?"

"It does. By the way, earlier you mentioned that we need a barrister, and you're absolutely right. I hope money isn't an issue? Because I think we should hire the very best to argue your case, and I have one such barrister in mind. The best there is in London, if not in the whole country."

"Money is not a problem. You should get the best, of course."

"Then, after I have briefed him, prepare yourself for a meeting with the somewhat eccentric QC Tom Fowley."

"QC?"

"Queen's Counsel; the most prominent title rewarded to a barrister in this country."

*

As the Eurostar train began to move, a sleazy-looking middle-aged man dropped into the seat next to Georgie and unfolded his newspaper without even bothering with a polite "good morning". Georgie grimaced, then turned his thoughts to his future plans while looking out the window as the train rushed through London.

Suddenly, he felt one of his mobiles starting to vibrate. He brought out both his phones. The screen of the one buzzing flashed Mister Fisherman as the caller. Georgie hesitated. Should he take the call? The Fisherman had called several times over the past days and he had ignored him because the calls had occurred when he was at work with colleagues. *Well, now I'm on the Eurostar and there can't be any harm in answering,* he decided.

"Yes?" Georgie said. Although no one was able to hear what his caller would say, he knew he needed to be careful with his own replies.

"I've been calling you repeatedly for days and I've left you a ton of messages! When I call, you pick up the phone, understood?"

"It's been impossible. You have no idea how busy it's been at the Yard, with all ..."

"I have a pretty good idea what's going on because ..." Georgie couldn't hear the rest because the man next to him loudly turned a page of his newspaper.

"What is it that you want?"

"I want your complete update on the ongoing investigation. Who has been arrested, what locations have been closed down, what will the police do next and everything concerning Arexim and Moorgate."

"Moorgate I know of, but Arexim …?"

"You look it up, then send me a message and I'll call you. If I don't hear from you, don't think for a second I won't blow the whistle on you and your comfy little Parisian love nest."

"I'll have to get back to you after the weekend. I won't have access to anything you ask for until then."

"I warn you", the angry voice of the caller growled. "Need I say more?"

Berlosky hung up without waiting for Georgie's reply. Worried, Georgie wondered what he should do. Maybe the time had come to reconsider his strategy and discreetly move from Paris. It meant giving up Nathalie, of course, but there were many million attractive young women available around the world. His thoughts went to Samantha. *Maybe I should move to Australia? However, to get to her, I first must make certain Callaghan gets convicted for the murder charge.*

The conductor was working his way through the carriage asking for the passengers' tickets. He addressed everyone with their surnames after he had examined them

"Your tickets, please", the conductor demanded as he came up to where Georgie and the man in a crumpled suit and no tie were sitting.

Georgie was the first of the two to hand his over.

"Thank you, Mister Forrester", the conductor said as he

gave it back.

"And thank you, Mister Porter", he added after he had checked the ticket of his fellow passenger.

*

How did the police get the recording that, at the time, I suspected Flint was making? I once again wondered when I was back in my cell. *How had the sound of the motorbike I was racing been erased? Who knew about the recording being made in the first place?* I knew I needed to solve these questions if I wanted to be a free man again. All the rest was insignificant. The recording of me impersonating the deceased Mahfouz was key to the prosecution's case.

Flint made the recording of me posing as Mahfouz when I asked him to kill Rathbone in exchange for the money he said my father owed him. Then, presumably, he went back to his office above the pub and listened to what he had recorded. Flint never used it against me, because the motorbike effectively drowned out our conversation. At some later date, the recording was cleaned up — perhaps not too surprising in this digital age when the remastering of vinyls is the rage of the times.

Then Flint died, not too long afterwards ... when was that? I vaguely remembered it to have occurred three years before I went to the police with my story. Counting backwards, that meant he died in his pub in or around 2009. *What had then been the fate of this and surely many more of his recordings? Most likely the heir to the pub had taken over his tapes.*

I felt my urgency to understand the chain of events make a knot in my belly. Philip Jones was Flint's heir, according to Porter. When he had died in 2014, his son George had inherited the pub and then sold it. The warrant for my arrest had been issued in October that year, meaning the police must have received the recording of our conversation around that time and somehow succeeded to digitally suppress the noise from my motorbike.

Surely George Jones must be the key. After his father's death, he had gone through the things at the pub before he had sold the place. He had handed over the recording, and perhaps other incriminating evidence of Flint's criminal activities, to the police as any upstanding citizen would do. Since Flint was a known criminal, the police had gone through the material and finally found a suspect to the unsolved Rathbone killing.

What about the other recordings Flint must have made of me acting as Mahfouz? I began to sweat. As independent recordings, I felt fairly sure they didn't amount to much of anything, consisting merely of negotiations regarding my father's debts.

I recalled the day I went to see Flint for the first time in the office above the pub. That proved I was in contact with him while wearing Mahfouz's face and using the same voice as on the motorbike recording. Then there were all the phone calls I had made to Flint. On the other hand, the only recording mentioned in the murder charge was the one in which I negotiated Rathbone's assassination.

I felt how I, once again, was drawn into the quagmire of the past.

*

After they had ordered lunch at the small French bistro not far from the Savoy, Yuliana began telling Samantha about what she had learnt from Wilclair Bartlett.

"Yesterday a lawyer called me to say he represents my husband who disappeared three days ago. It turns out he's in police custody, accused of money-laundering. He claims his innocence, but … but I know that the situation is more complex than he could possibly understand."

Samantha could see that Yuliana was on the verge of breaking out in tears.

"Why do say that?"

"I … I don't know where to begin … but I have reason to believe that the same people who were behind both the past torture of Matthias and his recent disappearance have set up my husband to become a scapegoat. And now he has been detained for a crime I'm certain he didn't commit. I know him, there's not a single dishonest bone in Frank."

"Why do you believe this?" Samantha wondered, incredulous. "Who are these people?"

"It's complicated", Yuliana replied after a prolonged pause, wondering how much she could tell Samantha. "You see, Frank is accused of laundering money for the Russian Mafia. The same people …"

Yuliana stopped when she saw Samantha put up her tiny fists against her mouth. Her words made Samantha recall the horrifying details Matthias had told her when they had sailed from Australia to Bali more than five years ago.

"How did your husband end up with these criminals?"

"I don't know", Yuliana said and began to sob. "He's been in financial services ever since he graduated, so I suppose he was offered a significant economic incentive to take the job."

"And the job is?"

"General manager for a financial institute called Full Sails Financing Limited. According to Frank's solicitor, the police has incriminating evidence showing that Frank has actively laundered money across Europe."

"You must insist on seeing him in jail. I've a friend who works with the Metropolitan Police. He helped me get access to see Matthias. I'll see if I can't get him to help you, too."

Saturday May 16, 2015

Samantha arrived in the morning for her second one-hour visit allowed to close family three times a week. After expressing her concern for my well-being, she looked happy over the news that I had great hopes to be released after the pre-trial that would take place in the next couple of days. Then Samantha said she had something important that she needed to share with me.

"It's a bit awkward for me to be telling you this", she

began, sounding unusually insecure. "With the limited time allowed us on the last occasion, I really didn't have the chance to tell you about it during my last visit. Nevertheless, I have to tell you the truth of how things stand."

She's leaving me! was my immediate reaction, and my stomach churned out despair at the thought.

"When you disappeared, I was in contact with Julie, your ex-wife", she continued. *This can't lead anywhere good,* was my next thought, my stomach still upset. "I was desperate, and she was willing to listen to me. Actually, I find her to be a very nice person. Through her, I learnt something that has nothing to do with you, only with me. Life is indeed a strange time and place. When she was a teenager, long before meeting you, she was adopted by a couple in London who had lost their daughter …"

Samantha's voice broke down and tears began rolling down her cheeks. She looked exceptionally beautiful that moment, although I only felt fear that whatever she was going to tell me was something awful and irreparable.

"I've never told you this, because you've lived your own tremendous tragedy of losing your identity."

"I'm not sure I understand what you're trying to tell me, Samantha."

"You see, that little girl that Julie's stepparents lost, that was me." Now she cried openly.

I was stunned. When I rose to embrace her, the warder standing in the corner keeping an eye on us started barking.

"No touching! Sit down, or the visit's over!"

There was nothing we could do but remain seated by the table that anyway was too wide for holding hands.

"Please, tell me", I half whispered.

And she told me her story, how she had been abducted in Istanbul as a 3-year-old, before later having been adopted by her Australian parents, who had paid a substantial amount to a fake adoption centre.

"At least I've now found out that I have some blood relatives here in England, Matthias", she finished, drying her tears.

When Samantha left the detention centre, she still considered it wise to not have mentioned her lunch with Julie the previous day, nor the detention of Julie's husband allegedly fronting the business of the men who had destroyed Matthias's life. *Why should I burden him with more worries, now that he has to concentrate on his own situation?*

Sunday May 17, 2015

As *La Tour d'Argent's* maître d' escorted Georgie and Nathalie to a window table for lunch overlooking the Seine and the Notre-Dame Cathedral, Georgie felt his mobile vibrate. He excused himself when he saw that it was Samantha calling, allowing for the pompous maître d' in tailcoat and white gloves to pull out the chair for Nathalie.

"George, I'm sorry to call on your day off, but I want to ask you if you can repeat the same favour you did for me for a dear friend of mine. You see, just like mine was, her husband has been detained and the police won't let her visit him."

All Georgie could feel was irritation. *Is that how Samantha perceives me – to be some facilitator every time she or her friends end up having trouble that the police may be able to solve?*

He controlled his annoyance before he replied.

"Of course, Samantha", he told her. "I'm a little busy now, since I'm just about to enter an international summit concerning police business. Perhaps you could message me the details of your request and I'll look into it the moment I get the chance to during the next couple of days?"

"Oh, thank you so much, George!" Samantha exclaimed, happy for Yuliana.

Although it never was Georgie's intention to make an attempt to help Samantha's friend, the following week's events would anyway have made it impossible to facilitate Yuliana's access to her jailed husband.

Monday May 18, 2015

Sandhurst arrived after lunch accompanied by a man in his sixties who carried an umbrella despite the cloudless sky that I had watched from my cell window before being escorted to our meeting. He shook my hand and presented himself as Thomas J. Fowley, QC. I thought Sandhurst had joked with me when he had used the title some days ago, but apparently the initials were a serious matter.

Fowley looked like someone who enjoyed a generous dinner together with a good bottle of claret. But I could also perceive the intelligence that shone in his eyes, which were surrounded by a pair of bushy eyebrows and a nose that was as prominent as his credentials.

Sandhurst made an introduction before confirming that the preliminary hearing had been set for the following day with the court's explanation that "due to the extraordinary circumstances that surround this particular case, in concordance with the prosecutor's office the court has decided to accede to Matthias Callaghan's petition that a pre-trial hearing shall take place without any unnecessary delay".

He continued by telling me that QC Fowley was indeed informed of the details as to my case, and had assured him that there were several legal antecedents that could be argued in my favour when it came to my exit and entrance into the UK.

"Although your forced exit leaving the country cannot be proven in the strictest sense of the law, the photographs you have provided of yourself and the two men speak more than a million words", Fowley weighed in.

Fowley had a peculiar way of addressing his audience, an audience that, at this point, merely consisted of Sandhurst and myself. Fowley spoke as if he were making a speech to a full jury, although only the two of us were present. I got a feeling that he was doing a private rehearsal before the actual trial, with his head leaning to one side as if listening for divine advice; eyes that looked to the ceiling for the same reason; and then sudden, heavy breathing to underline some argument. I could only agree with Sandhurst's opinion that Fowley was as eccentric as they come. Nevertheless, he inspired a lot of confidence with the learned way he argued, so I felt good about Sandhurst's choice.

"Now that I've come to the end of the easy part, the one that no court in England will convict you of, we still have to clear up the issue of the essential crime that you've been accused of", Fowley continued, turning his eyes heavenwards. "That is, the death of Charles Rathbone in March two thousand and nine. The purported proof for your guilt in connection with his assassination, which undeniably took place as the police have described it, is a recording where you are imitating a voice that is not yours. This recording is the only evidence presented by the prosecutor's office. Am I right in presuming that this is correct, Mister Sandhurst?"

"That is correct. As far as I'm aware, the prosecutor has not presented any other evidence or witness."

"It is indeed interesting, because I cannot recall a single case – and I have read through the vast majority of any consequence that have occurred during the past one hundred and seventy years or so – where the prosecutor claims guilt for the instigator because he imitates a voice of a deceased man, and certainly not while wearing his face. Now, Mister Callaghan, I need you to truthfully explain a few things to have me tools to defend you successfully come tomorrow."

"Of course, Mister Fowley", knowingly lying.

"There are three factors we have to consider. The first is the circumstances when the recording took place – place, time, date, surroundings, even the weather." He briefly patted his umbrella. "The second is the contents expressed in the recording. And the third one is the motive behind such a request. All this will lead us to the 'who'."

The man was really brilliant at deduction. I decided that the best way to convince him that I was an innocent victim of circumstance was to continue along the idea that he found my case unique. Surely that, more than anything, should keep his interest alive.

"In my mind, that is a very concise approach."

Sandhurst simultaneously nodded his approval.

"I have been asking my contacts in the police a few questions concerning your particular case", Fowley continued. "Henceforth, do interrupt me, should I express anything that you disagree with."

Again, I nodded my agreement.

"On March twenty-first, two thousand and nine, the police received an anonymous call reporting a murder. Charles Rathbone was found in the cellar of the building where he lived, after being strangled a day earlier. It occurred to me that perhaps we should compare the voices on the recording the police claims carries your voice and the one reporting the murder. Eureka! It turns out that Jeremiah Flint's voice undoubtedly is on both recordings – he reported the murder the day after it had taken place. That certainly implicates him in the case, although, since he's now deceased, it will bear little consequence.

"After establishing that Flint did in fact have knowledge of the murder, and probably ordered it as explained on the

461

recording, we have to get answers to the remaining questions. How long after the conversation, in which the murder was bargained for, did the murder take place? What relevance has the recording to the actual killing of Rathbone? Is this a recording made one day, one week or even a year earlier? Could it even have been made *after* the murder? Did somebody, after Flint's death that same year, concoct this recording to deflect any special interests?

"Now to the most interesting part from a legal point of view. I've been informed by Mister Sandhurst here that you were subject to a transplant that gave you a face from a man named Abdul Mahfouz. It's claimed by the prosecution that you adopted a raspy voice, the very one we hear on the recording. That rounds off my analysis of your case, Mister Callaghan. To be able to argue it successfully tomorrow, I need one very clear answer from you."

He inhaled and held his breath for a brief moment, looking into my eyes instead of, for once, raising his own to the ceiling. The man was truly impressive. I understood why he was so successful arguing in court. Then came his question.

"Are you the man talking to Flint in that recording?"

The question caught me off guard, because I hadn't expected it. It was rude, it was unacceptable if the man was representing me, it was … and in that moment I was saved by the gods living in the clouds on Olympus, because divine inspiration dawned on me.

"Of course not. I'm sorry to point it out, but, as impressive as it may sound, your logic is faltering." From his knitted eyebrows, I could see that Fowley didn't appreciate my assertion. "You were talking about 'the time' and 'the place'. In July two thousand and eight, that is, nine months before Rathbone was assassinated, I was in a Swiss clinic, where the doctors removed Mahfouz's face for that of my father's. Which, by the way, is the one you see now."

In a blink, I had realised that everyone assumed that I was wearing Mahfouz's face when I spoke with Flint about the assassination of Rathbone. With Flint and Thumps dead, no one alive knew that I had been wearing a helmet to conceal my present face when I met with Flint.

Now, a statement like that is likely to catch just about everybody's breath, and QC Fowley was no exception. Again, and this time for a full minute, he stared at me rather than up at the ceiling.

"My dear man, why didn't you tell me before? Sandhurst, can you confirm this?"

"I can. I heard his Swiss doctor confirm it three years ago at a reunion with the police at Scotland Yard."

Fowley rose with a happy smile and extended his hand.

"Dear Mister Callaghan, consider yourself a free man. I know just the trick that will persuade the judge to throw your case out the window."

Tuesday May 19, 2015

My handcuffs were removed as I entered the courtroom. Since it was a closed hearing, the audience consisted of less than a dozen persons. Although her preoccupation showed, Samantha looked fabulous wearing an exotic white dress that I didn't recall having seen before. Sandhurst gave me a confident smile and showed me where to sit. Fowley greeted me with a distant air; he seemed to be mulling over something related to the trial.

The proceedings was still ten minutes away from beginning, when Blackmoore entered the room, very elegant in his newly pressed uniform, walking up to where I was sitting.

"Time for you to keep your side of the bargain, Mister Callaghan", he said, offering me an insincere smile.

I asked Sandhurst to walk over to Samantha and request the envelope she had prepared on my behalf. It contained the pictures I'd taken of Vasily in the garage, together with a very clear, blow-up of him printed both in colour and black-and-white. After having looked at them briefly, I handed them to Blackmoore. He looked unusually pleased.

"As I promised, I've written down some things about Vasily Ivanovich that I think you may find useful in your search for him", I said and handed over two handwritten pages with everything – well, almost everything – that I knew about him.

"Everybody rise!" a clerk shouted. "The court is now in session."

Envelope in hand, Blackmoore strode out of the room the moment the judge entered.

464

*

"Look here, Jones", Blackmoore said in that superior voice of his that Georgie had learnt to dislike. "I want you to contact Interpol with new information about the leader of the Russian Mafia we're working to dismantle. In this folder you'll find a summary of the latest information we have on him, together with some recently taken photographs. That will certainly speed things up, I'd say. While you're at it, make sure all of it is uploaded on our own database."

"I'll get on to it right away, sir."

"By the way, how is the investigation going with the people at internal affairs?"

"As per your instructions, I've informed them discreetly and in depth about the possibility of a mole, sir", Georgie replied truthfully, before he started lying about the rest. "We are off to a good start and I believe we will solve the issue before the end of the month."

"Good. Keep me informed of any development." Blackmoore picked up a report and thus announced that the interview was over.

Not before he was back behind his own desk did Georgie remove the contents from the envelope Blackmoore had given him. He looked at the pictures. Despite the reluctance he felt, and wary of the consequences this might cause himself, he followed Blackmoore's instructions to the letter. Less than half an hour later, Georgie could confirm that Vasily's picture had been uploaded on Interpol's official web site.

He still had a week and a half to go before his official leave would start; his last workday was on Friday May 29. Georgie felt very nervous over how fast the case with the Russians was developing. He could only assume that Fisherman worked closely with Vasily Ivanovich. *What if they get to Fisherman, and Fisherman gives me up or uses me as a bargain chip in some plea negotiation? Or, worse yet, if this Vasily Ivanovich gets captured and uses his knowledge of me for his own gains?* The safest solution, he knew, was to terminate his employment with the Metropolitan Police that very afternoon by calling in sick the following morning.

Georgie exited the New Scotland Yard building at 5 p.m. for what he believed would be the last time. As soon as he could talk safely, he called Berlosky.

"You should know that your boss has been identified this afternoon."

"My boss?" Berlosky said, trying to act ignorant. "Who do you mean?"

"Does the name Vasily Ivanovich ring a bell?" Georgie taunted him. "Interpol is splashing his picture as breaking news on their website now, if you'd care to look it up."

"I'll check on it. Don't call me again, it's too risky as things are right now. I'll call you when everything calms down."

"A done deal", Georgie said, relieved. With the intention of packing his suitcases, he drove towards his childhood working-class semi-detached home that he had come to despise. He had kept it for appearance's sake instead of putting it up for sale. If he had tried to sell it, he reckoned he could perhaps net 15,000 pounds after the mortgages had been paid. It simply wasn't worth the trouble, he had thought, a mere drop in the ocean compared to the riches he was selling through the fences.

Every weekend he had gone to Paris, Georgie had by and by taken unsold gems and jewellery, gold bullion, cash and hard drives, recordings on CDs and Flint's minutely kept accounting ledger with him. On the weekends in questions, he had also taken either the Friday or the Monday off, thus in a piecemeal way using up the holidays he was entitled to instead of taking week-long vacations going to Mallorca or Greece, in the preferred way of his colleagues. Each time, he had opened a new account in a different bank, depositing a modest sum of money, which had allowed him the possibility to also rent a safety box. When he had finished transferring all his riches out of the country, he had twenty-one official Parisian savings accounts with a total balance of 253,000 euros. Between his salary, the sale of his dead father's mortgage-free house and the sale of the pub he had inherited, Georgie could easily prove the sources of the money as legal, should anyone check on him. No, the real money was in the safety boxes. Easily two million pounds in gems alone, based on what he had been paid so far by Milton Cooper, and 550,000 in pound notes. Twenty gold bullion that would be untraceable after they had been melted, which at today's price would be worth another million and a half.

Then there were the hard disk drives and the CD

recordings he and his dad had rescued from Uncle Flint's lair before his pub had been searched by the police. Georgie wasn't very interested in keeping them, although over the years he had taken the trouble to listen to each and every one. Despite the abundant and salacious details that would perhaps enthuse others at Scotland Yard, Georgie hadn't found any potential in them from a personal perspective. The only one he had made use of was the recording that he, to spite Callaghan, had mailed anonymously to the Metropolitan Police.

Georgie had moved the recordings to Paris because he felt he couldn't afford the risk of being connected with his uncle Jeremiah's illegal activities. How could he explain his role if someone within the police corps found Flint's recordings in his possession? A known criminal's recordings – why hadn't they been turned in? And how come the Mahfouz/Callaghan tape had been received by the police anonymously? He could imagine an endless session of cross-examination.

He had listened to several other recordings of Callaghan acting as Mahfouz discussing business and debts, but as far as Georgie was concerned, the one he had posted to Blackmoore should be more than enough to make Callaghan's life miserable and put him behind bars for a decade or two. If not, Georgie had decided not to pursue his luck. Once settled in permanently in Paris, he was determined to find a way to destroy Flint's tapes for good.

*

Berlosky called Vasily at once after learning the news from Georgie. It was Sonia who answered his phone.

"Mikhail, this is not a good time. You should call back tomorrow."

"Now is the only time", Berlosky insisted, "unless Vasily wants to be imprisoned for life. Tell him it's urgent. He needs to hear what I have to tell him."

Sonia went to look for Vasily, who was being entertained by a curvaceous redhead that Oleg had somehow managed to find for him on short notice. Sonia felt jealous, not because of the woman who had suddenly taken over one of her roles, but because her power had been diminished by it.

She walked into the bedroom and held out the telephone to the nude Vasily lying next to the redhead.

"Some urgent business that can't wait", she said curtly, turned and walked out without waiting for his reaction.

That Sonia had entered his bedroom contrary to his instructions left him flabbergasted. *It must be serious indeed,* he concluded. Vasily shooed the woman out of bed and signalled to her to get out of the room before he took the call.

"Da?"

"This is Mikhail. I have some bad news, and you won't like it. Go to the Interpol web site and look under 'Wanted Persons'. I'll call you later."

Vasily used the browser on the phone and less than a minute later he watched, horrified, how his picture opened up on the page with the details about his background, age, nationality and the charges made against him. *Leader of a criminal organisation; murder on behalf of a criminal organisation; drug trafficking including heroin, cocaine, amphetamines, cannabis and cannabis resin,* he read. There were two things he had always been protective of: never to have his face photographed and publicised, and not to give away his true position in his organisation. That's why he had always let Mikhail Berlosky to be the one to negotiate deals following his instructions.

Filled with fury, Vasily did a close-up of the photo. The suit and tie he wore were the same he had used when he had fled to his English country house on Monday. The parked car behind him was the Mercedes he had been driven in to Arexim that day. *The picture was taken in the garage on Park Lane,* he decided, *when I left for work. He was waiting there, specifically to take my picture. Then he went up to the flat, collected all the evidence I had left lying around before trotting off to the police.*

We will meet again, Matthias Callaghan, he seethed. *Count on it.*

The Callaghan Septology VII

THE FINAL FACEDOWN

by

KIM EKEMAR

The last of seven books in the septology
covering the terrible fate
of losing your identity
and the right to recover your stolen life.

PART XIII

In a game of life and death
pawns and kings alike are fair game.

Tuesday May 19, 2015

The counsel for the prosecution, on behalf of the Crown, and QC Fowley, representing me, went through the ridiculous-looking, centuries-old procedure clad in their symbolic wigs. They both – noisily, and hinting heavily on obscure (for a layman like myself, at least) legal antecedents – made their introductory views of the case for and against me in what had been labelled as my plea and trial preparation hearing. I had been warned beforehand by the judge that, should the arguments in my defence be unconvincing, I would remain incarcerated with no further conditional liberty on bail.

The judge asked me to stand up and indicate whether I pleaded guilty or not to the prosecutor's allegation that I had instigated the murder of Charles Rathbone. I declared myself not guilty. After that, the judge allowed the prosecutor to proceed with the details of the case. He argued known facts about me – no surprise there, really – and my past as a businessman. Turning up the heat a little, he continued with details about my interactions with Rathbone: Rathbone's lawsuit against me, acting on Allan Gould's behalf, and later against my father. He argued that Allan had been sentenced for a credit card fraud that I alone had committed, and that, on my insistence, my father had used the EVI company as a front to coerce an economically distressed Allan to sell his assets far too cheaply. He then played the recording of me talking to Flint in spring 2009, which ended thus:

"Listen closely, Flint. My third and last condition to complete our transaction is that you take care of the demise of a certain Charles Rathbone before the end of this month. Here is his picture and his contact details. If Rathbone is dead by April first, then I'll personally see to it that you'll receive the money you say Callaghan owes you."

"I don't go around and order people killed."

"Sure you do, Flint. Just have another look at the movie I gave you. By the way, keep it as a souvenir. I've got plenty of them."

"All right, assuming that this Rathbone bloke has an accident, how can I be certain that I'll get paid what's owed me? And how will I know that all copies of the video will be given to me?"

So far, it showed some impressive homework. However, there was more to come.

"A first attempt to understand the motive for the killing of Charles Rathbone, the roles of Abdul Mahfouz and the two

Matthias Callaghans, father and son, become very confusing. The recording Jeremiah Flint secretly made shows that Mahfouz ordered the murder. Callaghan the son is blamed as the sole perpetrator of the credit card scam that Gould had been convicted of. And Callaghan the father was accused of profiting greatly from Gould's economic distress. How does that make Callaghan the son the one who orchestrated Rathbone's death?"

The rhetorical question seemed to stir the judge's interest.

"The answer is not an easy one to digest, but it's nevertheless the truth", the prosecutor continued. "In this case, all three are the same person, namely Matthias Callaghan the son, born in the year nineteen seventy-one."

That statement made the judge really sit up in his comfortable chair.

"I have here a transcript of a recording made at the Metropolitan Police headquarters on September fifth, two thousand and twelve. It's a truly interesting document, and I'll read to you the passages pertinent to the case at hand."

He hemmed and hawed as he searched for the right page before moving in with his killer argument.

"While in a coma", he began reading out loud, *"the length of which the doctors couldn't predict, they made a face surgery on me with the consent of my then wife. Medically speaking, the face was a fit, but now I looked like a man who had died of a heart attack the same day I had been taken to the hospital. Completely different, believe me.*

"Since I had been transferred to a hospital in Switzerland on somebody else's passport – please do remember that my face had been carved into a bloody pulp – I travelled back to the UK on my donor's passport. His name was Abdul Mahfouz. You can confirm with immigration that I arrived under that name on March seven, two thousand and eight.

"Anyway, Flint claimed that my father owed him a significant amount of money that he had lost at cards. To guarantee the debt, my father had signed promissory notes that, including the accrued interest by spring 2009, had jumped to eight hundred and seventy-five thousand pounds. Again, Mister Sandhurst here can confirm this, because he has copies of these documents in his files.

"I was later told that the doctor who had tried to save my father's life met with his colleague who was treating me for my post-surgery complications. They discussed the rejection issues I was having with Abdul Mahfouz's face. They came to the conclusion that I'd be much better off with my dead father's face, which was a ninety-nine point six per cent match, genetically speaking. And that's why you now see my father's face in front of you."

"Mister Groening, you may remember that I met with you and Mr Barker in May two thousand and nine, here at New Scotland Yard?"

"Yes, of course", Groening replied.

"On that occasion, I gave you a recording made at the restaurant in question. I had started the video function on my mobile phone to record my conversation with my father. As he was shown towards my table, a man got up as he passed him and stabbed him in the chest; well, you've seen the video. The assassin, as you know, was

476

Richard Thompson, also known as Thumps. At the time, he was employed by Jeremiah Flint. I think it's logical to assume that Flint ordered my father to be killed for not paying his soaring debts. Flint later visited me at home, in the belief he could put pressure on my father's heir to get paid. He came accompanied by Thumps and another man."

The prosecutor looked up.

"The last passage I will read to you concerns an exchange between Callaghan and Detective Sergeant George Jones."

When I heard him say the name, it all came to me. Of course! George Jones was the officer who had asked me those clever questions and had looked awkward when I had mentioned Flint's name. The very same man who had inherited and sold Flint's pub, where he must have retrieved the recording from Flint's office.

"Some time after the opening of the account at the bank branch", the prosecutor read, *"the lawyer representing this fictional character 'Mahfouz' got suspended from all activities as a solicitor. He had used false witnesses to confirm Mahfouz's signature when setting up the bank account."*

"Sorry, I don't know about this."

"Yet you do recognise that the one who played the role of Mahfouz starting two thousand and eight was you?"

"Yes."

Finished, he put aside the sheaf of papers and looked sternly in my direction. Although I had permitted the recording at the time, I somehow felt betrayed that this ...

INTIMATE … information was now on display. In hindsight, the only relief I felt was that I had taken the precaution to order the tape recorder turned off when Dr Brown had entered the room to talk about the specifics of my two face transplants.

"Based on the evidence presented, the Crown claims that the defendant impersonated the then deceased Abdul Mahfouz while negotiating Charles Rathbone's murder with the known criminal Jeremiah Flint. Flint ordered Richard Thompson to carry out the murder, which took place on Garrick Street number twenty-five on March twentieth, two thousand and nine."

"You are not calling Flint and Thompson as witnesses?" the judge asked.

"They are both deceased, your honour."

"And the motive?"

"Rathbone, a distinguished and very skilled solicitor, was successfully arguing in court how Callaghan had benefitted financially from Gould, and how Gould had taken the fall for Callaghan's credit card scam. Callaghan was afraid that more of his secrets and shady dealings would come to light, and it's likely Rathbone had found out about his transplants and switching of personas. Callaghan wanted to avoid this information becoming known at a public trial.

"In addition to the murder charge, Callaghan was recently released on bail. Upon leaving prison, he broke the conditions for his release, immediately removed his ankle monitor and went into hiding. For this reason alone, he should

478

not be allowed renewed bail, and the previously deposited surety of two hundred and fifty thousand pounds shall be forfeited. However, when sentenced for this crime, it's the Crown's view that lenience shall be considered since Callaghan two weeks later voluntarily gave himself up to the police."

When he had finished, the judge asked me if I understood what the prosecutor had accused me of. I confirmed that I did, reiterating that I was innocent of instigating the murder I had been charged with (which I knew, technically but not morally, was a lie) and that the accusation of evasion after being granted bail was groundless, because I had been abducted against my will.

With that the judge slammed the gavel onto the bench and adjourned the court for a two-hour lunch recess.

*

Has Matthias done this crime he's accused of? Samantha wondered. She wouldn't put it beyond him, but if he had, he must have had a good reason to ask a hoodlum to kill Rathbone. She respected him enormously, and from all these years living with him, she knew him as a kind and generous man who had had the misfortune of being caught in a web of misconceptions. Matthias had fiercely defended himself, and now he was on trial for having done so.

He had on a couple of occasions expressed to her his disdain for the double-dealing solicitor Rathbone, who had betrayed him while secretly representing the Russian Mafia. Rathbone's murder was not a concern of his, Samantha remembered him telling her; that's what happens to bad, duplicitous men.

She knew that this was merely a pre-trial hearing to determine a timetable for the upcoming trial in perhaps six months' time. As for herself, she knew too much of his terrible past to even consider passing judgment of anything concerning the father of her present and unborn children. *It's all so frightening. Poor Matthias.*

*

Takeaway food was brought to the court conference room, where Sandhurst and Fowley were eager to make me clarify various issues brought up by the prosecution. Two warders outside the door were making sure that I wouldn't escape. With Sandhurst posing the questions, I could see how Fowley made mental notes of my answers.

A few minutes before two o'clock, the door opened and the two warders came inside to once again secure the handcuffs around my wrists. Followed by my lawyers, I was led to the courtroom, where the handcuffs were removed. Samantha smiled weakly at me as I passed by her. I tried my best to return a more encouraging one.

The judge came in, his horsehair wig a little askew, and announced that the court was once again in session. He now gave the floor to the defence. Fowley rose with a majestic motion and, staring at the ceiling, started his delivery.

Fowley began by shredding the prosecution's argument about the credit card fraud to pieces. He refuted that I had in any way benefitted from Allan's economic distress. He presented a copy of the statement in which the credit card companies confirmed that the claim of a fraud had been unfounded and caused due to an internal computer-related problem. Vincent Lyle had confirmed in writing that he was willing to testify that he had acted on his own in the company's best interest when helping Gould solve his economic problems, and at no time was acting on behalf of myself or anybody else. There couldn't be any truth in the prosecution's claim that I feared that Rathbone would somehow use his knowledge about my face transplants to blackmail me by making them public. As proof that I didn't fear a public understanding of my two traumatic face transplants, I had volunteered that very same information to the police three years ago – which now, in the most reprehensible way, was used by the prosecution to argue the very opposite.

Fowley's learned monologue was peppered with memorised legal precedents. The judge was apparently quite impressed by this, since he more than once raised his left eyebrow before jotting down a note. Fowley then moved into second gear, changing the order that the prosecutor had presented things, while building up the suspense.

"The claim by the prosecution that Charles Rathbone was, and I quote, 'a distinguished and very skilled solicitor', unquote, is a false, not to say a bizarre, claim in the light of recent developments. Rathbone was the legal expertise hired by a Russian drug cartel, which last week – thanks to the laudable and unselfish efforts of my distinguished client, I might add – was dismantled by the Metropolitan Police in the very city where we now conduct the hearing of this innocent man."

Wow. Horse wig and all, the man was good. Notwithstanding the fact that I know the truth better than anyone alive, and the moral and necessary steps I had been obliged to take to remain both sane and alive, I bought his pompous delivery hook, line and sinker just by watching and listening to him. He certainly knew how to deliver his lines. What a performer.

Fowley expanded on the theme that Rathbone had run the errands for the Russian Mafia for fifteen years, backing up his statements with irrefutable evidence.

"Charles Rathbone", he concluded, "is to me not the kind of legal ombudsman our honourable métier wants to embrace. Using the law to let drug cartels get away with murder and torture was never the purpose of those who, over the centuries, have distilled human interactions to be met with justice and fairness. No, sir. Charles Rathbone was not at all a 'distinguished and very skilled' solicitor.

Fowley's presentation of my case was so dramatic in language and gestures that he by now had the whole courtroom, from the judge down to the warders there to prevent me from escaping, in a thrall. And there was more to come.

"The truth is, and the facts prove, that the prosecution is attempting to pin a murder on an innocent man. The truth is, and the facts prove, that Rathbone was a legal adviser to one of the largest drug empires the United Kingdom has ever seen. The truth is, and the facts prove, that contrary to what the prosecution claims, it was Rathbone who was afraid of Matthias Callaghan's knowledge of his work with the Russian Mafia."

On purpose, I noted, Fowley repeated his statement at the beginning of three consecutive sentences. I remembered a study I had once read: "If you want someone to believe you, repeat it thrice in a slightly different context." I've found this to be true: search the fairy tales and you will see that any argument to convince you is based on three takes of the same issue (*Goldilocks and the Three Bears* is among the more innocent ones.)

"Rathbone", Fowley continued reciting from his impressive memory, "was a solicitor in the pay of an organisation in the business of selling illegal drugs that scarred Matthias Callaghan beyond recognition in December two thousand and seven. Now I will tell this honourable court what really took place", he thundered with his impressive voice, "contradicting the false information that the prosecution for some unfathomable reason has decided to present. To do that, I must first read from the official statement issued by the Metropolitan Police yesterday."

He read it slowly while stressing the key words, in my

mind evoking an image of Cicero in the Roman senate in doing so. It was a no-nonsense official press release about the dismantling of Vasily's organisation and the hunt of its principal leaders, presented with a flair for drama.

"Do we stand in this courtroom to accuse an innocent citizen for crimes he didn't commit, or are we standing up to applaud him, despite the daunting, physical consequences for himself, for his unselfish, sterling, to not say patriotic, efforts to do the right thing against the abominable drug trade that today is plaguing not only our country, but the world?"

I felt quite the hero after his bombastic speech, but I can't say the euphoria stayed with me for long. I have done what I've done for reasons known, and most of the decisions I made, I don't regret. Laws are made by humans, based on concepts of ethics, rights and history. But who defined the ethics and human rights? To me, there also exists the right to execute personal justice when the law or other circumstances don't permit you to.

"Shame! Shame on the prosecution. Shame on those who cast a shadow of doubt on this hero of civic courage!" cried Fowley, letting his robes flow dramatically as if he were talking on the role of a super hero.

I didn't know where all that came from, but when I cast a brief glance over my shoulder, I saw Samantha beaming, leaning forward with her hands clasped in front of her.

"Last but not least, my client cannot, I repeat, cannot", Fowley said, getting ready for the killer (so to speak) argument, "be the man who argues with Jeremiah Flint on the recording, because, as the prosecution so correctly has claimed, it must have taken place in March two thousand and nine. Why can it not be the defendant speaking on the recording? Because the voice says, and here I quote again: *'Listen closely, Flint. My third and last condition to complete our transaction is that you take care of the demise of a certain Charles Rathbone before the end of this month. Here is his picture and his contact details. If Rathbone is dead by April first, then I'll personally see to it that you'll receive the money you say Callaghan owed you.'* Unquote."

Fowley returned to the desk to drink some water and clear his throat. Everybody waited in suspense for the conclusive argument he was certain to deliver. Fowley, looking as if he thoroughly enjoyed being the centre of attention, before taking the floor again, robe swishing around him.

"That Flint was talking to someone he addressed as 'Mahfouz' is evident since on the recording he says: 'Look, Mahfouz. You told me I was going to get paid for Callaghan's debt.' It's also clear that we are talking about March two thousand and nine, because Charles Rathbone's killing occurred on March twentieth that same year.

"The Metropolitan Police received ample evidence from the renowned hospital Saint Puys on September twelfth, two thousand and twelve, that Matthias Callaghan received his second face transplant, namely that of his deceased father, in July, two thousand and eight. The previous donor face, from Abdul Mahfouz, was removed in the process. This surgery was made a full eight months before the recording with Flint took place.

"Flint met with Matthias Callaghan after his second surgery. He made an unannounced visit to Callaghan's flat on January nine, two thousand and nine, as shown by CCTV pictures recorded as he entered the building, which I'm entering as evidence. During this meeting, he dealt with Matthias Callaghan face to face. Two months later, Flint addressed the person on the recording as 'Mahfouz', negotiating in a familiar way, which shows that Flint knew the man well. In other words, the man he talks to simply cannot have been the defendant, Matthias Callaghan, since Mister Callaghan had been wearing his father's face since the previous summer.

"I've also ordered an investigation into the name Mahfouz, assuming it isn't merely a nickname. A simple search using Google shows that there are hundreds of people named Abdul Mahfouz, and many, many thousands with that surname. The bizarre circumstance that my client unwillingly and unwittingly, while in a coma, received a transplant from a man with that particular name combination is by no stretch of imagination whatsoever evidence that he ordered the assassination of the lawyer employed by the Russian Mafia operating in London. In fact, there's a high probability that that very same criminal organisation used the Mahfouz name to lure Flint into killing their solicitor for reasons known only to them. It's not hard to imagine those criminals, who were not aware of my client's second transplant, using someone who looked like Mahfouz to order Rathbone's assassination, record it and then blame it on Matthias Callaghan.

"One last observation: the recording the prosecution has presented was sent to the Metropolitan Police last year by courier service – with the sender specified as Abdul Mahfouz, no less! It was left with the DHL courier service in London on October fourteenth, when Mister Callaghan here was halfway around the world in Australia, where he now resides. From this, one can only draw the conclusion that somebody was interested in framing him for the murder of Charles Rathbone, close to six years after Rathbone's death.

"Then we have the lesser incident of Callaghan's evasion while on bail. The evidence submitted consists of photographs of him and two dead victims in the Sahara Desert within twenty-four hours of his release from prison, and two prison receipts given to him on that day. The police have concluded that he was abducted by the same Russian Mafia, now disbanded thanks to Mister Callaghan's achievement after he miraculously managed to make it all the way back to London to report the crimes committed to the police. Because of the abduction, he shall be considered not guilty of said offence, and the money rendered as surety should be reimbursed to him without delay."

After that, Fowley rounded up his magnificent performance with a salvo of legal antecedents to further support his case, before ending it by demanding my immediate acquittal and release.

The judge turned to the prosecutor, who rose with an

overwhelmed look on his face.

"In view of the recent evidence presented by the defence," the prosecutor announced in a loud voice, "the Crown rests its case and agrees to the acquittal of the defendant and his immediate release."

The judge let the gavel confirm his words.

What a relief, I silently applauded QC Fowley. *The most well-spent 20,000 pounds in my entire life.*

*

After the court hearing, Samantha and I travelled back to the Savoy in high spirits. It was a relief to finally have a decent shower and get into my own clothes that I'd brought from Australia. Then, while Samantha showered, I had a quick look at my emails. There was one from Porter. Although incomplete, the information was compelling to say the least.

Besides some basic facts that I was already aware of, Porter insisted that he needed more time on the background to Allan's death. As for George Jones, he reported that the man was leading a double life. His home in a London suburb was a mortgaged, run-down semi. Surprisingly, he also kept a luxury flat in the poshest *arrondissement* in Paris along with a weekend lover, who he liked to spoil by taking her shopping for high heels and expensive handbags. The address to the flat was attached.

There was more. After hiring him on several occasions over the years, I now distinguished Porter's *modus operandi*.

He was obviously well connected with a talent what to look for and where to retrieve information. Besides, I had noticed that he took great trouble in understanding the daily chores and activities of the people he researched, as if to understand them on a trivial basis. Perhaps he even went as far as looking through their trash, from which you undoubtedly can learn a lot about people's habits. What I did know was that Porter had so far always delivered impeccable information on the requested subjects.

In his email, he added that George Jones, over three days spent in Paris the past weekend, had on his own taken early morning walks to the same café, *Y a mieux*, located next to the Seine. Around eleven o'clock, he returned to his flat and, a few hours later, emerged with his mistress Nathalie Solange to drive away in an expensive sports car. During the time they had been under observation, the couple had returned well after midnight. The daily pattern had been consistent.

The most earth-shattering piece of information came at the end. According to Porter, George Jones had been in contact with a certain Mister Fisherman, who Porter had reason to believe was a member of the Russian Mafia. There were indications that Jones, who travelled on a false passport, was an informer for said Mafia.

Porter's news was unsettling, but it wasn't the moment to react on it. *Never act in anger,* I kept telling myself. That I had to do something about it before we went back to Australia was clear to me. *Keep your head cool, you'll think of something.* I thought of my beautiful wife and wondered how I could tell her that I needed more time before returning to Sydney. *I'm sure I'll think of something.*

I had barely had the time to finish Porter's email before Samantha, with a towel wrapped around her head and dressed in a thick morning gown, entered the room of the suite where I was sitting.

"You can't imagine how relieved I am that this nightmare has come to an end!" she beamed.

"I can. I do."

"Of course, you do. How stupid of me! Let's get back home as soon as possible, shall we? Besides, I think I felt the baby kicking."

She let me touch her belly and, smiling, we both imagined that we felt a hint of the life moving inside her.

"I imagined you went terrified to Morocco when they reported that prison receipt for my things", I asked her.

"I was terrified. I truly thought that you had become a victim, and for some incomprehensible reason had ended up in the desert. I will be forever grateful to the detective from Scotland Yard who invited me to accompany him. If not, I wouldn't have known until the Foreign Office had brought the bodies home."

"Who was this detective?"

"Detective Sergeant George Jones … or Georgie, as he says everyone calls him. He told me he was the officer in charge of the investigation surrounding any British victims in the Sahara, and of supervising their return to the UK."

The events never ceased to wonder. So, Georgie had

decided to take a holiday in Morocco with my wife, with the presumption that I was dead.

"Tell me more."

She told me about the chief of police, Goulla; her relief when I wasn't one of the victims; how Georgie Jones had been very polite and comforting; and that they had spent a total of five days away.

Something held me back when I thought about sharing what I knew about her recent acquaintance. Instead I changed the subject. At the back of my mind, however, I felt a strong desire to have a prolonged chat with Georgie.

*

The little Italian restaurant in lower Manhattan sported a sign on its entrance notifying that it had been closed for a private event. Ten people and no guns had been allowed inside, while the chauffeurs and armed bodyguards of the bosses outside glared at each other watching over the place outside.

"Welcome to a family meal and some interesting intelligence that has come to my attention", Benny Botana opened the meeting after having greeted each of the participants individually. "I can assure you that the information is first class, and the food even better."

There was scattered laughter among the expectant audience. Botana was indifferent to the classic Italian food served at the restaurant, but he had carefully considered it as a requisite to appease the older generation, now present, that still dominated the New York mob. Personally, he preferred sushi or tacos with guacamole.

Large plates with *spaghetti alla Bolognese*, the restaurant's trademark dish, were served to all present. Botana knew that this dish was almost never served in Italy, although it somehow had gathered foothold in New York, of all places, believed to be an Italian signature recipe.

"I hope you'll enjoy the food as much as the news I intend to share with you today."

An appreciative mumbling could be heard as his guests slurped on their spaghetti.

"The big news I want to break to you", Botana continued, "is that the thieving rat Harry Jordan died a couple of months ago, still a wealthy man. This time around, however, he didn't manage to get away with the spoils."

A few guffaws and some expectant mumbling where this would lead could be heard.

"We were all hit by Harry's breach of trust. Among us all, he stole about eight hundred and fifty million dollars that we in confidence invested through him. Now the time has come to get that money back. I have a pretty good idea how to do it, but I must add that any money stolen by Harry and returned to you will come with a twenty per cent commission to cover the costs involved."

Botana could immediately sense the shift as the ambience became frostier. *Still,* he reckoned, *although they didn't like the recovery fee, they would be keen enough to get the lion share of their lost money back.*

Wednesday May 20, 2015

After he had reported sick for work – coming down with severe influenza given as the reason – Georgie again took an early Eurostar train to Paris. To board the train, he used one of his three forged passports as identification. *From now on, I have to be careful about how I use my passports*, he thought as the train disappeared into the darkness under the English Channel. *I can't disappear completely, because such a disappearance will eventually create awkward questions. Or maybe I should? Scotland Yard may start looking for me – perhaps worried about me, or because they've found some unfortunate link between me and the Russians.*

Georgie nevertheless felt great relief that he had been able to get out from the looming mess in time. *To arrive in time is an effort, but to leave in time is an art,* he reflected.

Three hours later he entered his Paris flat where Nathalie welcomed him from between the silk sheets.

Georgie looked at his watch. It was 11:35.

"You're always in bed when I arrive. How come?"

"Does it bother you?" she smiled sleepily, and with the slightest force pulled him down next to her.

Never regret what you have done, he thought as she breathily kissed him, *only the things you didn't find the time to pursue.*

*

Checking my email inbox, I found a recent one from Porter in which he informed me why Allan had been killed. His report was brief and, as usual, very much to the point. Somehow, the lack of emotion in his reply made me deeply sad for a mate and a talented man who I had been close to when we were young. I saw the later version of Allan – the one who had betrayed me and my father, and whose actions had got me tortured – as a different person altogether. That version of Allan was the one I would never be able to forgive.

As for Allan's death, Porter wrote that he had been shot once in the head in a building in Wimbledon with flats for rent on a weekly basis. Allan had stayed there registered under a false name. After matching the data of his whereabouts, his last appearance, and the discovery of his body in Morocco, the time and date of his assassination could be fairly ascertained to have taken place in the afternoon on April 27. There were no known witnesses to the murder or when he had been removed from the building.

Who had killed him? Impossible to say, Porter wrote, but it definitely was a professional hit – most likely a hired gun. Who was behind his killing? A somewhat easier question to answer, because he had been released from prison on bail. The surety for the bail had been paid through the disbarred solicitor Jason Longhorn, who for some time had been heavily involved in solving legal problems for the company called Anglo-Russian Export and Import Limited, or Arexim for short … Did that name ring a bell?

It can't get any clearer, I thought. *The Russians killed Allan for reasons of their own, then sent his body and that of the third man along with me to make us disappear in the Sahara Desert.*

Oh, and by the way, Porter ended his report: Jones had left on the Eurostar for Paris that very morning, after reporting to his employer New Scotland Yard that he had come down with the flu.

*

Trudy entered Trevor Burns' office in a hurry, without bothering to knock.

"Look, Callaghan was acquitted and released yesterday. Which means that …"

"Forget about him, Trudy. That's yesterday's news in every sense", Burns said and looked up over the rim of his glasses. "Right now, we have bigger fish to fry. The Yard has a large investigation working day and night regarding a crime organisation that's behind a significant share of narcotics entering Europe. The kingpin, by the name of Mikhail Berlosky, has fled along with his closest collaborators. They're now sought after by Interpol. It has been confirmed that they laundered the proceeds through the company called Full Sails Financing Limited that you wrote about. It's been kept under wraps by the police for a couple of days now. I want you to follow up on this story right away. Take one of the photographers and rush down to Moorgate where the commotion is. There will also be a press conference at four by the commissioner himself, so it's bound to be big. Oh, and this will be front page news so make it good, will you?"

Trudy for once looked at him with appreciation, Burns noticed, before she slammed the door behind her and he returned to his papers.

There's never a dull day in this business, he thought before eyeing the report he had been reading before the interruption.

*

Vasily considered the most shattering blow to his existence up until then was to have his photo published on Interpol's web site. To him, it was far worse than the substantial economic loss that he had no choice but to accept. He understood perfectly that its publication meant the picture had automatically been spread to an infinite number of other Internet sites. Vasily also knew that, once something was published on the World Wide Web, it was extremely difficult, not to say impossible, to get it removed. In his particular case, he was sure that it would be an impossible task.

Put simply, his face would from now on be associated with drug trafficking. Vasily cursed again, because he would no longer be able to relish that precious freedom he had enjoyed since moving to London: the museums, the auctions, theatre, opera, travelling freely and a million more things that are the privileges of the very rich who live an anonymous life. Because of the arrest warrant out for him, with a description of his alleged crimes and a recently taken picture posted on the Interpol web site, that life was now behind him.

496

With the extensive coverage in the media, Vasily went through a completely unfamiliar experience. The ferocity the media demonstrated in their attempts to expose his activities surprised him. After all, he was merely a businessman supplying the demand of merchandise that willing customers were looking for. Having the press and the cable news showing his picture over and over made him nauseous.

If his soul were to be stripped to its essence, Vasily only adhered to one belief: his own importance. He was an orphan who had grown up with his adoptive parents, who in their turn had succumbed to the Soviet power game. Vasily had not only survived, but he had managed to thrive in its wake. Thanks to his intelligence, he had over and over proved that he was superior to those who challenged him. *This time will be no exception,* he silently vowed.

*

I won't deny that there were tears in my eyes when my passport was returned to me the day after the trial. Samantha was present when I received it and the clerk, on behalf of the justice system, read to me an official excuse for "the troubles caused in search of truth". Sandhurst was also present.

Afterwards, the three of us had lunch in a quiet corner at a seafood restaurant. It was the first time Samantha and Sandhurst met socially, which, frankly, kept me on my toes throughout the meal. What would they comment on or puzzle over about my chequered past? I wanted this to be a celebratory meal with no new surprises. In particular, I didn't want to expand on any more details in front of Sandhurst – he knew more than enough as it was.

Not surprisingly, they both insisted on talking about the details offered during the previous day's court hearing, which, for obvious reasons, I didn't care to discuss. I had been cleared by the court of any guilt, right? Why should they continue the legal discussion in my presence after the case had been closed?

"I've had a month of this ordeal", I said quietly, "can't we talk about something else?"

They both looked at me in surprise, as if this topic should be the very one that should interest me. Well, I told them, it did interest me, but only to the extent that I had been able to put the experience of being arrested and drugged and waking up in a desert and locked up in a prison behind me.

Instead of changing the subject, they both insisted on convincing me we should specifically talk about the events the past month, because now I was a hero who had brought down a major drug organisation. They were wrong, of course. I had known about the Russians' drug empire for years and done nothing about it until I was threatened. Only luck had got me to my old flat, where I had recognised a stolen painting that I, by coincidence, had read about in an inflight magazine.

Now the nightmare was finally over.

*

That night, when Samantha and I lingered over a light dinner at the hotel, I reluctantly did describe to her in detail what I had gone through the past month. Appalled, she asked some questions for clarification, and I'm sure she added my recent brushes with death to my unpleasant experience preceding my face transplants. Then came her turn to tell me how she had fared during my time in jail and in particular when I had been abducted. She continued to express her appreciation of Detective Sergeant George Jones's courteous considerations during the voyage to Morocco, where she had gone with him to identify my supposed corpse. After not having spent time together with her for nearly two months, I did feel jealousy creep upon me when she praised the man's attentions and glorious qualities. Still, I kept my tongue.

She then got very emotional when she explained how she had been reunited with a grandmother, two uncles, an aunt, five cousins and some other relatives. Samantha had spent time with them on three occasions and felt very relaxed in their company. They accepted her as a long-lost relative, and seemed happy to be in contact with her, creating family history.

"Let's buy flight tickets back to Australia for Saturday", I finally ventured. "This will allow you to get together with your newly discovered kin again for another two days. And, if you feel you want to be absolutely sure they are family, perhaps it would be best to formally confirm it? I mean, by taking some DNA samples and send them to a lab?"

"I would like you to meet them, Matthias."

"I would very much like to do so, but there is something that I need to settle first: the damage made to my reputation."

"What is it that you're planning, Matthias?" she asked with a suspicious look.

"I browsed through some of the dirt recently published about me in the media", I replied. "I'm particularly upset with the *Daily Mirror*, and I've decided to confront that paper by making a personal visit." I saw her alarmed look, and smiled. "Don't worry. Remember, I was acquitted and I think I have a card or two up my sleeve to get them to publish a formal apology. It'll be my way to start a discussion about the media's way of reporting before someone has been convicted, and I plan to get vindicated in the public eye at the same time."

"How on earth are you going to pull that off?"

"I'm still working on how to do that in my head, but I need a day or two to pull it off, and then we'll go home", I tried to persuade her, feeling the time to tell her the truth about George Jones hadn't come yet. I really should confirm Porter's report firsthand myself. "I promise I'll tell you all about it on the very long flight we have going back home. It's nothing dangerous; it's only that I haven't decided yet exactly how to go about it. It's just something I know I have to do."

She hesitated, because both she and I had been through separate hells recently, and now Samantha wanted us to spend time together in a tranquil environment.

"All right, Matthias", she finally gave in, "I'll let you do this on the two conditions that together we buy the tickets right away and that you don't leave my side for the next eighty years or so after we get on the flight on Saturday. Remember, a few more months and you will be a father of three."

"A done deal!" I laughed, still unaware that it was one of the biggest lies I was ever going to tell her.

"By the way, I think you're right about doing a DNA test", she continued. "That will remove any doubts whatsoever, and it'll also be a good, legal argument to establish who my real parents were. Once I have the test result, perhaps David Sandhurst can help me with the process in the British courts?"

"Of course he can."

"Thinking further, I assume that will make me a British citizen, too. Won't it?"

"Of course it will", I smiled at her, happy over seeing her being so positive. "What name will you ask for in your passport?"

"At thirty-five, I'm sort of used to 'Samantha', but you're right. I have to think this through … Maybe having two perfectly legal passports with different names isn't such a bad idea …"

"I've been through that phase, love. I'm not sure I would recommend it."

We both laughed.

Returning to our room at 10 p.m., and seeing that the time in Sydney was seven in the morning, Samantha dialled Jack's number. I could finally speak with our children, who hadn't seen their father since he had been arrested at Rome's airport. When they asked me where I had been, I promised to tell them of a strange adventure that I had been through as soon as we were back in Sydney, which would be very, very soon. It was one that beat any adventure they'd ever heard before, I promised them.

I would make up something on the flight back. There were plenty of adventures to choose from.

Thursday May 21, 2015

After breakfast, we bought the flight tickets to Sydney with the help of the hotel's travel agency and then went to an American Express office, where Samantha withdrew enough cash to keep me afloat for a couple of days. I had decided that I would wait until I got back to Sydney before applying for new debit and credit cards to replace those that had been stolen from me when I was abducted. I promised Samantha that I would meet her at the hotel later that evening. She kissed me with all the tenderness she could muster and whispered that I should take good care of myself and to never let her down. At this moment, the doorman came to announce that the cab I had ordered had arrived. I patted my briefcase to show her that I had everything under control and then placed my hand over my heart with a reassuring smile.

*

The task of responding to Special Agent Vaughn's request about Samantha Kirby's whereabouts in Australia was eventually assigned to First Constable Dwayne Bartlett. His commander, Sterling Dunaway, had received the FBI's formal petition, to which a note had been attached to give it low priority. Since Bartlett was considered one of the laziest officers on his watch besides previously having been in contact with that woman Kirby, it became easy to order him to do the follow-up.

When he eventually reported back, Bartlett wrote that he had on three occasions visited the address where Samantha Kirby owned a small house, but no one answered the doorbell. The phone service had been discontinued two months earlier. Looking into the kitchen area through the unwashed, curtainless windows, left no doubt the place was uninhabited. Bartlett concluded his report by confirming he had talked to several neighbours, and not one of them had any idea where she, her husband and their twins had gone. No one remembered the name displayed on the side of the moving van, and there was no registration of a forwarding address at the post office.

*

I entered the vast office landscape at the *Daily Mirror*, guided by a security guard whose job was to make sure that I wouldn't stray. He knocked on a glass door announcing that it was occupied by *Trevor Burns, Editor-in-Chief*. After a muttered exchange that I didn't catch, I was allowed inside Burns' office. Without being asked, I took a chair, gave him my best smile and extended my hand to celebrate that we had finally met.

"I'm Matthias Callaghan. Pleased to meet you."

For some reason, Trevor Burns seemed a bit apprehensive when he shook my hand. Was that, perhaps, because he had authorised articles questioning my innocence, which had later been proven in court? Well, he had managed to sell a few extra papers, and, although he didn't know it yet, I had come to help him sell a few more.

"I honestly think that I have an iron-clad case against your paper for libel", I told Burns. "I'm sure that by now you're aware that two days ago the court cleared me of all charges. However, I'm not interested to return to court over your ... mistaken reporting, because you will shortly publish the paper's sincere apology – and, mind you, one that covers at least a quarter of the front page."

"Dear Mister Callaghan, I see no reason whatsoever for doing so", Burns replied. "You were officially subject to extradition, allegedly charged with murder and skipped bail, and this paper merely did its job reporting on the details."

"For someone who runs the news section of a large paper" I said, "I don't find you particularly sensitive to what kind of news helps your paper sell copies."

"Although I can empathise with your thoughts", the smug bastard actually had the nerve to tell me, "I'm only an employee at this paper who does his best to interpret the ever-changing stories of the day. I understand you are upset about spending time in prison after being jailed for, what, a month or more? Who wouldn't be? Surely you understand that our readers ..."

There was more of the sort and I turned a deaf ear to his ongoing verbiage. My wait for him to end his nonsensical flow of words reminded me of once sitting above Flint's pub while he was shouting down my throat. Why is it that people have such a hard time to listen and instead immediately want to impose their predetermined opinion, when there is so much more to gain from merely paying attention?

After two minutes, I tuned in again and decided to interrupt Burns.

"Hold it there for a second, Mister Burns", I tried to deter him, raising the palm of my hand. "You see, I've come here not to be bored by your whining about why you posted false stories about me in your paper, but to offer you a chance to write an award-winning story about the largest drug-dealing organisation in Europe. Now, did that catch your attention, or should I go to your competition?"

To show I was serious, I rose and walked towards the door.

"May I ask what you mean by your last comment?"

I turned and studied him. All considered, he looked pitiful behind his powerful desk. There were at least two different-coloured sauce stains on his white shirt. Did he live alone and only changed his shirt every two days? It was obvious he preferred to eat takeaway food at his desk, like they do in those abominable American TV shows in which everyone expresses his or her opinion out loud while chewing on fast food.

"Yes. I was about to discuss with you the scoop of the year for this paper, but you just convinced me differently. I was the one who gave the police the necessary clues to dismantle the Russian Mafia here in London, but they still haven't caught the man at the top. I was going to discuss the present situation with you, but it has become obvious to me that you're someone who prefers to promote false news instead of the truth."

"Rest assured that you're wrong about that, Mister Callaghan", he said, making a half-hearted attempt to rise from his chair while inviting me to take the seat in front of him again.

Showing reluctance, I sat down again.

"Please explain why you've come here. If it's reasonable, we'll come to some arrangement."

"All right", I said, "so now I've got your attention. I know how you can find the head of the drug association that the police are looking for. Of course, in exchange I want your public apology on page one."

"Vasily Ivanovich? Everybody knows that, it's on Interpol's web site."

"Yes, and I was the one who took his picture. He's not the head, though, he's merely the figurehead", I bluffed. "The real boss is presently hiding in England."

"Tell me more."

"You are aware that I was the person who brought down this drug organisation?"

"I am. I do have a contact or two at Scotland Yard."

"Yet you didn't choose to mention that particular fact when you published the story."

"There were other facts that took precedence."

"It didn't occur to you that this whole charade of me in prison and going to trial was merely my cover to expose the Russian Mafia and their money laundering? You see, I knew someone within their organisation and I was eventually persuaded by the NCA – "

"NCA?"

"Yes – the National Crime Agency. My task was to help them reach the Russian Mafia's leadership. To enable me to do so, I was given a cover story as an alleged murderer."

This time he looked at me with sudden respect in his eyes.

"My work is done. Now I want my respectability and good name back. To my utter frustration, the NCA can't or won't do it despite the favour I've done them, since they argue that on principle they never reveal their agents under cover. If you post an apology to me in your paper, it will be a great twist in your story about me and the rest of the media are sure to follow. In exchange, I will give you my story and the kingpin. Let's imagine that we can't reach an agreement here and now. It would mean that I'd have to wait two years or longer before a court decision obliges you to publish that apology. By then, no one will remember the case and anyway

507

you'll publish it on page twenty-four, which nobody reads. Needless to say, of course it's going to cost the paper a pretty penny, which today I'm willing to forfeit if my conditions are met."

I had his ear now, all right, and I could see how he mulled the alternatives over in his mind. In the end, I think it was the promised scoop that won him over.

"OK, we'll do it", Burns said, leaned over and pressed a button on his intercom. "Mary, find one of our legal advisers in a hurry and send him to my office."

Minutes later, a man in his forties entered dressed in a suit and tie. Burns presented him as Frederick Aspinall.

"Fred, this is Matthias Callaghan, who we've been writing about lately. A few days ago, he was acquitted of a murder he was accused of. He has now offered an explanation that makes our paper wish to offer a public apology on the front page. We're willing to do this on the day that we publish a scoop that he has promised us along with his own story about helping the police to unravel the Russian Mafia headquartered in London. I want you to put together a contract to this effect, which at the same time clarifies that Mister Callaghan here exonerates the paper of any potential wrongdoing in the past and waives all claims, economic or otherwise."

He turned to me.

"Does this cover our agreement?"

It became obvious that he had done similar deals in the past and knew the ropes. If I didn't deliver the scoop and tell my story, I wouldn't get the paper's public apology. At the same time, signing the agreement meant I would renounce my rights to sue the paper for the stories published about me. Very clever.

"That's the essence of our agreement, yes. Just one more thing – it should be explicit that it only covers any incident or action before today."

"Please get it done at once, Fred, very straightforward and no hidden meanings between the lines, please", Burns ordered his legal adviser and then turned to me. "Meanwhile, I hope you don't mind if I let one of our reporters interview you about your personal involvement? It will gain us time, you know."

I hesitated. What if Burns for some reason didn't make good on our, so far, verbal agreement? On the other hand, I wouldn't tell him or his reporter anything beyond what could only improve my standing in the public eye if it were published. Once the written contract had been signed, I no longer cared if my lie about being an undercover agent for the NCA was discovered, although I doubted it would be. Burns had admitted to contacts at the Metropolitan Police, but he had asked me what NCA stood for.

"Yes, I'm fine with that, as long as you have no problem with me recording the interview, too."

Burns smiled knowingly. If the paper published something from the interview that was false, I would have my own proof on record.

"Mary, send for Trudy, I need to see her at once", he

barked into his intercom.

"There's one more thing you need to know before we get started", I told him as we waited for Trudy. "To give you the kingpin, I need to go with your reporter to Paris."

"You said he was in hiding in the UK – "

"He is, but the key to get to him is in Paris."

"It all sounds very mysterious to me – "

"You won't publish your apology unless I deliver the scoop, so what's your worry? The cost of a return ticket on the Eurostar and a night in Paris for your reporter? Don't worry, I'll reimburse you if you don't get what you expect."

"You're quite an enigma, Mister Callaghan", he reluctantly replied, painted into a corner.

A pale, thin woman, who was in dire need to wash her hair that was dyed a matte black, entered the room.

"Trudy, this is Matthias Callaghan, whom you've written so much about lately. He has some interesting follow-up stories to tell that will undo most of your previous work. If he delivers, we will publish an apology on the front page with your next story alongside it."

She looked at him surprised, lifting one eyebrow with a piece of metal dangling from it.

"Oh, and by the way, I'm authorising an overnight trip for you to go to Paris with Mister Callaghan this afternoon."

*

I can't say that her aspect of half-mortician, half-corpse adorned with piercings caused any admiration or attraction whatsoever, but it didn't take long for me to discover that the young woman was bright despite her appearance. I went through the interview at a slow pace, thinking hard before giving any answer that could be contradictory or a giveaway to other parts of my difficult life that I under no circumstance wanted to become public knowledge. This is how the interview went:

"Tell me about your first contact with the Russian Mafia in London."

"It was through a solicitor I had hired, who happened to also give advice to the Russians, although at the time I was unaware of the fact."

"When was this?"

"About five or six years ago."

"Who was this solicitor?"

"His name was Charles Rathbone."

"The same man whose death you were accused of ordering, and later acquitted of having ordered?"

"Yes."

"Can you share the names of the initial contacts you had with the Russian criminal organisation?"

"I can. The boss at the time was a certain Kiril Medzinki, working out of Moscow. The man in charge of his London operation was Yuri Petroff. However, I believe both men are dead now."

"What was your involvement with the Russian Mafia?

511

Did you have any business with them or some deal that you hoped to gain from?"

"No, I didn't have any business with them whatsoever, not then, not now, not ever. In fact, I wasn't aware of the extent of their activities and organisation until quite recently."

"You say you know who the head of the organisation is. Have you ever met him?"

"Yes, I've met him on a few occasions, although I didn't know then of his position in the organisation."

"Who is this man, the head of the Russian Mafia in London?"

"It's something you will learn about tomorrow, after we get to Paris."

"Now, turning to the NCA's recruitment of you to bring the Russian Mafia down, how did that happen?"

"I was approached by two of the NCA's agents, who told me that I unknowingly had had dealings with the Russians, namely the sale of my flat on Park Lane. They wanted my help to penetrate their organisation. I don't want to expand on that subject, though, because I've been instructed it could challenge other ongoing investigations. I'm sure you understand."

"Is that the same flat that was raided by the police recently?"

"It is, indeed."

"What was the purpose of your recruitment by the NCA?"

"To infiltrate their organisation, find hard evidence and

bring about its downfall."

"How did you approach the Russian Mafia after having accepted the recruitment?"

"Sorry, that's privileged information."

"At their latest press conference, the Metropolitan Police stated that they have arrested a number of Russian gangsters and, in the process, located and closed down several illegal laboratories of synthetic drugs. Also, your participation revealed an enormous money-laundering operation going on in Moorgate and the recovery of stolen artworks worth millions of pounds. Did you really accomplish this on your own?"

"That's a question I prefer to pass on to detective inspectors Anne Slater and John Blackmoore at Scotland Yard, who were the ones overseeing the operations you refer to."

There were more questions of the sort, and in the end I think I got away scot-free while successfully correcting any previous speculation the paper had published.

*

While I went over the contract with Burns and Aspinall, Trudy went home to pick up a few personal things for the trip to Paris. Without letting on to Samantha that I had anticipated going away for the night, I had packed a change of clothes and toiletries in my briefcase.

Waiting for Trudy to show up at the railway station, I called Samantha. She sounded exuberant over today's meeting with her relatives, which had included ones she hadn't previously met, and she marvelled that they seemed to like her.

"Did you ever meet anyone who doesn't like you, love?" I asked her. "Of course they like you. By the way, my plans for the day have run into some complications. I need to go to Paris for one night, but I'll be back at the hotel late tomorrow afternoon, come rain or come shine."

I could hear the resentment in her voice, but my insistence that I had an opportunity to clear my name eventually calmed her. I told her the *Daily Mirror* had signed a contract obliging them to publish an apology as long as I gave them my story. Samantha reminded me sternly that our flight to Australia on Saturday was sacred: she wouldn't accept any more changes to plans made.

Later that evening Trudy and I took the Eurostar from St Pancras to Paris. I invited her to a late dinner in Saint-Germain-des-Prés after we had checked into separate rooms at a small hotel that met the limit of her travel allowance. I didn't mind. The accommodation was infinitely better than spending a night at Wormwood Scrubs.

Friday May 22, 2015
Georgie took his usual thirty-minute morning walk from his flat to his favourite café in Paris overlooking the Seine and the Eiffel Tower. He liked to get there early, just after it opened at eight, watching the dawn and listening to the bird twitter.

Nathalie was still in bed, never one to get up before noon, but he didn't mind; he enjoyed his solitary walks, watching Paris waking up. *The morning air today is unusually chilly and foggy,* Georgie thought as he munched on a croissant, *but it won't take long before the sun makes it another beautiful, warm day. I'm a privileged man in every sense.*

He was sitting outside wearing a ridiculously expensive leather jacket he had bought the previous day while shopping with Nathalie. She had insisted in that sexy voice of hers that he should buy it "because it is just right for your personality". He didn't mind, although he didn't particularly like it, because buying it had made her think she could influence him. By making her think that she had that power over him, he had fooled her. Over lobsters for dinner, Nathalie had declared that she was "very 'appy" that he had finally decided to permanently move to Paris.

Sitting at his favourite café, he watched how more clients arrived for either a quick coffee or a complete, robust breakfast. He had found people-watching to be one of the greater enjoyments in Paris, now that he had decided to live there. *Paris is my home,* he reflected. *It's where I will live from now on, in unrestricted luxury and with no need to punch the clock and report to stiff upper-lip superiors.*

A couple sat down at the table next to him. The man, who wore a hat, sunglasses and an elegant scarf wrapped around the lower part of his face, ordered two espressos from the waiter.

"*Nous attend un très bel jour aujourd'hui, n'est-ce pas,*

monsieur?" the man suddenly asked Georgie.

"I'm sorry, I don't speak the French language very well", Georgie responded and followed up on his comment with one of his most endearing puppy smiles. "That is, not yet."

"This means that you plan on staying in France for an extended period, then, I presume?" the man replied in an upper-class British accent as he removed his scarf and sunglasses.

Georgie blinked thrice in surprise, before he paled and wondered what trouble he had landed himself in.

*

At Vasily's insistence, Sonia and Pyotr had worked for the past twenty-four hours to determine in detail the damage his business had suffered in strategic terms since the raids on his British operations.

Out of five meth laboratories in the UK, only two remained undiscovered. However, since no one was there to supervise the distribution or enforce any trespassing of the rules, it was becoming clear that those working at the labs had begun to sell the synthetic drugs on the side, pocketing the profits.

The same pattern had emerged in Holland, Belgium, France, Spain and Germany, although the harm so far was less than what had occurred in the UK. A few laboratories had been shut down and also here – for lack of enforcement – the workers had become less enthusiastic to produce the drugs for their owners while selling the product on the sly. Discipline had to be reimposed.

The news being broadcast certainly travelled fast, far and wide. With the arrest orders out for Berlosky, Vasily and others, the usual suppliers were reluctant to ship any additional merchandise. Sonia's hard-edged, Russian-accented voice when she called them on Vasily's behalf wasn't enough to convince them. Instead the suppliers had begun to hedge their bets by negotiating the sales of reduced quantities to a number of smaller, local distributors.

The recent raids on Vasily's drug empire had caused sudden price spikes for heroin and cocaine across Europe. No case is more obvious than the business of narcotics to confirm how the laws of supply and demand work. When supply is on the rise, the price comes down along with special offers to tempt more customers to try the products. If supply later, for whatever reason, is reduced, it's obvious that the price rockets leaving the burgeoning clientele no options but to pay the price increase or go cold turkey. *Such a beautiful business, with its built-in carrot-and-stick formula*, as Vasily more than once had pointed out to Sonia.

Sonia thought all these details through before she decided to confront Vasily with the facts. Vasily's drug empire had been severely affected, but its foundation was intact and still strong. Despite the cash that had been confiscated from the Moorgate vault and the various meth laboratories that had been shut down, this had had only minor effect on the cash flow. Even if 30 per cent of the meth laboratories in the West

517

had been dismantled by the police, the Moscow operation remained unaffected. The reduced profit from the diminished sales of cocaine and heroin had in great part been offset by the higher market prices. When it came to hashish, which never had been Vasily's strong suit, the losses were negligible.

The only bank account that had been seized by the police was the one on the Isle of Man. Fortunately, at the time there had only been around five million pounds in it. To avoid future impoundments of the fifty or so accounts that Vasily maintained across the globe, Sonia knew that a reshuffle was urgently needed in case the police found further proof of the accounts' existence. Moving the money around the world would be Pyotr's job.

Sonia had been tasked with finding replacements for the more than fifty people in Vasily's organisation who had been arrested. However, her priority was to put all the distributors back in line and for this she needed Vasily's help.

*

After I had removed my sunglasses and my scarf, I returned Georgie's gaze and smiled insouciantly at him. I placed my mobile on the table with its screen facing down. Well, my smile wasn't really intended to be pleasant, and it delighted me that he took it the right way, because his face projected instant worry. I'm sure he wondered how I could have found him at this particular café in Paris, one day after he had fled London. Did I work for Scotland Yard, did I work for the

Russians, or was I there by coincidence …? No – definitely not by coincidence. He then looked at the woman by my side, who stared back at him. How come the two of us were sitting there? How had I survived the Sahara? And who was that woman with her piercings and her depressing black clothes?

I could read all this from his face in the seconds that followed after he had realised who I was. I had his attention, all right. To show that my intentions weren't hostile (although, quite frankly, they were), I signalled the waiter for two more coffees. We didn't speak before they arrived. The lad was bright: I remembered how he had questioned me back in the days when I went to the Yard to tell my story so that I could get my life and identity back. Georgie was no doubt thinking at the speed of light about the unfortunate factors that had brought me to Paris. Sitting next to him at his favourite café by the Seine, he surely understood that if I had found him here, I also knew where he lived, who was in his flat, and what he kept in his garage. He looked scared.

The coffee arrived.

"The coffee in Paris is the best, don't you agree, George?", I offered, breaking our silence.

"How did you find me?" was his reply.

"I have my, shall we call them … private sources?" I told him. "Up until this moment, I haven't cared to share them with the police. But I do think we should chat, man to man, before things derail and you become a train wreck – what do you say?"

"I say, I'm all ears."

"Why is it I have such a clear impression that you tried to seduce my wife when you took her on a trip to Morocco?"

My question caught him off guard, probably because he expected one about how he had come by his fortune or that I'd found out about his Uncle Jeremiah. Besides, here I was accompanied by another, younger woman, although by far not as fetching as Samantha. He took his good time to respond.

"She's a very attractive woman. We both thought you were dead, as reported by the Moroccan police. What's the harm in that?"

Then he thought he suddenly had a handle on me; his time with Samantha and her warm feelings about his gentlemanly manners.

"Jealousy is, no doubt, the most flawless form of flattery", he concluded with a smirk.

The remark and his smirk infuriated me. I had to take several deep breaths to remind me that I was there for a completely different purpose, and that I shouldn't let myself be carried away by his insolence.

"Working with the public enemy is the assured way to end up in prison", I retorted.

"What's that supposed to mean ...?" he asked, as he visibly paled.

"It means that you've been much too friendly with Mister Fisherman. Does the name ring a bell?"

He responded with total silence, but by the look of him, I could see that he was frightened. I had to choose my words carefully, because Trudy was using her phone to record our conversation for future publication.

"I have some intriguing evidence that you have collaborated with the Russian Mafia in London. Would you like me to share the details with you or with the police?" I asked and pulled out a thick envelope from the briefcase I had brought.

I held up the envelope to him. It was stuffed with blank papers. On it, I had written the number plate of his Lamborghini. I was obliged to bluff, because I had no firm proof of Georgie working with the Russians; only Porter's word for it. My hope was that my knowledge of his secret life in Paris would do the trick.

"Considering all this information that you claim you have", Georgie finally said, "whether true or not, what is it you suggest that I do?"

"That, I think, is the first sensible question you've asked since we arrived", I replied. "I want something from you, and in exchange I'll give you an opportunity to disappear."

"Disappear?"

"Scarper. Run into the woods. Change identity. Waste your inherited fortune on some faraway island. Whatever."

That kept Georgie silent for a good three minutes while he thought through his options.

"All right", he finally said, "so what do you want in return?"

"Three things. One: you will give my reporter friend Trudy here an exclusive interview concerning everything you know about the Russian Mafia organisation presently

521

crumbling in London. The good part is, Trudy and her boss have agreed to not include your name in the story, so you'll only be referred to in it as 'an anonymous source'."

"How can I be sure of that?" Georgie asked.

"Secondly", I continued, ignoring his question, "Mister Fisherman communicated with you on a regular basis, and I know it was through a mobile phone. I want that phone number before we leave this café."

"What –"

"And lastly, there's something I need to talk to you about in private."

I turned to Trudy, who was still recording the conversation.

"Trudy, what I now have to discuss with our interviewee is something personal. I would greatly appreciate if you could go to that corner across the street and get me a crêpe suzette."

Reluctantly, she obeyed, collecting her mobile before lumbering towards the zebra crossing to get to the other side in the, by now, quite heavy traffic.

"The third thing I want from you", I told Georgie when Trudy no longer could overhear us, "before I allow you to run away, is the tapes – that is, every single tape in your possession that you inherited from your Uncle Jeremiah. Yes, I know about them and I'm quite familiar with your kinship to Flint."

It took a few seconds before a smile spread across Georgie's face when he understood what I was after. Georgie was a smart cookie, all right. He had immediately found my weak spot.

"I can't give you any tapes, but perhaps I can give you my Russian contact, the one who's been extorting me."

"And, his name is …?"

"I only know him by the nickname you mentioned – Mister Fisherman." Georgie seemed to find some inspiration as he sat up with a hint of a smirk. "I have reason to believe that he's the big boss; the man in charge; the kingpin, no less. I'll give you the opportunity to locate him in exchange for not mentioning me to anyone, meaning anyone, at any time in the future." Georgie paused again before giving me an insincere smile. "This should only be about the bad guys."

"It's about the 'main guys' *and* the 'bad guys', Georgie", I retorted. "As far as my opinion carries, you certainly belong among the bad guys while this Fisherman of yours certainly isn't the main guy. The man in charge has been someone called Vasily Ivanovich. Have you ever heard of him?"

"Well, perhaps I have", Georgie reluctantly admitted, recalling the information Blackmoore had instructed him to transmit to Interpol. "But I know that Fisherman is the important one, the man at the top of the chain of command."

There was no reason for me to get into a discussion with Georgie about the finer points of the Russian Mafia's hierarchy, so I let it pass.

"Well, you're the one who's been working with this so-called Fisherman, so I can only assume that you're right", I said, encouraging him. "Personally, I don't care what you do or where you go if that's what it takes to put all these big-time sturgeons behind bars. But how can I know you will tell me the truth if I agree?"

"Listen to this."

From across the table, Georgie brought out a mobile from his pocket and rapidly searched it before activating a voicemail with the loudspeaker on. No names were mentioned, but my heart made an extra beat when I recognised Berlosky's voice.

"Listen closely to what I have to say, Minnow. As I've told you over and over again – I need to know where Scotland Yard is concentrating its resources after the raids they've made! I expect you to return my call immediately!"

Georgie held up the mobile at a distance to show me the screen of his phone.

"As you can see, this message was left yesterday at eighteen past nine p.m. – French time." A smile of confidence appeared on his face. He leaned back in his chair, with a calculating look to see how far he could negotiate.

"I'll give you this phone, and you can give it to Blackmoore for all I care, as long as you leave my name out of it. Tell him the phone was mailed to you, or that you found it in that Park Lane flat that you broke into ... whatever. Then you can use the information on it to bait and catch the Fisherman."

"I'm sure I can think of something, should it be necessary."

"I've listened to 'Uncle Jeremiah's recordings', as you refer to them, on several occasions. Quite a few of them are

524

interesting – especially those that involve Abdul Mahfouz, deceased for a great many years. Of course you would like those recordings back! If not, you'll be caught in a big lie."

"Considering your options, I think your situation is far worse than the one you now suggest my own to be", I retorted. "All I need to do is place a phone call, and within minutes you'll have Interpol breathing down your neck."

We both kept our silence for a minute, pondering the options and their implications. From the corner of my eye, I could see Trudy crossing the street to get back to the café.

"Let's use our heads and make a trade", I finally said. "Give me the phone number that your Mister Fisherman uses to communicate with you, and I won't reveal your name to anyone. Your insurance is Flint's tapes that you claim have a hold on me."

He delayed before responding.

"All right, it seems a fair enough exchange."

"You know what?" I told him. "For me, this whole business is quite simple. I really don't care whether you are caught or not, although I must confess that a few things you and Flint have done upset me. Still, they don't compare with the damage the Russian Mafia has caused … to me, and to many others."

Trudy sat down and gave me the crêpe suzette she had purchased.

"Thank you, Trudy", I told her. "Mr Jones here is now all yours, since he has amicably accepted to do the interview you wished for."

Special FBI Agent Solomon Vaughn began to suspect he had reached a dead end in the case of the Englishman who had died underneath the cactus in Arizona.

He was puzzled, to say the least, over the disinterested response from the Australians. Kirby no longer lived at the address she was officially registered to, he had been told. There was no forwarding or other address given.

Samantha Kirby could not be found by the Australian police. Andrew Reese had disappeared without a trace while travelling on a train in motion. Matthias Callaghan, Thompson's apparent assassin, had also vanished. The last trace of him was at the Mexican border with the USA the day of the murder. That was six years ago. *How would these disappearances be possible in the age of real-time connection and ubiquitous surveillance cameras?*

The only one Vaughn had found related to the alleged assassin, but not to Thompson's death, was his son who had the same name as his father. The file on Matthias Callaghan III made for interesting reading. A millionaire, accused of grand theft from credit card companies, later absolved from the accusation, only to instead be charged with the murder of a British lawyer upon his recent arrival to Europe. Vaughn pondered any possible links between Thompson's death and Callaghan the son's arrest, but couldn't imagine one.

Then, another vanishing act had occurred. According to an investigation report made by the Metropolitan Police,

Callaghan the son was released on bail on April 26. Fifteen minutes later, he had vanished into thin air after removing his anklet monitor. Yet another mysterious disappearance.

However, unless they were on US soil, Vaughn couldn't insist on questioning any of the four with the exception of Matthias Callaghan the father. Reading through the details in Interpol's database over wanted persons, he found the information uploaded in 2009 incomplete compared to what he had learnt since taking over the case. Vaughn decided to request an update for Thompson's alleged killer.

To his surprise, less than an hour later he had a response from Interpol's headquarters in Lyon, France. *Someone over there must be working overtime,* he thought.

Matthias Callaghan, born 1953, was confirmed killed in 2008, the missive stated. Hence, the update was refused, and the warrant for his arrest was being retracted.

Who then, Vaughn wondered, incredulous, *was the man who had pushed the cactus on top of Thompson at the spa a year after Callaghan's death?*

*

Since I needed Georgie's phone to hand it over to the police, and Trudy needed it to get the story past her editor for publishing, we agreed on a plan on the train back to London. I would keep the phone, but she would copy its contents.

"Here we are, doing our best to duplicate the evidence", I said in jest to Trudy. It was the only time I ever heard her laugh (albeit her laughter couldn't have lasted more than three seconds). Thus reassured that somehow, somewhere deep inside her serious-looking appearance, Trudy had a sense of tumour, I tried to provoke one more laugh from her on the train trip. I didn't succeed.

I played the messages Berlosky had left on Georgie's phone and Trudy recorded them with her mobile. Finished, she brought out her iPad and began to rapidly type away.

When we came out of the Chunnel on the British side, Trudy called her editor while I placed a call to Blackmoore. Getting off the Eurostar, I was allowed to pass security check without even as much as a raised eyebrow, which confirmed that the police had removed any previous arrest alert.

I took a cab to New Scotland Yard and, soon afterwards, I was ushered into Detective Inspector Blackmoore's private office, no less. On all previous occasions, we had faced each other in rooms intended for interrogation. *Does this mean he's finally accepted that I'm not one of the villains?* I asked myself, smiling inwardly. The fact that Blackmoore received me on his home turf made me feel … how can I put it … even better than I deserved?

"Thank you for receiving me at this late hour, Inspector," I greeted him as we shook hands. I sat down, obeying his hand gesture. "I'm here, because I believe you have a good chance to apprehend Mikhail Berlosky, the head of Arexim."

Blackmoore merely stared at me with polite interest, as if he didn't quite believe, or perhaps because he thought that I had come with some ulterior motive.

"Continue."

I took Georgie's mobile out of my pocket and placed it on his desk. Georgie had been careful to wipe it clean before handing it over to me.

"Using this phone, you should be able to track him down. The only person who has this phone's number is Mikhail Berlosky. It also works the reverse way: the only number registered on this phone goes to Berlosky. If you can get him to talk long enough, I'm sure your technical team will be able to pinpoint his whereabouts. That's what you want, isn't it?"

I noticed a hint of reluctant respect in Blackmoore's eyes. Without responding, he grabbed the phone and ordered half a dozen people to immediately present themselves in his office.

Two hours later I was received at the Savoy in the welcoming arms of Samantha.

Saturday May 23, 2015

Four policemen, dressed in civilian clothes, discreetly positioned themselves near the house in the London suburb. When everyone was in place, the leader gave the code phrase "the fox is in the hen house" to his command centre. Less than a minute later, a Puma HC Mk2 helicopter carrying twelve troops deployed by the UK Special Forces landed on the lawn.

The ear-deafening sound from the whirling rotor blades alerted Berlosky. As he looked out through the curtains and saw the men in military clothing jump out of the helicopter, he immediately knew that the game was over.

"Stay here", he told his wife and son, "they're coming for me. The police have no reason to touch you. Remember what I told you about the accounts, Tania, if you and Sasha need money, but don't – under any circumstance – give away that information to anyone, understand? Not to anyone."

"Yes, Mikhail", she half-whispered, worried about Sasha and their future.

"I'll be locked up for some time, but you must come and visit me as often as you can."

"Yes, Mikhail, I promise."

A tremendous sound announced that the front door had been broken down. Mikhail rose to face the troops.

"I will need your help and the money I've got tucked away to get out of prison someday. I count on you, Tania. And, please take good care of Sasha ..."

He didn't get further. Just as he was to embrace Sasha farewell, the troops poured into the bedroom, pointing their weapons at him.

*

At the time of Mikhail Berlosky's arrest, which I was unaware of until much later, I was sitting next to Samantha on our flight back to Australia. I felt drained and exhausted, and I wondered what I could do to get my former energy back upon our return to Sydney. Our European vacation had turned into a nightmare. The experience had left me wondering if I should ever want to travel abroad again.

"Discovering my true identity and who my parents were, has been a profound relief, Matthias", Samantha said. "At the same time the impact makes me feel, I don't know … as if I've aged a century."

"You don't look one minute older than the moment I met you", I replied. "That is one of the great mysteries of amazing women like yourself."

"Flatterer!"

"No, I mean it. And to pour gasoline on my own pyre, I think – no, I know – that in the last month or so, I've aged faster than the portrait of Dorian Gray."

"You're exaggerating, of course", Samantha claimed, patting my hand affectionately. But I could see in her eyes that I wasn't exaggerating at all.

"Although it's more or less noticeable, getting older is the only thing we all truly share on equal terms… and it can only be a good thing. The single alternative – and, honestly, I find it the less attractive of the two – is to be dead. It's something I've lately been too close to for my liking."

"We're all learning by the day, and, I assure you, this trip to Europe has taught me to appreciate everything I have – you, our children, the unborn." Samantha patted her belly, which by now was showing a slight bump.

"Darling, can I ask you something that's been bothering me since the pretrial hearing?" she then asked.

I didn't like the sound of her question, but there was no way for me to tell her no.

"Yes, of course. Tell me, what is it that bothers you?"

"You told me once – remember, on the sailboat leaving Australia for Bali – that by coincidence you filmed your father's assassination at the Croydon restaurant. I wonder how the Mahfouz impostor, the one the court now has determined wasn't you, could have handed over copies of that video to Flint? How did this impostor get his hands on it, since I assume only you and the police had copies of it?"

Bright girl, my Samantha, but fortunately I had an ace up my sleeve.

"Because someone at the Metropolitan Police gave it to him. I don't know how he did it, but I do know who it was."

"Please explain."

"It has to do with why I needed an extra day before going home. I need to talk to you about your compassionate travel companion, who, by the way, resigned from Scotland Yard before he took you to Morocco."

My assertion made her move her seat into an upright position.

"What do you mean?" Her voice suddenly carried a sharper, almost accusing, note.

"Two days ago, I told you I had something to do before we went back to Sydney. Together with a reporter from the *Daily Mirror*, I went to Paris to look up a man who turned out to be a clue to one of the chief orchestrators of my near-death experience in the Sahara."

"What has this to do with George Jones?"

"The man we met with in Paris was the very same

George Jones with whom you travelled to Morocco. It turns out that George is the lucky heir to Jeremiah Flint's illicit fortune. If you recall, Flint was the gangster who sent an assassin to murder me in Arizona, believing I was my father."

"Of course I remember", she said, tartly.

"To cut a long story short", I told her, looking her straight in the eye without blinking, "George turned out to be working for the very same Russian organisation that once mutilated me and recently left me for dead in the Sahara."

As she always did when confronted with brutal news that was hard for her to digest, Samantha put her small fists up against her face and looked at with me with wide-opened eyes.

"How do you know? When I was with George in Marrakech, his words and actions never even ... hinted at the possibility. He was chivalry and kindness incarnated. How do you know?"

"I know, because I persuaded him to give up his mobile, given to him by the Russians so he could communicate with them. To reveal information about police business, no less."

"Why would he do that?"

I could see that she wasn't convinced that I was telling her the truth.

"Because we made a deal. Georgie gave me the phone, the reporter got her story, I'll get my apology printed on page one and Scotland Yard got the phone Berlosky used to talk to Georgie. In exchange, I was obliged to give Georgie some leeway to escape."

"Georgie … Flint's heir … working for the Russians?"

I could see that she had a hard time believing it. I brought out my mobile, on which I surreptitiously had recorded the conversation at the café where I and Trudy had confronted Georgie. I had previously edited out any mention of Flint's tapes and that Trudy briefly left us alone.

"After you have listened to this, you will know."

She listened to it by plugging in her headphones to my phone. After that, she wouldn't speak to me for the remainder of the flight.

*

"Look here, everyone", Burns shouted over the general clamour ruling the *Daily Mirror*'s newsroom. "Can you please stop yelling at each other and listen instead to what I have to say."

The noise abruptly disappeared. The forty people or so in the room looked expectantly at Burns, who rarely came out of his office to make a grand speech.

"Today's circulation stunned all expectations by at least twenty per cent. Although we all contribute to the stories that need to be told, I think it's only fair to today especially mention Trudy Swift's spectacular story as the one that propelled our paper to new heights."

Unaccustomed to flattery, especially since it was unexpected, Trudy was seen blushing deep. Although neither she nor anyone else present knew it at the moment, Burns' words were transformative for her future actions. It was the first time she had received official praise for anything she had done.

"Tomorrow we will run Trudy's follow-up story about the Russian Mafia on page one. Well done, Trudy!"

Monday May 25, 2015

The *Daily Mirror*'s Sunday edition was brought to Vasily on Sonia's instructions. He was sitting in the yacht's state room wearing his favourite hand-painted Japanese silk robe drinking tea when Ilya handed it over to him.

"Who wants yesterday's paper?" Vasily asked him when he saw the date.

"Sonia said it might interest you", Ilya replied.

On the front page was the same picture of Vasily that could be found on the Interpol website, next to that of Berlosky being carried off in handcuffs. "The scum drugging Europe", the black headline screamed. Vasily felt how the veins in his temples began to throb.

The article described in a disturbingly precise way how his organisation had managed to become the most dominant drug importer in the UK and on the continent. It described the variety of drugs sold; the presumed origins of the drugs; the dismantling of several laboratories; the extraordinary amount of money involved as proven by the staggering amount of cash found at the Moorgate facility; and the arrests made so far. The piece finished with a few paragraphs about the social costs and health issues provoked in society, which Vasily couldn't be bothered reading about. There were also some pictures from his flat and an enlarged one of the stolen Modigliani painting he had bought from Jeffrey Foley.

He was furious. *It's all Callaghan's fault!* he raged inwardly. *How on earth did the police catch up with Mikhail? I will get to the bottom of this, but I can't do it with my face plastered all over the place. First of all, I must think about my safety.*

Monday June 1, 2015

Detective Inspector John Blackmoore was flabbergasted by the news that George Jones had disappeared a good week before the end of his employment. After calling in sick, Jones had simply vanished. He didn't answer his phone at home or his mobile. Blackmoore was unsure what he should make of it. Eventually, he resorted to his favourite motto, "wait and see", but not before sending a constable to Jones's home in the suburb. The constable's assertion was that, although it looked as if someone lived there when peeking through the windows, no one was at home.

Wednesday June 3, 2015

Empowered by his associates in New York, Benny Botana patiently stalked the entrance to Ludmila Jordan's home in Paris for several days. His patience eventually paid off. On the fifth day, a Bentley pulled up outside the building that Botana had learnt Ludmila was the proprietor of. He also knew that she occupied the two upper floors in the building. *And now she's coming home,* he noted contentedly when he saw her Bentley stop outside her building. *It's time to get to work.*

Tuesday June 23, 2015

We were back in Sydney after the two months of nightmare in Europe. After fending off the twins' questions about our prolonged absence with toys bought in a tax-free shop and inventing tales about the things that had prevented our return, Samantha and I slowly returned to normalcy. The new house with its envious view; seeing the kids again; relaxed again, after, in a coordinated way, having satisfied Jack's incredulous questions; happy as larks expecting the new baby – it all helped us to eventually get settled into a life that had the semblance of the one we had enjoyed before our disastrous trip to Europe.

At Jack's insistence, I began analysing the new project he wanted us to embark on. The twins were excited that they were going to get a new sibling sometime in October. Samantha put up our previous home for sale after we had got organised in our spacious new one. The garden around our house was beginning to take shape. A lot of work, but it was of the agreeable kind.

*

The staff at the St Puys clinic looked out the window to see what caused the extraordinary noise that rarely affected their quiet surroundings. They watched how eight people jumped out of a huge helicopter after its rotors had slowed down.

A blond woman with cropped hair and an Eastern European accent led the party into the reception area.

"Good morning", she said with a mirthless smile. "We're here to see Doctor Sternmacher."

A few minutes later, she and two others of her team were admitted inside Dr Sternmacher's ample office. The remaining five men returned outside to wait by the helicopter and its pilot. She shook hands with the doctor before sitting down. Her two companions remained standing behind her, maintaining a respectful distance.

"My name is Daria Kuznetsov from Ukraine." While her real name was Sonia Malkovich, she had chosen 'Kuznetsov' for her new passport because it translated into 'Smith' – a surname as anonymous as they come. "I want to talk with you about my cousin's need of a face transplant."

"Well, Miss Kuznetsov, in that case you've chosen the right place to do so", Sternmacher smiled benevolently. "That is what we specialise in doing here at the Saint Puys clinic. May I ask what kind of accident your cousin has suffered? Or, better still, perhaps you have some photographs of him?"

"No, I don't have any pictures, there's no need for that", she replied. "I have something much better. I brought him here in the flesh for you to study."

"I'm not quite sure I follow you, Miss Kuznetsov?"

A short, dapper man dressed in a tailor-made silk suit stepped forward with a sardonic smile on his face.

"Please, let me introduce myself. I am Alexey Popov. I'm the one who needs the face transplant. Doubtlessly, it's not going to be easy, but I have complete trust in your experienced hands, Doctor."

Dr Sternmacher looked at the people crowding his office as if they were aliens.

"I don't understand a word you're saying", he finally offered. "Mister Popov here is in no need of a face – "

"Oh yes, but I am, Doctor," Vasily interrupted him and sat down in the chair next to Sonia. "You see, my face has been severely burnt in a different setting than a fire. I know for a fact that you're undoubtedly the best in the world performing this kind of surgery, so of course I come to you."

"Why … why would you need a … a face transplant?" Doctor Sternmacher stuttered. "You look perfectly healthy in that respect."

"Let's not waste time on arguments whether or not you will go through with my face transplant – it was settled the moment I walked into this room."

"Already settled?"

"Yes, because of this little souvenir that I brought you", Vasily giggled and placed a disk drive on Sternmacher's desk.

Sternmacher looked at the object uncomprehending.

"It's a copy of the first eight face transplants you made during the last decade", Vasily giggled. "Most notably, I believe, it includes the repeat surgery you made on a certain

... now, what was his name ... yes! Now I remember – Matthias Callaghan!"

Dr Sternmacher started to sweat copiously. If these recordings were made public, his career as a physician would be over. No one would request his expertise any longer, because he knew that the clients would no longer trust their highly private information to be safe at the clinic. Besides, although he was the major shareholder in the St Puys clinic, the other investors would no doubt be prone to distance themselves from both him and his business.

Caught between a rock a hard place ... what should I do? Dr Sternmacher wondered as he discreetly wiped some sweat off his forehead.

Vasily, watching him intently with his intelligent eyes, made what he was sure would be the closer of the deal.

"Besides getting these interesting videos back instead of finding them posted on YouTube, you'll get five million euros for operating on my face – tax free, any account, anywhere in the world. Does it sound sufficiently attractive for you? I mean it should ... you're securing both your reputation and getting a big fat cheque for a couple of hours of work. What do you think?"

Vasily had thought deeply about his situation before arriving at St Puys. He really didn't have much of a choice if he wanted a face transplant – there are only so many top doctors working in the field worldwide. Making a simple facelift didn't appeal to him, because he was aware that Interpol had software that could detect alterations or deformations of the face structure. The only solution, he had deduced, after weeks of contemplating the issue of how to regain his anonymity, was to physically become a completely different person as far as his face was concerned. Now, doing that with false passports or taking on identities of other people was risky business in the long run, Vasily knew. The only answer, long-term, was to adapt a truly different identity.

Vasily didn't enjoy the prospect of having his face cut off and getting it replaced by one that belonged to a dead person. On the other hand, he was acutely aware that the recent picture of him spread by Interpol had made him a subject that worldwide law enforcement was on the lookout for. Despite his immense wealth, there was nowhere he could go, since just about every country in the world is a member of Interpol. To avoid being arrested, he would have to flee to North Korea or some equally undesirable place, which every fibre in his being found to be out of the question.

Vasily realised he had been left with three alternatives.

He could go underground and stay under the radar incommunicado on a Pacific island or some other distant place, which would bring an end to his business with him as its leader. Besides weakening his position by in practice handing over the reins of his empire to whoever he would assign to take over after him, he wouldn't solve the real problem at hand. He would still remain a target for the police organisations determined to hunt him down.

If he were to stay at the helm of his growing business, it would be essential that he supervised it from some secret place in Europe and not some faraway island. So, his second option was to remain in hiding somewhere in Europe; a high-risk choice that didn't make good business sense should he be caught and end up in prison. No, this was the least viable of the solutions he could imagine. He must remain firmly at the helm of the business and make no show of weakness, but in order to make that work, he had to return to his former anonymity. Vasily also wanted the freedom of movement to pursue what he considered the pleasures in life, and he obviously couldn't do that if he locked himself up in some hiding place and threw away the key.

The last of his options would oblige Vasily to transform himself in such a way that no one beyond those in his inner circle knew that he was still in power. A facelift, with a tweak here and there to make him unrecognisable? Vasily had watched himself for hours in the bathroom mirror to study the delicate, clean-shaven face; the pointed nose; the black eyes without empathy; and the thin-lipped mouth. He had arrived at the conclusion that he never had liked the way he looked. This was an opportunity to change it for the better, his vanity prodded him, and simultaneously it would solve the nuisance of having his present face announced on Interpol's web site of wanted criminals. He had started to giggle uncontrollably. *How many people can buy themselves a new face?*

Dr Sternmacher was reaching his own conclusions regarding the blatant extortion Vasily was making for his services. *The best way out of this would be to perform the surgery requested, and then act is if it never happened,* he knew. He could keep it a secret if he were able to convince his personnel that it was a legitimate transplant. Five million euros wasn't a sum to be sneezed at, but, significantly more important: he simply couldn't allow the videos of his former face transplants to become public – they would destroy him.

"When would you want this to be done?"

"As soon as it's medically possible, Doctor", Vasily, in a carefree manner, replied. "However, before we continue, I need to ask you something vital. What are the requisites for transferring a dead man's face to a living man's skull? How does it work?"

By now, Dr Sternmacher had connected the hair-raising truths about the videos stolen from the clinic's hard drives; the torture that had made it necessary for Matthias Callaghan to go through two face transplants; and that, once having performed the requested face transplant on Alexey Popov, he might be killed just the same – in order to secure the secret of his client's face. *Something in the vein of the legend that Ivan the Terrible, impressed by the beauty of the finished St. Basil's Cathedral in Moscow, blinded its architect so he never would repeat the feat,* he recalled.

A long pause followed Vasily's questions while Sternmacher thought through his options. After much deliberation, there was no doubt in Dr Sternmacher's mind that his least worst choice was to perform the surgery that was requested of him. Then he thought about whether there was some way to escape his dilemma. *If I oblige these people to find the donor,* he thought, *they are likely to fail. Finding one in a hurry isn't easy without the right contacts.*

"I consent. I will give you the criteria for a successful face transplant. When you find a donor, I will perform the operation."

Vasily giggled, pleased. After he had recovered from the transplant, no one except those he would carefully choose as his immediate confidantes would be able to identify him. Wiser from past experiences, he would from now on work solely by relaying his orders and strategy through Sonia or Oleg, or whoever might possibly replace them in the future.

Perhaps I should create some code word so that the key distributors or suppliers I talk to over the phone will know that they're talking with the man at the top? Vasily smiled to himself. He would use the same name he had given Paddy the pilot: *Ben*. To deflect from his physical stature, he would add "big". Yes, Big Ben. It was a name that hinted at London from where he no longer could operate, and it certainly was a timely name.

As for Mikhail Berlosky, his most experienced operative, he was now languishing behind bars in a British jail. Vasily doubted Berlosky would be released any time soon, and he had through Sonia instructed his lawyers – Longhorn being one of them – to redirect all accusations and evidence towards Berlosky. By necessity, he had seen it necessary to assign Berlosky the role of scapegoat and allow the law enforcement to perceive him as the true leader of his drug business.

*

Gérard Mokrani was a third-generation Algerian immigrant to France. After the upheaval in Algeria in 1956, his Arabic grandparents had immigrated to a Parisian suburb, where his Algerian-born parents had met. As a result, Gérard had in 1979 been the first of the Mokrani family to be born on French soil.

Despite being born in France, culturally he had never been able to rid himself of his immigrant status. As a descendant of Algerian *pieds noirs* living in a *banlieue*, a Parisian suburb, he was regarded as a lesser citizen in the eyes of those French citizens who didn't suffer immigrant grandparents. It was a challenge very few with his background had been able to shake off, with the exceptions of a handful of film stars and successful soccer players.

The banlieue turned out to be both exclusive and inclusive as Gérard got older. Exclusive in the sense that those, with different backgrounds than the pure-bred French, were excluded from certain social activities the French enjoyed. Inclusive, because the banlieue in which Gérard grew up, like many others, reacted by becoming a close-knitted society on the edge and eventually beyond the control of the authorities.

As a teenager, Gérard participated in demonstrations against perceived grievances caused by the French government. He had joined the protests throwing Molotov cocktails, burning rubber tyres in the street and building barricades on entrance points to his suburb. The protests had complicated life for the suburb's inhabitants.

Still, the poverty he experienced in his teenage years had

formed and forged him into the person he had become. There had never been enough money around, and his family and their neighbours were equally dissatisfied. When one neighbour, a year older than Gérard, asked him if he would be interested in earning some extra money delivering a few packages, Gérard didn't hesitate before confirming that of course he was.

The simple task of going from one place to another delivering an envelope, which, with the return trip included, added up to less than one hour's work, paid him 200 francs. At 16, it was more money than he, up until then, had managed to save his entire life. The enormity of the financial benefit for such a simple effort made a great impression on Gérard. Playing truant, he was soon doing several deliveries a day. His parents, always fighting over something as far back as Gérard could remember, were suddenly jointly attacking him about his sudden wealth and lack of good grades at school. The family discordance rapidly mounted into a scene of passion and accusations between the parents and their son, which the following day resulted in his leaving his parents' home to never see them again. Instead, he took up residence in the 11th *arrondissement* in central Paris.

Bright and streetwise, Gérard soon flourished as a businessman. "Business is like water", he liked to say to those who listened. "Water always finds a way to level. Knowing how the tide flows is the secret to making money." This simple metaphor, embellished or to the point depending on the audience, was to guide him personally through the remainder of his life.

Gérard quickly adapted to the demand and supply flow of the drug business, and, thanks to his cunning, he was quite successful at it. The more involved he got, the richer his rewards. A natural-born leader, he soon had people working for him. He was now, at 36, the main supplier of illegal drugs in metropolitan Paris. This was very much thanks to a deal of regional exclusivity that he had struck with Mikhail Berlosky two years earlier. Thanks to the influence and the protection of the Russian Mafia, no one dared to lift a finger against him.

With his spoils, Gérard lived an easy, sybaritic life, and no one was there admonishing him not to. He was making so much money that he didn't know where to hide the soiled bills that he earned from junkies shooting heroin or snorting cocaine. Yet, he still aimed for more, much more.

The supply deal he had reached with Berlosky had been verbal, and the message had been very direct: "Two simple rules apply. You pay us on time, and you don't do business with anyone except us."

Then, in June 2015, the bombshell news reached his ears: Berlosky had been jailed and the Russians' organisation disrupted. Besides Berlosky, dozens of other people close to him had been arrested. As proof that the news was true, the price on hard drugs immediately skyrocketed.

What now? Gérard thought, worried about his business as usual. Soon afterwards he was contacted by a woman, who with an Eastern European accent told him that she had taken over the business from Berlosky and that Gérard could call her

Daria. Gérard didn't like taking orders from women. All those who had tried to control him, including his mother, had ended up with a bloodied nose or worse. Her commanding voice made him boil with fury.

Then, he began to see the changing situation in a different light. *Perhaps this is my big opportunity to make some real money,* he realised. *That woman Daria be damned. With Berlosky and his people out of the way, I can buy the drugs directly from the producers. I'll climb the career ladder in one swift run. I'll be the main supplier in France ... perhaps I can even expand into other countries.*

What Gérard didn't know when he began contacting potential suppliers in Mexico, Morocco, Afghanistan and Pakistan, was that the jailed Berlosky wasn't the man at the top of the Russian Mafia's hierarchy.

*

Things are slowly coming back together again after the great catastrophe Callaghan caused, Vasily thought as he, Sonia and Oleg stepped out of Dr Sternmacher's office. *I will pull through this, all right, even if the setback cost me close to half a billion. The meth laboratories are still intact except for those few ones raided by the police. The new shipments on the way from Asia and Mexico can't be touched; I just need to figure out some new routes into Europe.* He giggled out loud. *Why on earth am I giving my worries swimming lessons when I can let them drown?*

Sonia gave him a sideways look but knew better than to

ask him about what was on his mind. A couple of minutes later, the helicopter was up in the air and they headed back to the mansion in southern Germany. *The upcoming challenge is to quickly find someone not only handsome enough to become my new face and identity,* Vasily pondered as they flew across the stunningly beautiful Swiss landscape, *but also compatible with the ideal conditions Sternmacher listed.*

With the resources he had at his disposal, Vasily didn't doubt for a second that he eventually would find the right candidate. Vasily knew and lived by the observation that the difference between the possible and the impossible is a mere question of time and money, with a stress on the latter.

Thursday June 25, 2015

The helicopter took Vasily, Sonia and the closest members of his crew across the Alps to land at their destination, a helipad in Monte Carlo. From there, the two dark red Rolls-Royces drove them the short distance to his new yacht. These movements were nothing out of the ordinary in Monaco with its billionaires' playground where a life free of tax was bought with a half-a-million-euro-per-person entrance fee deposited into one of the principality's banks.

After having taken yet another tour around the yacht, relishing his newest plaything, a pleased Vasily summoned Sonia to the lavish stateroom where they could talk in privacy.

"Listen, Sonia, you know I've given a lot of thought to whether I should go through with the surgery", Vasily began.

"As things stand, with my face on Interpol's website for everyone to see, and as a consequence also everywhere on the Internet, I really can't think of a better solution to avoid the, shall we call it ... negative effects on business. We wouldn't want that, now, would we?"

Sonia nodded affirmatively to indicate that she agreed.

"This transplant thing sounds more complicated than I thought it would be, you know, with the blood type and the HLA typing and all the rest. You have the information to make the best match. Now take it and find me a perfect match!" Vasily giggled. "That last bit sounded as if I was looking for a date with someone ... well, in a way, you could say I am."

"Apart from the obvious necessary medical criteria", Sonia asked calmly, "what do you want me to look for?"

"Hmm, good question", Vasily replied as he got up and started walking around. "First of all, he shouldn't look remotely like me, of course. And, as the good doctor explained, he should have my facial bone structure. He should have my skin and hair colours. I don't want him to look like an ogre, naturally – more like a Hollywood star. Hm, hm; well, I think that completes my wish list."

"Nothing else?" Sonia said in her most ironic voice. "Consider it done."

"Actually, there *is* one more thing", Vasily retorted, immediately detecting her sarcasm. "I want to see pictures of your best three options by next week."

Sonia merely shook her head before leaving the stateroom.

Wednesday July 1, 2015

It was winter in Sydney. The June rains were finally coming to an end. It was the time of year I really enjoyed, with cooler weather that made for easier work conditions. The sales from the housing development we had recently finished were going great, and money kept flowing in. I relished getting my teeth into a new construction site, and thanks to Jack we had found one that was really interesting, besides having an extraordinary profit potential.

We were pouring over the plans and the papers for our new and very ambitious waterfront project in Sydney on 40 hectares that the local government wanted to resuscitate from its present abandoned and dilapidated state as a former shipyard. Thanks to a contact Jack had, we had been offered the deal as long as we complied with certain conditions: the project had to be centred around the teaching of crafts and ecological issues. There was to be an aquarium; a botanical garden; a planetarium; a butterfly sanctuary; a snake and lizard terrarium; a children's hands-on tech discovery centre; a street entertainment plaza; and an artisan centre where techniques in how to work leather, glass, textiles, painting, lithography, metal forging, and many other skills would be available for anyone to learn for a token cost. We would provide the design and the infrastructure, and the government would take care of and pay for the details. All this would cover 50 per cent of the area. With some restrictions, we would be allowed to develop the remaining area for profit: a hotel; restaurants, as long as they weren't franchises; lots of small and quaint boutiques; a cinema complex; a multimedia centre; a couple of venues for open air shows; a six-floor "food tower" where everything was dedicated to food and drink in all its forms (exotic herbs and vegetables, utensils and crockery, chefs giving cooking classes, wine tasting and much more).

Samantha was once again her old, relaxed self, and kept herself busy entertaining the twins. Her pregnancy was progressing just fine, about which she self-assuredly smiled in an affirmative way every time I asked. Fortunately, the horrific experiences of the past months were rapidly fading, because – in all honesty – there were issues that I felt I hadn't been able to explain satisfactorily to her. Samantha, however, never again questioned any of the loose ends that I had left untied in my explanations.

She did talk a lot about her new-found British family and her origins, which brought great joy to both of us. Samantha said she wanted to dig into her mother Violet's past as soon as our new baby was born. Our new house also kept her busy, with her choosing curtains, decorating the children's bedroom and all the rest that a woman instinctively knows to make a home a habitable place.

Friday August 8, 2015
It didn't take one week, but six, for Sonia to come up with three potential candidates for Vasily's face transplant. During that time, he didn't leave the ship, and all business was

conducted either through intermediaries employed by him or through encrypted messages relayed over secure lines. Vasily found these methods both antiquated and boring, due to the slow results, but he was aware that at this particular moment in his life he had to be more careful than ever. Despite Berlosky's incarceration, and the lawyers' successful hints that Berlosky was the brain who had lorded over the collapsing drug empire, the hunt was still on for Vasily. Although now considered by Interpol to have played a minor role under Berlosky's leadership, Vasily continued to be wanted in connection with narcotics crime.

Daily, Vasily pestered Sonia for results. She insisted that he had to choose between quality or speed. Which would he prefer? Vasily always deferred, because of course he prioritised the quality of his new face above anything else.

This was a time for Vasily when the events made his life increasingly more confusing. On the one hand, he was among the richest men in Europe, if not in the world. On the other hand, he had no freedom to express or explore his wealth. Every law enforcement was looking for him. If he were to disappear at a moment's notice, he suspected that all the secret wealth that he controlled through offshore companies would be transferred into the wallets of the vultures that inevitably would circle above his carcass.

So, at the same time that Vasily had a sense of being on top of the world and still in control of a vast part of the European narcotics business that had made him successful, he also felt utterly vulnerable. He liked the power that came with being fabulously rich, but he understood perfectly that it was more ephemeral than a house of cards. For some time, Vasily had been thinking of getting into politics behind the scenes, because he realised that it's through the executive branch of a democracy that power is wielded. The same rule, he knew, applied to a dictatorship, but Vasily preferred the idea of politics in a democracy. He considered the opportunities and the loopholes greater in a democracy than in a country run by a dictator, where a reduced number of oligarchs sliced the pie between themselves. The world's democracies moved more money, had more conscience through their human rights organisations and as a consequence offered more opportunities to corrupt. Not that corruption didn't exist where dictators ruled – on the contrary – but, as a rule, the bigger the oppression, the smaller the clique with influence. In democracies, the power was distributed among more hands and the general population was better off, which in Vasily's mind meant that money and its inherent power made it so much easier to manipulate to benefit his business interests. Vasily knew first-hand that the countries where he made the most money, were those with the highest average income among the middle class.

I should really begin to look into politics next, he concluded. *The question is, where do I begin?*

*

"Vasily, I need to talk to you", Sonia addressed him. "I've finally completed the task you charged me with."

They went to the stateroom, where she read out load the options from her notes.

"From a medical viewpoint, I believe I've found seven candidates", she began her introduction. "I've found all candidates among soldiers wounded during Russia's recent annexation of Crimea. Two are from Ukraine, the rest are Russian citizens. All have been more or less severely wounded, albeit not their faces. Their HLA typing, which Sternmacher stressed to be so important, are all between eighty-three and ninety-four per cent. All of them share your blood type. However, they're all a few years younger than you are."

"I'm impressed, Sonia", Vasily smiled, leaned back and clasped his hands behind his neck. "I really don't mind if I will appear a bit younger. My concern is what I will look like after the surgery."

Sonia turned on her laptop and swung it around to allow Vasily to watch its screen.

"It's your choice", she said, as she flipped through the photographs of the seven men.

Vasily immediately discarded four of the men as "unacceptable-looking".

"So, we now have three options for you to choose from", Sonia concluded with a wry smile. "Look at them, but you should also study the HLA value for each one, noted at the bottom of the screen."

Vasily seemed as fascinated as a child restricted to buy one single item in a toy store, Sonia noted. It took him a good hour to finally settle for one of the men.

"*This one*, he's my favourite choice", he said and put his finger on one of the photographs.

"Osip Shevchenko, a Ukrainian corporal wounded in the battle for Crimea in March 2014. In June 2015, he stepped on a landmine and one leg had to be amputated. In all other aspects he's a healthy man", Sonia read. "Shevchenko is twenty-seven years old and has a wife and three children. Presently, he's convalescing in a hospital at the outskirts of Odessa. And, not less importantly, he has a ninety-two per cent HLA match compared to yours, which will alleviate any negative effects according to Doctor Sternmacher."

"Sounds absolutely perfect!" Vasily got up to pace the room and giggled. "Finally, I'm getting a new face! And, Russia will be conquering another piece of Ukrainian identity. A lost leg, you say?" Vasily began to dance from exhilaration. "I'll make the man whole again!"

Sonia, surprised as always, wondered how a man could look forward to having his face removed and giggle about it. But, wise from experience, she held her tongue to ensure she wouldn't risk losing it.

Saturday August 15, 2015

"Everything is now ready for the operation", Sonia, who was responsible for its coordination, reported to Vasily.

"Sternmacher will receive you on the twentieth of August. The operation is estimated to take thirty to thirty-five hours. You will be anaesthetised for most of that time. No cameras will be allowed to film in the operation theatre. Oleg will provide security both inside and outside the clinic, and I will be supervising everything."

"Excellent, Sonia!" Vasily giggled with glee. "You're very good at these things. Now, what about my donor's face?"

"Oleg and some of his men will take care of that as soon as you give your go-ahead."

"You have it. While you're at it, make sure that all my donor's documents, like birth certificate and ID cards, are collected."

"I've already taken that into consideration, Vasily", she replied coolly.

Vasily couldn't help admiring her amazing efficiency. As soon as he had recovered from the transplant, he would consider letting her take over more of Berlosky's former duties, which he himself had lately been obliged to assume.

They were now staying at the chalet in the south of Germany again, for two reasons. It was a close distance away from St Puys, and Vasily didn't want to risk his face to be seen by moving around. He had dedicated his time since their flight from London to rescue as much as possible of his former organisation. Berlosky was of course now no longer operative, spending time in jail awaiting his trial. Sonia had meanwhile turned out to be a goldmine of proficiency in the way she calmly and methodically solved the smallest problem, and he had come to trust her with more, and increasingly important, tasks.

The last three months hadn't been easy, but Vasily felt convinced that he was on the road of straightening everything that had gone awry since Callaghan's break-in at his flat on Park Lane. He only needed to have his anonymity returned to him once more, and, after that, he was certain he could put together his lost business pyramid again – and this time made of steel instead of bricks. Vasily estimated that the setback would be solved in six to nine months, and then he'd be back at the top of the game again. *Those half a billion pounds in losses for lost property, money and business opportunities that Pyotr so gloomily has declared,* he thought, *will in the long run be a drop in the ocean.*

Sunday August 16, 2015

With a stop-over in Vienna after boarding the flight in Munich, Oleg and his two most trusted soldiers, Vladimir and Ilya, landed in Odessa in the early afternoon. Oleg rented a mid-size Volkswagen at the Avis counter using false documents and a cloned credit card. The car's GPS guided them to an inconspicuous hotel that carried a smell of mildew. Oleg was adamant: they couldn't risk travelling in an ostentatious manner, since that might later raise unwanted suspicions.

They spent the rest of the afternoon in Oleg's room with pizzas that tasted like rubber (Vladimir's opinion about the salami) and rancid fish (Ilya's opinion about the anchovy) and a map of Europe that covered the area from Ukraine to France.

"I'm much less concerned about entering and exiting the convalescent centre when compared to the difficulty of getting back to Germany", Oleg pointed out when Ilya wondered why he worried so much. "We have to cross at least two countries to go from here to there. One option is via Poland – it's a detour that will take extra time, but I believe the Polish border is the least controlled of all to enter the European Union."

"This tastes like a five-week-old chewing gum", Vladimir complained again, as he suspiciously masticated a thick, greasy slice of pizza with salami on it.

Oleg gave Vladimir a hard look to warn him he should pay attention to what he was saying.

"Two alternatives are to drive either through Slovakia or Hungary, and from there on through Austria. That would be faster and less road to travel, but the borders of these countries are on high alert because of the influx of refugees from the Middle East."

"Are there no other options?" Ilya asked.

"If we could go through Russia, I have contacts that could fly us back to Germany. The problem is that, since the Crimean annexation last year, the border between Ukraine and Russia is closely watched by everyone including spy satellites and drones. Further south, via Romania, would mean more borders to cross, and the refugee situation there makes that even more difficult. No, our best option will be to go back by crossing the Polish border."

He checked Google Maps on his computer.

"Two thousand and four hundred kilometres in twenty-seven hours, if we take turns at the wheel. Add to that time for fuelling up, meals and mishaps, and we should consider at least two days and two nights. To meet the deadline Vasily has set, this leaves us with less than twenty-four hours to pick up Shevchenko."

Monday August 17, 2015

After a hearty breakfast, the three Russians left their accommodation and drove to the veterans' care home outside Odessa where Shevchenko was convalescing according to Sonia. After parking the car outside the grey Soviet-era building that displayed a complete lack of embellishment or any architectural thought beyond that it was standing, Oleg went inside. While he reconnoitered the place, Ilya and Vladimir obeyed his caution that they should make themselves as unobtrusive as possible.

The building was equipped with different medical and therapy facilities on the ground floor, Oleg deduced from the plaques on the doors. A broad staircase and two elevators led up to the other five floors of the building. He took one of the elevators to the top floor, which turned out to merely house administrative offices. People he met in the hallway only cast casual glances at him, which he found reassuring.

Oleg took the staircase down to the next floor and found a hallway lined with doors. Next to each door there was a printed piece of cardboard inserted in a metal frame. The cardboards stated the person, or patient, who occupied the living space along with a date that Oleg assumed was the individual's arrival date to the facility. Methodically he went from door to door and read the nameplates that were spelled in Cyrillic. None of them coincided with the name Sonia had given him, until he went down another floor and found it at the end of the hallway. *Osip Shevchenko*, he read.

He had not seen any people walking about except on the top floor. *I can't believe it's going to be this simple*, he thought, as he hurried down the remaining stairs and out to the rental car. Ilya and Vladimir looked at him askingly as he entered the car and slammed the door shut.

"I've found the man we're looking for", he said with a smile. "Relax, this one will be easy as pie. Let me explain."

*

Accompanied by Ilya and Vladimir, Oleg rapped twice on Osip Shevchenko's door. Through the paper-thin door, they could hear how someone shuffled across the floor inside.

"Who is it?" a voice inquired in Ukrainian as the shuffling sound came closer.

Oleg merely mumbled some incomprehensible words barely loud enough to be heard through the door.

Muttering, Shevchenko shuffled closer and unlocked the door. He frowned as he saw the three men in the corridor, then with the quick grasp of an observant soldier understood that

561

they had come with bad intentions. He tried to slam the door shut and lock it, but not before Oleg had put his foot in the doorway.

Oleg pushed the invalid with force, and the one-legged Shevchenko fell helplessly to the floor. Ilya brought out the syringe he had prepared earlier at the hotel and, while Vladimir and Oleg held the screaming veteran down, inserted the syringe in the jugular vein. The screams promptly subsided.

Ilya got up and checked the corridor outside for any unwanted attention. There was none. He closed the door.

"Let's wait another few minutes to allow for the propofol to take full effect", Oleg said and got up from his knees. "Then we'll move him to the car."

With Vladimir still holding Shevchenko pinned to the floor, Oleg studied the man they had been ordered to abduct. He was in his late twenties and quite good-looking, with rosy cheeks announcing a healthy outdoors lifestyle. Apart from his amputated leg, he looked as if he were a very fit man. A well-trained soldier, no less.

Wearing latex gloves, Oleg and Ilya began to search the flat for ID cards and other documents that may become useful. The only thing of interest they found was Shevchenko's wallet with a driver's licence and his army-issued identity card. Fifteen minutes later, the three Russians had safely placed Shevchenko in the centre of the backseat, with Ilya and Vladimir on each side of him. On the way out of the building, they had only met two persons who had merely cast a brief glance at the three comrades helping the one-legged man to the exit.

Oleg left Odessa driving north-west towards the Polish border. Sonia had repeatedly insisted that time was of the essence, and that he must make it to Stuttgart no later than on August 18 – and the earlier, the better. There, the object of interest would be transferred to a waiting lorry.

It was getting dark when they reached Ukraine's border with Poland. Shevchenko lay slumped between the two Russians, with his jaw hanging low on his chest. As their car crept forward among the queuing vehicles waiting to get through the Polish immigration checkpoint, Oleg viewed Shevchenko's appearance in the rearview mirror.

"Ilya, try to make him appear as if he were awake", he ordered. "Right now, he looks like a corpse. We don't want any trouble here at the border."

After the slow-moving queue of cars finally made it Oleg's turn to present their passports, the uniformed Polish immigration officer motioned him to lower the window. Ilya and Vladimir were sitting on each side of the fast-asleep Shevchenko in the backseat. There was no way that anyone would believe he was awake. Oleg decided to change strategy.

"Pretend that you are asleep, too", Oleg hissed to his companions. Ilya and Vladimir obeyed.

Oleg opened the window and presented their four passports, all forged, with Osip Shevchenko's announcing him as a German by the name of Klaus Wolfgang Goldstein. After carefully leafing through them, the official compared the photographs to the faces of the passengers.

"You in the backseat, tell me your names out loud", the suspicious migration officer said.

"It's late and they're tired", Oleg protested. "It's been a long journey and we've been taking turns at the wheel."

At that precise moment, both Ilya and Vladimir moved. After yawning without opening their eyes, they apparently went to sleep again after finding a more comfortable position.

"Where are you going?" the immigration officer insisted.

"To visit some old friends in Hamburg", Oleg lied.

After the car's boot had been checked for contraband, the official went back to the office and returned with their passports stamped.

"Have a good trip to Hamburg", he grinned knowingly. "My advice is that you avoid Reeperbahn, though, because rumour has it that it's a place where even grown men can get both lost and unwanted diseases."

He waved them through.

In the first town after having crossed the border, Oleg stopped to get petrol. Bored and weary from crossing Ukraine's uninteresting landscape, both Ilya and Vladimir got out and stretched. Oleg looked at his watch. It showed 21:16. Vladimir went inside the shop to buy some beers to last them to Wrocław. Oleg followed him to pay for the petrol. A late-model Porsche pulled up, which caught Ilya's interest as he stood leaning against the boot of their rented Volkswagen with his arms crossed. He got even more interested when a ravishing blonde stepped outside and looked around the bleak and disappointing surroundings while the driver, a man in his sixties, replenished the car with petrol. She smiled at Ilya as their eyes met. Although it meant nothing beyond the fleeting moment, it made him feel pleased.

Ilya and Oleg came out together. Oleg nodded to Vladimir to indicate that it was his turn to take the wheel. When he opened the rear door, Shevchenko was no longer in the backseat.

*

Henrik Sternmacher was so distraught that he for months had had a difficult time to get a full night's sleep. To his daughter, friends and colleagues, he blamed his insomnia on the workload he was facing, but the real cause for it was the threat Alexey Popov had presented him with. He couldn't help churning the alternatives and consequences over and over in his mind. His career was challenged by a rogue who held him hostage using video tapes stolen from his hospital. Dr Sternmacher simply couldn't allow these video tapes to be made public. If they were, what would happen to the recognition he presently enjoyed on the highest international level?

Dr Sternmacher knew he had been caught between the devil and the deep blue sea. If he didn't perform the face transplant, the videos would be published, or worse still – he might be killed because of his knowledge. Dr Sternmacher held no illusions regarding the brutality these people would resort to in order to get their way. The 5-million-euro carrot offered for the transplant showed that money was not an issue; it only indicated that Popov and his people were either dealing drugs, laundering cash or siphoning off money in some corrupt, political scheme.

On the other hand, if he went ahead with the surgery, he would automatically be complicit in helping to shield a criminal. That is, helping the kind of criminal that was a pariah in society, and should Dr Sternmacher be caught having assisted him with a face transplant, he understood that life as he knew it would be over. Still, after weeks of weighing one option against the other, he reckoned that his odds were slightly better if he went through with the transplant.

Dr Sternmacher began surfing the Internet for information and eventually found a picture of his future patient "Alexey Popov" on Interpol's website where wanted persons were announced. His real name was Vasily Ivanovich, he read, who was accused of a number of criminal offences, including drug trafficking. So now Dr Sternmacher was faced with losing his reputation, getting killed or going to prison for helping one of Interpol's most sought-after criminals. He knew he needed to do something to solve his quandary, but he was at a loss as to what that something should be.

The only thing that kept his hopes up to somehow get out of his awkward situation was the assured difficulty for Vasily Ivanovich to find an acceptable match for his face transplant.

Somehow, Oleg discovered, Shevchenko had managed to crawl to the back of the station building, where they eventually found him. He was dragged back to the vehicle he had escaped from. Despite considering it, Oleg decided that there was no need to beat him or in some other way punish him. After all, it was only natural that a man attempted to regain his freedom. Instead, he gave him another propofol injection that rendered him unconscious.

With Vladimir now at the wheel, Oleg scolded the remorseful Ilya for fifteen minutes straight for Shevchenko's brief escape.

Tuesday August 18, 2015

Ilya and Vladimir complained about being hungry. No more petrol station sandwiches and lukewarm beer: they required a healthy portion of meat and potatoes to be able to keep up with their side of the work.

Reluctantly, Oleg – who was driving and also felt hungry – gave in to their request. A little later, he pulled over at a roadside restaurant with a flashing sign that in Polish announced itself as "The Hungry Driver's Grill". Not that any of them understood what the sign said apart from the word "Grill" and the promising neon image of a sizzling steak.

They would have to take turns, Oleg decided. Someone had to stay in the car in case Shevchenko woke up – they couldn't risk another incident where he disappeared. It was decided that Ilya and Vladimir would enter first, making their meal a quick one. Upon their return, Oleg would go inside to get some food.

The two disappeared beyond the fake doors made to look like a nostalgia Wild West saloon. Forty minutes later, a roaring Ilya came flying through the flapping saloon doors before he with an audible thud fell on the wooden stairs leading up to the entrance. The next moment, a large, bald man came sailing after him. A furious Vladimir appeared red-faced in the doorway.

All this happened in a matter of seconds. Oleg stole a glance at Shevchenko. Sedated, he continued to appear completely oblivious of his surroundings.

The moment Oleg opened the door to the car, Vladimir was attacked from behind by two tattooed men with rolled-up shirt sleeves who looked very much like the one Vladimir had thrown down the stairs. They shouted insults in broken Russian about the presence of Russian troops in Ukraine.

What should I do? Oleg asked himself, remembering that his number one task was to bring Shevchenko to Stuttgart on time. If not, there would be hell to pay.

Talking frantically, offering apologetic words he never would have dreamed of using under other circumstances because he thought them to be beneath his macho dignity, he somehow managed to distract the Ukrainians enough to allow Vladimir and Ilya to return to their car without further assault.

Ilya got behind the wheel and drove off in haste. To

Oleg's relief, they weren't followed.

"You're crazy, both of you!" he scolded his two companions. "Don't you understand that we need to get to Stuttgart with our package here as instructed, and there'll be hell to pay if we don't get there on time! We can't risk stupid brawls like the one you were just in."

Neither Ilya, nor Vladimir, made an attempt to contradict him. Silence reigned in the vehicle for another forty minutes, while Oleg was reminded by his stomach that he was getting increasingly hungry.

"I think we should –", he began, when, in mid-sentence, thudding sounds interrupted him. Ilya swore and stopped the car.

Oleg went outside, only to find that the left rear tyre was flat. They were stranded on a Polish highway, and he estimated that Wrocław, the closest city, to be perhaps 100 kilometres away. *There must be some village between here and Wrocław"*, Oleg thought and wondered how he would reach Stuttgart not later than the hour Sonia Vasily stipulated. Oleg didn't understand why there was such a rush to deliver Shevchenko, but he did know that he would be punished if he failed to get him there on time.

They were still at least twelve hours away from the agreed meeting point in Stuttgart. He had to rapidly get the tyre changed and then risk being flagged down by the Polish police for speeding. Fortunately, there were no speed limits on the Autobahn once they had crossed into Germany.

Ilya and Vladimir changed the flat tyre for the skinny

spare one, which had a label adhered to it that warned that, when in use, the car shouldn't be driven at a velocity exceeding 80 kilometres per hour. To make sure they would get to the rendezvous place in time, Oleg took the wheel again and drove the car at twice the cautionary speed.

Two hours later, without further incidents, they crossed the unmanned border crossing between Poland and Germany.

Wednesday August 19, 2015

Two hours past the deadline that Sonia, on Vasily's orders, had imposed on them, Oleg passed the sign that announced their arrival in Stuttgart. Dead tired and numb with hunger, he wondered if they would be punished for appearing late with their kidnap victim. He hoped not. Oleg felt they had been successful despite the repeated mishaps on their trip from Ukraine.

Oleg found the industrial park where they had agreed to meet. A lone lorry, announcing its business as a carrier of refrigerated produce, stood parked with its motor idling. Sonia was sitting in a car nearby. She was bored and her throat felt raw after smoking two packs of cigarettes over the past eight hours. She looked at her watch as she saw Oleg walking up to her. *There's still time*, she decided, *although there's not much of it left.*

Sonia got out of her rental car and curtly greeted Oleg.

"Do you have him?" she asked. "Is he sedated?"

"Yes, to both questions", Oleg replied, "but I think he's

about to wake up. We gave him the last shot about six hours ago."

"Get him and yourself up on the lorry over there", she ordered. "I'll take over from here."

Ilya and Vladimir dragged the semi-conscious Shevchenko out of the car and pushed him inside the lorry's cargo space. They jumped in after him, followed by Oleg. Sonia climbed into the lorry's passenger seat and ordered the driver to head towards Switzerland.

The lorry crossed the Swiss border without any incident. When they came to a rural area between two villages, Sonia checked her watch again. She dialled Oleg's number. He sounded tired when he answered.

"*Da.*"

"Prepare for the next phase. You've got exactly three minutes before I tell the driver to stop."

"Ok, will do", Oleg said. Sonia detected an inaudible sigh behind his words.

Thursday August 20, 2015

At 8:00 a.m. sharp, Dr Sternmacher arrived at St Puys hoping that he wouldn't have to perform the surgery he had agreed to carry out on this day. His heart sank as he saw Sonia waiting with her arms crossed next to a large BMW van. After he had parked his car, Dr Sternmacher walked up to her. He discerned three shadowy figures sitting behind the darkened windows of her van.

"Is the patient prepared to go through the transplant?" he asked.

She merely nodded to confirm that Vasily was ready.

"Then the only thing amiss is the donor's face", Dr Sternmacher observed.

Sonia walked over to the boot of the car, which snapped open with a distinct sound when she pressed a button. Inside was a large, commercial icebox. Taking the cue, the car doors opened and Vasily, Oleg and Ilya stepped outside.

Dr Sternmacher was an intelligent man, and he understood that no words were necessary. These people had come prepared to go through the transplant no matter the cost or the strong-arming it would take. He walked up to the clinic and entered the reception, followed by the others. Ilya carried the icebox.

They all squeezed inside his office. The personnel present at the reception had rarely, if ever, seen him allow so many people inside his personal office simultaneously. Soon the clinic was buzzing with rumours about the tough-looking persons who had returned bringing an icebox to Dr Sternmacher's office. Dr Sternmacher had a week earlier only given vague instructions to his surgical and administrative teams to stand by for a possible face transplant, although he thought it was improbable that it would take place since the client was unlikely to meet the criteria he had established to go through with the surgery. He had, nonetheless, shared basic medical information, charts and X-rays regarding the patient in question, Alexey Popov, with his staff for further study.

Dr Sternmacher made a vague gesture with his open hand, palm up, inviting anyone to follow his example as he sat down. There were only two more chairs in the office, which Vasily and Sonia took. With his head, Vasily gestured to Ilya that he should walk over to the doctor. Ilya put the icebox down next to the doctor's chair.

"Please, Doctor Sternmacher, have a look at the future me", Vasily encouraged him and giggled as if the thought was hilarious. "As you can see, I'm making good on my promise to deliver you the perfect donor. Now the time has come for you to make good on your promise to operate on my face." He turned to Sonia. "Give him the documents; the doctor will undoubtedly need them."

Sonia obeyed without a word and placed a large Manila envelope on his desk.

Dr Sternmacher hesitated briefly before taking out the contents from the envelope and putting on his reading glasses. In silence, he read through the medical history of the donor, which had any information concerning his name, identity and nationality erased.

He frowned and nodded to confirm that the information was satisfactory.

"I see that you have taken great care to cover every issue according to my directives", he then said, striking his chin pensively. "I think that is promising. What I now need to do is to have a look at the state of the donor's face."

Vasily giggled. Sonia offered the doctor the hint of a

smile. Oleg and Ilya waited eagerly for the doctor to open the icebox.

Doctor Sternmacher, a man who had seen his fair share of blood and mutilation in the operating room, still couldn't help feeling shocked when he opened the icebox.

Inside the icebox, the eyes in the head of a recently decapitated man stared back at him.

*

After three months in Istanbul, Georgie felt he had finally been able to settle in. He had spent his first weeks in a hotel before finally getting a lease for a fabulous flat with a terrace overlooking the Bosporus from the European side. He had made new friends with some young Turks impressed with the Porsche 911 he had immediately bought and now cruised in to make the nightclub rounds. Through them he had been introduced to stunning young ladies, even more exotic than Nathalie, who now remained all but forgotten back in Paris along with his abandoned Lamborghini.

*

Once Dr Sternmacher was able to focus entirely on the mechanics of the procedure, the discomfort – present since the Russians had walked through the doors of the clinic – vanished. Despite the supervision in the operating theatre by the two thugs and the woman, looking ridiculous now, dressed in surgical clothing that didn't fit them, he felt calm and assured because he was going to do what he was best at.

Although Dr Sternmacher projected a tranquil appearance, as if nothing were out of the ordinary, there was a tangible tension in the air among the dozen junior surgeons and nurses who were assisting him. Dr Sternmacher sensed, correctly, that they were suspicious about the surgery they were about to perform. No video cameras were whirring, recording the transplant. There was the unprecedented presence of the three "observers", as Dr Sternmacher had presented Sonia and the two other Russians. More than any other among the disturbing signals, it was obvious to his team that this patient was a 37-year-old man who had no need of a face transplant whatsoever.

What can I do? Sternmacher thought, and mentally shrugged off his staff's suspicions. *If I don't go ahead with this operation, my career – or worse, my life – will come to an end. All the personnel's questions, that no doubt will be asked after this surgery is over, will have to be parried with convincing arguments. Perhaps by explaining that the patient suffers from skin cancer in the facial area? Or that he has a severe psychological conflict watching his face in the mirror because of his murdered twin brother? Or something else, along those lines ... surely I'll be able to come up with some plausible explanation.*

Friday August 21, 2015
Tired after being on his feet for thirty-six hours without pause;

no food or anything else beyond sips of water and an occasional trip to the lavatory, Dr Sternmacher put the final touches to the face skin he had detached from the skull of the donor. He had done the surgery entirely on his own, since he didn't want to be questioned about the procedure by his junior medics. Still, he couldn't avoid noticing his surgical team's unusual silence and asking looks over their face masks.

The Russians had taken turns supervising the operation. Sometimes adopting a tough-guy attitude, sometimes feeling queasy as the transplant advanced, they had nevertheless stayed put throughout.

*

Sonia considered herself a person hardened when it came to executing violence, watching people being tortured until they confessed and ordering individuals being killed. Without having thought too deeply beforehand about what awaited her as she stood next to Ilya and Oleg in a corner of the theatre, dressed as a nurse, she for once felt nausea as Vasily's transplant proceeded. To watch his facial skin being carefully removed and thrown into a bucket was the hardest. *Looking at the tissue,* which bled surprisingly little, *is like looking death in the face,* Sonia thought, both fascinated and revolted over what she observed.

Then came the moment when the donor's face was to be fastened to Vasily's skull. Shevchenko's face, which previously had been detached from his skull by Dr Sternmacher personally with no one else present, was carefully extracted from the icebox and put on top of the bloody remnants of Vasily's face. *How can any person voluntarily go through a surgery like this?* she wondered, as she watched the procedure, simultaneously disgusted and mesmerised.

The doctor began to connect Vasily's arteries to Shevchenko's face, the one that Sonia understood she would be reporting to from now on when she received Vasily's commands. She remembered having ordered Oleg to kill its previous owner after parking in a wooded area in Switzerland. She had instructed him that it had to be done by knife to the heart, not causing any damage to the face. While the driver, paid well enough to look the other way, ignored what was going on, Ilya and Vladimir had dragged the still unconscious Shevchenko into the woods. Oleg had followed with the icebox. They had returned half an hour later.

Dr Sternmacher threw his hands in the air thanking everyone for the successful outcome. There was a muted mumbling instead of the usual cheer. Everybody now longed to go home to enjoy the extra three-day holiday that automatically came with these extensive, complicated transplants.

It was only natural that Dr Sternmacher felt mentally and physically more exhausted than any of his personnel. This time he had carried out the surgery almost entirely on his own while peering into the faces either removed or replaced during the long hours. He abhorred the idea of having done so, in front of strange, non-professional people in the operating theatre. To be extorted the way he had been, to perform one of the most ethically complicated surgeries that exists, was repugnant to him. And, from a professional viewpoint, he rejected the idea that he had been prevented to film every step of such an important, life-changing operation.

Fortunately, there was a minor, discreet, but nonetheless important detail that had taken place during the transplant that he had hopes would eventually make up for the distress he had experienced the past two months. During the time leading up to Vasily's surgery, Dr Sternmacher had turned every possible and impossible alternative at his disposal over in his mind. He had finally come to the conclusion that, although it was by no means guaranteed to be a perfect solution, there was something he could do that might, or might not, secure his future safety.

The hard disk with the recordings of the eight face transplants had been returned to him, but of course he couldn't be certain whether copies had been made. Dr Sternmacher was desperate enough to go to any length to make sure that he wouldn't be killed or get his career compromised. Two of the transplants recorded were the ones he had made on Callaghan.

The solution he had come up with to eliminate the threats against him was to find a way to get Matthias Callaghan involved.

Sunday August 23, 2015

Walking through the tranquil woods with their two dogs, the Swiss couple was startled when their pets suddenly began to bark and rushed through the underbrush without heeding their masters' commands. Apprehensive, the couple followed the dogs until they found them barking near a riverbed. Close to where they were standing, there was a mound of earth that looked as if wild animals had been trying to dig out something. The dogs didn't cease their barking.

When the couple cautiously moved closer, they realised why the dogs had reacted. Inside a shallow grave lay the body of a man, partially dug out by wild animals. He had been decapitated. Both his hands had been removed, and one of his legs was missing.

Tuesday August 25, 2015

When he woke up again, on the fourth day after the transplant, Vasily finally felt that most of the drowsiness and the fatigue had left him. The blood circulating in his face didn't pulsate quite as intensely as previously. Moreover, he was finally able to think clearly without the irresistible desire to go back to sleep. He took these to be good signs.

He had no recall of anything concerning the transplant itself due to the general anaesthesia he had been given throughout the operation. The days following the surgery had been a haze during the short moments he had been awake, and his bandaged face had felt extremely sensitive even to the lightest touch when he had tried it with his fingertips.

Although his face still remained sore and untouchable, he was now past that initial sensation, *I've turned into another man ... no – I'm the same man*, he thought, *but with this, I've paid the necessary price to return to my previous, anonymous life. I've lost my official identity and the face that went with it.*

Sonia came into his field of view.

"Is there anything you need, Vasily?" she asked.

He tried to talk for the first time after the transplant, but his tongue felt strangely thick. He only managed to grunt back.

"You need more rest." She leaned forward to adjust his pillow.

Suddenly he was filled with fury that he had had to go through the inconvenience of his surgery. *It's all Callaghan's fault*, he fumed. *If he hadn't meddled with things that were of no concern of his, I'd still be in London wearing my old, perhaps not very pretty but quite comfortable face.*

The sudden thought of Matthias Callaghan that cropped up in his mind infuriated him. *Callaghan made me feel this way. Callaghan forced me to lose face. Callaghan ... Callaghan ... Callaghan ...* His thoughts became a jumble, before he fell into a sleep that lasted a mere minute. *Callaghan,* he remembered, conscious again. *He will regret he ever stood up against me.* Vasily was overcome with a fury that he never before had experienced.

"Do you ... do you remember Misha?" he finally half-whispered to Sonia.

She nodded that she did remember Misha, the son of Sergei Gagarin, owner of Caspian Sea restaurants in London.

"The time has now come for Misha to atone for what he did to me", Vasily lectured Sonia in a weak, tired voice. "As soon as I get my strength back, I'll explain to you what he must do."

Friday August 28, 2015

As his face was recovering astonishingly quickly after the surgery – at least, that was what Vasily was told repeatedly by a seemingly surprised Dr Sternmacher upon his three daily inspections – Vasily was getting increasingly jittery about remaining at the St Puys clinic. He was aware of Dr Sternmacher's admonishment before the surgery that he should expect at least two months before he could re-enter society again, and probably another three months before he was perfectly healed – assuming all went well and that there was no tissue rejection.

However, after a week at the clinic – with the nurses coming and going, not trusting his own men to be vigilant enough and having a visceral feeling that the calm Dr Sternmacher had some trick up his sleeve – Vasily suddenly decided he had had enough.

"Sonia!" he called for her in the most stentorian voice he could muster.

She hurried to his bedside, sat beside him and looked at his pitiful, bandaged head. *What has become of this, once brilliant, man?* she wondered. Vasily looked at her darkly through the slits of his bandages.

"I want you to arrange my departure from this place", he said in a low voice so only she could hear. "Take me to my place outside Konstanz. But, be very careful – none of the people here, and in particular not Doctor Sternmacher, must know where we have gone. How long will it take to drive there?"

"About two hours."

"Good. Talk with Sternmacher, too, about visiting me on a daily basis. He'll understand that I need his attention. Still, take notice that I don't trust him a bit – he's too self-assured for my liking. Once we get to the villa by the Bodensee, you will bring the doctor to me blindfolded. Blindfolded – do you understand!?"

"I understand", Sonia reassured him, thinking that Vasily sounded more paranoid by each passing day.

"No slip-ups", Vasily insisted. "I can't afford to have my surgery known to anyone outside those who I trust."

"I said, I understand – I'm not deaf", Sonia rebuked him as she rose. "I'll see to it at once. Give me an hour, and then we'll leave."

Satisfied with her answer, Vasily relaxed on his pillows.

That woman is my salvation, he thought when she left the room, closing the door behind her. *What a pity she wasn't born a redhead and a little more voluptuous.*

Saturday August 29 – Monday September 14, 2015

From his Bodensee villa in Germany, Vasily impatiently went through his slow convalescence. By and by Vasily recovered his control of the business operation that Sonia had managed for him during his absence. Although Sonia during this period had claimed that she was acting on behalf of Big Ben, Berlosky's replacement, the results had been mixed or downright disappointing.

Together, they daily discussed how to solve the cracks in Vasily's previously seemingly impenetrable drug business fortress. Now that local drug lords had got wind of Berlosky's imprisonment, everyone was vying for a boost in their operation, seeking to buy directly from the producers.

During Vasily's recovery, not one of the distributors had shown her the necessary respect or loyalty. A woman, however tough she sounded, could not just burst in and take over after crafty old Berlosky. These months of rebellion against a female, who in practice was in charge, taught Sonia several important lessons that she wasn't going to forget.

Vasily eventually recovered sufficient strength to help her address the problems. Although he remained bedridden, he was able to dispatch his people to enforce payments or order those distributors who were reluctant to continue working for him to be killed. Such tactics would seem as if Sonia, who in many practical matters now had taken over Berlosky's role, was acting on an unknown but ruthless boss's behalf. It was Vasily's way of preparing Sonia to become the face of the new drug empire rising from its former ashes.

Sonia complained a lot about the unwillingness of the distributors to work with her. As a case in point, she emphasised the rebelliousness of their distributor in Paris, Gérard Mokrani. Vasily understood the issue clearly and knew that he had to come up with some solution to correct it. He decided that the best way to do so was to make an example out of Gérard. *That will make the rest of them think twice before breaking ranks*, he decided.

Dr Sternmacher, brought to the villa blindfolded by Vasily's bodyguards, visited him daily to supervise the face transplant progress. Although Dr Sternmacher went through the motions that any doctor would after performing an important surgery, Vasily sensed a certain nervousness about him that he couldn't define. *Has he done something he shouldn't have done while I was in his hands? Will I look like a monster instead of the soldier in the photograph I chose?* Yet, each day, with Dr Sternmacher driven back to Switzerland with a hood covering his face, Vasily never could understand what had made Dr Sternmacher seem more jittery after his operation than before it had been performed.

Monday September 21, 2015

Vasily's first coherent thoughts, after waking up from a nightmare, jumped from concern to concern. The first of those was whether the face transplant had been a success or not. The one immediately following was that he needed Sonia to report to him. He cried out for her, or rather, he croaked for someone to fetch her. Waiting for Sonia to arrive, he dwelled once again on the facts of why he had landed in a situation where the only solution was to exchange his face for someone else's. The answer, as always, boiled down to Matthias Callaghan.

*

As usual, Dr Sternmacher was picked up around ten in the morning and driven to the German lakeside villa with a hood covering his face. As he inspected his latest transplant patient, he was sincere when he, astonished, uttered:

"I have never seen such rapid recovery after a face surgery. I think that you will be able to confront sunlight and any outdoor activities within a week at the most. Actually, I would encourage it."

Vasily felt jubilant.

"Thank you, Doctor", he smiled as much as he was able, grabbing the doctor's hand with both of his and shaking it vigorously. "Now the time has come to keep my part of our bargain. When you return tomorrow, bring me the details of the bank account you want your fee to be transferred to."

Boris came into the room and handed over a mobile to Vasily.

"It's my Hungarian contact", Boris said in Russian. "The one who has helped me investigate the doctor, like you asked me to."

Vasily gently put the phone against his ear.

"Yes? What news do you have for me?"

He listened as the Hungarian, who spoke good English, gave him the information.

"I see. Good work", Vasily replied while giving Dr Sternmacher an amused look. "Now I'll hand you over to Boris. He'll make sure that you'll get paid."

Since Boris was wanted by Interpol after his removal of the anklet, Vasily had ordered Boris to stay in the villa with him and make the necessary research through third parties. The Hungarian was a professional investigator with a criminal background that Boris had used on occasion.

"I was just informed that your dog hasn't run away for several weeks now. A Belgian Shepherd, is it? Fine dogs, that breed. It would be a pity if it got lost. By the way, I'm not sure if you're aware of this, but your daughter – a lovely girl, I'm told – stayed at home from school today. Is that because she has a cold, I wonder, or because she's playing truant? Anyway, I've seen pictures of your house, a lovely place, as is the clinic you run. May I assume that you have both places amply insured against fire and other calamities, Doctor?"

Vasily giggled. Dr Sternmacher realised that, instead of showing gratitude, his patient was threatening him. The moment a wire transfer would be sent to his account, he'd become an accomplice who had helped a fugitive criminal escape justice. The dog, his daughter, the threat of burning down of his properties ... This was Vasily's way of telling Dr Sternmacher that, unless he kept his mouth shut about the transplant, he could count all kinds of assorted misfortunes.

Vasily nodded to Oleg. Again, the doctor's head was

covered with a hood that prevented him from seeing anything while waiting to be led outside to the car that would take him back to St Puys. Hooded, uncomfortable and afraid, he stood there, near the exit, expecting someone to take charge of his return. From a distance, he could hear Vasily addressing one of his courtiers.

"Do you remember that I told you Misha has to atone for what he did to me?" he asked Sonia in Russian. "Now the time has come to send him to Australia. I want Misha to go together with Vladimir to supervise him."

"Why do you want them to do that?" Sonia asked, unable to hide her surprise. "What's in Australia?"

"Australia is where Matthias Callaghan lives with his family", Vasily explained, irritated that she had posed the question. "I want Misha to find him, snatch him and then wait for my instructions. Once Misha has him secured, I will have the personal pleasure of executing Callaghan's appropriate punishment."

"Do you think this will be wise, Vasily, now that we – "

"Just do as I say."

"Of course, Vasily", Sonia replied. "I'll talk to Vladimir and Misha right away."

Although she knew that Vasily was a patient man who never made a rash decision, Sonia wondered briefly why it had taken Vasily longer than usual to decide how he would avenge himself on Callaghan.

Friday September 25, 2015

My recently purchased iPhone made the sound of a growling jaguar to announce that someone had sent me a WhatsApp message. My boys, now effortlessly showing more tech savvy at three than I at my present age of 44, had somehow managed to change the tune for incoming messages on my phone. For some time, I had steeled myself against looking at it every time it made an announcement. This time was no different, because I was discussing the adjustments for our planned construction project with Jack. At this point, we had developed the initial idea in various ways. Instead of making one botanical garden, we would make "botanical islands" all over the area with scientific explanatory signs. The self-sustaining hotel, a concept we had sold before it had been constructed, was to be 100 per cent ecological, incorporating ideas from all over the world including solar power, water recycling and hydroponic plants. This would be built next to an open-air modern amphitheatre that would be used for plays, fashion events and concerts. Moreover, we had decided to add several mini museums circling the hotel, which we planned to make the central building of the project. Namely: museums for clocks, glass, design, exotic clothing, precious stones, inventions and the evolution of ideas. However, in my opinion, the best idea of all was to make the place a living port by receiving fishermen and their boats bringing fresh catch every morning to the restaurants. The local council loved the concept.

We were at Jack's office in central Sydney as we

discussed the latest changes. When it became time for lunch, we decided to take a break and stroll down to Darling Harbour. While I was waiting for Jack to tidy up some issue before we left, I looked at my phone. There was a message from Dr Sternmacher. I immediately felt alarm wrench my guts. "Call me URGENTLY", was all it said, apart from a phone number.

The message had been received on my mobile at 9:16 a.m., Sydney time. This meant Sternmacher had sent me his message, his first ever, at 1:16 a.m., Swiss time. What on earth could be so important that he sent me a message in the middle of the night requesting my call?

Jack came into the room and announced with a big smile that he was hungry as a wallaby and ready to leave.

"Just wait a minute, Jack, apparently something very important just came up and I need to make a phone call in private. Lend me your office, will you?"

"Sure, go ahead."

Closing the door, I dialled the number Dr Sternmacher had sent me. The call went through, but no one picked up the phone. I felt apprehensive and looked at my watch. It showed 1:45 p.m., which meant it was 4:45 a.m. in Switzerland. After six rings, somebody finally picked up the phone at the other end and replied in a sleepy voice.

"*Ja?*"

One word, but it was enough for me to immediately recognise Dr Sternmacher's voice.

"This is Matthias Callaghan. I received your message

that you urgently need to consult something with me?"

"Thank you for getting back to me so soon." He cleared his voice and now sounded more awake. "Yes, there's an important issue at hand, and over the phone, I'm sorry to say, I can only give you the general idea of a threat that I'm, frankly, very concerned about. It's a serious one, directed at you."

I frowned.

"I'm sorry, doctor, but I have no way of understanding what you're talking about."

"I know", he replied, wearily. "That's why I want you to take the first available flight to Zürich."

"Fly to Zürich? Why should I fly to Zürich? I just came back from Europe."

"There's some serious danger that concerns you and your family", Dr Sternmacher responded, in a more tired voice than I had ever heard him speak. "It's imperative for you to come here so I can explain the details to you. I can't talk about it over the phone. It's not safe."

I didn't know what to think.

"Let me consider it, and I'll let you know, OK?"

"Time is of the essence, Mister Callaghan. Don't delay your response. It's too dangerous."

*

Later, with the children asleep in their beds, I discussed Dr Sternmacher's call with Samantha. She became even more concerned than I, wondering out loud about whether our curse would ever end. The argument we had wasn't so much a disagreement as it was an expression of our worries about what would happen whether I did go or if I didn't. After all these years, it was the only time that Dr Sternmacher had contacted me, which certainly made the situation sound serious. Finally, we agreed that I'd better travel to Switzerland to hear the details of whatever Dr Sternmacher was upset about.

Although I had Samantha's reluctant agreement that I should return to Europe to meet with Dr Sternmacher, there was also the question of the birth of our daughter, a mere three weeks or so away. This time I wanted to be present.

I'll give Sternmacher a week, no more, I thought, *then I'll be heading back home to Sydney.*

Saturday September 26, 2015

I bought an open round-trip ticket Sydney-Zürich that left the same afternoon. Our twins and a worried Samantha saw me off at the airport after taking me there.

Travelling with the clock, I landed only a few hours later, local time. It was still early evening in Zürich. The largest city in the vicinity of St Puys was Berne, which is where I had agreed to meet with Dr Sternmacher early the following day. The regional train took me to Berne in less than two hours, where I checked into a hotel and, exhausted, immediately fell asleep.

Sunday September 27, 2015

"Thank you for joining me so soon, Mister Callaghan", Dr Sternmacher began after we were seated in my Berne hotel suite. "I wouldn't have insisted on it, if it weren't for something I overheard by chance just a few days ago."

"Please rest assured I'm curious to learn what it is that compelled you to contact me", I replied.

"To do so, I must first give you the background story. You see, at first I didn't realise who this recent patient of mine was, although of course I suspected he was someone up to no good."

"Who is this patient you're referring to?" I asked him.

"Let me start from the beginning. A little over two months ago, a man walked into my office at Saint Puys, requesting a face transplant. It took me some time before I discovered that he wanted it for himself, despite having a perfectly healthy face. He didn't want a facelift, he told me, but a transplant. Later still, I understood that he wanted to go through the surgery so he could let his former self disappear while he adopted a new, foolproof identity. Now, what kind of man is needlessly willing to submit himself to a transplant conditioned to life-long medication while offering to pay a huge sum of money to secure it? I could only guess, so privately I started to investigate the man."

"What did you find?"

"I'll come to that part soon. Despite my findings, I couldn't go to the police, because I was also blackmailed into doing the surgery on his face. And this is when your name first popped up."

He paused. Filled with apprehension, I waited for Dr Sternmacher to continue.

"You see, Mister Callaghan, he presented me with …", he hesitated, "… the stolen recordings of your two face transplants and threatened to upload these to YouTube together with six similar recordings of other patients. Of course I couldn't permit that, so I agreed to perform the face surgery he requested from me."

I felt the hair stand up as I realised what Dr Sternmacher was implying.

"In exchange, I would get the stolen recordings back, and I thought that would be the end of it. It wasn't. After a chaotic week at the clinic, during which I tried to keep my personnel from asking questions like: 'Why have you accepted to perform a transplant on a man with a healthy face?' and others more difficult still, the patient abruptly decided to move to an undisclosed place where he would finish his convalescence. His decision, however, meant that I was obliged to travel daily to his new accommodations. The time involved was a total of five hours: a two-hour trip each direction to be with the patient less than one hour … I'm sure you can appreciate the toll these compulsory, unexpected visits have taken on me, my work and the business of the Saint Puys clinic."

I nodded in agreement, although, despite my respect for his professional skills, I'd always felt a certain dislike for him as a person and for his puffed-up ego.

"Then, during my daily visit four days ago, I overheard by accident a conversation where your name came up again. It was made in Russian, a language I don't speak, but there were a few key words that came across clearly: 'Australia', 'Matthias Callaghan'. They were repeated several times by my transplant patient, something he did in a tone of controlled rage and with an occasional giggle. He was talking to a female assistant of his, and the tone of their voices was menacing, not to say aggressive. In my mind, there was no way to misinterpret the message: he ordered his people to 'pick up Callaghan in Australia'."

I was sitting on the edge of my chair, horrified over what I was hearing.

"You're talking about Vasily Ivanovich, no doubt."

"The very same", Dr Sternmacher confirmed.

"And now, what is he planning to do?"

"I haven't the slightest doubt that he intends to kill you for causing harm to his business empire."

"How do you know that?"

"I looked him up on Interpol's website. He must have stolen the transplant video recordings of you for some reason, and there were also references he made about you when he first came here. I also know from the news that you caused his drug empire in London to fall apart. With that information, it wasn't too hard to put two and two together."

Sternmacher's assertion certainly sounded plausible. I had disrupted Vasily's organisation, although I didn't know to what extent. Weren't the police doing their job? What was I going to do about it? Australia was a long way off, but I was sure that if Vasily was bent on revenge, he could surely make it halfway around the world if he set his mind to it.

"I'm sorry for imparting this sinister news", Dr Sternmacher continued after a brief silence, "but I felt it to be my obligation to share this information with you. Yet, there is something on a more positive note that I think you'll be interested to learn."

"I'm all ears."

"The preparations before the transplant lasted more than two months. The principal problem was finding a suitable donor … well, there's no need for me to dwell on that particular detail. Suffice to say that it gave me time to think through the situation, and, helped by my dog, I eventually came up with a solution."

"Your dog?"

"Yes, I have a young Belgian Shepherd who was escaping every week or so. Finally, I found a way to track him – I equipped his collar with a chip."

"Surely you didn't equip Vasily with a collar and a chip?" I asked him, incredulous.

"Of course not." Dr Sternmacher smiled weakly. "I did something much better. I developed the idea behind the collar. In short, while doing the transplant, I inserted the chip of the dog-tracking device underneath his new face. Then I connected it to one of those minuscule batteries that you yourself used for a brief time for your artificial fingers – remember?"

What an ignorant question. Of course I remembered.

"The signal from the chip itself is not as strong as needed to reach a relay tower and then onto a satellite. But, every time Vasily is near a mobile that is switched on, that mobile reinforces the signal, and that's how it gets to the satellite."

"Which, in other words", I asked, intrigued by the possibilities, "means that anyone with the necessary application will know where Vasily can be found?"

"Exactly." He leaned forward to show me his mobile. "As you can see, here on this Google Map there's a blinking red light near the town of Konstanz, close to the Swiss border. That's where Vasily has been holed up for the last four weeks and to date still remains."

We both remained silent for some time. I was chewing on the unsettling news of Vasily's intent on revenge for my meddling in his affairs. *How far is his reach, with billions of euros at his disposal? Can he reach me and my family in Australia? Of course he can, if he is incensed enough. Should I tip off the police where to find him? That is the wise course to take, but what if he already has set plans in motion to find me in Sydney? Is my family at risk?*

"Tell me, doctor, how long will this minuscule battery last before it needs to be replaced?"

"Three months, at the most."

"And it was installed … when?"

"A month ago."

It meant the chip would allow tracking Vasily until sometime in November.

"Here, take this." Dr Sternmacher gave me a USB stick. "After downloading this application, you too will be able to follow Vasily's movements."

"What does he look like now, after the transplant?"

"I have to describe him at the best of my recall, because I was closely watched all the time during and following the surgery. While it lasted, I was never allowed to make any video recordings or take pictures. The facial hair continues to be an unchanged dark brown, since it's still his own. His skin is now coarser, and slightly darker than before. His mouth is wider and his lips are fuller. The nose, instead of previously being slightly pointed, is now straighter and a little longer. The lips are larger. His cheeks are fuller and have dimples should he smile, with the one on the right side more pronounced."

"What about his medical profile?"

"He is R negative; no diabetes; the blood pressure normal while the cholesterol is somewhat elevated. Really nothing out of the ordinary. A man with his medical chart can live to be a hundred."

"He needs to be stopped", I concluded between clenched teeth.

"I've told you this in confidence", Dr Sternmacher added. "I've also told you that I can't go to the police, because should I do that, it would be the end of my career, my reputation, my clinic, my life ... My hope is that you can find a way to stop him."

I suddenly understood why he had contacted me and

gave him a look of contempt. So, this had been Sternmacher's intention all along. He had prepared the stage and then called me with the hope that I would somehow take care of the dirty work that would save his reputation and his livelihood.

Monday September 28 – Sunday October 18, 2015

In a nearby town, I bought two high-grade Swiss binoculars: one pair for daylight use and the other with night sight. For the next three weeks, I checked my phone screen at least five times a day for the red blip that represented Vasily's location. Unsurprisingly, it didn't move from the Bodensee Lake.

I made several excursions to study the property through my binoculars, but I had no success whatsoever in catching a glimpse of any of its occupants. Every day, I questioned myself about why I kept doing it, when all I wanted was to be back in Sydney to be present at the imminent birth of my daughter. It wasn't a question easily answered, but somewhere in the back of my head I was pestered by the notion that I and my family remained at risk unless I could find a way to remove the threat Vasily presented. Perhaps he perceived me as a menace, but more than anything I feared that he would retaliate for the nuisance I had caused him by exposing his business empire when I had entered my old flat.

By now, three weeks had passed since my departure from Australia. My absence meant that I missed the last weeks of Samantha's pregnancy, time with my boys and first-hand presence of the development I was doing on Jack's latest pet project. Moreover, there was the understandable vexation Samantha expressed over my prolonged absence every time I spoke with her. Still, I was convinced that there was nothing I could do differently. Sternmacher's warning words rang true: as soon as he had recovered, Vasily was coming for me. And, if he was targeting me, there was also a possibility that he would go after my family if necessary. Anything to bend me to his will. I couldn't allow that to happen.

The solitary wait gave me plenty of time to contemplate the situation and the options I faced. Vasily wanted to kill me for revealing his business activities to the police. As I saw it, the only way I could remove the threat that Vasily presented was if he were apprehended by the police with no clue about any involvement on my part. Maybe it was possible, should I anonymously tip off Interpol about his whereabouts along with a picture of his new face? But how would I be able to snap his picture up close?

Another crucial circumstance was that Berlosky remained in custody, awaiting trial. Perhaps he wouldn't reveal anything of importance to the police, but surely it meant that Vasily must be affected by not having his key operator around. Besides Berlosky, more than fifty of Vasily's minor operators were in jail, and he had lost an enormous fortune in cash found in his vault – that much I knew. I was also aware that his organisation had tentacles like an octopus enveloping most of Europe with a reach to the Americas, Africa and Asia. The people he had lost to British justice during the raids would no doubt eventually be replaced. I really didn't know, but who could tell whether Vasily had 1,000, or 10,000, or even 100,000, people working for him, directly or indirectly?

I was still hesitant whether I should return to share my recent knowledge about Vasily with the police. Something held me back. I had helped Scotland Yard breaking up his drug empire, confiscating millions of illicit money, finding stolen masterpieces and solving Allan's murder. Then, by confronting Georgie, I had found them Berlosky who had been in hiding. My participation in bringing down the Russian drug organisation had tacitly been acknowledged by the court when I was set free, but, as far as the police and the British authorities were concerned, they certainly hadn't demonstrated much gratitude.

Now, here I was, dragged into this quagmire again, unable to severe myself from the past and free myself from the Russians. What would happen if I decided to go to the police? They would give me a brief smile, before thanking me for having the sense of a dutiful citizen to report my concerns – and that would be it. Vasily, in prison or outside, would still have the power to order me killed. Revenge was in his blood. He didn't care if he was a billion euros richer or a billion euros poorer – he cared about the power he could yield sustained by his money. He cared about his prestige and the challenges he found in accumulating more money and power. I had slighted his prestige and his ego, and I had caused him enormous losses. Could I go to the police with that information? I decided that I couldn't.

At least I had one advantage: Vasily and his people had no idea that I was in Europe, while I – for as long as the battery implant lasted, at least – would know exactly where Vasily could be found by merely looking at my mobile.

*

The weeks went by idly with little or nothing of interest. Vasily's red blip didn't move from the Bodensee Lake. I had daily conversations with Samantha and the twins, and also with Jack at least three times a week. To not faint from boredom sitting in my hotel room, I continued to work on the project at the outskirts of Sydney that Jack and I had in progress, thankful for the conversations we could maintain over the Internet.

Friday October 2, 2015

Misha and Vladimir stepped out into the blinding sunlight outside Kingsford Smith Airport near Sydney after briefly having their forged passports scrutinised and collecting their luggage.

Two hours later, they were drinking beer by the poolside at the hotel they had checked into. Although fourteen years younger than Vladimir, Misha had with his usual youthful self-assuredness assumed the leadership of their mission. His immature approach amused Vladimir, who had received strict orders from Vasily to leave Misha free reins unless he bungled

601

their assignment.

"First of all, we need to find Callaghan's address", Misha told his companion. He had absolutely no idea where to find Callaghan or how they would bring him back to Europe in case that was what Vasily would order.

"Nowadays everything can be found on the Internet", Vladimir said, assuming his role as Misha's baby-sitting supervisor.

"You're right, I was thinking of that, too", Misha quickly responded before bringing out his mobile. Although there was a lot of information of various people either named 'Matthias' or 'Callaghan', he soon had his search narrowed down by adding 'Australia'. There were merely three mentions, and all three had to do with a construction project. The only address mentioned was the company's offices in central Sydney.

"On Monday morning, we'll rent a car and go to the place where Callaghan works", Misha announced triumphantly and got up from his chair. "Meanwhile, let's enjoy the pool and a few drinks."

Monday October 5, 2015

Under Misha's direction, he and Vladimir positioned themselves across the street from the office tower that had a plaque confirming that the company where Callaghan was one of directors occupied an office on the tenth floor.

Six hours later, bored and hungry, they gave up the illusion of watching Callaghan step out from the office building. Instead Misha and Vladimir retreated to a restaurant nearby that promised "a tail-spinning jumpstart for the remainder of the day" if ordering a dish of the succulent kangaroo meat served at the establishment. While they waited for the food to arrive, they discussed different approaches that would allow them to corner Callaghan.

Tuesday October 6, 2015

More determined than ever, Misha and Vladimir returned to the office complex well before seven in the morning to study those who arrived for work in the building. By ten o'clock, comparing the men who entered with the photo of Callaghan that Oleg had provided them with, they acknowledged that Matthias Callaghan hadn't walked through its front door. Still, there was always the possibility that he had arrived by entering the underground garage. Due to the disappointing result so far, Misha decided to take a more direct approach. He walked into the building's reception area and asked the young lady behind the counter for Matthias Callaghan.

"I don't know which company he's with, sir. It would be helpful if you can give me the company's name."

"Sajama Construction Limited."

The woman took her time to study the computer to find the requested information.

"It seems Mister Callaghan hasn't been in his office for the past three weeks", the woman at the reception desk finally informed Misha. "I can take a message and ask him to contact you. Would you like that?"

"I appreciate your concern", Misha replied, flashing his most endearing smile. "However, I have this urgent need to converse with Mister Callaghan concerning a business deal with my father that is not going according to plan. Any further delay could be disastrous for our common interests. Perhaps you know of some other way I could contact him?"

"I don't have his phone number", the girl said after searching her virtual Rolodex, "but I have his home address, if that would be of any use to you."

"It certainly would be a great help", Misha said, relieved.

After the young woman had written it down for him, he went outside to the waiting Vladimir.

"Callaghan hasn't been in his office for three weeks", Misha announced, triumphantly waving the piece of paper with the address, "but we now know where he lives."

An hour later the GPS had taken them to the address Misha had obtained. The only windows of the house they could look through were those of the kitchen. To their disappointment the building looked as if no one lived in it.

Misha rang the doorbells of their three closest neighbours, but they all shook their heads when asked if they knew how he could get in touch Matthias Callaghan in house number four. They hadn't seen him or his family for six months or so, they all assured him.

"His family?" Misha asked. "Meaning?"

"Well, his wife Samantha and their twins."

"Twins?"

"Yes, two identical boys around three or four years old."

"A growing family, no doubt, with a need for a bigger place. Do you have any idea where they could have gone?"

"None whatsoever."

Thursday October 15, 2015

Misha suddenly had an inspired idea how they could find Callaghan through his family. One of the neighbours he had interviewed the day before had mentioned that their children were still not old enough to go to school. However, there was a good chance they went to some nearby day care centre. Full of enthusiasm over the possibility, he searched the Internet for any kindergarten within five kilometres of the family's former home. He found three.

Misha and Vladimir were in luck. At the first one they visited, the young administrator confirmed that the Callaghan twins had attended this particular day care centre for two years before leaving it about six months ago. Their mother had explained that they were moving to a different part of Sydney.

"We are working on an identical twin study under the direction of our university, and Missis Callaghan has helped us in the past", Misha lied. "We're interested in discussing some follow-up questions with her to close the investigation. Do you have any idea how we could reach her?"

"Yes, I do. Just let me look at my records."

It didn't take the young woman long to find the requested information.

"Here's the address she told me she and her family were moving to."

Misha copied it onto a piece of paper and blew the blushing girl a kiss.

"Thank you! You've made my day."

*

To reach the recently constructed Callaghan residence, the car Misha and Vladimir had rented had to climb a steep hill that revealed increasingly breathtaking views as they rounded each curve. Finally, they reached the end of the dead-end road. For security purposes, Misha decided to return down the same road for a kilometre or so before telling Vladimir to abandon their car behind some bushes. Afterwards, they returned on foot to Callaghan's new residence.

It was still before noon. While watching the place during the following six hours, they noted a lot of activity but no presence of their target. A good-looking blonde, heavily pregnant and presumably Callaghan's wife, occasionally came outside to give instructions to the workers about removal of the debris still present after the construction and where to plant fruit trees in the garden. On two of these occasions, she was accompanied by two identical-looking boys, who apparently enjoyed running through the mud.

"We have to wait until Callaghan turns up", Vladimir mumbled as they watched the house and the happy family. "Then we'll decide our next move."

Monday October 19, 2015

My phone woke me up. The screen flashed Samantha's number.

"The water broke half an hour ago, Matthias", I heard her say. Her voice was even. "Jack's taking me to the hospital now."

Her words made me feel awful that I wasn't by her side. I explained to her once again that the danger of the Russians' revenge remained imminent. She didn't sound happy, and neither was I. We talked for a little longer before Samantha said she needed to hang up.

I can't go back to be present at my daughter's birth, because I may put my family at risk. The threat from the recovering Vasily is still present. What can I do? What can I do!

Tuesday October 20, 2015

Jack called as I was having breakfast.

"Your daughter Ruby was born less than an hour ago!" he exclaimed. "Congratulations! A perfect, shapely little girl! Hold on. I'll pass my phone to Samantha."

"Darling, I'm so sorry not to be able to be with you at this important moment", I told her, "yet I'm so happy that everything's went well and that our family now is richer than before."

We talked for another half an hour. Not until I had disconnected the call did I notice that my cheeks were wet with tears.

Monday October 26, 2015

Vasily, now up and walking, was doing constant exercises, moving his face and jaw to make the stiffness go away. Most of the swellings had settled, and he could sit for hours in front of a mirror plucking at his face, watching it, giggling, and sometimes act almost normally to the silent opinion of those who were allowed to observe him. He liked his new face. Except for the underlying bone structure, it had very little in common with how he used to look. He increasingly found his new face more handsome, less feminine and definitely more interesting than his former one.

Although he tired easily and still slept a lot, he was rapidly on his way to full recovery. By now, Dr Sternmacher visited him only twice a week. On his last visit, the doctor had declared that in another ten days Vasily would be as good as new, and that his services would no longer be needed.

During his hours awake, Vasily worked with Sonia to get his drug empire back on its feet. There were shipments in transit that needed to be taken care of; bribes to be paid; methamphetamine laboratories that required more raw materials. The suppliers in Afghanistan, Mexico and elsewhere had immediately learnt about Scotland Yard's successful raid. Now they worried whether they would get paid or not, should they go through the trouble of shipping more merchandise. Smaller competitors had taken notice of the sudden vacuum and did their best to take advantage. Gang shootings occurred when established turfs were challenged.

The concern that more than anything provoked this restlessness was that no one of importance in the underworld had seen or met with either the jailed Berlosky, or his replacement referred to as Big Ben, for five months. They all had had to deal with Sonia over the phone, an unknown woman they knew as Daria, who only offered tough deals and no tangible proof that the Russian Mafia was still truly in business.

*

"It's Misha calling from Australia", Sonia informed Vasily as she held out the phone to him.

Vasily's thoughts were elsewhere, and at first he wasn't keen on taking the call. Then Callaghan's name flashed through his mind and he grabbed the phone.

"What news do you have for me, Misha?" he barked into the mouthpiece. "Something worthwhile this time, no doubt?"

"I'm afraid I don't." Misha sounded miserable. "I've tracked down the place to where Callaghan and his family recently moved, but he hasn't been around even once. He must be out of the country, or maybe he's divorced, because we have watched the comings and goings to his house for ten days now. He doesn't live here, and he doesn't visit his wife and kids. What should I do?"

Vasily chewed on the information for a moment.

"You say that his wife and children are in the house, carrying on a normal life?"

"Sure. And you can tell they've just finished building it. The garden is still a mess, and there's some excess construction material waiting to be taken away. I don't think anyone builds a house, especially a very nice one like this with a terrific view, unless you intend to live in it. That's why I didn't call before, because I thought his absence was only temporary."

So Callaghan is staying away from his home, Vasily thought. *Does he know I'm targeting him? No, that's impossible, unless someone in the know who is close to me has warned him. Highly unlikely. Only a handful of my people know I sent Misha and Vladimir on this mission. But there's a simple solution to flush him out into the open. After all, the weakest spot of any family man is his family.*

"Misha, grab his wife or one of his kids", Vasily ordered him with a giggle. "That, for sure, will make Callaghan appear. Call again when you have one of them, and then I'll set things in motion from here."

Thursday November 5, 2015

During Mikhail Berlosky's three-day October trial, the jury had found him guilty on all thirteen charges including wholesale distribution of illegal drugs and money-laundering. The time had come for his sentencing. The judge of the case called for attention in his courtroom by rapping his gavel twice.

"After due consideration upon hearing the jury's

assessment of guilt, I have arrived at the following decision."

He went on to explain in detail each crime and the punishment each offence merited.

"To sum it up", the judge ended his litany, "the defendant is hereby sentenced to thirty-two years and eight months of imprisonment in one of Her Majesty's high-security prisons.

For once, Berlosky didn't sparkle his gold-capped tooth with one his self-assured smiles. Unless he could make a successful appeal in the meantime, he would be 84 years old on the day of his release.

The warder in charge of his custody expertly snapped the handcuffs around his wrists and, with the help of a colleague, led Berlosky out of the courtroom past a crying Tania.

Friday November 6, 2015

On Vasily's orders, everybody in the Bodensee villa was getting prepared to leave. The company had by now grown to twenty-two persons living on the property since more of Pyotr's accountants and Oleg's henchmen had managed to get out of the UK. This meant that the helicopter, with a capacity of twelve, would have to make two trips to the destination that Vasily wouldn't reveal to anyone except Sonia – and only because he now depended more than ever on her to execute his plans. In spite of being the owner of several dozen large, anonymously owned properties around Europe, Vasily had decided they would return to the yacht in Monte Carlo.

Things are finally improving since the catastrophe six months ago, Vasily thought as he got into the helicopter. *Berlosky has taken most of the heat, now that everyone thinks he was the one who ran my organisation. Since then, I've been able to get most of the pieces back on my chessboard onto the squares where they belong. I've started up two new laboratories, with half a dozen more of them soon ready to begin production. The merchandise from Afghanistan, Mexico and elsewhere keeps coming in, because, fortunately, my cash flow wasn't too severely interrupted. The losses Callaghan's meddling caused me, though highly annoying, are not critical. Now the only main remaining irritant is reports that people, like that nuisance Gérard in Paris, still think they're strong enough to become independent. I have to address that soon. Best of all, at last I now feel physically as well as before the surgery. It was a dreadful experience, but well worth it. Now no one knows what I look like, except for the limited few people I've decided I can trust. I have regained my anonymity, and,* Vasily giggled at the thought, *with the unexpected bonus that I now look even more handsome than I expected.*

Sonia got into the seat next to him. Pyotr, Boris and some of his bodyguards filled up the rest of the seats available.

"Let's go", Vasily shouted at the pilot in order to be heard over the deafening sound of the rotors as the helicopter left the ground.

"Monaco is still on?"

"Monaco, it is", Vasily confirmed with a contented look on his face.

*

Since being informed by Dr Sternmacher after my reluctant return to Europe, my daily routine included checking my mobile for the red blip of Vasily's whereabouts three times a day. Now, for the first time in a month, it no longer appeared.

Has the battery died already? I asked myself. *Or, has Vasily somehow discovered that, courtesy Dr Sternmacher, he has a chip buried inside him?*

I didn't know what to do, really, and the best idea I could come up with was travelling to the villa where Vasily had been recovering the past months. A little over two hours later, I was lying in the long grass on a hill overlooking the villa and the lake beyond with a pair of binoculars glued to my eyes. As far as I could tell, after half an hour's watching, no one was living in the house. There was no movement whatsoever to be seen. All I could see were two empty Mercedes on the driveway.

The Russian eagle has fled his German nest, I concluded.

I waited outside the lake villa for several hours in the hope that Vasily would return. Every five minutes or so, I checked the application on my phone to see if the blip would reappear. Nothing.

After two hours of waiting, I returned to my hotel in Switzerland. I realised that I had lost Vasily. Either the tracking device that Dr Sternmacher had implanted was malfunctioning, or the battery had gone dead. Disappointed and concerned, I decided to go back to Australia the next day.

I was prepared to go to bed when I glanced a last time at my phone before turning off the lights. The red blip was pulsing again, and the application automatically zoomed in on its location.

The blip revealed that Vasily was on the French Riviera, next to the Italian border.

Saturday November 7, 2017

"I want you to pick up some guests flying in today, Sonia", Vasily told her. "They will arrive by helicopter from Nice at three o'clock, landing on helipad six. Take one of the Rolls and pick them up, will you?"

Although Vasily said all this in an even voice as if he were asking her a favour, she knew perfectly well it was an order that had to be obeyed without further discussion.

Two hours later, she was sipping a martini in Vasily's custom-made Rolls-Royce, which was parked near the heliport. The whirring sound of an approaching helicopter announced the arrival of Vasily's guests. Two minutes after it had landed and the rotor blades had stopped stirring up too much air, two spectacular, large-breasted redheads in tight-clinging dresses stepped outside while taking in the principality's impressive views of the Mediterranean through their designer sunglasses.

Sonia felt hurt and, yes, a sting of jealousy, when she immediately understood the purpose of the visit of the generously endowed redheads. At the same time, she knew perfectly well she could never be the object of Vasily's desires, since he obviously preferred true redheads in lieu of her wigged London impersonation. *Well, every dog has its day*, she thought, teeth clenched.

She got out of the car and amicably welcomed the girls, whose ages Sonia estimated to be between 25 and 30. With the three of them seated in the car, she offered them drinks from the bar cabinet. They both opted for a gin and tonic.

While Sonia chatted with them about things of no consequence to get some understanding of their personalities, Ilya drove the car through the winding streets of the small principality. Ten minutes later, he stopped the car next to the yacht that now served as Vasily's residence.

There, the yacht's diminutive, handsome-looking owner appeared with outstretched arms to welcome his guests.

*

My flight arrived before schedule at the Nice Côte d'Azur Airport after the short shuttle from Germany. The moment the wheels touched the ground, I again checked my mobile. Yes, there it was, the red blip on the map, although by now it had moved to Monte Carlo.

A taxi took me from the airport into central Nice. I found an establishment where I bought a black, longhair wig. In another shop, I bought the largest reflecting sunglasses I could find.

From there, I went to an agency that rented luxury cars.

Less than an hour later, I was driving a Maserati cabriolet following the GPS instructions on how to get out of Nice. Soon I was on the beautiful lower Corniche road that would take me to Monaco in less than half an hour.

Descending the road into Monte Carlo, I constantly checked my phone for the blip that remained constant. The map on the screen automatically became enlarged as I closed in on the blip. I cruised the streets and soon found myself next to the principal harbour with its many hundreds of sailboats and luxury yachts.

I parked the car on Avenue de Monte-Carlo and walked over to a lookout with my mobile and the binoculars. Carefully comparing the information on my phone with what I was seeing, I scanned this particular port of Monaco until I could pinpoint the blip as coming from a huge yacht bearing the name *Twinkle*. It was moored to Quai Rainer III.

Got you, Vasily.

I continued up the hill and soon found that the Hotel Hermitage – one block from the Place du Casino, behind Hôtel de Paris – had a perfect view overlooking the harbour where Vasily was holed up on his yacht. The decoration of the junior suite was far from my liking; I wouldn't have stayed in it if it hadn't been for the view from its ample balcony. Some interior designer with an affinity for kitsch had decided that a honeymooner's dream had to be propped up by frilly pillows, pastel colours and watercolours depicting cherubs. To me, the only thing of importance was its balcony overlooking the harbour where Vasily's yacht was moored.

Saturday November 8 – Monday November 9, 2015

Using my binoculars, I rarely left the balcony during the next couple of days. I noted everything that occurred on the yacht's deck, not forgetting to jot down the detailed description of everyone who showed his or her face on board.

Two eye-catching redheads enjoyed long, bare-breasted sessions in the sun. At least six thugs – overweight and with one hand across the belly grabbing the wrist of the other – were present above deck at all times. Apparently, they didn't mind the show that the redheads put on.

Two men were in charge of the food catering, besides leaving the yacht for other presumed errands of that nature. Twice a day, a man dressed in typical chef's clothing came outside to inspect the boxes delivered by a van announcing itself as "catering service". I could see that the wooden boxes filled with ice were laden with lobsters, fish and other delicatessen. The imposing musclemen who lived on the yacht carried the heavy boxes on board.

Then, on the second day, a small, handsome man appeared blinking in the sunlight. He turned to the two sun-bathing redheads and said something that made them laugh.

I looked at my phone. The red dot kept blinking, now strongly, confirming that Vasily definitely was on the yacht. I raised my binoculars to my eyes and focused on the diminutive man who by now had the girls falling over with laughter. He turned around, and for the first time I got a clear, unobstructed view of his face. A good-looking man, beyond doubt, whose face I had never before set my eyes on.

I felt confused. Then it dawned on me. This had to be Vasily. Yes, the same body build, the same manners, the gesturing. The face, which I didn't recognise at all, must of course be the very face Dr Sternmacher had transplanted.

I was too far away to take any pictures, but I studied him carefully through the binoculars before he disappeared into the yacht's belly.

I now knew what Vasily looked like and where to find him until the chip's battery died. The question was – what should I do with the information I had?

Tuesday October 27 – Tuesday November 10, 2015
Vladimir felt uncomfortable about kidnapping 3-year-old toddlers, and he told Misha that he vehemently disagreed with Misha's initial plan despite it being easier to abduct a small child when compared to kidnapping an adult.

Misha eventually relented, and they agreed that, in the absence of Matthias Callaghan himself, his wife alone would have to become the necessary target to flush him out. To abduct her turned out to not be an easy task, something they discovered as they lay for days on end in the long grass with binoculars watching the comings and goings from the Callaghan residence. During the day, there were always workers present, with one or two entering the building and several more intent on putting the garden in shape.

For weeks, Callaghan's wife didn't leave the house. *How could they get close enough to abduct her with all these people around?* Misha wondered. Then, one morning he could observe through his binoculars that Samantha made sure her two lookalike boys were safely strapped in their seats and that a pram was stowed in the back of her van. Finally, she carried a basket with a baby that she placed in the backseat. At a slow pace, she started driving downhill.

Misha and Vladimir quickly retreated to their own vehicle and barely managed to get it on the main road before the jeep Samantha was driving had disappeared out of sight. They followed her to a kindergarten, where they watched the twins disembark with loud cries of joy. Twenty minutes later, she parked her vehicle outside a large supermarket.

Samantha got out and went to the back of the jeep to get the pram out. The moment she pulled the hatchback open, Misha drove up and stopped next to her. Wearing balaclavas to mask their faces, Misha and Vladimir quickly exited and grabbed her arms from behind. She was pushed into the backseat of their rented car, followed by Vladimir, who pulled a black hood over Samantha's face.

"Wait!" Vladimir shouted when Misha got into the driver's seat. "You forgot to leave the message in her car."

Misha cursed, went back to Samantha's jeep and threw the message they had prepared earlier inside. The baby had begun to cry. *I can't stand crying babies,* he thought angrily before slamming the hatchback shut. He got back into the car and scanned the parking lot as he left it at a leisurely pace.

"Don't remove the hood, unless you want to get killed", Vladimir growled to the trembling woman who was trying to recover her wits. He pulled her tiny hands behind her back and secured them with tape. He then proceeded by wrapping the same duct tape several times across Samantha's mouth on top of her hood.

At the supermarket exit there was a token fee to be paid for using the parking lot, but Misha simply sped through it. The plastic bar flew high and landed on an incoming car. Misha laughed out loud. *This really is my cup of tea*, he decided, after enduring the long, boring wait studying the Callaghan household.

A few kilometres down the road, they switched the car for a camper van that Misha had rented earlier. Not until then did Misha and Vladimir take off the balaclavas and the gloves they were wearing.

Throughout this, Samantha felt confusion and fear. *Why was she being abducted? What about my baby left in the backseat of the jeep? Had this something to do with Matthias's past?*

The questions swirled through her mind as she, unseeing, was raced to her unknown destination

"Give me her phone", Misha demanded. Vladimir searched the woman's belongings until he found it. He handed it over to Misha.

"Ask her who her closest relative is, or whoever she thinks we need to contact if she wants to get out of this alive."

Vladimir put the question to her, and Samantha reluctantly gave him Jack's phone number. Sitting up front, Misha dialled it and on the fourth ring got a man's voice on the line.

"I've been told by a certain lady that you're someone close to her. I'm afraid that she's no longer with her baby at the supermarket on Old South Head Road where she went this morning. I suggest you go there immediately. Understood? And don't bother to contact the police; it will only make things worse."

"What is this? Some kind of sick joke?" Jack protested, bewildered by the unexpected call.

"Of course it isn't. Until Callaghan appears, we will keep his wife. I should worry about the baby crying at the parking lot, if I were you. And, by the way, next to the baby you'll find the instructions you should immediately relay to Callaghan."

Misha disconnected the call and, using the rearview mirror, grinned at Vladimir.

"The mission is going as smoothly as could be expected. The Aussies aren't used to surprises like this one. Now, let's drive our guest to the place outside the city."

He drove the van for a little over two hours before they reached the camping ground next to a little lake that they had researched earlier. It was located within the Blue Mountains National Park, and Misha turned off the highway onto an almost invisible road that took them there. There were no houses or people to be seen anywhere.

Vladimir struggled with the task of putting together the tent they had bought. They had decided that Samantha would remain alone in the camper van, chained to a metal bar in the small kitchenette, and with its windows blackened with spray paint. The chain was measured to be long enough to allow her

621

complete freedom inside the vehicle. Since there was a toilet facility inside, there was no need for them to let her leave the van under any pretext.

*

"In Paris, Gérard no longer takes my calls", Sonia complained to Vasily. "And he still owes us eight million euros and change from the June shipment."

It had taken her considerable time to get used to his new face, one that she now found expressed surprise over Sonia's report.

"Why, Gérard must think that just because Mikhail has landed a prison sentence, Big Ben isn't strong enough to watch out for his business interests", he mused referring to his latest code name. "It sounds like Gérard has joined somebody else, or, more likely, that he has decided strike out on his own."

"He doesn't have a clue about you running the organisation, Vasily", Sonia retorted, "and I don't think he believes me when I claim to be working on Big Ben's orders. He clings to the idea that Mikhail, the only one of importance that he has ever negotiated with, is the boss."

"Well, judging by the lengthy sentence Mikhail was handed down, so does the British legal system."

"I've tried to both threaten and cajole Gérard, but he doesn't listen to me. I suspect it's because he refuses to take instructions from a woman."

"But you're such a competent one", Vasily giggled.

"Don't worry, we'll teach him to listen. You're the best lieutenant one could wish for. What we need to do is to give our French distributor the choice of some wholesome advice that should correct his ways regarding misogyny or a bullet between his eyes."

Wednesday November 11, 2016

I had just finished lunch on the balcony that came with my room, when I noticed that the red blip revealing Vasily's position appeared to move for the first time since I had arrived in Monaco. Using my binoculars, I could see that a Rolls-Royce and a large, black van had pulled up on the quay next to the ship. Vasily, three women and another five people got into the two vehicles.

The Rolls-Royce, immediately followed by the van, drove slowly along the pier and then took a turn up on Quai des États-Unis – just below my balcony.

My mind was working fast. Since the cars hadn't taken the road to the main artery going from Nice in France to Ventimiglia on the Italian side of the border, it could only mean that the passengers intended to do some sightseeing in Monaco. Being such a small place, it wasn't difficult to guess that they were headed to the main plaza, where the casino was the principality's main attraction.

I put on the wig and the large sunglasses I had bought in Nice, hurried out from the hotel and walked up to the Place du Casino. When I got there, Vasily's Rolls-Royce had already stopped next to the Café de Paris. Vasily, the two redheads and a third woman, whom I recognised as the one who had threatened me with a gun when I had visited my former flat, stepped out of the car. The Rolls-Royce and the van left while the four strolled over to a table that carried a sign that it had been reserved. Three bodyguards followed them.

I casually walked past the table where Vasily entertained and could hear him order two bottles of champagne from the waiter. Vasily and the three women were sitting with a front view of the street that allowed them to watch the glitterati and the continuous parade of exotic luxury cars passing by. The bodyguards sat down at a table immediately behind them.

As I slowly passed them while pretending to limp, I got a close look at Vasily's new face for the first time. Considering myself somewhat of an expert on the subject, I could tell that his face transplant had gone miraculously well. There were no bruises to be seen, only some minor swellings that no doubt would disappear within another week or two. Dr Sternmacher had told me that he had performed Vasily's surgery on August 20; that is, twelve weeks earlier. By now, it was impossible to say that he had gone through the transplant unless you knew about it or went up close enough to see the scars.

There was no doubt that Vasily was a different person when comparing his new face with his previous one. Yes, there were some similarities if you knew where to look for them, but only if you were in the know. My immediate impression was that he was better-looking than previously. The nose was linear, the chin was fuller and dimples appeared on his cheeks when he giggled. The eyes looked the same, however: black, impenetrable and with no laughter whatsoever in them.

I found a free table at the back, far from the coveted front-row seats from where the café's customers wanted to ogle the parading muscle cars. A waiter appeared the moment I sat down. I ordered a Kir Royal and a daily paper in English from him. My watch showed 2:10 The voluptuous redheads laughed as Vasily made conversation, while the blonde with the cropped hair didn't seem particularly amused by his comments. The bodyguards, wearing gaudy shirts and heavy gold chains, merely grunted when the waiter put down a bottle of beer in front of each.

I knew where Vasily lived, what he looked like and the company he kept. What I now needed was a high-definition picture of Vasily's face before I went to the police with what I knew about him. How was I going to take it without being spotted, or worse, killed by his henchmen?

Ferraris, Lamborghinis and Aston Martins kept rolling by. Across the street, outside the Hôtel de Paris, half a dozen Rolls-Royces stood abandoned in the no-parking zone. *Surely Vasily, vastly rich and now anonymous again, must feel that he's both secure and in a place where he belongs. But he doesn't know that I'm working on springing him a surprise.* I had barely finished my thought before my phone rang, only to learn that it was Vasily who had sprung a surprise on me.

"Matthias? Jack here. I'm so, so sorry, but I have terrible news. Samantha has been kidnapped."

PART XIV

Life is a lottery

with the winners impossible to predict.

Wednesday November 11, 2015

Oleg's mobile rang. He listened to the voice asking for his boss, then rose and approached the table where Vasily was entertaining the ladies.

"It's Misha", Oleg said, "calling from Australia. He needs to talk to you."

"Yes, Misha?" Vasily greeted him.

"I've got her – Callaghan's lady. She's locked up in a van outside the city."

"Finally some good news, Misha", Vasily thanked him with a giggle. "This is certain to bring Callaghan out in the light, wherever he may be holed up."

*

"I didn't want to call the police before I talked to you", Jack said. "The man who rang me using Samantha's mobile warned me about contacting them."

"You did right, Jack", I replied, my heart beating violently from anxiety and anger. "Were the children with her? What about the baby?"

"She left the twins at the kindergarten before going to the supermarket. It appears she was abducted as she was preparing to get the pram out of the jeep. Ruby is all right, although she was screaming red-faced when I got to her. Alice is taking care of her now. As for the twins, I'll pick them up later. To sum it up: no worries about the kids, mate. "

"Tell me what you know about Samantha's kidnapping."

"The call was bone-chilling, Matthias. The voice sounded like a younger man. In the background, there were some muffled sounds, but I couldn't tell if they were made by Samantha. The call was very quick and to the point: 'We will keep Samantha captive until Callaghan appears.' Afterwards, I tried to call her mobile several times, but I only got her voice mail. I drove to the supermarket on Old South Head Road and found her car, unlocked, on the parking lot. In the back, there was a written message that I have here in front of me. It says: *I lost my paintings. Don't lose your wife. The Ritz, Paris, immediately. Stay put and wait.*' It isn't too hard to deduce that someone is using Samantha to get you to go to Paris. But what's this about the lost paintings?"

The thoughts rushed through my head. *The man sitting three tables away from me has ordered Samantha's kidnapping to flush me out. He's looking to avenge the harm I've caused his drug empire.*

"I don't know what to say, Jack", I finally told him. "Our concern must be to find Samantha before she comes to any harm. I will do what I can from my end. Now, report at once to the police that she's missing, but do not, under any circumstance, show them that message. Please, Jack, it's important."

"What's going on, Matthias?"

"Do you remember what I told you when I returned to Sydney about being extorted by some bad people for things that happened, oh, fifteen, twenty years ago?"

"How can I forget", he replied. "A terrible yarn, that one."

"I can't go into any details right now, Jack, please understand. The main thing is to get Samantha back safely. I repeat: go to the police, while I'll go to Paris, as requested. I promise I'll keep in touch with you on a regular basis. Any new development, text me if you can't get me on the phone."

"You seem to continuously end up in these strange situations, where you get arrested or abducted, and now extorted with Samantha as –"

"I know, Jack, and it all comes with a logical but very long explanation", I interrupted, feeling overcome with helplessness. "I repeat, the important thing now is to get Samantha released unharmed."

"All right, Matthias", he replied, not sounding very convinced by my attempted explanation, "but I'm sure you can appreciate that this is a strange situation with you ordered to travel to Paris over some paintings and we here worried to death about Samantha's disappearance."

"Believe me, Jack, I understand perfectly." I watched how Vasily and his entourage got up from their tables. "I have to hang up now, but we'll talk again soon."

"Yes, let's talk soon." He said it in a voice as if he had doubts about me.

Chatting, the Russians passed not too far from my table. I lowered my head so the long hair of my wig covered my face. Vasily, the women and the bodyguards went inside to the restaurant. I remained outside, paralysed at the thought that something had happened to Samantha.

In a very intelligent way, Vasily had found a way to get to me. *If I give myself up, he will release Samantha. If not, I will lose her ... Will he kill her?* I simply couldn't risk it, because one way he could seek revenge was by doing precisely that. It didn't take me long to understand that I had no choice except to go to Paris on Vasily's conditions.

Despite all the many difficult things I'd been through, I couldn't recall a moment in my life when I had felt more powerless.

*

Feeling elated, Vasily entered the private gambling room at the upper floor of the casino with one redhead hanging onto each arm. He was followed by a less enthusiastic Sonia and his bodyguards. They were offered seats around the roulette table. Giggling more than usual, Vasily ordered another two bottles of champagne and 100,000 euros in chips each for the three women and himself.

The two redheads placed their bets randomly. Sonia, who didn't like games where the odds were stacked against the player, bet cautiously. Vasily, she noticed, placed his bets in a systematic way. Surprisingly, his approach seemed to work because his winnings slowly began to pile up.

Half of his chips he placed on numbers, and the other half on red. Whenever he lost on red, he doubled the bet until he won. Then he went back to his original bet of 1,000 euros on red. The bets on the numbers were pure luck, but doubling his bets on red until it came up was an assured way of winning, Sonia realised.

Two hours later, the redheads were out of chips while Sonia had lost half of hers. Vasily, to his great delight, now had considerably more chips when compared to his original stack. The money didn't matter to him, but winning did. He was content.

How curious, Sonia thought as they walked out of the casino. *Adding up the numbers, Vasily lost over 200,000 euros of his money at the table. Yet he's happy because as an individual player he won despite the money the rest of us lost? Perhaps he felt that he was in competition with us, not the casino.*

Vasily asked the redheads to travel in the van with his bodyguards, since he had some business to discuss with Sonia.

"Tomorrow I will go to Paris", he told her when they were alone in the Rolls-Royce's backseat. "You will stay on the yacht and supervise all ongoing concerns."

"Why Paris?" she asked him. "Your presence here is important to get the business back on its feet again. Besides, we have two large shipments coming – "

"I know, believe me, I understand everything that you're telling me. But I have some unfinished business to take care of in Paris, and actually", and here he started giggling almost uncontrollably, "I think my short trip there will kill two bothersome birds with one stone, your ungrateful friend Gérard being one of them." He extended his tiny fist to show his resolution to crush the birds in question.

As they rode back to the yacht, Sonia reflected on Vasily's new face and how he'd changed since his transplant.

He is better-looking now, despite some persistent swelling that is sure to disappear soon. Vasily's becoming both richer and more dapper as time goes by, yes; but the price has been a change of personality for the worse.

Every time the car silently passed by a street light, Sonia thought she could detect Vasily's countenance going through a rapid sequence of different emotions: hatred, comfort, suspicion, tranquillity, the intent to murder. What she couldn't see was the pleasure of being alive. *No, no, that can't be true,* she corrected herself. *The only way to really come alive is by being rich. As rich as Vasily. Not until then do you get total freedom; the power to give free rein to anything and everything imaginable. Not until you've reached that pinnacle, will you know that you're truly alive.*

Money buys you everything, Sonia, wise from her observations, concluded, *but only as long as you have enough of it.*

Thursday November 12, 2015

Early in the morning, I checked out from the hotel and drove to Nice where I returned the car. A cab took me to the airport. Just to be sure I wouldn't run into Vasily on my way to Paris, I constantly checked if his blip was moving off the yacht. It never did. I was able to get a ticket on an Air France flight that left Nice at 9:30.

Two hours later, I was sitting in a cab on my way to the Ritz. Now the red blip had moved to central Nice. *So Vasily has left Monaco. Is he on his way to Paris?*

The cab let me off at the hotel, where a bellboy took care of my suitcase. Although far from the pleasant Riviera weather, Paris was still reasonably warm, which was fine with me since I hadn't taken the precaution to bring any clothes for cold weather. At the reception, I was asked how many nights I was going to stay. I had no idea, of course, so I said two nights with a possible extension for another two or three nights.

"No problem, monsieur, this is low season, so there's plenty of availability."

I was taken to my room. When I had been left alone, I checked my mobile for the red blip. It was moving towards Lyon, and judging by its speed it could hardly be a car. The only explanation was that Vasily and his retinue had got on a bullet train in Nice. That meant they would arrive in the afternoon, so I had better prepare myself if Vasily would get in touch with me after he'd arrived.

More than anything, getting prepared meant stuffing my pockets with ciclosporin pills in case I would be held hostage for an extended time, and Dr Sternmacher's prescription in case I needed more. Cash, credit cards, passport … no, they were no doubt likely to be removed during a body search. I did stuff a credit card inside one of my socks, however. My mobile? My first impulse was to bring it with me hidden somewhere, but remembering the software on it that traced Vasily, it would definitely be more prudent to leave it behind. Since I needed to be able to call Jack, if I later would somehow be able to do so, I took the precaution of memorising his phone number.

What else was there that I could do? I felt upset and nervous. What was going to happen to me? Was Samantha going to be set free? Should I contact the police? I decided to call Jack. In Sydney, it was 9:30 in the evening. Jack picked up on the third ring.

"Any news about Samantha, Jack?"

"None. I went to the police as you told me to, and they took the whole thing very seriously."

"Did you show them the note you found?"

"No, I didn't, but now I feel bad about it. It could help them find her, you know. Fingerprints and other evidence – "

"No, Jack, it won't help them. The message was clearly directed to me, and I've now arrived at the Ritz in Paris as instructed. I have reasons to believe that the man who ordered Samantha's kidnapping will pick me up later today. My cooperation will set her free."

"This is terrible, mate! What have you got yourself into?"

"Some difficulties, no doubt, which I'll explain to you over a beer when we next meet in Sydney." I tried to sound cheerful, but I doubt that Jack noticed. "What about our kids? Are they asking for their mom? Or me?"

"At first the twins were puzzled that both of you are absent again, but Alice and I keep them busy. Don't worry about them. Worry about yourself, because I certainly do. Your newborn is with us, too, with Alice taking care of the little girl. Since our own firstborn is only six months older than Ruby, Alice says there's really no extra trouble. I can confirm that, although I'm extremely concerned about the two of you, the one thing you don't need to worry about are your kids."

"I really, really appreciate what you and Alice are doing for us, Jack. There are forces at large that I can't speak about now, but that I have to face. Unfortunately, Samantha has become a pawn in this involuntary game. What more can I say?"

"Please solve the situation as quickly as you can, mate", Jack replied, sounding troubled, "and then hurry back to Sydney. I already suspect that the explanation you owe me will last longer than a single beer."

"Thanks, Jack, I'm very grateful. Send me a message whenever you have some update from the police, although I'm not certain I'll be able to read it right away."

"I will, Matthias. Take care."

After the call with Jack, I went outside to buy an overcoat in anticipation of colder weather. When I returned to the hotel, I went to one of its restaurants and ordered a hearty meal, not knowing when I would be able to have my next one.

Friday November 13 – Saturday November 14, 2015

Vasily chose not to contact me upon his arrival in Paris. After some research, the red blip on my phone's screen showed that he could be found at the hotel Le Meurice a mere five minutes walking distance away. I had breakfast and an early lunch, and I felt as prepared as I could possibly be. The waiting nevertheless made me feel increasingly nervous with the sensation of butterflies in my stomach.

With nothing better to do, I watched the news on television. When I got bored, I tried to watch Hollywood's latest best picture Oscar winner, but I couldn't concentrate on the plot. Then, just as I was thinking going downstairs for dinner, the phone rang. The sudden sound made my stomach feel as if kicked by a mule. I looked at my watch. It showed 20:31.

"Callaghan, right?" a male voice with a thick Russian accent growled. He didn't wait for my confirmation. "I'm waiting in lobby. You better come quick quick, hurry hurry."

I left my room and went to the ground floor by taking the stairs. In the lobby, I could see nothing but the polished marble floor, the marble pillars and the huge flower arrangements with their peculiar fragrance that enveloped the space. Vasily wasn't there waiting for me, nor was the blonde who had threatened me with a gun on Park Lane. When I approached the elevators, I noticed a large man in a light trench coat and a brown hat studying them. He was the only one present in the lobby apart from the uniformed hotel personnel.

I silently walked up to him from behind and tapped him on the shoulder. He turned around surprised, and made a gesture as if he wanted to grab something beneath his coat.

"You're perhaps the gentleman who called my room a few minutes ago?" I asked him. "I assume you work for Vasily?"

His face shifted from concern to recognition to fury for having been outfoxed by the quarry.

"You come with me, Callaghan", he ordered me in broken English. "Vasily waits you."

He led the way out of the hotel to a black van with tinted windows. The van was standing between two street lamps where the light was faint. Vasily's man ordered me to spread my legs and raise my arms before he patted me down in a professional way. Then he angrily pulled the sliding door open and pointed at the interior to make it clear that I should get inside. I obeyed. The door immediately slammed shut behind me.

The interior of the van had been redesigned to have two facing leather chairs on each side of a small table crammed with electronics and communications gear. In the backseat at the rear, Vasily was sitting next to one of his bodyguards. He looked sharp dressed in an exquisitely tailor-made three-piece suit with a handkerchief flowing out of the breast pocket of the jacket. There was a mohair coat neatly folded across his lap. I took the only remaining seat opposite him, next to another of his bodyguards. The man who had fetched me inside the hotel got into the driver's seat.

The tension was tangible. I felt a knot in my stomach. *This is it, this is the end of the road.*

"Matthias Callaghan", Vasily interrupted my thoughts. "although we've met before, I believe this is the first time we meet face to face in our new incarnations, so to speak ... courtesy of Doctor Sternmacher, of course!"

I couldn't think of anything to reply to his taunt, so I remained silent.

"You had me fooled the last time we met, Callaghan", Vasily continued. "This time I fooled you. I've done some research lately, with a little help from the good doctor we both share. You are, of course, far ahead of me when it comes to face-switching. An interesting experience, don't you think?" He giggled. "After repeated trials, I can't help noticing that you've chosen to go back to the one is most reminiscent of your original face."

"Who are you? What do you want from me?" I asked,

reminding myself that Vasily had no knowledge that I knew of his recent face transplant.

"Who am I? What do I want from you?" Vasily mimicked and giggled. "You should know who I am. We met once at Victoria station ... remember? You looked quite different then, of course. As did I." He giggled again. "What I want is for you to compensate me for my losses after you broke into my flat and went to the police. Does that sound unreasonable to you? Tell me, does it? Well, it shouldn't."

His voice hardened.

"Your meddling this past summer cost me half a billion pounds, Callaghan. It's a sum that isn't easily lost or forgotten."

His words felt like iced water poured down my spine.

"I'm here", I said, simply. "I got your message, and I'm here at your request. Now, release my wife."

"Yes, yes. Later." All of a sudden, Vasily had no interest in talking to me. "First I have some business to take care of. Then we'll see. Oleg", he called out to the driver, "take us to the café."

He leaned back and closed his eyes. Ever the great chess player, I imagined that he was now walking through his next moves with Samantha and myself as two of his pawns.

The van started moving through the streets that had taken on a more ominous darkness thanks to the tinted windows.

*

Gérard was sitting with three of his men at *La Belle Équipe*, a café on Rue de Charonne in Paris's 11th arrondissement. This district was his home turf, and he knew every inch of it like the palm of his hand. Unlike other parts of Paris and its banlieues where he had sales, he felt safe here. Everybody of any interest or importance to him in the neighbourhood knew who he was, that he had money to burn, and that he could make generous donations if he was in the right mood or when he found it to be to his advantage.

With the night temperature at twelve degrees Celsius, the evening was still pleasant enough to sit outside if you wore a jacket. Despite the promise of rain in the air, there were hardly any free tables at the popular café.

That Russian woman, Daria something, Gérard thought, *had called him several times the past week, insisting that he must meet with some key people who had taken over Berlosky's job.* She had given him a great sales pitch about their work together so far, and that fresh leaders had stepped in after the recent unfortunate events that had occurred in London. Although she had sounded professional and seemed to know what she was talking about, he still intensely disliked obeying instructions from a woman.

"The risks are part of the business", Sonia had concluded before making him a veiled threat. "If I were in your shoes, I would minimise those risks and any losses by continuing our, so far, successful business relationship."

More out of curiosity than from feeling threatened, he had agreed to meet with the new bosses Sonia was promoting.

Gérard was about to receive his first big shipment from his suppliers in Mexico and thought it wise to learn first-hand about his competition's intentions.

*

Everybody remained silent after Vasily had stopped talking and the van continued at a leisurely pace through the streets of Paris. He had closed his eyes, but the vivid eye movements beneath his lids betrayed that he was thinking intensely about one thing or other. I imagined that I formed part of whatever plot he was devising.

The van came to a stop and the side door slid open. Vasily opened his eyes and nodded. The bodyguard sitting next to me immediately shoved me outside. The others followed, with Vasily the last one to exit. The evening air had become slightly chillier. Vasily secured his mohair coat upon his shoulders and, despite the evening darkness, put on a pair of sunglasses that looked enormous on his small face.

We had disembarked on the corner of a crossing in one of Paris's less attractive *quartiers*. The call from a man, sitting with a plastic cup and unfocused eyes imploring us to fill it with a coin or two, went unheeded. The unembellished apartment buildings had small businesses occupying the street level: pharmacies, cafés, a plumber, some Asian takeaway food. *What is Vasily's intention by bringing me here?*

We crossed the street with my two guardians three steps behind me. Vasily walked as if he didn't have a worry in the world. On the other side of the zebra crossing was an establishment that on the awning promoted itself as *La Belle Équipe.* The driver, who had parked the van further down the street, hurried to join us. Less than a dozen tables were placed outside on the pavement, with another two dozen tables inside. Self-assuredly, Vasily, swaying elegantly with his coat resting across his shoulders, walked up to a table where four men, with tattoos and proudly displayed piercings, sat huddled together over glasses of whisky and bottles of beers. I was prodded to never be less than two steps behind Vasily. It became increasingly obvious that I was meant to be part of whatever he had planned for the evening.

"Vous-êtes Monsieur Gérard, n'est-ce pas?" Vasily asked in passable French. I never would have guessed it: Vasily turned out to be a polyglot.

Three of the men at the table looked up at him with a mixture of curiosity, bother and animosity. Two of them put their hands inside their motorcycle jackets. The fourth, their apparent leader and the one who Vasily had called Gérard, rose from his chair with his face red and menacing.

"Who are you? What do you want?" he defied him aggressively while sizing Vasily up.

Cool as you please, Vasily sat down at the table next to Gérard's and gestured to me and his four ruffians to join him. I was getting increasingly apprehensive about witnessing some kind of settlement between them, but there was nothing I could do about it, of course.

"Take it easy, Monsieur Gérard, I'm only the translator",

Vasily continued in English. "We have come because Daria wanted my boss here to have a serious conversation with you." He nodded towards me. I felt horrified. Vasily was posing me as his organisation's leader. "You have talked to Daria, yes? She told me she wasn't happy with your recent lack of, shall we say, enthusiasm for our shared business relationship. Although she's all for improving our existing business bonds, my boss here isn't too sure he agrees. That's why he insisted we should look you up and get your opinion directly from the horse's mouth."

"Daria this, Daria that!" Gérard responded, forcefully slamming the palm of his hand down on the tabletop. "I don't know who you are, but no woman is my boss, do you understand? And I have no idea why you are telling me this!"

The final comment made Vasily giggle. Still bristling, Gérard nevertheless looked perturbed by Vasily's self-assured attitude, elegant clothing and obvious knowledge of the racket he was in. Gérard appeared curious about why we had come, or maybe he was only impressed by the rugged companions who watched out for Vasily and myself.

Vasily ordered espresso from the waiter for the five of us and waited patiently for Gérard to say something.

"Get to the point, quickly", Gérard finally barked, "or get out of my sight. I've no interest in conducting any sort of business with you."

At this, Vasily couldn't help laughing out loud, but I noticed that his eyes didn't. *Is Vasily here to provoke this apparent low-life Gérard to get a pretext to kill him?* I wondered. *If so, does he really need a pretext? And why is he allowing me to witness all this? Where do I fit in?*

There was some commotion on the pavement. As I turned around, I saw a scruffy man in his thirties with hollow cheeks shuffling around with his hand extended asking the café customers for money. When he got closer to our tables, Vasily's two men immediately rose and pushed him towards the street where he had come from in such a way that he fell crashing into the surrounding tables and hit the pavement. The waiter hurried outside when he heard the disturbance and the loud protests from the upset customers.

"Jean-Luc, I've told you time and time again that you can't come here begging for money!" he shouted as he tried to pull the man onto his feet. As he did, I got a clear look at Jean-Luc's naked arms, with their veins marked from years of drug abuse.

With everyone momentarily watching, the waiter eventually managed to get Jean-Luc on his way from the café. Discreetly, I looked at my watch. It displayed 21:33.

The talk at the tables returned to normal levels after the unpleasant interruption. Vasily took the opportunity to lock his gaze onto Gérard's.

"I won't be able to make some delightful small talk that will last all night, Gérard", he told him. He nodded in my direction to imply I had somehow given him such an instruction. I didn't dare to protest, and anyway it wouldn't have served any purpose.

"Big Ben strongly suggests that you immediately accept

a return to our previous arrangement", Vasily continued. "He's told me that, if you do, any recent infidelity will be forgotten. If not, I have doubts that you'll survive the competitive situation that my boss says he will unleash."

Gérard's eyes had been reduced to mere slits that fluttered back and forth between me and Vasily.

"You see, Big Ben has found out that since July you've been ordering merchandise from Mendoza in Mexico", Vasily continued after unsuccessfully waiting for Gérard's reply. "He doesn't like disloyal distributors, but he has assured me that, should you immediately return to our previous arrangement, I repeat – your missteps will be forgotten."

"If we tell you must take orders from Sonia, you do", Oleg told Gérard in broken English. "If not obey, punishment will not be nice, not nice at all."

Red-faced, Gérard looked at the three of us. There was suddenly a hint of insecurity in his eyes, provoked by the superior way that the petit and elegantly clad Vasily – whom he probably perceived to be an accountant of sorts – addressed him. Looking at Oleg, Gérard merely bristled unimpressed. His eyes narrowed as he turned to study me, the supposed boss as introduced by Vasily. I tried my best to not reveal my apprehension and merely stared back at him. Perhaps Gérard found my silence menacing; in any case, he didn't challenge me.

Sipping my espresso, I was sitting next to Vasily with a clear view of the street. Not giving it much importance, I noticed a black Seat stopping next to our café.

"Look, I have – "

Gérard was that instant interrupted by two men who jumped out of the black Seat and opened fire with their semi-automatic weapons, indiscriminately spraying bullets that targeted the customers at the café. I dived beneath the table and found myself looking into the surprised eyes of Vasily. He hadn't expected this, I instinctively understood. *If Vasily hasn't ordered this massacre, then who did? Gérard?* No, it couldn't be, because I saw Gérard bleeding from a chest wound while breathing with a wheezing sound. One of his men wearing a motorcycle jacket lay unmoving on the floor with glazed eyes. *What the hell is happening?* I wondered in panic, trying to grasp at some straw of explanation. *What's going on? Who are these people raining bullets? Why are they doing it?*

The screams from the café guests replaced the bursts of gunfire. The watch on the man dressed in the motorcycle jacket showed 21:40. The killing spree had lasted for four minutes. When I looked for the black Seat, it was gone.

The yelling, the sobbing and the blood splattered around us made a horrifying scene. There, in the relative shelter beneath the marble coffee tables, Vasily and I locked eyes for the first and only time without some intent to sway one another. Strangely, it was a brief moment of bonding, because we were sharing a moment of mutual terror. Some madmen had been shooting at random without an apparent purpose or specific target. We were both afraid of being killed. It was a strong bond, momentarily even stronger than my contempt for a man for whom I only felt abhorrence. For a few seconds,

I forgot that he had kidnapped my wife, that he was likely to kill me in the cruellest way possible, and that he remained free to flood Europe with illegal drugs.

I heard sirens approaching. By and by, I got my senses back after the immediate shock. Vasily began crawling away from the café. Two of Vasily's bodyguards, who had been seated with their backs toward the street when the shooting had begun, lay dead on the ground. They had involuntarily protected me and Vasily from the bullets by becoming victims. One of them had had the time to react by pulling out his gun, which now lay next to him. By impulse, not thinking, I grabbed it before I rose to take stock of the unexpected mayhem.

Several dozens of people lay on the ground, either dead or injured. The driver Vasily had called Oleg, who embraced himself while inexplicably holding on to Vasily's lost sunglasses, sat dazed on the pavement bleeding from several wounds. There were screams and sobs in the air, an air that vibrated with incredulity. The shots kept ringing loud in my ears, and I couldn't get the ringing to stop. The first ambulance arrived, immediately followed by two police cars.

The howling sirens caused my initial refusal to comprehend the situation to change abruptly. My head cleared from the daze. I saw Vasily hurrying away from the café and realised that he had all of a sudden become vulnerable in every sense. He could no longer count on his bodyguards to protect him. His reaction had been to run away in fear from this inexplicable scene of terror, because there was no longer

646

anyone on his payroll here to protect him.

And it was for that very reason I started to pursue him.

*

Samantha felt both angry and helpless. She had been kept for days in complete darkness chained to the kitchenette inside a camper van. Only on a few occasions did one of her captors venture inside the camper with food and drink. Before entering, he shouted to her to pull the hood over her head unless she wanted to put her life at risk. Samantha was too afraid to disobey.

To her great relief, her captors turned out to be uninterested in her as a woman. Samantha took the lack of further violence and sexual advances to be good signs. She soon got the impression that they were a couple of professionals who had been tasked with tracking down Matthias and wanted the whole circus to be over as quickly as possible.

She wondered about the message they had left in her jeep for Jack. It must have been something sinister, a threat about what they would do to her and their children unless he complied. Since she was still held as their prisoner, she assumed that Matthias had not yet been reached. *Did they know he was in Europe? No, how could they? More mysterious still, how come they hadn't try to interrogate her about Matthias's whereabouts?*

*

After having been the prey, it felt surreal with the tables so suddenly turned leaving me to act as the predator. The street lamps on the abandoned streets provoked a sense of loneliness. There was not a soul to be seen. An autumn fog had descended on the city, which made the surroundings eerie. Paris, the city of light, always full of people, yet a magic wand had suddenly made them disappear.

No people on the streets made it easier for me to catch up with Vasily. As I stalked him, it soon became obvious that I was in a much better physical condition than he was. An occasional car, none of them a taxi, passed us on the empty, narrow streets that we travelled. I saw his shape as he walked with a limp as quickly as he could through the fog, running away from the terror that he, for once, had not unleashed but had become a victim of. I wondered what I should do when I caught up with him. I constantly reminded myself that my priority was to obtain Samantha's release.

He eventually reached a wider street, Rue du Faubourg Saint-Antoine, which he followed in the direction of central Paris. Cars were still scarce, and when Vasily tried to hail the only taxi that passed on the opposite side of the street, he was ignored. Apparently, it didn't occur to Vasily that he was being followed, because not once did he turn around. The autumn fog suddenly got thicker, and momentarily I lost sight of him. There was no wind to disperse the fog, and I could feel rain in the air as I hurried to reduce the distance between us.

Minutes later, I saw him again as he reached the Place de la Bastille. He crossed it before taking the boulevard next to

Canal Saint-Martin that I knew flowed into the River Seine. I pulled out the gun I had picked up at the café and ran until I caught up with him. He heard me coming and swung around with a surprised look on his face. It disappeared when he saw the gun in my hand.

"We're going to have a talk, you and I", I told him, teeth clenched, "to sort out a few misconceptions on your part. Turn around and walk. The moment you don't obey my instructions, I swear I will kill you without any hesitation whatsoever."

Vasily chose to believe that my threat was real enough – which it was. I felt ready to kill him, but before I did, I needed him to get Samantha released. He turned around and walked straight ahead. I stayed behind him at some distance in case he would make an attempt to overwhelm me.

In the canal, parallel to the boulevard where we were walking, there were several barges moored. Only a few were lit up with light bulbs to indicate that the owners were on board. Most of the barges had the appearance of being abandoned, or at least inhabited. I chose one that looked easy to break into.

"Get on the barge", I ordered Vasily.

He obeyed by jumping from the quay onto the barge. I followed him, passed him and rapidly kicked in the door using all the force I could muster. I waved my gun at Vasily to indicate that he should go inside. Vasily reluctantly obeyed. I closed the door behind us.

Using the flashlight on my smartphone, I found some

candlelights that I lit.

"Sit down in that chair", I ordered him, my gun trained on him.

Again, he obeyed. I sat down on a chair facing him. The air inside was cold and carried a smell of mould. It gave the impression that no one had lived on the barge for some time. It suited my intentions perfectly.

"What was all the shooting about?" I asked him as I kept pointing the gun at him. "Did you arrange that surprise?"

"Of course, not." Vasily looked at me with indignation. "Why would I have my own men killed?"

"So, what happened?"

"I don't know. Perhaps it was an attempt by Gérard to eliminate me that went wrong … I was there to correct his ways. He wasn't performing as he should."

We studied each other without speaking for several minutes. While I considered how I could best negotiate Samantha's release, Vasily no doubt contemplated his options to get away from me unharmed. It occurred to me I had better search him for weapons and means of communication; who knew what tricks a resourceful man like Vasily had up his sleeve. I found no guns or other weapons as I frisked him, but something more interesting – a blister pack containing ciclosporin pills.

When I put them in my pocket, Vasily paled for the first time since we had entered the cabin of the barge.

"I need those", he said. "You, of all, know why."

"Yes, I do", I replied and continued the search that

650

resulted in nothing more of interest beyond Vasily's mobile, which I slipped into one of my pockets.

*

Unsuccessful, Samantha had tried to peer through the windows of the camper van. They had been painstakingly spray-painted from the outside until not even the slightest hint of daylight slipped through. She didn't dare to try opening the sliding door for fear that one of her kidnappers would become aggressive.

Samantha had been warned on several occasions by the one with the younger voice who spoke with a cockney accent that, if she saw their faces, she had automatically given herself a death sentence. Although it sounded a bit melodramatic, it also carried some logic. If she couldn't identify her kidnappers, there was no need for them to kill her before they released her.

My release must be a mere question of time, she concluded, *and it will all depend on whether Matthias complies with whatever he is supposed to do.* She feared more for him than for herself. While she was merely a pawn locked up somewhere in the Australian bush, Matthias was somewhere in Europe faced with some impossible choice if he wanted her to be released.

Samantha despaired. *Will I ever see him again?*

*

"These are the rules", I advised Vasily. "If you make any sudden move, I will shoot you. If you don't obey my instructions, I will shoot you. If you refuse to call your man in Australia and tell him to release my wife unharmed, I will shoot you. Nod if you understand. If you don't, rest assured that I will execute you without any hesitation whatsoever."

Vasily nodded. His unfathomable peppercorn eyes stared back at me. He maintained an eerie calm despite facing the gun. It made me wonder if he had some unexpected surprise in store for me.

A quick look around the interior of the barge gave the impression no one had set foot on it for many months. Dust, spider-webs and a raw cold pervaded the atmosphere. Despite his overcoat, Vasily shivered and wrapped it closer around his body.

Not taking my eyes or the pistol off him, we sat opposite one another without talking. We studied one another, wondering where this situation would take us. *Will one of us, or both, walk out from the barge? What arguments will Vasily give me for letting him go? Money? Am I capable of shooting him, should he disobey me?*

"I will speak my next words very slowly to avoid any misunderstanding", I finally said. "You will give me the password to open up your mobile. After that, you will speak with the man in Australia that you sent to kidnap my wife so you could get to me. Well, here I am. You succeeded."

Vasily gave me a bleak smile but didn't say anything.

"What's your password?"

After some hesitation, Vasily gave it to me. It worked on my first attempt.

"I will dial the number, because I don't trust you. Then I'll turn on the phone's loudspeaker, and you will unequivocally instruct your man there to immediately release my wife. This is your only and very slim chance of getting a free ticket out of here … do you understand?"

Vasily nodded slowly in agreement that he did.

"What's the number I should call?" I asked him, waving Vasily's phone at him.

"Look for Misha", he said.

I found Misha in the directory, dialled the number and placed the phone on the chair between us with the loudspeaker on.

"Vasily, so good of you to call me. I – "

"Misha, shut up and listen to me. I want you to immediately release the woman you kidnapped, without harming her."

"Wow, 'immediately' sounds a bit difficult because right now I'm in Sydney, doing some errands, and she's in a van, you know, some two hours driving from here – "

"Make sure you release her at once, and as soon as it has been done, call me. I want you back here in Europe."

"OK, boss, I understand", a subdued Misha confirmed, "I'll take care of it."

I hung up by stabbing my finger on Vasily's phone, and then leaned back in my chair. Thus we sat for ten or fifteen minutes, glaring at each other and without talking.

*

Misha, confused by the new instructions that he had received from Vasily, drove out of Sydney towards the Blue Mountains where he and Vladimir had decided to park the rented van out of the public eye.

Due to some extensive roadworks that slowed the traffic down, it took him almost three hours to get there.

"Vladi", he called out as he got out of his car, "come here!"

Vladimir appeared from the tent where he had been asleep with a surprised look on his face.

"What is it? You sound upset – "

"You're right, I'm upset! Vasily sent us here to kidnap the woman, and now I got a call from him that we should release her and immediately return to Europe."

Vladimir's face lit up.

"That's great news, don't you think? Instead of sitting here in the Australian bush, within hours we'll be back to civilisation and decent food."

"I don't like it", Misha said, shaking his head. "I simply don't like it. All our work for nothing." He sighed. "What we have to do now is erase our presence in Australia – do you understand?"

Her head covered, Samantha was led out of the camper van. She was cautioned to keep the hood on and stay inactive seated in the car Misha had rented. She was careful to obey her kidnappers to the letter.

With Samantha in the car, Vladimir and Misha proceeded by collecting everything that could be traced to them, including the tent, and threw it inside the van. When they were satisfied that there was nothing left to prove they had ever been at the site, Misha set fire to the van after pouring gasoline on it from a spare tank.

With the camper still burning behind them, Misha began the drive back to Sydney.

*

It turns out that pointing a gun at a man for hours on end, however dangerous he is, is physically not an easy task. You get weary. Your wrist gets weary. Threatening another human with a deadly weapon for hours on end wears you down. The monotony gets to you.

I slowly realised all this as I kept the gun aimed at Vasily's heart. I was absolutely convinced – and I believe Vasily knew this, since he made no attempt to trick me – that I would shoot him if he attacked me or tried to escape.

One hour, two hours, passed without a word between us. We were both waiting for the call from Australia. Vasily realised that, if Samantha was killed or harmed in any way, I would go berserk and kill him. I wanted her to come out of her trial alive, because I couldn't imagine life without her.

The river water lapped against the hull. A solitary sea gull suddenly screeched above us. In the far distance, there was a constant blaring of sirens from emergency vehicles.

Meanwhile, the silence that existed between us was so profound that I imagined I could hear the worms devouring the rotting barge's wooden framework.

So, here I was, doing something that really was no business of mine except that I needed to protect myself and my family. I was holding a gun that felt heavier for every minute that passed. I thought I detected a cat-like patience in Vasily's eyes, meaning he would jump on me if I nodded off or became distracted by something.

I finally decided that the best recipe against falling asleep from inactivity while waiting for news about Samantha was to engage Vasily in a conversation.

"You abducted my wife. Why?"

More than two hours had gone by since we had made the call to Misha before I finally broke the silence between us. Vasily took his time before he answered me.

"Obviously, I wanted to get your attention. I couldn't find you, but I could find your wife. I thought that her ... disappearance would flush you out, and it did, didn't it?"

"True. It did. I assume her abduction was an intent to get even with me; to trade her safety for my appearance so you could get back at me for destroying your cozy little business empire back in London?"

"I don't know about 'little', Matthias", Vasily replied calmly. "I moved half a billion pounds worth of merchandise across Europe last year, with vast expectations of expansion in the Americas, Asia and North Africa. I wouldn't put a 'little' tag to a successful operation like that one."

"Selling narcotics worth billions … You're obviously a very intelligent man, and I'm sure you could make more than enough money working legally doing just about anything. Why did you choose this career?"

My question provoked a prolonged giggle from Vasily.

"I didn't choose it – it chose me. And once you've been chosen, you either go to the top or you go under – it's merely a question of time. So here I am. But I understand the essence of what you're asking me … Why pursue stratospheric amounts of money when you can only drive one car at a time or eat one steak each meal? The answer is simple. Money gives you power. Power is a gift that allows you to move mountains and makes other people do your bidding and removes those who stand in your way. And, rest assured, so far I haven't encountered a single person who is incorruptible."

Vasily told me all this in an even-handed way, as if he were unaware of the gun I was still pointing at him.

"It's possible to corrupt people because they *want* to be corrupted", he continued, apparently enjoying discussing the topic. "I haven't known anyone who isn't interested in a free lunch, or easy money, or an effortless career move, or whatever benefits him or her. Everybody's looking for a deal that gives him an advantage. The only detail that varies is the amount of money it takes."

"I don't agree. You wouldn't be able suborn me for a start."

That, Vasily found hilarious.

"Of course you're willing to take a bribe if it means that

you can benefit from it!"

"What do you mean?"

It took Vasily a good while to collect his thoughts, I could see. He was in no hurry. Vasily gave me a weak smile.

"Let me see if I remember the story correctly", he started. "You and Allan Gould stole millions of pounds from the credit card companies by hacking them. There's no need to deny this, because Allan told me this with all the exquisite details."

"You had Allan killed", I argued, not very logically.

"Yes, I did, but his death was not random. It was necessary. And, please, don't insult me by switching the topic when it suddenly concerns you."

"Meaning?"

"Meaning that I'm fully aware of the theft you orchestrated from the credit card companies. Quite clever, actually. I know that you used your old partner Allan to do it. He worked for me, too, you know, and he told me all about it. He was scared for his life. The law was coming after him instead of Matthias Callaghan who had set him up, he said. Do you want me to go on?"

He snickered.

"That's ridiculous", I answered with an effort to remain cool despite the anger over the provocation swelling up inside. *He's at a disadvantage and now he's merely trying to get me to lose my temper,* I told myself.

"A moment ago, you were taking the moral high ground claiming that you wouldn't accept a bribe."

"I resent that. What are you getting at?"

"Isn't a bribe a theft of sorts, committed in secret? I can't see the difference between stealing millions in a credit card scam or bribing someone to secure an advantage to make money. You use your brains and money and connections and you leave those without your resources behind in the dust. That, of course, is the way the game is played. What I object to is that you're looking down your nose at me and my business, when in reality you're just another lucky player in life's lottery. Either you come out a winner or you don't. I think you and I are the same kind – winners. Yes, you're definitely a winner. I'm in awe and admiration that you made it back from Sahara."

"You murder people."

"So, I understand, do you."

"Don't be absurd, Vasily."

"I don't think I am", Vasily giggled, "I'm just stating facts. Rathbone was one victim, that Thumps fellow another. I've studied you. I've investigated you. You're an interesting exception to my theory that no one escapes me unless I decide to. I know a lot more about you than you imagine."

"Your threat is not improving your present situation."

"Your wife is being released as we speak."

"Don't for a second think that I won't make sure of that."

Vasily shifted his position and suddenly seemed more contemplative, changing the subject somewhat.

"Perhaps you can agree that there's something special about making more money than most people do – that is, the challenge that comes with making it. I think you do. You know, the moves of the chess game when you put everything together. The glorious sensation that descends on you when you know you've outsmarted the police, the competition and all those who want to topple you from your elevated position. It's exhilarating, to say the least, and certainly more stimulating than being your average citizen with a boring nine-to-five job commuting from some suburb."

"You have no remorse for the people squandering their lives or dying doing drugs?"

Vasily shrugged.

"Why should I? Everyone has a choice, and some choose drugs. The rule of demand and availability applies. My business is to supply what the market demands. What's wrong with that?" He giggled. "And, if I was suddenly overcome with scruples, it would only result in someone else stepping forward to take my place."

"That includes no scruples ordering the killing of people?"

"That's just business", Vasily said in a cold voice, "and quite necessary if you want to stay at the top of your game. A firm response is required when you've been slighted or lied to or stolen from or, worse, betrayed or challenged for shows of strength. Just study the great kings in history, or Machiavelli's treatise on the subject." He smiled wryly. "A lot of people believe that success is a question of luck. Just ask anyone who didn't make it."

The easiest way to fascinate people is to let them talk about themselves, I reminded myself. Vasily reached inside the pocket of his jacket, then recalled that I had removed his ciclosporin pills.

"I can feel my face is pulsating a little, which is always a sign that I need to take my pills. With your superior experience on the subject, I'm sure you're familiar with the tingling sensation? Do you mind giving me my pills back?"

I glanced at my watch. It showed that the time was nearly two in the morning.

"When did you last take ciclosporin?" I asked him, making no effort to find the pills that I had confiscated. The question seemed to make him uncomfortable.

"Around four, I think. Dr Sternmacher instructed me to take one every eight hours."

"Funny", I replied with a smile filled with sarcasm. "He told me to take one every twenty-four hours. It makes it less hard on the liver, he claimed. But, then again, thanks to you and your people, I was recently without the pills for two weeks ... Remember when I was dropped off in the Sahara and left for dead?"

Vasily didn't reply, but he looked concerned. Suddenly, we both heard a scurrying noise coming from behind me. I reacted by turning around with my gun raised. In the weak candlelight, I saw a big rat running across the boards. The same moment, Vasily threw himself across the space that separated us and attempted to knock the pistol from my hand. Brave man, considering that I was both larger and in better shape than he was. I smashed the pistol against his temple, but not hard enough. He came at me again, his teeth exposed.

On the spur of the moment, feeling challenged and desperate, I shot him.

*

"Climb outside when I stop", Misha admonished Samantha, "then wait for three minutes before you remove your hood. Cross the parking lot. Someone will pick you up."

"You've played by our rules so far", she heard the usually taciturn man, who spoke with a heavy accent, warn her. "That is in your favour. You're being released. Don't do anything stupid that might make us change our opinion."

Samantha felt considerably more frightened by the advice from the elder man with a notable Eastern European accent. She merely nodded her consent.

Misha parked the rental car away from the supermarket entrance. Shielded by a pickup truck, Vladimir opened the door and pushed the hooded Samantha outside. Helpless, she fell onto her knees. Vladimir shut the door and Misha quickly moved the vehicle towards the exit.

They had decided to return Callaghan's wife to the same location where they had previously picked her up. When they were a few blocks away, Misha fast-dialled the prerecorded number Samantha had told him was that of her closest next of kin.

"Samantha!" a relieved voice answered. "We've been so worried! Where are …"

"You can pick her up at the same supermarket where she

got lost."

Misha turned off the phone and gave it to Vladimir, who stamped on it with his military boot until it broke. He opened the window and flung the remains of it outside.

*

The bullet struck Vasily's upper left arm. He screamed. Blood spread over his trench coat.

"I recommend that you tear off a strip of your shirt and tie it above the wound to stop the bleeding", I said, calm as you like. Vasily's reaction to his wound reeled between rage and hysteria. *Serves the bastard right,* I thought, with the pistol pointed at his heart.

After some indecision, he decided to heed my advice. Groaning, he removed his trench coat and jacket. With some difficulty, he tore open the sleeve of his shirt using his right hand and his teeth. He tied it hard above the injury and succeeded in stemming the flowing blood. There was murder in his eyes as he looked at me, but fortunately I was the one with the firearm.

"Just so you'll know, the next time you try something, I'll shoot you in the kneecaps."

I said this very slowly to again mark the rules while we were waiting for the confirmation of Samantha's release. Now he knew I could be as cold-blooded as he was. Vasily, however, was both cunning and resourceful. I needed to stay alert.

Ten or fifteen minutes passed without either of us uttering a word. I felt tired, but I knew I couldn't relax for a second. Again, I glanced at my watch. It showed 2.30.

"I can't see the purpose of not allowing me my ciclosporin pills", Vasily suddenly said. *So he's beginning to feel the effect,* I thought, remembering the agony I lived travelling from the Sahara to Switzerland.

I had three options. I could give him his pills. I could deny him the pills. Or I could force him to swallow, let's say, a twentyfold of his regular dose. Between his and my own, I had enough of them, all right. I had never asked Dr Sternmacher what would happen if one was to exceed the prescribed amount, and made a mental note that I would when I next got the opportunity. I knew the drug weakened the immune system, so I speculated that if I forced Vasily to take an overdose of ciclosporin tonight, perhaps he would die from a liver breakdown; or perhaps a common cold the next time he sneezed.

I recognised my fury, and I tried to reason with myself, because I knew losing my head would only make things worse. As always, I tried to focus on my objectives. I wanted Samantha set free; that was my top priority. I wanted peace in my life, without being targeted by Vasily and his henchmen; or people like Flint and Georgie; or for that matter, the police.

"Once you've got the confirmation from your family in Australia that your wife's been released", Vasily said, trying another tack since I hadn't responded to his request, "I'm willing to return the money you gave me a few years ago ...

remember, the money stolen from us by your ex-partner who wound up in the Sahara?"

"I do remember."

"I now recognise that you weren't responsible, and I'm willing to give it back to you. Not only that, I'm going to double it to compensate you for all the … unfair troubles you've gone through. Give me a bank account number anywhere in the world, and I'll deposit thirty million pounds immediately after you have confirmed that your wife is free and unharmed – as I assure you that she soon will be."

"You're offering me thirty million pounds out of the blue … for what?"

"For letting me leave this barge, alone and alive", Vasily replied.

So, we were back to the bribing game, were we? Vasily thought his freedom was worth 30 million pounds, and that I could be bought for that amount. Did he expect me to negotiate for a higher sum? Probably, and if I did, he would know that he had beaten me.

Once in a while life comes up with an unexpected situation in which you're faced with choosing a tempting offer and compromising your beliefs. To me, Vasily's offer was not one of those moments, and for many reasons. My core belief was against any kind of corruption. Yes, I had made some deplorable mistakes in my life like stealing from the credit card companies, but I had atoned for them. Besides, I was a successful entrepreneur in my own right, and I had no interest in his offer, even if 30 million pounds is an impressive sum of

665

money. Then there was my fury over his attempt to kill me and having abducted Samantha. Of course he couldn't buy me, for 30 million or any other amount of money. Greed had stolen my life; how could I allow it to corrupt me now?

"To be fair, it wasn't you who ordered my torture. You didn't cause me to lose my physical and legal identities. That was Petroff's doing."

"Yes, I remember him. He drowned in the Moskva River on Kiril's order."

Vasily seemed to muster hope over my words. He was mistaken.

"Still – your values, your manipulations, your single-mindedness of enriching only yourself, is in every essence contrary to what I believe. Your money is worthless. You will die a rich man, and you will take nothing with you. Worse, you will leave nothing worthwhile behind you – only death and misery and poverty."

After my outburst, we remained in silence again for another fifteen minutes. I felt convinced that Vasily was gauging me to see in what way he could overcome me. He had tried using my wife and offering me millions of pounds. Yet, there he was, sitting bleeding in a broken chair with no one around to help him out of his predicament despite having accumulated a now worthless billion-dollar fortune. Why? Because I called the shots.

Despite his diminutive appearance, it was an eerie feeling controlling Europe's most powerful drug trafficker with a pistol I never before that night had used or had any knowledge whatsoever about.

That was the moment I decided I wouldn't allow Vasily any of the immunosuppressant pills I had confiscated from him. An eye for an eye, a tooth for a tooth? Of course. Wasn't that the lesson that Vasily, and his predecessor Yuri, had sown in my heart?

Then it finally occurred to me that I had the means to hold Vasily hostage by extorting him and thus secure my and my family's safety. Yes, that was it! With the flash function on, I raised Vasily's mobile and rapidly took two pictures of him before he had a chance to turn away his face. Nothing I had said or done so far had enraged him as much as me taking pictures of his transplanted face.

"I've taken these photos so I can be sure you won't come after me and my family again", I informed him. "I won't publish them or hand them over to the police unless you come after any of my family members. They will be my assurance that you won't seek revenge for however you think I may have wronged you."

Throughout the night, sirens from patrol cars and ambulances had contaminated the usual city calm. There were no more words to be exchanged. All that had been said only confirmed that our positions were incompatible.

Vasily's mobile rang; once, twice. After the third ring, I picked it up and activated the loudspeaker. The clock on the screen showed the time to be 5:15 in the morning, which meant it was 1:15 p.m. in Sydney.

Using the gun, I indicated that Vasily should be careful

with his words when he took the call.

"Misha, what news do you have?"

"We released the lady outside the same supermarket where we picked her up. No one was around, so Vlad and I got away …"

"Spare me the details, Misha. Now get back to Europe. Your mission is over."

I disconnected and then, without using the loudspeaker, called Jack to verify the information.

"Matthias, good news!" Jack greeted me. "Samantha has just been released. She was found, unhurt in every sense, on the same parking lot where she was kidnapped."

Keeping my gun pointed at Vasily, I rejoiced in the good news. The looming question was: What should I do with the Russian drug mastermind sitting opposite me? Was my family the only thing that interested me? Weren't there hundreds or thousands or millions of cases where the victims of drug abuse were the result of the greed of kingpins like Vasily?

"How are things with you in Paris?" Jack continued. "We're all concerned – the news is terrifying, mate."

The hair on my back rose as I heard his words.

"What terrifying news?"

"Don't tell me you're not aware of the attacks, Matthias! Several places in Paris have been hit simultaneously by terrorists and suicide bombers: four cafés, a stadium and a concert hall. Hundreds have been killed. Everyone's worried to death. Surely you must have heard?"

Terrorist attacks? Then it all came to me. The people who

had attacked the café last evening didn't belong to some local drug gang working for or avenging Gérard ... they had been terrorists.

"Jack, I truly don't know what happened here", I told him, weary to my bones. "What I can tell you is that I've concentrated my efforts to get Samantha released, and my next effort will be to hop on a plane to Sydney without further delay. How's that?"

"Thumbs up, mate. We'll discuss it all when you're back home."

"Yes, Jack, we'll do that. Please tell Samantha I'm fine. I'm a little busy at the moment, so I'll have to call her later, OK?"

Bleary-eyed, I noticed that the dawn was announcing itself through the unwashed windows of the barge I had broken into. There was a steady drizzle making the morning hour drearier still. Man, was I tired. I hadn't had a satisfactory night's sleep in a week. Police sirens continued to contaminate the dawn and the capital's sensitive ears. A new day was arriving.

Samantha has been released. Now, what on earth should I do with Vasily?

Interesting, isn't it? You do your best trying to solve a perceived, titanic problem, and once it's done – once it's actually done! – you're left with other tasks you never thought you'd be confronting. Like the one now facing me. Should I shoot Vasily? He no doubt deserved to be shot, but it would make me a judge, jury and executioner in one stroke ... would

I be able to live with that? Possibly, because of the things I knew and that I'd been through.

After hanging up on Jack, Vasily and I stared at each other. Vasily, very perceptive, knew I was making up my mind about something I'd been told over the phone.

I agonised. Should I kill this man for all the evil he had done? No, that definitely wasn't my call. Should I avenge myself because he abducted my wife? No, that wasn't my call either; it was for the police to investigate. What about all the attacks against me? If I released him, would he make renewed attempts to hurt me and my family? No, the pictures of his new face were my insurance policy.

"Your wife was freed", Vasily said. "Now, are you letting me go? If not, I suppose you have to shoot me again", he taunted me, "and this time it has to be fatal."

I was very tired and tried to think clearly. Vasily didn't know that I could find him for perhaps another week or two before the battery implanted in his head stopped functioning. Unaware to Vasily, during the gasping last days of its signal, I would be controlling his destiny. It was safer to let him go, and, when I was back in Australia, I could decide whether I'd let Interpol know where to find him.

"Leave", I told him, lowering the pistol, "but never again come looking for me or my family."

"Of course not, Callaghan. This is the end of it all, as far as you're concerned. I promise you a long and healthy life."

Vasily gave me an inscrutable smile, wrapped his mohair coat tighter against the cold and the drizzle outside, and swept past me towards the exit door. A moment later, I was alone and felt an immense fatigue come over me. Beyond the dirty windowpanes, the bleak dawn, reflected on the dark waters, made the new day feel more dismal still.

*

Vasily walked hurriedly through the empty streets of the Marais quarter clutching his wounded arm. The light rain made the morning miserable and the chilly air added to his discomfort. Vasily was chewing with rage. *Held at gunpoint for a whole night! Shot at; insulted; left powerless! Pictures of my new face taken! What good will my transplant have served if ... I must think of something to prevent Callaghan from ... but first things first: I urgently need to get back to the hotel for my pills.*

A constant question on his mind over the last months was whether the face transplant really had been a good idea. Despite the pain and the convalescence he had gone through, Vasily always ended up with the same answer: yes. Besides being the most convenient solution, it was also the most astute one. He had become a completely different person, one not wanted by Interpol. Vasily mentally kicked his shin for the thousandth time for not having made sure that Callaghan had been killed. Callaghan was a nuisance who knew too much. It was urgent to take him out of the equation, but before he did, Vasily had to make sure he recovered the pictures taken of his precious new face.

Vasily fumed as he hobbled along the streets looking for

a cab that could take him back to his suite at the Le Meurice hotel. His arm hurt intensely. *Callaghan shot me, but that bullet comes with a very high price. Come tomorrow, Callaghan is a dead man.*

The fog hovering over the empty streets was caused by a light but persistent rain. Vasily shivered as the humidity penetrated the clothes he wore. *Where is the bloody hotel? Where is the Seine? Where is everybody?* The sound of sirens could no longer be heard. With not a soul out on the streets, Vasily had a vague, uncomfortable sensation that he was completely alone in this great metropolitan city.

That is, until suddenly a vaguely familiar figure stepped in front of him and wielded a knife to show that he was serious.

*

There was a mist hanging on to the feeble morning light as I clumsily stepped off the barge. A soft rain was falling. In addition to my exhaustion, the November morning chill promptly penetrated my body to the bones. I wondered what I should do next. Go to the Ritz? Well, that's where Vasily and his thugs knew I had a room, so I immediately struck that option off my list. He had gone livid when I had taken his picture, so I had to assume he would make immediate efforts to recover his mobile. It reminded me that I should send backup copies to Samantha's phone, just in case. As for my luggage at the Ritz, I could arrange for it to be shipped to wherever I wanted to pick it up later. Now, I just felt too tired to bother with solving all these minute details. I needed a bed to sleep in.

Why me? I wondered over and over as I thought through the past seven years of my life. *Why me? Why me? Why me? Did I ever have a choice?*

I walked up to the Place de la Bastille and, after some hesitation, took the Boulevard Henri IV towards the Seine. After crossing the bridge, I found myself on the Île Saint-Louis. There, on a side street, I saw a flickering neon sign promising rooms in letters alternating between green and red next to a two-star promise.

I walked into the small hotel. With a hard rap on the counter, I woke up the night manager. Ruffling his hair, he inexplicably yelled at some unseen employee to "do room number fifteen", as if this action would excuse the fact that he had been asleep on the job.

After some exchange, during which I merely expressed my desire for a clean room where I could sleep, I was finally given a key. It was given to me after I had settled my bill in advance with an excess charge for having the affront of paying with a credit card that I had pulled out of my sock. Not bothering to undress, I immediately fell asleep on top of the king-size bed after wrapping myself in the bedspread.

*

The wavering, haggard figure brandishing a knife seemed familiar to Vasily. At first, he couldn't recall where he had seen him, although he knew it must have been recently. As a million clues raced through his brain's memory bank, one finally came to a stop at his centre of attention. The man threatening him was the same individual who had come begging at the café the previous night … *What was it the waiter had called him? Jean-Luc?*

"I need your wallet and your watch and your phone", Jean-Luc addressed him in a shaky voice. "Give them to me and you'll walk away without being hurt."

He noticed how his attacker rolled his eyes towards the grey skies, which, unknown to Vasily, was part of Jean-Luc's withdrawal symptoms. On an impulse, Vasily jumped at the chance offered and bit his opponent's nose at the same time as he made a karate strike against the hand that held the knife. Surprised, Jean-Luc took three steps back, but he didn't drop his weapon. Instead, furious, he raised it and rushed towards Vasily, burying the knife in his chest close to his heart. Vasily toppled over and hit the cobblestones.

Quickly, Jean-Luc rifled through the pockets of the bleeding, unconscious man in search of anything of value that could pay for his badly needed fix. A diamond-incrusted Piaget gold watch looked like it could fetch a couple of hundred. No phone, no wallet, no jewellery around his neck. Exasperated, Jean-Luc started to run from the scene of the robbery. The thuds when his shoes hit the pavement echoed against the walls of the buildings lining the narrow streets.

Meanwhile, Vasily lay bleeding to death on Rue de la Cerisaie, a mere block away from the police prefecture that supervised the security of the citizens in the Marais. However, the Paris police were at that moment kept busy with things of higher priority than patrolling streets to prevent muggings.

Thirty-five minutes after Vasily had been stabbed, a passerby noticed the immobile body lying in a pool of blood. Calling the local emergency number, he reported the incident and then left the scene. Three minutes later, with the police and the security forces still on high alert after the previous night's terror attacks, a patrol and an ambulance arrived at the scene of Vasily's murder. Photos were taken; information was shared. Afterwards, Vasily's body was taken to the morgue for autopsy.

Sunday November 15, 2015

With his usual confident, spoilt rich-kid attitude, 19-year-old Misha handed over his passport to the immigration officer at Kingsford Smith Airport outside Sydney. As a precaution, Vladimir had beforehand insisted that they would travel as two independent passengers who merely happened to go on the same Quantas flight via Dubai to Zürich, Switzerland.

The immigration official leafed through Misha's passport before he slid it through his magnetic reader. Immediately, his screen flashed that there had been no corresponding entrance to the country with that particular passport. The official discreetly buzzed a button to alert the airport security personnel that something unusual was afoot. He continued to leaf through the passport pages until two sturdy policemen appeared next to Misha.

"You better come with us, mate. We need to check out a few details before you get on your flight."

Three lines away, Vladimir watched how Misha was led away by the police. He became apprehensive. Would he confront the same fate?

He didn't. Instead, he was quickly waved through.

Misha and Vladimir had both arrived with two sets of forged passports and driving licences. Misha's error was that he had used the same set of identification to rent the vehicles as the one he had presented when entering the country. Saving his unused passport for his return to Europe, he hadn't anticipated Australia's sophisticated immigration software. As a tourist exiting the country, a corresponding entrance, had to exist.

*

I was able to buy a ticket for a midnight flight to Sydney with a stopover in Hong Kong. Despite my excessive share of the darker surprises in life, I felt mentally more exhausted even when compared with my trip out of the Sahara. I arrived two hours early to check in at Charles de Gaulle Airport. Despite the weariness that I still couldn't shake off, I started watching all the stupid information via the apps on my new smartphone that I had missed out on for days and days.

Emails from Samantha and Jack, WhatsApp messages from my kids and friends, Twitter, the BBC World News ... you name it. Not until a notice flashed that my mobile was nearing the end of its battery life, it occurred to me that I should check up on Vasily's whereabouts.

The red blip that flashed on the phone's screen seemed somewhat intermittent now. Perhaps the battery was finally getting near its depletion? The signal, however, was stationary.

I looked up the signal's coordinates on Google Maps. Unsurprisingly, the red blip indicated that he was still in Paris. When I closed in on the search function, it marked Vasily's location to be in one of the city's morgues.

Monday November 16, 2015

Sonia, who had remained on board the yacht in Monaco as ordered by Vasily, had by now been informed by multiple sources about the terror attacks in Paris, and Gérard and Vasily's deaths. Ilya and another of Vasily's bodyguards had been shot dead, while Oleg had been taken to a hospital for treatment of his bullet wounds.

What am I going to do now? she pondered. Then the implication of the events dawned on her. With Vasily out of the game, there was no one in a better position than herself to take over his organisation. She had negotiated with all the major suppliers; she knew their every distributor down to the last detail; and she had knowledge and access to – although certainly not all of them – quite a few of Vasily's bank accounts. *The advantage of being the boss's trusted help, no doubt. I can make a deal with Pyotr, he surely has plenty of information that will complement what I already know.*

As Sonia pondered her situation and future sunbathing in a deckchair on the yacht that now would be hers, it didn't take her long to come to a conclusion.

Vasily, still in his thirties and surely invincible in his own mind, had never assigned an heir to his empire. There was no obvious crown prince to take over. As far as Sonia was aware, he had no close family. *This will be my opportunity*, she thought. *I can take on Vasily's role, because I know how the organisation works. I have the contacts. I have access to the distributors and I know their markets. I'm now taking over as Big Ben.*

But most important of all: I now control the cash flow.

EPILOGUE TO *THE CALLAGHAN SEPTOLOGY*

To the great surprise of everybody who had come to know both **Abdullah** and **Ghalib Mahfouz**, a few years after Abdullah's death, she gained their respect for her cunning and unexpected business acumen that by far surpassed that of her deceased husband. Investing the money she had recovered from his Swiss bank account, added to the generous compensation she had received for selling his face for a transplant surgery at a Swiss hospital, she increased her inherited fortune five-fold within ten years. In 2008, awed by her increasing fortune, she had pondered the best way to further invest her unexpected riches. The husband she had widowed had doubtlessly done well with his smuggling operations, so Ghalib decided to try her own hand at financing some trafficking. By 2017, she had made investments in more than a dozen joint ventures, in which she risked the capital while people like **Ahmed** did the actual work. She invested her profits in properties, with a preference for small hotels across Morocco. Ghalib was apprehensive of investing abroad for lack of knowledge and language skills. She did, however, also have a charitable side to her character, in that she helped launch projects across Africa that encouraged poor women to start their own businesses.

Advised by **Benny Botana**, the New York mob managed to milk from **Ludmila Jordan** close to everything that her deceased husband had left her. Destitute, she returned to Montenegro, where she, surprisingly, became a popular host of a reality show.

Sofia and **Andrew Reese** – who had married late in life – never had any children. They continued to live happily in Rome, where they successfully managed their trattoria. Andrew's acquired and restrained butler attitude that never abandoned him was in stark contrast to the ebullient Sofia and her large family. At first they found his emotional control suspicious, but eventually they became endeared by it. Although they occasionally were in contact by email, Andrew never again met Matthias Callaghan face to face.

Georgie Jones fled Paris the same evening that Matthias and Trudy returned to London after interviewing him. He left behind his expensive flat, his expensive sports car and his even more expensive lover, **Nathalie Solange**. She was evicted from the flat seven months later because its upkeep hadn't been paid and for running up hefty bills in Georgie's name. Georgie crisscrossed Europe for three weeks, going to Spain, Italy and Greece before finally settling for Istanbul, Turkey. He found life in the cosmopolitan city enchanting, and to boot, much less expensive than his former life in Paris. He soon entertained three mistresses and invested in various properties. He bought himself a Porsche, which caught everyone's eye and many men's envy as he zipped down the streets with one of his mistresses in the passenger seat. In the summer of 2016, his carefree life got increasingly complicated when there was an attempted coup against the president Recep Tayyip Erdoğan. The coup didn't succeed, and Erdoğan immediately started his reprisals against the participants in the coup in addition to a few others that he found inconvenient for different reasons. Unfortunately for Georgie, these were the very same people he had bribed to care for his interests. By the end of 2016, he saw himself forced to leave the country after hastily selling off his properties at a loss. Georgie decided to mothball his Porsche in a garage because he was unable to find anyone willing or able to pay even a reasonable sum close to the 350,000 dollars he had paid for it. He continued to Saudi Arabia and some of the emirates, none of which he found to be to his liking, mainly due to the strict rules regarding alcohol and contact with women. He moved on to Mumbai in India, where he managed to acquire a membership to an exclusive club for the very rich, and very soon picked up where he had left off in Turkey. By now, his only real concern was that his fortune was dwindling at a worrying speed.

Eight months after the raid of the Park Lane flat, when the last pieces of the Russians' drug-dealing jigsaw puzzle had been solved to reveal the full picture, Detective Inspector **John Blackmoore** was awarded an extra pip along with his promotion to Detective Chief Inspector. He received this promotion despite that, in Blackmoore's opinion and to his great frustration, there were still some pieces missing in the investigation into the Russian Mafia's drug empire. Vasily Ivanovich's role and death had never been satisfactorily explained after he had ended up as a corpse in a Paris city morgue. Paddy O'Hare's murderer was never found. When he received his promotion, the drug business was once again flourishing and prices had come down as a sign that supply was indeed abundant.

After **Frank O'Hare** received the severe prison sentence of eight years and six months for overseeing the international money-laundering scheme that Mikhail Berlosky had conjectured, he lashed out against the injustice. His appeal didn't change his sentence, however. When he eventually deduced the hard facts about the way his brother had died in a helicopter in Germany accused of piloting for Berlosky's drug cartel, he started to draw his conclusions. As the months and years in prison wore him down, he became more withdrawn and hardly talked to anyone besides his wife and his solicitor.

Yuliana Korzha, known in the entertainment world as Julie Cross, had a hard time overcoming her husband's prison sentence. Feeling depressed and lonely, she lost interest in acting after a season's lacklustre performances in the musical in which she starred. Yuliana found it difficult to get another role, and dedicated her time to lobbying for Frank's release through appeals and costly lawyers. She and **Samantha Callaghan** had struck up a friendship and were in contact through emails and Skype. Samantha also met with her on the occasions she visited London.

Mikhail Berlosky, sentenced to life in prison and forfeiture of his known fortune (although most of it was kept hidden from the law enforcers) for drug offences and money laundering, soon became the leader of a gang of Eastern European convicts in Her Majesty's Prison Wormwood Scrubs.

Though on a much lesser scale than before his arrest, he soon ran the drug business inside the jail, and also had runners on the outside who sold hard drugs in the London area. For this, he came to rely on **Jason Longhorn**, the lawyer he had employed as a coordinator and adviser during his trial, and for which Longhorn hired the best criminal solicitors that money could get. Regardless of the enormous amount of cash confiscated in the Moorgate facility, Berlosky had a personal fortune stashed away. He cunningly used it for his personal benefit, and to plot and pay for his escape from prison with his wife and Jason Longhorn's unwitting assistance.

Misha Gagarin was eventually found guilty of the abduction of Samantha Callaghan and sentenced to ten years and eight months in Her Majesty's Prison in Australia.

Not long after his return to Europe from Australia, **Vladimir Kutin** decided he had had enough of working for the now weakened organisation. With Sonia's reluctant blessing, he returned to Russia with his savings. He used a large part of his money to buy a *dacha* in the countryside 300 kilometres from Moscow. A year later, he married a local girl with whom he had two children and never discussed his past as an enforcer for the Mafia.

Although it took both effort and time, the cool-headed **Sonia Malkovich** managed to recover and consolidate a large part of Vasily's former drug empire, mostly thanks to her knowledge of key information like suppliers, distributors and where some of his fortune had been hidden in bank accounts and properties. This knowledge, along with the generous remunerations she judged necessary to hand out, allowed her to keep Vasily's enforcers and other employees on her payroll. She became particularly successful in bribing officials to look the other way when drug shipments were moved around the globe into the European market. She lasted a little over two years in this capacity, before being toppled by her second-in-command, the brutal **Oleg Volkov**. Before he killed Sonia, he made sure to extract all information she had about bank accounts and the business logistics by torturing her.

Despite being extremely apprehensive after the recent interaction with Vasily Ivanovich and his ruthless people, **Dr Henrik Sternmacher** eventually recovered his inner peace as the news came trickling back to him about Vasily's fate. To this day, he continues as the manager of his successful clinic in Switzerland. He succeeded in convincing the incredulous staff that had assisted him performing the surgery on Vasily by arguing that the patient had been diagnosed with a multiple personality syndrome, and that the case had been referred to him by a psychiatrist and close friend of his.

Samantha Callaghan, adopted Kirby, née Sandra Winthrop, and mother of three, continued to work part time as the accountant in the construction business she owned jointly with her husband and her brother. She travelled regularly to the United Kingdom to meet with cousins and other relatives to her biological parents, although Matthias never accompanied her on these trips. He did, however, get to meet her relatives when Samantha on occasions invited them to Australia for a family gathering.

And then, last but evidently not least, what happened to **Matthias Callaghan**? After his return to Australia in November 2015, he didn't leave the country even once during the following years. Physically, he aged very rapidly after his recent ordeals in Europe, and it didn't take long before friends and acquaintances mentioned in private how he looked much older than his actual age. Samantha, the only one in Australia who knew the full and tragic truth behind her husband's misfortunes, defended him at every turn without divulging anything relating to his past. She also effectively shielded him from the observations and comments made by outsiders. Mentally, however, he continued to be as agile as ever. He enjoyed his participation in the creation of innovative construction projects together with Jack and Samantha, and their business was very successful in what turned out to be the boom construction years in Australia. With Samantha's approval, he invested a large portion of the profits in a huge ranch in the Australian Outback, where he increasingly spent more time away from city life.

As the years passed, he became more melancholic and tended to seek out solitude. He often revisited his own past and studied the fate of others in history, from which he drew philosophical conclusions about the evil and, in particular, the stupidity men would stoop to, to satisfy their greed.

An overview of those who appear in this septology, a tale that stretches over twenty years, and some
(with the principal characters marked in **bold**)

THE CALLAGHANS

THE CALLAGHAN FAMILY

Matthias Callaghan I, grandfather (1926-1990)
Matthias Callaghan II, father (1953-2008)
Matthias Callaghan III (1971-)

THE WIVES AND CHILDREN OF MATTHIAS CALLAGHAN III

Sharon Callaghan
Yuliana Korzha, aka **Julia "Julie" Cross** (1970-)
Samantha Kirby, née **Sandra Winthrop** (1980-)
George Callaghan (2012-)
Owen Callaghan (2012-)
Ruby Callaghan (2015-)

OTHER PEOPLE IN MATTHIAS CALLAGHAN III's BUSINESS & PRIVATE LIVES

Andrew Reese (1961-) *MC III's butler*
Sofia Reese *Andrew Reese's wife*
Kevin Smith *A distant acquaintance with a knack for trouble*
Vincent "Vince" Lyle *MC III's occasional front when doing business*
Peter "Pete" Carter *Professional administrator of computer companies*
Lady Amelia Ashton-Bright *Widowed octogenarian, sharp as a whistle*
Ms Finn *Lady Ashton-Bright's private secretary*
Clemens Porter *Private detective*
Marjorie *An old school friend*
Cecil *Porter in the Park Lane building*
Henry "the Hoarse" *Porter in the Park Lane building*

YULIANA & ALLAN
IMPORTANT PEOPLE IN YULIANA'S LIFE

Nicolae *Her Romanian boyfriend*

Gregorio *People smuggler*

Tania *Childhood girlfriend who lives in Romania*

Alexandru Ilionesco (1937-2007) *Romanian diplomat; Yuliana's protector*

Violet Ilionesco (1940-2006) *Married to Alexandru, Yuliana's protector*

Karen *Actress friend*

Agnes *Actress friend*

Frank O'Hare *Yuliana's second husband; Paddy O'Hare's brother*

ALLAN GOULD & IMPORTANT PEOPLE IN HIS LIFE

Allan Gould (1971-) *MC III's university pal and business partner*

Belle *Allan's wife*

Bruno Fenwich *Allan's partner in his Internet café business venture*

THE RUSSIAN MAFIA
THE LEADERS

Kiril Medzinki (1978-2008) *The Russian Mafia organisation's leader*

Yuri Petroff (1961-2008) *The Russian Mafia's chief operator in London*

Mikhail Berlosky (1969-) *The Russian Mafia's number two in London*

Vasily Ivanovich (1978-2015) *Kiril's schoolmate and second-in-command; later the Russian Mafia's leader*

Bogdan Sokolov *Vasily's second-in-command supervising the Moscow business*

THE LIEUTENANTS & THE FOOT SOLDIERS

Jaime "Spanish" Hernandez (1966-2011) *Responsible for drug import logistics*

Oleg Volkov *Russian Mafia lieutenant in London*

Ilya Furo *Russian foot soldier in London*

Vladimir Kutin (1982-) *Russian foot soldier in London*

Igor *Foot soldier in Moscow; Kiril's bodyguard*

Leo *Foot soldier in Moscow; Kiril's bodyguard*

Mikhail "Misha" Gagarin *(1996-) Sergei Gagarin's son; foot soldier in London*

THE ADMINISTRATORS

Boris Orloff *The Russian Mafia's IT expert in London*

Sonia Malkovich (1985-2017) *Vasily's personal assistant and chief administrator*

Pyotr Litvinoff *Head accountant at the Russian Mafia's company front, Arexim*

THE ASSOCIATES

Sergei Gagarin *Owner of the Caspian Sea restaurants in London; Misha's father*

Karl "the Cat" Katzinger (1958 –) *Burglar; former East German spy*

Paddy O'Hare *The pilot; Frank O'Hare's brother*

Hamza Khalis *Paddy O'Hare's Moroccan co-pilot*

"One-eye" *An assassin for hire*

Gérard Mokrani (1979 – 2015) *A Paris-based drug distributor with fifty men working for him*

THE OTHERS

Tania Berlosky *Mikhail Berlosky's wife*

Sasha Berlosky (2003 –) *Mikhail Berlosky's son*

JEREMIAH FLINT

FLINT & HIS FAMILY

Jeremiah Flint (1941 – 2009) *The head of a criminal London-based organisation*

Clara Flint *Jeremiah Flint's mother*

Alfred Jones *Jeremiah Flint's stepfather; George Jones's grandfather*

Philip "Phil" Jones (1937 – 2014) *Jeremiah Flint's stepbrother; George Jones's father*

George "Georgie" Jones (1976 –) *Flint's step-nephew, who works for the police*

FLINT'S CREW

Richard "Thumps" Thompson (1972 – 2009) *Assassin employed by Flint*

"Charlie" Henderson *Enforcer employed by Jeremiah Flint*

"Tiger Tail" *Enforcer employed by Jeremiah Flint*

"Weasel" *Enforcer employed by Jeremiah Flint*

"Blowey" *Jeremiah Flint's bodyguard*

"Staples" *Jeremiah Flint's bodyguard*

Tim *Bartender at Jeremiah Flint's pub "The Lion's Head"*

FLINT'S OTHER ACQUAINTANCES

Ronnie Kray *London crime organisation boss; Reggie's twin brother*

Reggie Kray *London crime organisation boss; Ronnie's twin brother*

Christine Thompson *Thumps's Irish mother*

THE MOB

THE NEW YORK CITY MOB

"Benny" Botana *New York Mafia boss*

Robert "Bob" Robertson *New York mob made guy/assassin*

Tito *Mob lieutenant in Las Vegas*

Luigi Monticalli *Harry Jordan's protector*

THE MEXICAN CARTELS
THE SINALOA CARTEL
Joaquin "El Chapo" Guzman   *Cartel capo*
Pablo "Picapiedra" Chavez   *Cartel lieutenant*
"La Calavera"   *Cartel lieutenant*
Ignacio "Nacho" Gonzalez   *Cartel assassin*
Salvador "Chava" Sandoval   *Cartel assassin*

THE BELTRAN LEYVA CARTEL
Arturo "El Barbas" Beltran Leyva   *Cartel capo*
Edgar "La Barbie" Valdez   *Cartel lieutenant*
Enrique "El Loco" Garrido   *Cartel assassin*

THE GULF CARTEL/LOS ZETAS
Heriberto "El Lazca" Lazcano Lazcano   *Gulf cartel enforcer and leader of Los Zetas*
"Tony Tormenta"   *Gulf cartel capo*
"Z-40"   *Cartel lieutenant*
Carlos "El Capi" Valverde   *Cartel drug negotiator*
Rogelio "El Coqueto" Prieto   *Cartel assassin*

THE PEOPLE IN CHECHNYA & UKRAINE
THE CHECHNYA TERRORISTS
Khokha   *Chechen terrorist leader*
Axmed   *Chechen terrorist*

THE UKRAINIAN WAR VETERAN
Osip Shevchenko (1988 – 2015)   *Wounded corporal*

THE LONDON METROPOLITAN
POLICE FORCE
(NEW SCOTLAND YARD)

CHIEFS & BOSSES

John Stopper (1966 –) *Assistant Commissioner*

Robert Groening (1939 –) *Detective Chief Inspector; fraud division*

Ralph Ramsey *Chief Detective Inspector and head of the narcotics division*

Chief Inspector Corbett *Herbert Barker's boss in 2008*

DETECTIVES

Herbert "Herb" Barker (1960 – 2012) *Detective Sergeant; later Detective Inspector*

George Jones (1976 –) *Detective Constable; later Detective Sergeant*

John Blackmoore *Detective Sergeant: eventually promoted to Detective Chief Inspector*

Anne Slater *Detective Inspector and head of the art fraud division*

Peter Scarborough *Detective Constable*

OTHER POLICEMEN

Officer Paisley *Police officer*

Constable Cooper *Police constable*

Constable Jennings *Police constable*

Craig Williams *Police sergeant*

ADMINISTRATORS

Jenny *Secretary at the New Scotland Yard*

Maureen Arlington *Policewoman; Herbert Barker's girlfriend*

THE US LAW ENFORCEMENT
THE ARIZONA POLICE DEPARTMENT
Charles Durham *Police chief*
Jeff Carson *Police officer*
William "Billy" Edwards *Police officer*

US BORDER MIGRATION PERSONNEL
"Johnny" *US border migration officer in Nogales*
"Eddie" *US border migration officer in Nogales*

FBI
Solomon Vaughn *Special agent employed by the FBI*

THE VISA POLICE LIAISON DEPARTMENT
Michael McDougharty *Police liaison working for VISA*

THE LAWYERS
Charles Rathbone (1963 - 2009) *Solicitor in the Russian Mafia's employment*
David Sandhurst *Matthias Callaghan III's solicitor*
Jason Longhorn (1969 –) *Solicitor, specialising in estate settlements*
Clive Mason *Junior solicitor employed by David Sandhurst*
Brett Stevens *Solicitor employed by Jason Longhorn*
Aaron Constable *Solicitor employed by Allan Gould for his defence*
Tom Fowley *An eminent British barrister*
Latimer Stone *Jeremiah Flint's legal adviser*
Paul Penney *Solicitor working for the credit card companies*
Wilclair Bartlett *Frank O'Hare's solicitor*

THE OTHER PARTICIPANTS

THE PEOPLE IN SWITZERLAND

Dr Henrik Sternmacher *Part owner/head surgeon at the St Puys clinic*
Dr Wolfgang Braun *Psychiatrist employed by the St Puys clinic*
Dr Frank Hessel *Medical doctor employed at the Zürich morgue*
Hassan Bassir *Diplomat at the Moroccan Embassy in Berne*
Jeffrey Rose *Diplomat at the British Embassy in Berne*
Mr Stettinger *CEO hired by MC I to manage his business interests*

THE PEOPLE IN LONDON

Mrs Manning *Housekeeper at Matthias Callaghan II's rented house*
Florence Fotheringale *John Stopper's fiancée*
Harold Winthrop (1939 – 1986) *Violet Ilionesco's first husband*
Ralph Trollope (1964 –) *A shady art dealer*
Jeffrey Foley *A dealer in stolen artworks*
Milton Cooper *A passport forger*
Alistair Stewart *A fence*
Trevor Burns *Editor-in-chief at the* Daily Mirror
Trudy Swift (1987 -) *Journalist employed by the* Daily Mirror
Frederick Aspinall *Legal advisor employed by the* Daily Mirror
Mr Cairn *Bank vault specialist*

THE PEOPLE IN MONACO, FRANCE & ITALY

Paolo *Hired help in Umbria*
Vjeran Tomic, aka "Spiderman" *Burglar*
Yonathan Born *Fence*
Harry Jordan (1941 – 2015) *An ex-mob billionaire living on a yacht in Monaco*
Ludmila Jordan (1970 –) *The billionaire Harry Jordan's estranged wife*
Nathalie Solange *Georgie's Parisian mistress*
Nathan Ripley *Train passenger from Liverpool*
Commandant Rossi *Italian police officer*
Jean-Luc *Parisian drug addict*

THE PEOPLE IN SPAIN, MOROCCO & MAURITANIA

Jaime "Spanish" Hernandez (1966 – 2011) *Human trafficker and drug dealer*

Abdul Mahfouz *(1962 – 2007) Moroccan drug smuggler*

Ghalib Mahfouz (1964 –) *Abdul Mahfouz's estranged wife*

Masisi *Nubian girl, bought as sex slave by Abdul Mahfouz*

Ramón *Chauffeur employed to smuggle girls from Eastern Europe*

Ahmed (1973 –) *A Moroccan people trafficker, previously employed by "Spanish"*

Mustafa Goulla (1975 –) *Marrakech police chief; descendant of the Goulla sheiks in Ourrzazate*

Lamrani *Mustafa Goulla's personal assistant*

N'douro *A Mauritian people smuggling recruiter*

Bamba Boubacar *The Russian Mafia's local contact in Nouakchott*

Haroun *A berber caravan driver*

Omar *A poor Mauritian citizen looking for a better life in Europe*

Moammar *A Libyan overland people trafficker*

THE PEOPLE IN MEXICO

Bernardo Villamar *Hotel employee*

Porfirio "El Pollo" Yañez *Small-time thief*

Alberto "Beto" Sanchez *Police captain in the Sinaloa Cartel's employ*

Francisco "Pancho" Herrera *Recent university graduate*

Raul Perez *Recent university graduate*

Juan "Juanito" Barragan Kuri *Thief*

Jesus "Chucho" Navarro Garcia *Thief*

THE PEOPLE IN AUSTRALIA

Melvin Kirby *Samantha and Jack's adoptive father*

Janet Kirby *Samantha and Jack's adoptive mother*

Jack Kirby *Samantha Kirby's brother*

Alice Kirby *Jack Kirby's wife*

Sterling Dunaway *Commander with the Australian police*

Dwayne Bartlett *Sydney police detective*

THE BEAKED WHALE ASSIGNMENT TRILOGY

Greed, Past and Present

Threads Spun in the Dark

Shadows Etched in Stone

COLLECTED SHORT STORIES

Graveyard Grapevine

The Game & the Challenge

At the Heart of the Ivory Maze

Destiny Comes with Strings Attached

The Future Has a Discouraging Past

The Power of Greed

WORDS ON THE WING

When the Reds Fade from Purple (You're Left with the Blues)

Riddles & Madness

Dovetail Deals by the Devil's Door

Life in the Rearview Mirror

LIBROS EN ESPAÑOL

Escrito en Sangre

Más Allá del Límite

La Cara Oscura de la Moneda

El Reino del Terror